Echoes of Esteria

Resonance of Ruin

Stanley L. Garland Jr.

This book is dedicated to Leo. Love you dude!

Contents

Prologue

The continent of Esteria, a beautiful and immense land, has a history soaked in blood. In the early age, the goddess Astra created ten races to enjoy her majestic creation. All of her creation could use magic. For hundreds of years, the races lived in harmony, enjoying Astra's presence.

Humans were blessed with double the amount of land as the other races, and double the amount of time spent with Astra. In the year 350, the demon race, led by the vicious warlord, Helion, launched an attack on Esteria. His brute strength and charisma persuaded several other races to join forces against the humans, whom he saw as Astra's favorite creation, with the aim of extinguishing them all.

Astra withdrew from her creation to protect herself, for she saw no possibility of dissuading the warlord. However, she bestowed four human champions with angelic weapons to halt Helion's conquest across Esteria. These humans became the heroes of old who would slay Helion and create a new and peaceful Esteria.

Helion was defeated but at the cost of a million innocent souls. Astra wept for the loss of her creation. Earthquakes ravaged the land, separating all the different races as her tears flooded the lands and changed them into oceans. Esteria was broken into continents, and only a fraction of it remained the original Esteria. The demons were banished to far and uncharted territories for their many crimes against Astra, territories where the heroes of old created a magical seal to bind them. The Goddess sent four minor deities, one in each of the four kingdoms, to observe from afar and keep watch, in case the demon race should rise again.

Astra was the source of magic for her creation. Since her departure, magic can be inherited, learned, gifted, or obtained. All magic comes from the World Tree Elysium, located on an island in the middle of the Sela Ocean. It is a reminder of Astra's love for her people. No one who has sought the tree has ever returned.

Each child at the age of ten participates in an awakening ceremony to determine if the spirit of Astra will awaken their magical potential. A covenant is made to use magic for the enrichment of the world. Those who choose the path of wickedness will receive the Mark of Damnation from the Church of Astra, which will strip them of their magical powers.

After Helion's defeat, over three hundred years of peace passed until the untimely assassination of King Leo the First of the Northern Kingdom in the year 800 AS (after separation from Astra). His assassination became the catalyst of the Second Great War of Esteria, which lasted for twenty years. Since the end of the war, some nations have fared better than others.

Esteria has been at peace for twenty years. Yet even now, there are those in the shadows plotting its downfall.

Chapter 1

It is the year 845 AS, on the fifth day of the Month of Angels on the Astral Calendar. Adventurers roam the land in search of an ancient goddess, hidden deep in the Eastern Kingdom. Near the town of Dalton, south of the capital of Glashmere in the Eastern Kingdom, four friends from Ifer seek shelter from the rain.

Slash, a self-taught swordsman with lightly darkened skin, peers through the fog and heavy rainfall and spots a cave not far away. He brushes his short, black, wavy hair out of his eyes and looks back at his three companions.

"We can take refuge there," he says, pointing at the cave. His brown eyes reflect the rainfall.

His three companions hurry after him into the mouth of the cave. The most precious being his fiancé, Sodina. Many say she is the living image of the Goddess herself—with her long red hair, fair skin, and entrancing blue eyes that resemble the serene afternoon sky. Despite only being twenty years old, her wisdom and demeanor match those older in age. Her jaded green dress is soaked by the evening rain as she leans over, wringing out her hair.

"That rain came out of nowhere," Sodina says, looking over at Slash.

Slash smiles as he puts his hand on her head. Looking deeper into the cave, he sees a path leading inside. "It looks like luck is on our side," he says.

"Goddess Astra, grant us your light." Sodina points her staff forward as the blue orb near its end shines brightly.

Amanda, a short woman, twenty years of age with long brunette pigtails, and freckles covering fair skin, sits on the stony interior of the cave. "The last thing we need is more rain," she says with a disgruntled expression. Wiping her glasses, she looks back toward the torrential downpour. "The last few days were filled with rain. I'm tired of it all."

"Wet hair seems to be the latest fashion trend in the kingdom," Lorenz jokingly replies.

Being the oldest at twenty-two years old, Lorenz sees himself as somewhat of an older brother to his three friends. His lush, long purple hair and clear fair skin have made him a favorite amongst the women in Ifer. It helps that he's also the oldest son of the mayor.

"Are we sure no monsters are on our scent?" Lorenz asks, readying his short bow. He peers back out of the cave, squinting.

"The rain would cover our scent even if monsters were roaming this area," Slash says to Lorenz.

His calming voice eases the tension in Lorenz's shoulders. Putting the arrow back in its quiver, Lorenz turns toward his friends and lets out a sigh of relief.

"An ambush is the last thing we need," he says, "but you have yet to steer us wrong." Letting out a loud laugh, he takes a seat by Amanda and twirls her pigtails.

She pulls away from him with a scowl. "How many times have I told you not to play with my hair?"

Playing with his younger sister's hair has been a habit of his ever since they were young. Amanda finds it extremely annoying and always berates Lorenz for his behavior.

An hour passes by as the group nourishes themselves on pumpkin bread and water.

"We should explore this cave, since it's not on the map," Slash says to his friends. "We need your light magic to guide the way, Sodina."

Walking forward, Slash pulls out his sword and proceeds into the cave with Sodina right behind him. Amanda stays in the middle of the pack, while Lorenz guards the rear with his bow at the ready. The way forward holds an impenetrable darkness. The light from Sodina's staff illuminates the path.

Walking through the darkness, sounds of screeching echo throughout the cave, bouncing off the moist stone walls.

"What was that?" Amanda squeals as she grabs the hem of Sodina's green cloak. She is the least capable of combat in the group.

"Keep it down." Slash hushes her. A door appears ahead of them in the light.

"Strange," he mutters as he investigates the oddly placed entrance. "A door with no warnings or instructions right in the middle of a cave. Be at the ready—"

Without warning, the floor collapses beneath them. The group falls into the darkness, wailing and flailing as they tumble down.

"Illuminate!" Sodina yells.

She shoots a flash of white light from her scepter, revealing the ground they are plunging toward.

She closes her eyes as she chants a prayer. "Goddess Astra, hold away our graves." She looks at her friends once more before she shouts, "Levitate!"

With only a few feet to spare, the group's fall slows and they descend gently to the ground. Amanda collapses onto her knees, crying. "Surely Astra is with us, because our death was imminent," she yells out in frustration. "Why did I ever agree to come on these adventures? One of these days, we won't be so lucky."

Sodina walks up to Amanda, wrapping her arms around her. "Everything will be okay," she reassures her with a smile.

"It would appear far too many have met their death in this area," Lorenz says, pointing toward several decayed and broken skeletons littering the large pit. Amanda shudders.

"I think there are people around here," Lorenz adds as he points toward a path sparsely lit by torches. "That path might lead us out of here." He takes one step forward, but his right leg buckles under him, bringing him to his knees. He winces.

Slash walks over to him and offers a hand to help him back up. "You all right?"

"It's nothing but a piece of wood that went too deep," snaps Lorenz. "I already pulled it out."

"The way you're speaking leads me to believe otherwise." Amanda sighs, walking over to her brother. "Let us see it!"

Sodina leans her staff toward Lorenz's right leg, revealing a deep bloodied wound on his calf. Surveying the injury, Amanda pulls out a vial of blue liquid.

"This is going to sting a bit," Amanda warns her brother before pouring it on his calf.

Lorenz yells while covering his mouth, then inhales and exhales deeply. His heart pumps faster as he tries to resist the painful sting in his leg.

"Well, it's not a hug from the Goddess." Sodina giggles.

Slash chuckles, too. "Your humor brings a smile to my face."

"You always seem to keep the situation pleasant." Lorenz groans as he avoids looking at his wound.

"That should stop the bleeding," Amanda assures him.

Pulling out a large bandage, Slash wraps the exposed flesh, to Lorenz's relief. He makes sure to tightly secure the cloth around his calf, ensuring that he'll still be able to move.

"I am sorry for putting all of you in harm's way," Slash says as he bows his head, looking at Lorenz.

"We could have chosen to wait out the storm near the cave's entrance, but now there is no escape," Lorenz replies grimly.

Looking toward the darkness in front of him, Slash points his sword. "I will slay all who come our way."

"We believe in you, Slash," Sodina says with a smile.

She lifts up Lorenz and puts his arm around her shoulder. Slash looks at Sodina with an approving gaze. Her words always boost his confidence.

"We have a wedding to plan in the coming months." Sodina giggles.

"I'm going to scout ahead," Slash says.

"Be careful, love," Sodina cautions him before giving him a comforting kiss.

He nods to her and descends toward the illuminated path. It soon leads to a split. Slash takes the left pathing, walking into a large square room lined with lit torches.

A growl comes from the corner, and he spins toward it. There stands a wolfen, five foot tall with foam oozing from its mouth.

What in Astra's name? Terror climbs his spine as he looks into the eyes of the beast.

The wolfen, covered in thick brown fur, lunges toward Slash on all fours. Slash clenches his sword with both hands and sidesteps the attack, dodging the massive canine, and digs his blade into the beast's flesh. The wolfen snarls in pain, blood dripping from its shoulder. Turning around for a second attack at Slash, the creature jumps into the air, diving toward him, its mouth wide open.

"Off with you!" Slash yells, slamming the tip of his sword into the wolfen's neck.

The body of the beast flails as Slash slams the ferocious creature toward the ground. Soon, it falls limp.

* * *

The distant sound of snarls sends a trickle of worry down Sodina's spine. "Come on. Slash might need our help," she says to the others.

Walking slowly into the darkness, Sodina leads Amanda and Lorenz with her staff illuminating the path ahead. The split in the path appears before them. Looking down, she observes footsteps in the dirt.

"Let's go left," Sodina says.

"This cave gives me a bad feeling," says Amanda, her eyes flitting this way and that.

Walking through the hallway, the group makes it to Slash, who is looking around the room.

"Nice of you to join me," he says, crossing his arms. "There is a door over there, but I wanted all of us to be here before proceeding."

Slash starts to walk toward the door. A massive sound echoes from the darkness above. He jumps backwards as a massive ten-foot-tall spider drops to the ground before them.

"I hate these stupid things," Slash yells.

"What in Astra's name is that monstrosity?" Lorenz says.

The spider steps back, its eyes twitching in different directions.

"We need to take out its vision, or we have no chance of beating that thing," says Slash.

"Let's do this, baby!" Sodina shouts, charging forward, smacking Slash on the butt.

Slash runs toward the spider, tripping on an unseen hole in the ground, landing in front of the hairy arachnid. The spider takes one of its legs and slams it toward Slash. He rolls to the right, avoiding the crushing blow.

"Be careful, Sodina!" Slash yells.

Sodina nods, sprinting toward the spider and slamming her staff into its legs. The spider jumps back, baring its long, dark fangs.

Slash runs at the spider and jumps. He crashes his sword down onto the spider's back, just barely avoiding its fangs. The spider screeches and tries to buckle him off.

Distraught by the screeching pain of the sound, Slash is caught off balance and falls.

"Slash!" Sodina cries as the spider turns around quickly and lowers its fangs toward Slash.

He rolls to the left and right as the spider continues to attack him, with poison dripping from its chelicerae. Sodina runs toward the spider's backside and slams the pointed edge of her scepter into one of the spider's legs. The spider turns and swings a different leg at Sodina. Flying back, she slams against the stone wall then falls to the floor.

Coughing up blood, Sodina looks at the spider. Her vision blurs as she closes her eyes.

Amanda's wide eyes follow the spider as it turns back to Slash. She quickly moves to Sodina, crouches down, and puts Sodina's head in her lap. "Drink this." She gives her a bottle filled with green liquid.

Lorenz glances down at his leg, wishing he could join in the fight. He pulls out his bow and shoots three arrows in rapid succession. The arrows hit the spider on its underbelly as it beats its chest.

"Right in the cheeks." Lorenz chuckles.

The spider turns away from Slash and scuttles toward Lorenz.

"Not today!" Slash yells.

Slash runs behind the beast and cuts off one of its legs. The spider rises slightly, scuttling from its injury. Lorenz shoots three more arrows at the spider's abdomen. Slash runs up and cuts another two legs off, throwing the spider off balance. The spider lets out another screech.

"That noise is unbearable," Lorenz grunts, kneeling on the ground.

"Slash!" Sodina yells across the cave floor. "Go for the rest of the legs!"

Slash nods, charging once more toward the spider.

"Okay, here we go," Sodina says. "Freezing Tempest!"

She stands, lifts her staff in the air, and points it at the creature, unleashing a stream of ice wind toward the spider's legs and freezing them.

The spider tries to free itself from her spell's frozen grasp by squirming about, but topples over and slides across the room helplessly. Slash grips his sword once more and swings his blade, slamming it into the frozen legs of the creature. Shattering each leg with ease underneath his furious blows. Lorenz shoots five arrows at the spider, blinding the beast as it nears its imminent death. Slash runs around to the front of the spider, thrusting his sword between the beast's fangs. Green slime sprays out of the spider's mouth, covering him completely.

"Ugh." Amanda turns her head in disgust.

The spider's blood continues to ooze on the ground as Slash walks away from the carnage.

"That was a close call," Lorenz says.

Slash saunters over to Sodina.

"Give me a hug, baby," he says.

"Don't do it," Amanda shrieks.

Sodina ambles toward Slash and embraces his blood-covered body as her arms crawl and slide through the disgustingly sticky juices.

"True love," Lorenz says, slapping his chest.

"I couldn't do that," Amanda says, looking away in disgust.

"If you love someone, you love them in the most intense moments as well," Sodina says.

"Always cheerful, that one is," Lorenz adds.

Slash sits on the ground after the kiss, wiping the slime off his body. Sodina walks across the room, pressing her hand on the door and accidentally releasing the internal magical lock. A giant rock door slides open. Sodina's face lights up with excitement at the room beyond.

"Something amazing is in there," Sodina says. Her eyes wide with awe, she looks back at her friends.

Slash shoots straight up and runs toward the door, eyes wide open.

"Oh, by the Goddess." Slash's mouth drops open,

In front of them is a pool stretching to at least forty feet long, and a fountain giving off hot steam. The room has a welcoming atmosphere, with a twin twenty-step stone staircase at the end of it. Amanda puts Lorenz's arm over her shoulder, walking toward the door.

"Be cautious, you guys," Amanda reminds them.

Slash, with his sword still drawn, walks cautiously toward the step leading into the pool. It glows with a green light.

"Do not fear dear children of Astra, for you are safe." A female voice echoes throughout the room.

"Despite your calming voice, we have no reason to trust you," bellows Slash as he points his sword forward.

"You have the right to be skeptical, human," the female voice says.

A ten-foot-tall fairy emerges from behind the staircase near the end of the fountain. Her hair is white in color, emitting a brilliant light. Her translucent pink wings are massive, spanning ten feet wide. They give off a gentle breeze as she hovers slightly above the staircase.

"My name is Ella. I am one of the servants of the Goddess Astra." Ella flies down into the pool, standing in the water. She wears a light blue dress. "This is the water from the heavenly city of Arcadia."

Ella gazes down at the party of four with a smile that could illuminate the darkness.

Slash looks at the water and takes his boots off, followed by his tunic. Shaking ever so slightly, he steps forward. "As the leader, I will go first," he enthusiastically says. "It's just like taking a dip in the pool with a bathing suit on." He smiles playfully "But we are in a deep cave and could be attacked." He walks into the warm pool, lowering his body into the deep, soothing water.

Ella smiles, flying towards Slash. "You, brave warrior, have the faith to trust the unknown," she says.

Amanda sits Lorenz down so he can remove his weapons and armor. Then Amanda, still in full dress, runs toward the pool and jumps into the warm water.

"This pool feels like happiness." She grins. "This is wonderful! Oh, what a glorious story we have to tell our townspeople," she says, throwing her hands into the air.

Sodina takes off her shoes and walks into the pool near Slash.

"My love, you are wonderful," Sodina says, wrapping her arms around Slash and kissing his neck slowly.

Slash blushes as he splashes water toward Sodina's face.

"Oh, you!" Sodina says, putting her hands together and splashing him right back.

Ella smiles as she sits at the edge of the pool.

"Dear humans, you know of the legend. Correct?" she asks the party of four.

The group nods, looking at Ella.

"Goddess Astra closed off these areas to the public and built enormous caves, volcanoes, and structures filled with trials of all types," she says.

"Legends say fountains like these are used across Esteria," says Amanda. She adjusts her glasses to ensure the fairy goddess before her is no illusion. "The history books say this is one of the last four fountains left, because Helion defied the Goddess."

"You are the correct, young one, and our tears grant one hundred years of additional life," Ella adds. "You are practically like little brothers or sisters to us."

Ella grabs Amanda and lifts her into the air, holding her like a young child.

"How cool is this?" Amanda says, swinging her arms in the air as Ella flies around the room.

Ella strokes Amanda's hair and twirls her in the air. Amanda puts out her arms, enjoying the experience.

Sodina looks at Lorenz, sitting quietly near the edge of the pool. "What's wrong, Lorenz?" she asks.

Lorenz looks down at the pool. "My leg is fully healed, and I am at peace enjoying this moment," he assures her. He searches for a joke but is at a loss. "I'd rather not trouble you with my endless thoughts." Standing up, he does a backflip into the water.

Hours pass as the party of four enjoys their time with Ella and relaxes in the pool.

"I would like to reward you for finding this place," Ella says. "If you have any vials, please give them to me."

Slash holds out his bottle, and Ella lifts it toward her eye.

"These tears may come in handy as you travel Esteria," she says. Ella cries into sixteen small vials before handing them back.

"Drink up, young ones." Ella smiles.

Slash turns to his group, drinking his tear right away, feeling more refreshed than ever. Amanda raises her bottle to drink hers next.

"Bottoms up," she cheers.

"Look out!" yells Slash. His eyes trace an object rapidly approaching from the room's entrance.

A spear impales Amanda through her chest, killing her instantly.

"Amanda!" Sodina yells. "Amanda, come back to us!"

"Where did that come from?" Lorenz bellows.

"Who dares defile this place?" Ella cries, shaking. She looks around, trying to ascertain where the attack came from.

Sodina climbs out of the pool and rushes over to Amanda's lifeless body. She runs her fingers through Amanda's hair and then down to her eyes, closing them slowly. A pool of bright red blood surrounds Amanda's body, lying limp on the ground.

Lorenz runs to grab his bow.

"Augh!" he screams in pain.

Both of his legs are taken out by a twirling scythe.

"Augh!" he screams one last time as his upper body falls to the ground with a thud.

"Lorenz!" Slash yells, pulling out his sword.

The terror climbs through his back as he runs over to grab Sodina's hand. Lorenz crawls as the scythe comes around again and cuts his upper body in half.

Panic eclipses his mind. "You bastards, show your face!" Slash shouts, demanding the unknown assailants reveal themselves.

Ella puts up a magical barrier around Slash and Sodina.

"There is nothing you can do for them, young ones," she says with a sorrowful look.

Ella carves a circle in thin air as a portal opens, revealing the mouth of the cave. She puts out her hand as Slash and Sodina levitate, flying through the portal.

"Young ones, never come here again," Ella warns them as the portal closes behind them.

Slash slams his fist into the ground in frustration.

"We cannot get their bodies," Sodina says as tears slowly form in her eyes.

Slash screams towards the night sky, his lungs about to burst. Sodina puts her hands together, bowing toward the ground, tears flowing down her cheeks.

"Goddess Astra, please receive our dear friends into your presence," she says.

Slash looks around, lifting his view toward Sodina. He notices a small dart in her right shoulder. His eyes widen in fear.

"Sodina—"

Her eyes meet his, her lashes fluttering, and then she stumbles and falls forward. Slash runs over to catch her before she hits the ground.

He embraces Sodina in his arms, running down same the hill they came up a few hours ago. From the look of the dart, it must be poisonous. The area around her shoulder is already starting to turn a dark purple.

Slash makes for Dalton, the closest town to his location. He takes a right turn and runs through the night. The moonlight pierces through the gloomy fog, revealing the dirt road ahead. In the distance, he sees the light of town.

Chapter 2

Month of Dragons
Day 12

The human existence—a never-ending cycle of choices

    Those choices lead to actions that cannot be undone

    Two graves of those time will forget

    Where do I belong?

    Do we fight to free ourselves from oppression?

    What is life? What is freedom? Why does man bleed? Have the Gods betrayed us?

    I fall down in failure awaiting the stinging blade of death!

    Fight! Kill! We will rise above!

    What are we but humans? The breath in our lungs propelling us forward!

    We will create a new path toward the bright horizon!

On a hot summer's day, Slash stares at the graves of his two friends he swore to protect, Sodina's hand in his. Slash's wavy black hair blows in the wind, and his sword rests on his hip. Five years have passed since they set forth on that fated journey.

    There is such emptiness within my heart.

The minutes feel like hours and hours like days.

The grief of my decisions is almost too much to bear.

These past several years were difficult on them. The mayor exiled Slash and Sodina from their hometown of Ifer due to the deaths of his children Lorenz and Amanda.

That fated day when darkness intertwined with our lives.

Sodina started aging slowly, since she was poisoned in an attack by an unknown enemy. The poison gravely altered the effect of the tears they drank from the fairy goddess fountain. The tears from the fountain added one hundred years of life for each drop, and they had each drunk only one. The effects from the poison were slowed as a result, but Sodina still shows some pain. Her joints spasm for hours at a time without warning. She experiences weakness that is out of the ordinary for someone her age.

We will reverse this and claim back what was stolen from us.

* * *

In the outer realms of the Eastern Kingdom, near the border, lies the town of Jerut. The two lovers lie out in a field of high grass, their belongings strewn around them. The memory of that day by the gravestones floods Slash's mind as he sleeps.

"Slash, wake up…" Sodina's face shines from the afternoon sun as she looks down at him.

"How long have I been asleep?" Slash wonders aloud, sitting up to meet Sodina beaming at him.

"For some time now, silly." Sodina touches his smooth cheek lovingly. "I protected us with magic so we could sleep in broad daylight without being attacked."

"Thank you, baby, I appreciate that," he answers, staring at his beautiful wife.

Sodina smiles. "You're looking at my breasts, love, not my eyes."

"Sorry for my manly instincts."

"I know that my man is going to look." Sodina giggles while rising from the ground, offering her hand.

"You know me too well," he answers, letting her pull him up.

The pair begins to walk slowly toward the town in the distance. Just then, a wolfen runs out of the forest, heading right toward Slash.

Slash is ready. Seeing the beast approach, he pulls out his sword and cuts the wolfen across the chest leaving a gaping wound. The blood splatters over Sodina's skirts and Slash's coat as they continue to walk forward.

"Since we met Ella, there seems to be an increase in monsters throughout the kingdom," Sodina murmurs.

Slash sighs, looking off into the distance. "I know, love, it's tragic."

Sodina looks at the ground, wondering when the bloodshed will end.

"Don't look so gloomy," Slash says. "It is only part of our journey. We are merely warriors, trying our best to make it through this life. I know the blood will continue to bother you, but eventually, we will never have to fight again." He pulls in her for a sweet kiss before they move along. "Until then, cheer up and know that you husband is here for you."

Sodina looks up at the sky, at the sun glimmering with delight. "I know."

They approach the city gates of Jerut and walk through them. Clouds gather above the town.

"Everything is going to be okay," he says.

"These travels can be too much for me, love," Sodina whispers.

"We will need to explore as we continue to dive deeper into this mystery," Slash replies. "Whoever poisoned you is still out there."

Sodina runs forward with a skip and hop, trying to shake off the blood on her summer dress.

"If I could just use magic to clean my dress," she mutters.

"I know, baby. How great would it be if you could use magic every time you get dirty?" Slash looks over with a smirk on his face and waggles his brows.

"Hey, don't be like that." Sodina beams. Her long red hair blows in the wind.

Slash looked at her in admiration, knowing the poison is still impacting her significantly. *How does this woman do it? She continues to fight on with poison in her body*, he thinks to himself. *So brave.*

They still have so much to explore, and they need to find a way to remove the poison from Sodina. Traditional medicine yielded no results. All Slash can think about is her and the troubles she is going through. What an amazing wife he has, regardless of the pain and suffering.

Sodina skips forward, slightly off balance, jumping in the puddles of the city streets. Raindrops fall in a light drizzle.

"I just love how the rain feels on my body, Slash!" she exclaims. "It will wash the blood off my dress!"

Slash looks into the distance and sees stores upon stores that resemble every other city they have ventured into. This city is packed full of everything a traveler might need, even thugs.

"The local knights probably let the back alleys roam freely, full of crime," he mumbles, though Sodina can hear him clearly.

"I wonder how many unsolved murders happen because of those scoundrels who roam in the darkness." She shivers as they make their way through the busy cobblestone streets. Her eyes explore the two-story homes and business that all look the same except for the signs on the front of them.

I wonder if we can make some money being bounty hunters and bringing those criminals to justice, thinks Slash.

"Keep an eye out for a guild, my love," Slash yells after Sodina.

She looks back in approval as she continues to skip and hop through the puddles.

Slash grins at his wife, continuing to live her life with glee even with the impending doom of death lurking.

"What are you thinking about?" asks Sodina.

"I was thinking about the monsters that attacked us and if there is some sort of infestation around this area," says Slash. "I wish we knew what those monsters were called."

The city is still packed to the brim with people as they make their way through the streets. There is something eerily familiar about the place that Slash can't quite understand. The rain begins to pour harder, and the lovers raise their cloaks to shield them.

"We need to find a place to get out of the rain, Sodina!" Slash shouts over the downpour. *The rainy season in summer never ends,* he thinks to himself.

"There, love, a tavern!" Sodina points at a building about five hundred feet away from where they are. "We can take refuge there."

Sodina grabs Slash's hand as they run toward the tavern doors.

Slash looks up at the sign. The tavern sports the name, "Adventurers' Guild." *With luck, maybe we'll find a lead here that can help us score some gold coins!* he thinks.

Sodina pulls the door open, and to their delight, the tavern is open, with lots of people inside. "Let's grab a seat in the corner, okay." Sodina surveys the room and finds a table at the top right of the bar by the stairs. "Let's go, Slash, I found us a seat!"

"I have no choice, my love; you are gripping my hand so tightly!" Slash exclaims.

Inside the tavern are all types of people who may be of help to them. Slash looks around to see mages, swordsmen, knights, assassins, and a woman with a tail. Adventurers' Guild seems friendly to all.

One man, in particular, crosses eyes with Slash and gives him a disapproving look. He's dressed all in black, like some kind of assassin.

Slash frowns a little. *I wonder what that was all about.*

He won't forget the look in the man's eyes and the set of several daggers on his waist. The assassin looked ready to kill their prey silently and swiftly. Slash gulps and looks away, back to Sodina.

"Here we are, silly!" Sodina laughs as Slash sits down close beside her.

Her husband is always stuck in the stars, and it is her job to bring him back down to earth.

"This is…" Sodina tries to find the right word. "Cozy. But a little uncomfortable, no?"

"Yes, dear, these wooden chairs are nothing to write home about." Slash sighs.

A perky young lady walks up with a menu and places it down in front of them.

"Let me know when you're ready!" the waitress says before running off to assist another patron.

Slash picks up the list and looks at it. There is nothing on the menu but lamb, more lamb, and baked dragon meat, a seasonal special.

Wow. Dragon meat! I wonder if it tastes like chicken. What spices will they use? The spices Slash imagines dance around in his head like children playing in the streets on a summer's day.

At that moment, something clamors by the front tavern doors.

"Oh, my, we have a special guest tonight!" a plump man says.

A tall, fair-skinned, well-endowed woman with long pink hair and large hips starts to walk down the middle aisle of the tavern.

Slash's eyes follow her every step.

"That's Busty Bridget," the barkeeper, Chadwick, says to Sodina and Slash, who are looking on with curiosity.

Another man at the table next to them whispers, "She is the most beautiful woman in the land. They say she can slay a dragon just by looking at it."

Bridget approaches him and looks down at the man, who cowers in fear.

Her pupils turn purple with annoyance. "Say that again and my axe will crush your spine in an instant," she snaps.

Slash looks across at her, and Bridget catches his eyes. She winks at him and saunters toward the end of the bar. A single stool is pulled out just for her, and she orders a small glass of wine.

Oh, she is quite beautiful, Slash thinks to himself.

He turns back to Sodina, who is drinking a glass of water with an indifferent look upon her face.

"I wonder if she is famous because of her bouncing assets of joy," his wife mutters.

"All of the men must really like her," Slash says.

Another patron turns around to Sodina and smiles. "She is popular; all of the ladies want to be her, and the men want to be with her. She continues to bring in lots of money in the guild because of her hunting and killing skills. She is a bloodthirsty warrior, always traveling on quests to be the best in the land. I hear that she is loyal but will only give her loyalty to those who are worthy. She travels with groups but will never stay with one group too long."

Sodina smiles, hearing Bridget's story. She admires that she is more than her looks.

"I wonder if she will join us," she cheerfully states.

"Me too, my love," answers Slash, taking a chug of his beer.

"I doubt it," the barkeeper butts in as he wipes the counter clean. "You two are outsiders. This is an Adventurers' tavern, so new faces are usually stuck with weaker quests or tasks like watching some minor nobles or protecting caravans full of vegetables from foreign lands."

"What is that on her back, my love?" Sodina questions, and Slash looks over in Bridget's direction.

Draped over Bridget's back is a large cloak of dragon scales woven in silk.

Chadwick looks over at Slash and says matter-of-factly, "That cloak provides protection from enemies and untrained men. The dragon scales are from a rare dragon that can sense danger from afar."

"So, you're telling me those scales are alive?!" Slash's eyes widen in amazement.

"Yes, in a way... The scales act as a defense and may take on the emotions of the individual wearing them."

Slash looks slightly puzzled but also curious as to how a woman like this exists.

Sodina leans over to Slash, trying to hide the pain in her eyes. Her right arm violently shakes as she grips it with her left hand, steadying the shaking.

"I am feeling weak, love. I need to get some rest soon." Sodina closes her eyes and lets out a single tear before laying her head on her husband's shoulder.

Slash waves down the perky young waitress.

"I think I will try the dragon meat," he says. "We don't have much money. Do you need help with the dishes tonight?"

"You're that desperate, eh?" The waitress looks at Slash suggestively. "What else would you offer for some food?"

Chadwick hushes her. "We are a small staff, so you can wash the dishes for a piece of dragon meat. That meat isn't cheap, you know."

"Okay, boss, one slab of dragon meat with a free glass of our red wine coming right up for this handsome man!" The young lady winks as she walks back toward the kitchen.

Why do I have to have this handsome face that makes women want to flirt with me? Slash thinks. *Washing dishes is pretty bad, but I guess it could be worse.*

Slash looks over back at Bridget, who is now eating a leg of lamb with a huge fork, considering how to approach her.

Maybe I should have Sodina do it since they are both ladies. Slash glances at his wife, snoring lightly at his side. *But then what type of man would I be if I was not confident asking this beautiful unknown woman to help us or give us a lead to find something to heal Sodina?*

Slash continues to stare at the scene around the tavern. Individuals are enjoying themselves with wine, drinking their troubles away.

The rain that pelted the roof earlier transitions into a light drizzle as the evening starts to set in.

Sodina wakes up after an hour of resting on Slash's shoulder and shoots up immediately.

"I can't believe I slept that long! Why didn't you wake me up? Is my lamb's meat stale?"

"No, darling, everything is okay," Slash says. "You were so tired I did not want to wake you. Your meal should be here any minute."

Sodina relaxes and smooths down her hair and dress, her eyes still filled with sleep.

"My love, I'm going to try to talk to that Bridget lady and see if she knows anything." Slash rubs her gently on the head.

Sodina nods at him. "Okay, just be careful not to get your pocket picked. The tables are very close together."

Slash kisses her cheek before he stands up, headed for the end of the bar, leaving his sword with Sodina. Her food arrives and she digs in, watching her husband walk down to where Bridget is sitting.

Bridget is talking to Chadwick about the local news when he nears her.

"Hello, Bridget." He clears his throat. "My name is Slash. I'm a traveler. I just wanted a moment of your time."

Bridget stops talking as a small smile graces her face with delight.

"You must be a kindhearted man for the scales on the back of my cloak to not stand up."

Slash did not take time to notice the scales continued to lie flat, though still as beautiful as ever, protecting Bridget with pride.

"You were very courageous to come at me from behind, knowing that I could chop you down in an instant. You left your sword with your companion, knowing full well that you have no way of defending yourself." Bridget continues to stare at the bar, not turning toward Slash.

The whole tavern falls silent as they look from Slash back to Bridget. It is so quiet a needle could drop and everyone would hear it.

Slash stands there, confident, awaiting an answer. No sweat hits his eyebrows as he stares at the back of her cloak.

Bridget turns around with a gleeful smile and squeals, "I like you!"

Every man in the bar stares at Slash with sternness and awe.

Bridget, who is taller than Slash by a foot, leans over and hugs him, her enormous breasts hitting his face.

"He touched them!" a patron says, looking at Slash with jealous envy.

Slash yells, "Please, Bridget! I'm married!" His muffled scream can only be heard by a few people near the bar as Bridget grips him tightly.

Sodina blushes, knowing that her husband would never cheat on her, and just laughs.

Bridget looks down at Slash 's beet-red face, tucked in her bosom.

"Oh, you're married." Bridget frowns and loosens her grip on Slash, letting him go. "I apologize. And to your wife as well."

"Many thanks," Slash says, trying not to look at her assets.

"I can tell you're a kind man by how you approached me." Bridget smiles. "I watched as you interacted with people since I came in. You are a ray of light in this dark city, and I was automatically drawn to you.

"I will give you my loyalty still, even though I want to provide you with so much more." Bridget winks, leans down, and gives Slash a big kiss on the cheek.

Blushing, Slash can't take any more attention from the other patrons and sits down next to her at the bar.

"I guess my husband is still out there." Bridget sighs. "Maybe I will find him on our travels."

Slash looks at Bridget with confusion. "Our travels?"

"Yes," Bridget states. "I want to join you on whatever journey you are planning. Your meals and your inns are on me as well."

All of the patrons in the tavern, still staring in awe, start to go back to their activities.

"Does it ever get tiring being the center of attention?" Slash asks Bridget as she wipes the lamb oil off her mouth.

"Sometimes, I would rather not be the pun of many jokes of jealous women, or viewed as some mountain men want to conquer. All of the men around here are boys wishing they could ride this wagon, or so they say. I'm a mare that can't be tamed unless it is by one who claims my heart. Only one man can handle all of this excitement and bounciness."

Bridget starts to sway back and forth, intentionally causing her bosoms to bounce with glee.

Slash replies, "I understand, indeed. We are grateful for your assistance. Let me get back to Sodina."

Bridget slaps Slash on the back as he stands up and walks back to his wife. He wasn't gone for long, but it felt like a lifetime being away from his wife. All of the emotions of being embraced by a beautiful woman, the hug, and then a kiss, have left him in shock. He made a new friend but she already feels like family.

A woman who would die for me just like that… How did that happen?

Slash sits down next to Sodina, who is finishing up her wine.

"What type of wine did you get, my love?" Slash asks.

Sodina replies, "A strong white wine, the finest in the region."

"How expensive was it?"

"It doesn't matter, silly," Sodina giggles, "because Bridget is paying for it!"

Slash shakes his head, looking at his wife. "That is not the response I thought you were going to say."

"That was amazing what you did." Sodina kissed Slash lightly and looked into his eyes. "I saw your reaction to her beautiful body. You are my man for sure." She smiled from ear to ear, knowing that Slash went through a lot of craziness to get the help they needed. "But I do understand how someone that…large could rival me."

"Here you are. One piece of dragon meat for the two of you." The waitress puts down the plate of dragon meat and an extra glass of wine.

"This looks amazing!" Sodina says, doing a little dance in her chair before taking a bite. "While you were talking with Bridget, love, I tried to extract some of the poison out of my body with a healing spell. I got one drop out!"

"You did?" Slash's face lights up with excitement. "Oh, my goodness, what joy I have in my heart for you. Did you use Revival of the Goodness?"

"Yes," Sodina went on. "It took so much out of me. The lamb helped me, though, and gave me the strength to get at least one drop. That was the one good thing we learned at the church all those years ago—how to extract poison. But, love, I'll be dead soon if I do not get the rest of it out. Draining one drop of infected blood every six months is not going to cut it."

"I'm selfish and do not want to lose you." Slash sighs. "We will get this wretched curse out of your body."

As closing time draws near, Slash walks toward the waitress who brought him his meal.

"My wife is rather ill at the moment. I am here to wash the dishes for the meal, even though Bridget paid for it."

The waitress nods at him, showing him the path to the dish room.

Slash walks back to the kitchen, where the pile of dishes awaits him. *The things I must do to survive here. Why couldn't I have some magic power to clean them without lifting a hand?*

Slash puts on an apron and starts to fill the sink with soapy water.

"Well, if it's a hand you need, I am more than willing to help!" Bridget bolts into the kitchen, axe in hand. "I can just crush all the plates and you won't have to do them!"

"That's not going to work!" Slash proclaims.

"Well, I guess I will help you do them the normal way." Bridget takes off her cloak to put on an apron.

The waitress comes into the kitchen, surprised to see Bridget in such attire.

"Mistress Bridget, you must not do such a menial task!"

"It's okay, ma'am. I am helping out a friend who owes a debt." Bridget smiles as she turns her attention to the pile at hand. "So, why don't I wash and you dry?"

"Sounds like a plan," Slash says as he grabs a handful of towels.

"So, tell me, would you ever cheat on your wife?" Bridget speaks seriously.

Slash looks puzzled as he starts to dry the first dish handed to him. The giant bosom babe washes dishes quickly.

"I would not cheat on her because Sodina is my everything," he replies, drying more dishes as Bridget hands them over. "No matter how sexy the woman, I will run if I am in a situation where I could fall into temptation. I am still a man, and beauty is beauty. I must continuously be on my guard and not fall into any pitfalls where I could tarnish my love for her."

"That is so sweet." Bridget continues to wash the dirty dishes and pass them to Slash.

"I know that you are pure of heart, Slash, but I also sense a dark past full of regret in your heart. Could you tell me a little about what happened?" Bridget stops washing dishes and looks at Slash intently.

"Sodina was poisoned and we were with two of our childhood friends. We do not know what happened for sure." Slash clears his throat before going on. "We ventured deep into the Eastern Kingdom to search for the goddess of that region. We finally found her deep inside a damp, murky cavern. Our journey was full of monsters, traps, and all types of bewitched doors, but we had a competent party. We had two other childhood friends with us, Amanda and Lorenz. They were both murdered by the same individuals who poisoned Sodina."

"How awful!" Bridget exclaims.

"I was not able to carry their bodies out of the cavern. They died cruel deaths, my friends. I swore to protect them and…I couldn't do anything, nor could I see what was happening. It was as if the enemy manifested out of thin air or was waiting there for us all along."

Slash leans over the sink, his eyes squeezed shut, tears falling down at a rapid pace. He is afraid of what Bridget might think of him, but his heart needs to grieve once again. "I am the worst of the worst. What good is a man who can't keep his word?"

Bridget puts her damp hand on Slash's back. "You will make it. Your friends died knowing you did the best you could."

"How could you understand?! Has anyone died underneath your watch?" Slash turns toward Bridget, tears still streaming down his face. "I am a wreck, and I am sorry for saying that." He turns back to the sink.

Bridget stays quiet, observing the weeping man beside her.

"I promised their parents I would look after them. One of them was impaled with a spear, and the other cut down with a scythe. I swear I will find whoever killed them and put my sword through their throat. I remember the scythe being a light purple tint with a certain aura around it. That type of power doesn't go away." Slash shakes his head. "I am sure they are out there hurting and killing other people."

Bridget finishes cleaning the last dish.

"It's okay to feel that way," she says. "When you are cold, hurt, and beatdown on the inside, a shower on the outside will cleanse the soul, making your heart anew. Let those tears flow, dear."

She takes off her apron and puts on her cloak. "I will be waiting in the main lobby. "

Slash looks at the dishes left to dry. *I'm glad they have a lot of towels to use. Otherwise, I'd have to air dry all of these on a rack.* He finishes drying the dishes and takes off his apron.

It feels good to complete a task, even though Slash really didn't have to. Good deeds go a long way.

Slash tidies up the kitchen, leaving the area spotless, before heading back out into the main tavern room. Sodina and Bridget are waiting for him.

"Ready to go, silly?" Sodina asks Slash.

"Of course. I worked pretty hard back there, and it's time for some rest with my love."

"The inn is right down the street from here," Bridget states. "It's only two blocks, and I usually rent two rooms, just to be safe. You may have the other one."

The couple thanks her in unison, and Bridget laughs.

"When you're a powerful adventurer like me, people do want you dead often. I have yet to see a bounty hunter, but I am sure my name is being used in blacklisted guilds."

"You mean those guilds that are in the bad parts of town?" Sodina asks.

"Yes, those guilds." Bridget nods. "Many of them are run by merchants who trade on the black market. You can pick up some killer deals there, but I would not recommend going unless you have a party of four people or more. Any less and you are asking for trouble."

The trio heads for the door, waving goodbye to the waitress. Bridget walks outside and then jerks back, screaming, "Watch out!"

Three poison darts fly toward Bridget, and she turns around so the scales on her cloak act as an impenetrable shield. The trio runs toward the inn. Bridget spins back around to see a figure in black with a dagger ready to pounce.

"That's the man I saw earlier dressed in black back at the bar!" Slash says. "I knew there was something off about him."

"You know of the black market?" Bridget huffs. "I am sure this is one of the local enforcers. I heard rumors they sent one to the town to scope out potential scams they could execute."

The trio shields themselves from more darts as they back away.

"You messed with the wrong woman today, pal!" Bridget yells.

The evening summer breeze blows briskly across the stone road.

"You know when there is one, there is usually more!" Slash draws his sword and jumps in front of his wife to protect her.

Sodina puts out her hand and chants, "In the name of Goddess Astra, I channel fire to burn this evil to a crisp!" A small flame blooms and grows bigger and bigger in Sodina's hand, ready to throw.

Bridget draws her axe from her hip. "Get ready!"

She runs toward the masked figure, swinging furiously at his head.

The masked figure jumps into the air and kicks Bridget in the face.

"Nice one, you creep." Bridget wipes away the blood from her lip.

"It's going to take more than that to kill me. And I'm not alone this time!"

"Oh, I know," answers the masked figure. He clutches his dagger and lunges toward Bridget. Bridget spins around the blade; it hits the scales on her cloak. The blade snaps in half, and the masked figure jumps back.

"So, it is as they say," he spits. "That cloak is your powerful defense, but besides that, you're nothing but a slow, beautiful fighter. You will never hit me with that giant axe of yours. Tell your friend back there to stop chanting. I will be gone before she can cast her spell."

Sodina calls a flame storm, and a massive fireball flies toward the masked figure.

Before it can hit its mark, the masked assassin jumps onto the rooftop of a nearby shop and disappears into the night.

"That bastard got away," Bridget growls, wiping more blood trickling from her mouth. "That makes me so mad. I usually get attacked at least once a month, but that assassin was something different. We're going to have to watch our backs from now on. I'm sure that isn't the last time we'll run into characters like that."

Bridget puts her axe back on her hip, looking around for another attack. "I think we are in the clear. You know what, Slash, you didn't even react! What were you doing?!"

"I was trying to protect Sodina as she was chanting to cast her spell."

"Oh, I see. Sorry to doubt you." Bridget chuckles softly. "I guess I judged too quickly. I forget you're married."

She walks toward the inn and puts her hands behind her head. "You know, this town used to be much safer. Thugs and other groups have come in and supplied those with less money to join their cause. Eventually, there could be an uprising on the government's hands."

Sodina looks off into the distance and sees the inn coming into view. "I see," she says as she takes Slash's hand in hers.

The spell took a lot out of her, and Slash is frustrated that it was for nothing.

"This two-story inn is one of the nicer ones in town," Bridget says.

She leads them through the doors of the inn.

Bridget walks to the counter and speaks with the manager. "The normal, please, Carol."

"Of course," Carol says, and Bridget smiles at her.

"You're pretty popular with everyone," Sodina notes.

"Well, I saved her son from bandits last year, so she insists on giving me a discount on the rooms." Bridget takes the keys from Carol and proceeds up the stairs. "You guys are in 201, and I am in 202, okay?"

"Thank you so much for everything, Bridget." Slash bows his head in gratitude.

"Before you go to bed, though, I want to tell you some of my stories."

Slash and Sodina follow Bridget into room 201, and they sit down at a wooden table built for four.

Bridget yawns, stretching wildly and gazing at couple. "Now that we have officially had our first fight together, you should know the lady behind the axe."

Chapter 3

Month of Dragons
Day 12

The inns of Jerut are filled with the aromatic smell of wine, permeating the neat and mundane rooms of the old building. Bridget leans back in her chair and looks at Slash and Sodina with playful eyes.

"How much do you know about The Boarding School for Troubled Girls?" Bridget asks.

"Not much," Slash replies as Sodina stares at Bridget, puzzled by the question.

"The Boarding School for Troubled Girls is an academy for young women between the ages of fifteen and twenty, many of whom have been outcast by society. The Academy was founded by a rich duke who had a daughter who was possessed by a demon. The young woman was eventually exorcised by a priest of Astra.

"The duke later founded the Academy to help his daughter recover from the possession. He brought in the best scholars, priests, and rural workers, and put the university in the center of the four kingdoms so the travel time would be at an equal distance for everyone traveling," Bridget explains, staring out the window. "It was twelve years ago. I can still remember every detail of it. Like a bitter taste in my mouth that won't go away no matter how much I drink. The pain, the smiles, the eyes of those who preyed upon my body. It was a part of my life that still claws against the back of my head."

* * *

A hand smacked Bridget's face and she stumbled back, hitting her head against the wall behind her. Her face turned red as anger filled her eyes.

"Repeat it," a man commanded her.

"I won't say it," Bridget yelled. "I'm no slave-whore, especially to the likes of you."

A middle-aged bald man scaned Bridget up and down, with a paddle in his hand.

"Say it again," he said, slowly putting his face closer to Bridget's. "I will be a good wife, and please my husband to his utmost delight."

Bridget looked up at the man and snarled. She threw a quick jab at the man's crotch before pushing him down to the ground.

"You crazy tomboy!" the man yelled as he groaned in pain. "You were born with a beautiful body for that must be trained. No man will ever want to bed you with that attitude. You'll rot in a lonely unmarried life."

"I didn't even want to be in this dump of a place to start with," Bridget snapped.

She looked down at the man, grinning menacingly. The headmaster walked in with a cold, stern face as she stared at Bridget.

"Headmaster Anna," Bridget murmured.

Bridget stood up tall immediately, with her hand leaning on her chest, and bowed. Anna walked over to Bridget and looked down at the man.

"Care to explain to me what is the meaning of this?

"He was making me say horrible things, Anna."

"That's Headmaster Anna to you, young one. I will talk with Paul about your behavior. If I find that he is treating you in a horrible manner, we will take the appropriate actions."

Paul rolled over and lifted himself up slowly.

"That girl," Paul said as he wiped off the dust from his shoulders, "has some problematic issues with her brain. She will never be a proper lady and is better off becoming a cheap harlot."

"That is quite enough, Paul." Anna looked at him with a stern glance. "You can take your leave now and leave young Bridget to me."

Paul walked out of the room, throwing Bridget a look of contempt.

"Don't forget to put ice on it!" Bridget snickered.

"Bridget!"

"Yes, Headmaster?" Bridget responded, looking down at the floor.

Anna placed her finger under Bridget's chin, and lifted her head slowly.

"Eyes up here, young one," Anna commanded.

Bridget looked up slowly toward the eyes of Anna.

"That's a good girl. Now. What are the core values here at the Academy?"

Bridget let out a soft sigh, scratching her nape.

"*Love yourself. Love others. Love Goddess Astra.*"

"Now, that wasn't that so hard, was it now?" Anna asked.

"No. It wasn't," Bridget replied. "But I don't like being forced to be something I am not. I want to be free to make my own decisions and run wild in this world. Having relations with a man until the day I die does not sound like the best life possible."

"You do not have to get married if you do not want to," Anna said, looking at Bridget. "Marriage is not for everyone. Some women, like me, stay single and charge forward, making their own destiny. I believe you can do the same."

"You really think so?"

"Yes. Yes, I do," Anna replied. "But you cannot punch our faculty in their family heirlooms. They only get one set, so kindly refrain from taking them out of commission. Is that understood? Will you promise me not to do it again?"

"I promise, Headmaster. I will try not to punch any unruly men in the gentleman's area. Even if they do deserve it."

"Good enough, I suppose." Anna let out a small chuckle. "Now go. Get some rest, young one."

Bridget crouched down and picked up her books on martial tactics. She noticed Anna giving her weird glances.

Just because I want to study knight formations and other types of warfare doesn't make me weird, Bridget thought to herself. *Does Goddess Astra even care for us? They speak of such love of the Goddess, but people like Paul exist to torment me. I have a bad feeling about his intentions. He considers himself a devout believer, but most of the professors at the Academy are dirty crooks. They say one thing with their lips and another with their actions.*

Bridget proceeded to the Academy library for her afternoon studies. She picked a desk in the corner of the library, away from the traffic of the busy day. She chose a book from one of the nearby shelves—*Deri Meritari: On the Art of Military Formations Vol I,*

"I've been looking for this for so long and it's finally back!" said Bridget, grinning.

This book had been on Bridget's mind for the past three months. She quickly grabbed it and sat down at the nearby table.

Chapter 1: Formations of Military Knighthood

The pages showed her the formations knights used to attack their enemies in close quarters. She visualized a scene where knights were pinned down by their enemies and were back to back, pushing their way out of a critical situation.

The knights are so dreamy! She sighed. *As a female, I could never be a knight. Why is this world so cruel? I'm tough. I can definitely take on any of the girls here.*

"Hey, Bridget!"

Bridget looked over to where the voice was coming from. A young, short girl with chubby cheeks ran toward Bridget.

I'd know that voice anywhere. Bridget smiled. "Hey, Grace!"

Grace and Bridget slapped hands and punched each other's fists.

"Let's say our version of the Academy's motto," Grace said. "Okay, together now."

Goddess Astra Last
Treat yourself right first
Don't marry a crazy man
He will always thirst

Grow as a lady
Pursue the truth
Love yourself to no end
Be uniquely you

Bridget hugged Grace before they sat down together at the table. "I heard you had to go back home to your mother's funeral," said Bridget.

"Yes, she was killed by the bandits roaming the Eastern Kingdom," Grace replied, clenching her fingers together. "My father was stabbed in the arm, trying to protect her. Thankfully, the knights of the city arrived and killed the bandits."

"That's horrible," Bridget murmured, so no one else in the library would overhear them.

"Yes, it truly is." Grace looked down at the ground. "I have to continue to focus on my studies. Father paid my way through planting produce for the kingdom. Making the most of my time is essential. I must not bring shame to my family."

"At least you still have your father by your side. Both of my parents died when I was young, during the Second Great War, or at least that's what I was told," said Bridget.

Hours passed as the girls conversed about everything from which teacher was the worst to what dreams they wanted to achieve in the coming years.

"It's almost closing time. I can talk to you for hours," said Grace, looking at Bridget with a smile. "Off to the dorms then, shall we?"

"I'm going to hang out a little bit longer and put the books back. I'll catch up with you."

"I'll see you in a few minutes then," Grace said before waving goodbye.

"I will never understand magic." Bridget sighed, returning *Magic for Those Who Don't Like Magic* to the shelf. "I guess the title explains it all. I'd rather brawl with my fists or an axe rather than cast a spell."

Bridget placed the book neatly on the shelf before walking out of the library. A cool night breeze greeted her, stroking her cheeks. The peaceful sounds of evening time seemed to caress her, as though the evening kissed her softly. Bridget smiled. It was time to turn in for the night. She headed for the women's dorms, trudging slowly up the long stairway to a long night's rest.

Like a thief in the darkness, without warning, a hand grabbed her from behind, covering her mouth. A sharp blade touched her throat.

"You scream and you will suffer worse," a voice whispered in her ear.

Two men dragged Bridget into a dark back alley. Looking frantically around, she didn't recognize where they were taking her. It didn't look like anywhere in the school, though the smell still reminded her of school.

Where are they taking me? she wondered in panic. *What is going to happen to me?*

Bridget's eyes couldn't concentrate fast enough to see where they were going. The thought of yelling crossed her mind, but the sweat from the hand over her mouth reminded her she would be punched or knocked out. She wanted to be awake if something horrible happened.

The two men carrying Bridget stopped moving and knocked on a strange door. It opened, revealing a dimly lit room. The two men chained Bridget up against the wall by her wrist.

"Thank you, gentlemen," a voice murmured from the darkness.

"You thought you were going to get away with this, young Bridget," Paul said, emerging into the light. "You have been a bad little girl. You must be disciplined for your disrespect. I will punish you for embarrassing me in front of the headmaster."

Paul walked up to Bridget and eyed her whole body. He got near her face, breathing on her neck before licking her.

"Get away from me!" she yelled, her heart pounding.

"Oh, the taste of young meat," Paul said softly. "You're quite the catch, young one. I am going to enjoy lusting on your flesh today. Your spirit will be broken by the time I am done with you. You will be nothing more than a sack of flesh for my pleasure, without purpose or meaning."

Paul ran his hand through Bridget's long hair, rubbing her scalp in the process. He licked his lips before staring into Bridget's eyes.

"Yes, my dear, you will be my treat tonight."

* * *

"Paul proceeded to violate me by molesting my upper body and rubbing my thighs," Bridget tells Sodina and Slash. "It was horrible. He would have gotten farther, but Headmaster Anna found me after a student reported me missing, and I was rescued. I was powerless to do anything to stop him. Ever since that day, I vowed to never be powerless again. To become the most powerful warrior in Esteria."

* * *

That morning, Paul was taken by the military police. An assembly was held to see if any other girls had been victims. Seven girls came forth. All of them had been assaulted by Paul but were too scared to say anything, for fear of being cast out of the Academy. Headmaster Anna called the eight to the middle of the room and walked down the stairs.

"Let us pray for those afflicted by this monster," Anna started.

Goddess Astra thank you for loving our students

Thank you for your guidance and uncovering this evil

Keep us protected and safe in your love

Heal these young women from the pain they feel

Guide them as they grow into womanhood

We ask for swift justice for those involved

Amen

Anna lifted her head, and a single tear streamed down her left cheek as she brought the eight students close to her and looked them all in the eye.

"I love you all." Anna sobbed. "I am so sorry I could not protect you. Priests will be available for anyone who is in need of counseling or a shoulder to lean on. We will continue to investigate these crimes and bring any others who have hurt you all to justice. You're all dismissed now. Take it easy today."

Instant chatter broke out as Anna walked back to the stage.

I wonder what is next for us? Bridget asked herself.

* * *

Slash and Sodina look at Bridget with wide eyes.

"That event happened during my third year. Now you know why I killed that dragon to get this cloak. I graduated from the Academy at twenty years old. After that, I decided to become an adventurer making my claim in this world. I have been roaming the four kingdoms for the past seven years. Now that I am twenty-seven years of age, I still wonder when my true love will come. That is why I got so excited when you walked up to me, Slash. I felt like there was someone who understood me, because the dragon scales did not react."

"Yeah. That was a crazy situation," Slash replies.

"Let me explain," Bridget says. "Several years ago, I was on a quest with an advanced group of mages and warriors. There were fifteen of us. Seven people died while searching for the dragon. It was deep in a cave nestled in the Northern Kingdom. I delivered the killing blow, shrinking it in the neck after I climbed on its back. Those left alive after the battle skinned the dragon's scales. Some sold them, while others fashioned weapons. Since I have a hard time gaining speed, I wanted a great defense, so I had this cloak sewed together."

"Such bravery," Sodina says, smiling.

"Thank you." Bridget blushes slightly. "I then took the cloak for a trial run to see how much punishment the scales could take. It was then I felt a sensation like none other. I was traveling one day when a fierce solem attacked out of nowhere. The scales in a sense warned me. It was like they were one with my skin. I knew that I needed to dodge an attack. I guess in a way it was like a preemptive defense. I still do not understand it fully. One of these days, I want to travel to a magical blacksmith to see if they can uncover the true mystery of these scales."

"To think there are weapons like that around Esteria. It sounds truly legendary," Slash says, leaning back in his chair. *Maybe I can find a magical weapon soon to increase my swordsmanship.*

Bridget leans in toward Slash. "You're kind hearted, and I will follow you to the end of the Astra. I do not give my loyalty easily." She giggles. "You don't even have to pay me."

Sodina gave a wide grin to Bridget. "We are lucky to have someone as powerful as you on our side."

Bridget stands up and puts her hand on Sodina's shoulder. "We will leave at dawn to see if a connection I have in a nearby town knows anything about poison removal. Best we get some rest."

Bridget walks out of the hotel room to her room across the hall.

Sodina looks at Slash and walks over to the bed. "Come join me, sweetie, to rest."

Slash changes into his pajamas and lays his sword by the bed. "Never know when to be too careful. Someone could break in and try to kill us."

"Don't worry, honey. I'm a light sleeper. Anyone who tries to get into the door will be met with a dizziness spell."

Sodina walks over to the door and reaches out her hand.

"Goddess Astra, grant us thy protection."

A ray of light flashes out of Sodina's fingers, hitting the door before seeping into the wood.

"There we go." She smiles tenderly at her husband. "Anyone who touches the doors will instantly be paralyzed."

Sodina walks back to Slash, lying on the bed then snuggling beside him.

"Time to rest, Slash," Sodina whispers as she grabs him from behind.

She closes her eyes and soon falls asleep.

Slash looks out the window into the moonlight, thinking about today.

"I am not much of an individual who prays, but hopefully, Bridget knows someone who can help us. I will save you, Sodina," he whispers to himself as he closes his eyes. "I will travel to the end of the world just to see you smile in the future, smile with life and health. This I swear."

Chapter 4

Month of Dragons
Day 13

The thick fog covers the Uncharted Lands on a windy summer's afternoon. The castle built by the Exalted One stands tall amongst the small wooden houses.

This land is full of strife and is home to the forgotten, housing the generations of demons that were sealed away by the Heroes of Old.

A woman in a purple dress flies toward the castle, her black wings blending in with the darkened clouds. It is always cloudy in the Uncharted Lands that lie above the Eastern Kingdom. A curse from the exile that occurred hundreds of years ago still has a profound effect on the current demon population. Exhausted from her journey, the woman slowly descends from the sky onto the steps of the castle. She walks into a long, narrow hallway, making for the large horn-covered door at the end.

The door bursts open for the woman, and she ascends a flight of stairs to the second floor of the castle. After a short walk down a dimply lit hallway, she heads into the throne room. She is immediately greeted by a smartly dressed man, towering above her. Today, he smells of cedarwood and expensive oranges, she notes.

"You have returned, dearest Lisha!" the man exclaims, rushing her into the room happily before taking a seat on his golden throne. "Have you located my daughter?"

"Oh, Exalted One." Lisha bows on one knee, her body shivering with delight. "I am so pleased to see you."

"I hope that you are well, Lisha," He gestures for her to stand before him. "You may stand and call me by my real name, Gareth."

"I will do no such thing, my lord." Lisha gasps and blushes, tucking a piece of her black hair back behind her ear. The Exalted One always makes her feel as if she is a schoolgirl again.

"One day, I hope to hear you speak my name," Gareth says, rubbing his hands together suggestively.

A sadistic smile dances across Lisha's face as she raises her head to meet his gaze.

"I have yet to locate your daughter, my lord," she admits. "It's been some years, my lord... She could be...dead. The power we sought from the Gospel of Helion years ago to aid us was an error."

"Do not speak such things." Gareth raises his voice, darkness filling his stare.

Lisha's voice shakes, her body quivering with fear. "Yes, oh Exalted One."

"You are forgiven." Gareth huffs. "That is our child you speak of!"

Lisha nods sadly, trying to keep the tears from welling up in her eyes. She cannot show weakness to the most powerful man she knows, even for a moment.

"Do not lose hope, dearest." He raises his hand as if to touch her face.

"Why will you not make me your queen, my lord?" Lisha sighs, wishing he would reach out to her farther.

"If the humans were to hear that the Exalted One were to be married, they would try to exploit that weakness by capturing you." Gareth chuckles, adjusting his coat. "I could not bear to see my beautiful lover trapped and tormented by humans."

"Such simple creatures the humans are." Lisha snickers in reply. "Though...I would take any amount of punishment to be called your wife, my lord."

Lisha bows again in reverence of Gareth's great power, and Gareth blows her a kiss.

"One day, dearest," he bellows, sitting back in his throne brightly.

"Save the affection for another time, my lord," a deep voice growls from behind them.

A large, muscle-bound shape steps out of the darkness from the corner of the room to join the two. His spiked gauntlets cover the floor with dripping blood, fresh from a kill.

"Oh." Lisha straightens and looks at the man pointedly. "When did you arrive, Neron?"

"Some time ago." He rolls his eyes. "While you were talking about making love and babies."

Neron bows as he approaches Gareth and glares at Lisha, shaking the blood on his wrists toward her too pretty violet gown.

"And that's General Neron to you, Lisha," Neron adds, puffing out his chest. "Show some respect for your superior officer."

"You're only stronger than me by the slightest amount." Lisha glares back and punches him in the arm, leaving only a small mark. *How infuriating*, she thinks.

"Weak punches like that will never impress me!" Neron crosses his arms and laughs at Lisha's feeble attempt at a right jab.

"Enough, both of you," Gareth says. "Neron, how was your reconnaissance mission to the Northern Kingdom?"

Neron looks up at Gareth on his throne. "Well, the Northern Kingdom is indeed the second strongest, my lord. King Leo has his men well trained."

He went on, "I did some scouting in the villages, and each of the outer ones around the capital had elite-level knights and mages. But I did run into some trouble in one of the outer towns, hence the blood. That concludes my report."

Neron winces and continues, "Forgive me, my lord. You know I hate getting blood on my clothes."

"So, why is it you fight hand to hand with gauntlets then?" Lisha giggles. "You're so dramatic for being so muscular. 'Oh, I am so strong, but blood on my clothes will bring me to agony!'" Lisha mocks his voice, and Gareth bites back a laugh.

"Give me a break." Lisha throws her head back and guffaws.

"General, my pretty behind! You're nothing but a neat-freak bastard who happens to be good at killing people."

Neron turns toward Lisha, raising his fists. "You want to go right now, temptress? I'd love to shove your head into that pretty behind of yours."

"I'd rather not waste time on you, fool." Lisha sits on the nearest chair, crossing her legs and looking bored.

Neron sighs and looks down at his clothes with a pout. He really hates getting bloodstains out of his garments.

Gareth looks between his two generals and sighs. "What I am to do with you two?"

When neither of them answer, the Exalted One finally laughs with delight. "Come, let's enjoy a meal together."

Gareth leads his generals to the Igash Ballroom, two rooms down from his throne room.

"I wonder what is taking Magnar so long," Gareth thinks aloud.

"Wasn't he assigned to the Western Kingdom, my lord?" asks Lisha.

"That's correct," Neron mutters as they cross the hall. He hates being the third wheel between the Exalted One and Lisha the Lewd so often.

"From what I've heard, the Western Kingdom of Tamar is the strongest throughout the land. The Eastern Kingdom of Sol is on the brink of collapse!" Lisha squeals, bouncing with glee. "That should be our first target, my lord! I can kill, kill, kill all I want to. Crush and kill them all with my power! We've broken the barrier with the blood of the fairy we captured. Let me do the honors of taking Glashmere, the capital of Sol. We may find where our daughter is."

"They certainly may die when they see that outfit of yours, revealing everything," Neron says. "It doesn't leave much for the imagination."

Lisha glances over at Neron with contempt. "I like this outfit because of its functionality. And it's sexy."

She turns toward Gareth and bats her eyelashes. "Wouldn't you agree, my lord?"

The Exalted One smacks Lisha on the butt firmly before saying, "Yes, I do enjoy your outfit very much, dearest."

Neron turns his head away, not wanting to see any more public displays of lust, and walks into the Igash Ballroom first.

The room has been transformed into a dining hall with a long, oak table stretching down the center. Food of all kinds, gathered from all the lands of Esteria, covers the top as far as the eye can see.

"It took you long enough," General Magnar says, a sweet roll in both hands. He sits in the farthest corner from them, munching away. "I nearly finished my meal."

Magnar stands in the presence of Gareth and bows.

"It is rude to eat without the master, Maggie." Lisha shoots him an unapproving glance.

"It is all right, dearest," Gareth says. He gives Magnar a look of approval as the general sits down at the table, downing a keg of beer to wash down the rolls.

"You drink too much and that is going to be your downfall." Neron chuckles, taking the seat next to Magnar.

"I can still take down the humans, so I am going to keep drinking until I can drink no more." Magnar leans back in his seat, downing more beer. "Especially after that long mission."

"What of the Western Kingdom then, Magnar? How was your journey?" Gareth asks from his seat in the middle of the table. Lisha plops down next to him and spoons some soup into her mouth quietly.

Neron looks at the Exalted One and back at Magnar, waiting for his response. "I'm curious as well."

"Well," Magnar clears his throat, "it is definitely the strongest of the four kingdoms. The Western Kingdom is fortified in the desert, and sandstorms rage across the land. It was a brutal trek. It will be no small task to topple the queen and her men, my lord."

"What is her name again?" Gareth asks as he twirls his glass around, watching the red wine swirl in a small cyclone.

"She is Queen Victoria," Magnar says as he grabs another chicken leg. "She is a true queen of the people, they say. Strong, beautiful, and feared. Honestly, I would not want to clash with her."

Gareth looks at Magnar with disgust and speaks sternly. "Fear no human, *General* Magnar. You are leagues above those pests."

Magnar nods at the Exalted One. He continues to munch on his chicken leg.

"We will need to bolster our forces," Neron offers to the Exalted One. "The Eastern Kingdom could be the perfect place to take the land and turn it into our headquarters."

"I agree, the Uncharted Lands are nothing to look at." Lisha turns her attention toward Neron. "It's ugly, and the rivers are black, and there is barely anything to eat here."

"You mean Hilda, dearest," says Gareth.

"Yes, her, my lord." Lisha nods. "Forgive me. I forget her name because we never see her."

"Well, she and her goons are always hunting, making sure we have something to eat." Neron rolls his eyes again.

"For that, I thank her." Magnar waves his chicken leg bone in the air happily.

Gareth looks around the table, watching his generals enjoy their meals.

"I really enjoy your company, you lot." The Exalted One raises his glass proudly. "Being together is what is most important."

Lisha, Neron, and Magnar grin, listening to their ferocious leader go on. The sun shines into the room over all of them, as if the Heavens are bathing them in power.

Gareth's eyes glaze over. "We will rid Esteria of the curse of humanity and take over the land for ourselves. We will plunder, steal, and destroy all who stand in the way of our goal. We may even bring down Astra herself! You are the strongest demons in our army. Do me proud and continue to bolster our forces as you have been, so we will be prepared to launch our assault in the coming weeks."

Lisha stands up and slams her fist down on the table. "We can take the wretched human queen and her Eastern Kingdom for our own!"

"You are ravishing when you are excited, Lisha." Gareth smiles smugly.

"Thank you!" Lisha winks at Gareth. Groans come from Magnar and Neron. "I'm ready to crush some skulls in your name."

Lisha licks her lips and leans toward Gareth in his high chair. "What say you, oh Exalted One?"

Gareth looks at Lisha's awkward pose and answers, "Do what you like, dear. We know their kingdom is weaker than the others," he continues, staring at the other two generals before him. "If you are to overthrow the capital, make sure you take some wolfen. Take at least a hundred of them with you to ensure victory. Even though they seem weak, gentlemen, do not underestimate them. There are still some warriors in that part of the land, especially the War Master."

Magnar and Neron nod at their master and take that as a cue to continue eating. They must fill up for their next missions, after all.

Lisha adjusts her dress and leans forward so that Gareth has a full view of her breasts, covered in only the purple leather binding them at her bodice. Gareth raises his brow as she starts to saunter over to him.

"I will ensure that I take care of myself for you, my lord." Lisha comes close to his face before she licks his ear playfully.

"Wait for me," she whispers seductively.

Gareth shakes his head at the temptress with a grin.

Neron looks over, disgusted again, and lifts his fork to eat his salad. "Save some killing for us, Lisha."

"Who knows? You may need backup!" Magnar chuckles.

"You wish," Lisha spits. "But I would like to see more blood on your outfit, Neron."

Lisha walks over to the open window and jumps out of the window, her long, lavender skirts trailing behind her. Moments before she reaches the ground, her lavender wings stretch, propelling her into the sky.

Gareth looks at his remaining generals and smiles. "Do finish your meals, gentlemen, and take some time to rest. Our day of destiny is upon us."

With that, he gets up out of his chair, leaving the two behind to devour the remaining food and drink. He closes the doors behind him and makes his way to the foyer.

A shadowy figure awaits him patiently, sharpening a broadsword with his palm.

"What of your mission, Nagi?" Gareth asks, approaching the shadow.

The masked man bows in front of Gareth and breathes, "Exalted One..."

"You can rise, good servant."

"I have eliminated twenty-five high-level warriors throughout the Eastern Kingdom," Nagi says. "Without these warriors, our invasion of the Eastern Kingdom should be of no concern to you, my lord. You should not have to lift a finger traveling to our new home."

"Very good, Nagi!" The Exalted One smiles wide.

"But," Nagi gulps before continuing, "there was one warrior in particular, a female, whom I could not eliminate, my lord."

Gareth's smile fades into a frown. "You, bested by a female? Surely, you jest."

"She had a healer and another swordsman with her. I retreated before the situation became dire, my lord."

"Hmm…" Gareth strokes his chin. "Do go on."

"I'd rather eliminate my target than battle for long periods of time. Thus is the life of this assassin, my lord," Nagi says apologetically.

"Thank you, Nagi, for the honest report." The Exalted One pats his shoulder. "Do keep an eye on that group for me."

"Yes, my lord." Nagi bows a final time before disappearing into the shadows, leaving Gareth alone in the corridor.

To think that a common warrior could match up with the leader of the Dark Order. Gareth frowns deeper as he starts back toward his throne room, his hands clasped together. *That is most interesting indeed.*

Chapter 5

Month of Dragons
Day 14

Lisha looks over the Great Forest, the stars glimmering in the sky.

"What a beautiful view!" Lisha exclaims. "It's a shame there will be such death below the wonder of the stars. Astra is truly amazing, but who cares about the Goddess. I appreciate her creation but despise her teachings. This will be a great place to land."

Lisha's purple wings flap steadily, lowering her between ten solems. Covered in skin and rock, they resemble golems but differ greatly.

"These will do just fine," Lisha says as the solems look at her and bow in response.

For a bunch of dumb creatures, at least they know fighting me would be their end. Lisha shrugs her shoulders. *The great thing about this invasion is the humans will never see it coming. The Great Forest is right next to the town of Ifer. Ever since Nagi took out most of their elite warriors, I should have no problem wiping out their main force. We have to attack at full force. Then the capital of Glashmere will be right in our grasp. Once the capital falls, the rest will be as easy as taking candy from a baby. We will wipe the rest of the remaining villages off the map.*

"Well, not all of them. There may be some spoils for us to take." Lisha chuckles before bowing her head and closing her eyes, slowly chanting an ancient language unknown to most humans.

She breathes in silence followed by a distant roar. She hears the marching steps of multitudes gathering around her. Lisha opens her eyes to find many different solems, dark mages, and wolfen, all called upon by her energies. Her small army totals in the hundreds—a few dozen of each creature, more than enough to take two cities. With Sol's weakened economy, their troops will be poorly trained. A group of laborers turned into a lousy militia is nothing compared to the might of her demon army.

Lisha walks among the formation of her minions.

"Praise the wolfen!" she calls. "What fabulous creations by Gareth."

Twenty wolfen, all seven feet tall, stand covered with bristling dark hair, snarling as they bear their large teeth.

"Who would have thought to take human hair and blood then fuse it with a wolf. Some could call that a monstrosity, but I think they are quite cute." Lisha grins menacingly. "Their teeth tearing into human flesh will be a symphony I will relish."

Lisha peers into the gnarly mouth of her favorite demonic creature.

"Be sure to rip them to shreds, my lovelies." Lisha says, caressing the wolfen's chin.

The wolfmen howl as saliva drips from their mouths.

"I feel the heat of the night has taken its toll."

Lisha snaps her finger, and in an instant her dress fades away, revealing only her black bra, panties, fishnet stockings, and heels.

"That feels so much better." Reaching her arms to the sky and stretching, she says, "I love the early morning dew. It's showtime!"

Lisha walks through her small army, heading toward the front.

"We march to Ifer, my lovelies," Lisha commands.

She leads her army through the Great Forest. The wind blows across her cheeks gently as a small smile graces her face. *I wonder where my daughter is. We lost you twenty years ago to those warriors from the Eastern Kingdom. I will find you!*

Birds escape their roost, flying away, frightened by the heavy steps of the solems.

Lisha frowns. "There is no way to be stealthy with all of these solems. They barely fit on the path. Couldn't Gareth have just given me a hundred wolfen instead?" she ponders aloud, looking up at the moon, thinking of her daughter's last smile and training.

"Magical Arrow!" a voice shouts from the darkness.

"My lady!" A wolfman slashes the arrow of light just before it hits Lisha.

"I should have known there would be some futile resistance before getting to the humans," Lisha mutters.

"Stop right there!" the voice calls out.

A single fairy, around four feet tall, descends from the sky. She has fair skin and wears a cloth brown dress. Her green and blue wings flap quickly as she reaches the ground, setting her piercing green eyes against Lisha.

"You demons have killed too many of my people. If I can kill at least one of you and protect those humans, my life will have meaning," says the fairy.

"What is your name, twig?" Lisha asks, staring into the fairy's eyes.

"My name is Tori, and I am the defender of this section of the forest. I will not allow you to take another step forward," she snaps, glaring. "Magical Barrier!"

Tori puts her hands out as a hundred-foot barrier surrounds her, emitting a radiant green light.

"Crush her," Lisha orders the solems.

Fifteen solems charge forward and slam shoulder-first into the magical wall. Tori keeps her hands raised as the solems continuously pound against the barrier with tremendous force.

Lisha smiles, seeing the panic in the fairy's eyes. She's trying to hide it but she can't. The solems continue to bash their stony fists against the barrier.

Lisha waves her hand and points forward. Fifteen more solems run shoulder-first into the barrier.

A cackle breaks through the tremendous beating. The light of the barrier breaks into shards of glistening powder. Tori screams as the barrier breaks. A solem charges up to her and bashes its fist into her chest, sending her flying through layers of trees before crashing on a large boulder. She falls on the forest floor, coughing up blood as she lies on the ground crying.

"I need to get up," Tori grunts, trying to push herself up from the ground. "I'm sorry I couldn't prevent this disaster," she whispers, her eyelashes fluttering as she loses consciousness.

Lisha looks out into the distance toward where Tori fell.

"Solems, return to me," she commands. "I believe that the pathetic twig is dead. There is no need to find her. We are on a timeline to destiny."

Lisha walks forward towards the tree line. The sun is starting to show its smile over the horizon near Ifer. The solems emerge from the brush, a distance away from the outskirts of the town.

A sentry on a wooden lookout tower near the town's perimeter sees the solems walk out the woods.

"Ring the alarm!" he commands. "It looks like we'll be having company."

Another sentry nearby rushes to ring the bell.

"Oh, they rang the bell," Lisha says. "How pitiful. Well, it's time to launch a full assault. Go, my lovelies, and wreak havoc on those pathetic humans."

"They are about five hundred feet away!" the sentry shouts.

"Close the gates," the other man commands. "Now!"

Two knights rush in and close the ten-foot-tall gates to the city. Lisha flies toward the sentry in the wooden tower and grabs his head. Petrified with fear, he looks into Lisha's eyes as she licks his face.

"Oh, why did you ring the bell, sweetie?" Lisha asks. "I wanted our little visit to be a surprise."

Within a flash, Lisha snaps the neck of the sentry.

"Ah! The intoxicating sounds of bones breaking really vibrates my body." Lisha shivers with delight as she throws his body out of the tower. Underneath, the solems run headfirst into the gate, breaking it open in an instant.

"Run!"

The townsfolk cower as the solems grab people and throw them forty to fifty feet in the air.

"Where are our knights?" asks one of the townsfolk. "Quickly send a messenger to Glashmere, lest we let our town come to ruin."

Lisha flies down toward the middle of the town, gazing upon the chaos brought by her army. A grin forms on her face as the screams of innocent townsfolk surround her.

"I guess I can have a little fun." She laughs. "Set fire to the whole town and kill them all."

"You witch!" A man with a pitchfork runs toward Lisha.

She steps to the right, easily avoiding the attack before she manifests her scythe.

"You're a naughty boy, aren't you?" Lisha cackles before slicing off the man's right leg.

The man howls, groaning in agony. "You demons have no right to attack us. The king will make sure you pay."

"Do not waste your breath on this human, Mistress." A wolfen speaks behind Lisha. "Allow me, Mistress."

The wolfen digs his claws deep into the flesh of the man's neck, killing the man. His blood paints the claws red.

The wolfen laughs before running off to attack a woman, gnawing on her neck. The screams of villagers being slaughtered echo throughout the small town. Lisha relishes in their screams once more.

"Hellfire Storm!"

Lisha opens her hand as flames burst out. She yells as she throws fireballs. A maniacal smile graces her face. The flaming balls find their mark, slamming into the houses. The flames cackle as the wooden foundations crash upon the people inside, screaming for help, as the barrage of fire explodes around them.

"Oh. Here comes the backup."

Lisha looks toward the hills. Hundreds of knights are coming down the road. Lisha whistles, calling a few wolfmen around her.

"Lovelies, go and take out those archers before they can quiver a single arrow."

"Do not let them have any quarter!" a knight yells.

A volley of arrows rains down on Lisha.

"My lady!" A wolfen howls, running toward Lisha as he spreads his arms out, covering her. Five arrows pierce his back and neck, killing him immediately.

Lisha leaves his body on the ground as she stretches out her hands toward the archers, fifty feet away, pointing at them.

"Solems, crush them. Leave none alive."

Twenty solems charge toward the archers. The archers fire at them, but the arrows bounce off their rocky exterior.

"Retreat!" a knight commands the archers.

The archers shuffle back in the direction they came from, but the solems quickly grab them by their legs. Lifting them up then slamming them into the ground.

"This is a slaughter!" another knight shrieks. "We need reinforcements. 'Tis getting more dire by the moment!"

Lisha walks through the chaos, looking for anyone who might be left behind. She spots a solem lifting a group of children in its hands.

"Please spare the children," a woman begs.

Lisha looks over at the solem, signaling him to hold.

"You heard your momma," she says to the children. "Scram before I change my mind!"

"No, we won't leave her!" one of them cries out.

"Well, little brats, it's either your momma dies or you all die together," Lisha explains, lifting up a little boy by his ears.

"Run!" The mother pushes them away. "Run to the next town. Shekainah, take care of your brothers. Don't look back!"

The tallest amongst the children, Shekainah, drags her brothers away. One of them turns their head to look back as the solem pummels the woman on the ground, her body bursting into a fine red mist.

Lisha walks away from the carnage, not bothered in the slightest. *War isn't pretty, but it is necessary*. Lisha bows her head, thinking so much has already been lost to senseless violence. She forgot what grief or remorse feels like. *I've lost count of the dead, but there is still so much left to do. This scythe will never be satisfied.*

"My lady." A wolfen bows before Lisha. "We have killed all of the knights and townspeople here. Shall we proceed to Glashmere?"

"Not yet." Lisha waves her hand in the air, signaling all of the troops to come to the middle of town. "We need to account for our losses. While the carnage must go on, there is no need to be reckless. Gareth would have us all killed should we fail in our conquest."

* * *

Some time passes as Lisha's army regathers itself. She sits on the ground, pondering her daughter's existence.

Where are you, my daughter? You should be the spitting image of me! Busty, sexy, full of vigor, and virility.

Lost in thought, Lisha licks her lips as a wolfen walks up to her.

"My lady, we have a report that the knights of Glashmere are heading this way to stop our advances."

"Oh, what a pity. I didn't get enough time to even relax and enjoy the scenery." Lisha sighs, patting the dirt from her palms. "Well, I guess it's their grave."

Lisha stands up, walks over to an untouched fruit stand, and grabs an apple. *Such luscious fruit.* Taking a small bite, she smiles. *I will enjoy this apple before the slaughter begins again. Let's see what type of faith these men have. To make it fun, let's head back out to the field for a clash.*

"Gather to rest," she calls out. "We'll meet them on open ground."

"But, my lady. I mean no disrespect, but that would put us in a disadvantage."

"We have everything we need right here, brave warrior." Lisha's words are soft but her glare is piercing, holding the wolfen in place.

"Yes, my lady." The wolfen bows before leaving.

The flames continue to roar, burning many of the houses down in minutes. The only ones left standing are those built of stone and brick. What was once a bustling town has now been reduced to ashes.

Without saying a word, Lisha flies out of the village, followed by the rest of her troops. Time passes by before Lisha sees a group of around five hundred soldiers marching down the long road to Ifer.

"Oh, what joy. Here comes the cavalry," Lisha says in mockery.

The knights of Ifer pass through the village, searching for survivors. At last, they reach the plains on the other side.

"Lord Regal." One of the knights speaks. "There is none left alive, my lord. They killed them all.

"Divine, have mercy! What in Astra have they done?" Regal says, stunned by the situation.

Lisha flies toward them at a safe distance from above, to everyone's surprise. Signaling to Regal and his men that she wants to talk. Regal motions his archers to lower their weapons before dismounting to meet the demon mistress.

"Vile witch, if you have any honor, come meet me in the middle to negotiate. We will spare you and your men. We outnumber you. We are the shining knights of Glashmere. There is none better than us," Regal shouts.

He does not look like a knight, Lisha thinks to herself. *He wears not the heavy plates nor the brigandine that sports of combat. I wonder if he is some sort of significant figure among the knights.*

Lisha floats down to meet him.

"Speak your name, witch, and make it quick," Regal commands.

Lisha leans back, shaking with delight, greeting Regal with a malicious grin.

"Why the rush, human? You only need to hear it once and it will be the last name you ever hear," she replies, licking her lips seductively. "I am Lisha. I am one of the demon army's finest generals—serving the Exalted One, Lord Gareth, the future ruler of all of Esteria."

"Like hell, he's the next ruler," Regal yells. "I damn you all to hell."

Pulling two knives out of his pocket, Regal charges toward Lisha, swiping at her neck. Lisha narrowly dodges his attack.

"The poor wretched fool thinks he's fast," says Lisha, mocking him. "Tsk tsk. That's no way to treat a lady, pathetic worm. You did not even give me your name."

Lisha looks intently at Regal, eyeing him from top to bottom.

"A hasty one. Are you like this with all the wenches you meet?" asks Lisha, licking her lips again.

"Spare me your devilish tongue, vile creature. You speak to Lord Regal, the protector of the region before Glashmere. I am a knight and governing Lord. Your head will be decorated on a pike before you set foot in Glashmere."

"Good job, Regal. You did a pretty pathetic job of protecting your people. Going through you is naught but a chore."

Regal clenches his fist, snarling as he puffs his anger out of his nose, with sweat sliding from his head. Without a second to waste, Lisha flies with her foot aimed at Regal. He quickly sidesteps and takes an opportunity to swipe at her head, barely missing and cutting off a piece of Lisha's hair.

"Oh. How rude. You call yourself a lord, yet you act like a scared beast." Looking at the locks of her hair, Lisha narrows her eyes at him. "You need to be punished."

Lisha manifests her scythe, twirling it behind her back. A wolfen runs up beside her.

"You need not waste your energy, my lady."

"I appreciate your concern, warrior, but I will waste my energy how I see fit."

Lisha flies toward Regal, swinging her scythe wildly at his body. Regal jumps back and ducks, dodging the attack.

The knights, eager and anxious to charge, talk amongst themselves, discussing their battle plan. The flag-bearing knight on a horse blows a trumpet.

Lisha looks back to see five hundred knights running toward her, their weapons at the ready.

"It looks like you dogs are so impatient to die. Very well then. I was having fun toying with you, but playtime is over, boy!" Lisha cries out.

Lisha jumps behind Regal, swinging her scythe at his right arm. Regal, unable to dodge, falls to the ground, screaming, as his right arm lands in front of him, lying in a pool of blood.

"Well. It has been fun, my playful mutt!" Lisha cries out.

Lisha swings her scythe, aiming for Regal's head. He rolls away and manages to mark a cut across Lisha's leg.

"Lord Regal!" a knight calls out.

He charges toward Lisha with the sword gripped tightly in his hand. Lisha swings her scythe and slices his torso in half.

"Attack! Wreak havoc on these wretched scums!" A wolfen cries.

The rest of the demon army runs to meet the knights. A fierce battle clashes in the middle of the green and peaceful plains. The screams of warriors echo through the air as the wolfen claw and gnaw their way to the necks of the humans. The knights bounce their swords against the solems, unable to hit the skin in between the armored exterior of the towering giants.

Regal carries himself up and runs toward Lisha in the middle of the chaos. He readies his dagger, aiming at Lisha's neck.

"You're bleeding out, human, without any help. The end is near for you," Lisha berates him.

She sheaths her scythe and punches Regal in the chest. Regal gasps for air as he stumbles back, his stump of an arm still dripping blood.

"You vile witch!" a knight cries out, swinging his weapon toward Lisha.

Lisha sidesteps to the left, avoiding the blade before snapping the knight's neck.

"Broken like a twig. You humans are nothing but playthings," she says, smiling.

Regal, losing consciousness, peers up at Lisha, his eyes burning with anger and hatred. He continues to struggle breathing, keeping himself awake as the battle wages on.

Five hours have passed since the first sword was unsheathed, and only ten knights remain. The remaining knights surround Regal.

"My lord, we will defend you," a knight tells him.

Lisha walks over to the pool of blood. Her voluptuous body is covered in blood from the many knights she has slain. She and the remaining fifteen solems surround Regal and his knights.

"To think you knights would best my wolfen." Lisha mocks them as she grabs her bosoms with fondness. "I haven't had such fun in a long time. A few of your knights even managed to cut my precious thighs. That made me furious!"

A maniacal laugh leaves Lisha's mouth.

"I don't even need the solems to finish you off."

Lisha charges, jumping into the circle of knights protecting Regal.

"Enjoy the afterlife," she whispers, as a small grin forms on her face.

She pulls her scythe out and twirls it in a circle, cutting all of the knights in half. Killing them in one swift slash. Covered in blood still, Lisha stands before Regal, looking down at his dying body.

Regal looks up from his position, kneeling and crying. "Goddess! Receive my spirit for it is done," he cries out.

"I am surprised you lasted this long with that wound." Lisha spits on him. "You really have the stamina, don't you? Or perhaps you're some sort of potion addict? No matter. Let the worms remember you."

Lisha turns her back on Regal as the solems surround him. She smiles, relishing the beautiful harmony of pain, and closes her eyes before letting out a small chuckle.

Chapter 6

Month of Dragons
Day 15

The Southern Kingdom is home to golden-brown and black-skinned citizens. Goddess Astra made sure the sun favored her southern children, the legends say.

A young woman peers out of the back of an old wagon as it exits the Southern Gates. She always sticks out in this land, she thinks, with her emerald-colored pigtails and fair skin.

With her favored crossbow in hand, she watches for any monsters that may be tailing their caravan. For they are on a critical mission for the Eastern Kingdom, and it is imperative they make it out of the Southern Kingdom.

As they go along the dirt route, the woman makes sure to never take her eye off of the trail.

Most people she has come across so far on her journey called her Pint Size, since she is barely five feet tall. It never bothers her, though. She might be pretty small, but they know better. To get on Lea's wrong side means a hard kick in the shins or worse, where their unborn children swim.

She usually works alone on her trips, choosing to protect those in power who negotiate on behalf of the kingdom. The pay isn't that good, but the Goddess could have let her die a long time ago in the orphanage in Dalton, Lea notes as the sun streams in through the wagon, making her squint.

As long as I have a bow and arrow, I can make a living.

The caravan she's riding on today is four deep, with three decoy wagons and one holding the precious client. They have two fire elemental knights in front and two water mages in the back of the caravan.

Matthew, Duke of Glashmere, always rides in style and is prepared for anything. Lea does think his title is impressive, especially for a man of his stature, but she also knows he's a womanizing pig. She would love to put an arrow into his pretty little face if given a chance, but that isn't what she is being paid for. This time.

I can hit him while he is taking a leak at our next stop. Lea eyes his decked-out wagon in front of hers. It even has matching footmen. *What a prick.*

Shut up, Lea, or you're going to lose your job. She snaps herself out of it. Though, dreaming on road trips isn't such a bad thing. A little slip of the hand on the bow here and a little disappearing for the duke over there.

Lea smiles at the thought and begins to dust off her green overshirt and brown trousers. Her typical uniform.

As she puts her hood over her head, Lea sits back and sighs. *This journey took ten days, but it seemed like a whole lot more than that.*

Matthew, or The Duke as he calls himself, even if there is clearly more than one duke in Esteria, had to secure a trade route to increase the amount of steel needed to build swords. He gave the Southern Kingdom ten percent of his homeland's crops for the next year, and they gave twenty percent of their steel production in return. The southerners have to eat, so it isn't a bad trade-off.

At least Lea knows Matthew is good at something other than searching for the next woman to have relations with.

Her pigtails lift underneath the evening breeze that kisses the countryside at sunset. The sun, giving a silent goodbye, sinks as night dusk starts to creep slowly over the edge of the horizon. She loves watching the sunset ever since she was a girl. Though the places she travels to vary, the sun always rises in the morning and sets in the evening. It is a constant reminder of life.

With her honest heart, Lea believes this kingdom is headed in the wrong direction. The peace-loving king has no backbone, nor does he train long enough to hold his own in battle.

The evening sky starts to show its brilliance as the stars line the sky above her. In due time, guard duty will be upon her. Lea took the extra shift because a swordsman fell sick with a stomach virus. She can be nice if she wants to be.

"Halt the carriage!" calls out Captain Hubert, one of the knights on horseback, disturbing Lea's train of thought. "We will be staying the night here by this lake. We will depart in the morning. The night shift starts now, ladies."

Lea rolls her eyes and takes her hood off her head. She is definitely the only lady in this bunch of silly guardsmen.

"Prepare your weapons and protect the duke!" he yells to the motley crue.

"Sir, yes, sir!" Replies to the captain echo throughout the caravan, and Lea hears feet shuffling in the grass below them.

"What am I defending the duke from exactly, Captain? No one interrupting him during his alone time with his lady guards?" A newer knight chuckles.

Hubert hits the back side of his head. "Get to work, *guard*, and no faffing about the duke," he spits, and the knight hurries away.

Lea respects the hold Hubert has on his men, although sometimes his harshness is off-putting. As her caravan comes to a full stop, she stands and stretches her limbs. The breeze from the lake is cool and smells of pine. Hopefully, nothing is in the lake to disturb her rest.

Far east on the continent of Esteria lies the city of Glashmere. Glashmere is an important city in the trade route of the Eastern Kingdom. It has been under massive attack by demons or solem, as the locals call them, and other beasts because it is right by the Great Forest.

Lea knows that the Great Forest used to house the people of fairy descent, but lately, there have been great disturbances. The fairy people have closed themselves off from the modern world, so no one truly knows what is happening in the woods. It intrigues her.

Many believe a lot of the fairies perished because of the increase in solem in the forest. Glashmere sent out many expeditions of knights to venture into the forest. Unfortunately, knights came back through the bronze Glashmere gates with no head or half a body, still on horseback. It was as if the demons were organized, or making fun of the city's efforts to unveil the truth that lies beyond.

Lea walks towards the middle of the caravan, thinking about her favorite treat. Images of a decadent cake with chocolate and vanilla frosting dance in Lea's head as her pigtails wave in the wind.

A song plays in her head as she skips out of her caravan, onto the forest floor.

Cake, cake! I love the taste of cake

It is fluffy, so sweet!

My heart flutters with joy at the sight of this delight

Give me cake every single day and night!

Without noticing, Lea starts to drool, trotting up and down the road they parked in, singing in her head. Her bow is at the ready in case of any sudden attack.

The other members of the night guard look at her with questions in their heads.

One older knight whispers to the others, "I wonder what she is dancing on about."

Another shrugs. "Beats me." They look at Lea skeptically. "This area is roaming with monsters. I wouldn't exactly be dancing around here."

Although they are in the Southern Kingdom, there is still activity they need to be on the lookout for. The older knight stares at Lea, wondering if he should say anything, but keeps his mouth closed.

Lea walks back toward the end of their caravan, looking out into the night sky. Just then, Duke Matthew rolls out of his carriage.

"You there!" He points at Lea. "Come with me, archer."

"You know, my name is Lea, you entitled prat," she snaps.

"If you weren't an elite archer, I would have your head, you know." The duke snarls, and a smug smile creeps onto his face. "Or I can have you in bed, you know. Undoing those pigtails would be quite the delight."

Lea glares at Matthew, disgusted, and walks up to him anyway. "What do you need from me, Duke?"

"I need to take a leak," he begins, "and it's dark out there. I have a torch, but you'll need to protect me from monsters in the woods. It's *your* job."

Lea throws him a bothered look, but resigns and follows him into the woods.

"Not that I care or anything," Lea mutters, "but do you ever get tired of your playboy lifestyle? I mean, a different woman every week! That sort of activity can do damage to your body both physically and emotionally."

"I know very well what it can do." Matthew waves his torch around as they walk through the brush. "I have access to the best doctors in the city. To monitor me in case I catch something."

Lea nods, and Matthew looks back at her curiously. "Why does it matter to you anyway?"

She clears her throat. "As a devout follower of the Goddess Astra, I want the best for mankind. Watching you throw your life away despite having a head start on life due to your position seems like a waste. You are blessed with influence, yet you live in poverty mentally and spiritually. That is not the will of the Goddess."

"You do speak wisdom, arch—girl," Matthew mumbles. "I understand what you're saying. What is your name again?"

"It's Lea," she retorts, and Matthew frowns because he should have known that to begin with. "And your words are nothing but emptiness to my ears. If you hear wisdom, you better apply it, or what I have said to you will have been for naught." She adjusts her cloak on her shoulders and puffs her chest.

"Go ahead and do your business, Duke Matthew. I will stand guard fifteen feet from you." Lea walks away toward the head of the tree line, her back turned to Matthew.

Matthew peers into the darkness, his torch now perched on a nearby rock. He looks up toward the moon and instead sees two yellow eyes looking at him.

"HELP!" he screams.

Lea spins around to see an ogre with four arms, one club in each, swinging at Matthew.

Matthew ducks on the ground, wetting himself and cursing. He's wearing his favorite leather pants.

"Stay down!" Lea yells at Matthew and then turns int the direction of their camp. "We need backup! We need to wake up the day guards! We have an ogre, and it's one of the larger ones!"

The knights spring from their seats and run to gather more guards to help them.

Lea runs toward the ogre and sends an arrow at the knee of the beast. The ogre uses one of the clubs to block it.

"So, that's how it is!" Lea taunts. "Come and get me!"

The ogre roars in reply, hurling two clubs at her, and she dodges with no effort. The duke cowers behind a tree trunk and prays his laundry maid doesn't scold him for the mess in his pants.

"Matthew! Run toward me!" Lea yells.

"I can't!" he wails, trembling violently behind the tree trunk.

"Get up and run this way! I will lay down cover for you, moron!" Lea hides behind a nearby tree and shoots two more arrows from her crossbow, finally striking the ogre in the eye.

Screaming in pain, the ogre falls to one knee, covering his hurt eye, now gushing green blood.

"You need to run now!" Lea exclaims, and Matthew runs towards the tree line, shaking in fear.

"Protect me, please, Lea!" He blubbers into her cloak and she shakes him off her, keeping her eye on the fallen ogre.

"What do you think I'm doing, you stupid noble? Now, go get in your carriage! NOW!"

The ogre swings wildly, following the screams of Matthew. Lea steps back to the tree line.

Two mages with hands raised shoot fireballs at the ogre. *About damned time,* Lea thinks, dodging the ogre's clubs again.

"Keep him pinned down," Lea yells. She dashes toward the ogre, jumping on its back and stabbing five arrows into the skull of the creature, toppling it.

The ogre is down, she thinks in relief as the mages take the ogre into the woods to burn him to a crisp. If there were a few more, the whole convoy could have been overtaken. Hubert will have a piece of her mind in the morning.

Lea zips back over to the carriage, where another mage is checking Matthew for any damage.

"Are you okay, Matt—Duke?" She silently curses herself for calling him something so informal in front of others.

"I'm fine," says Matthew, shooing away the mage and straightening his stance.

"Thank you, Lea." He holds out his hand, and she tilts her head. "You saved my life back there."

"Eventually, I will shake your hand, Matthew," she answers and turns away from him. "Today is not that day."

The Duke of Glashmere stares as Lea walks back toward the convoy and slips into her caravan. *What a young woman,* he thinks.

Lea pulls out her small chest of items and takes out a small piece of cake, wrapped in baking linens.

She sighs. "I need to make this moment last."

Looking down at the tasty treat, she dives in. *It's just you and me, cakey.*

Humming along, she takes a large bite of the delicious pastry. Glashmere has some of the best bakers in Esteria, and she is grateful to have the reward after proving herself to the duke and his men.

Hours pass, and the only sounds keeping her company on watch are the distant howls of wolfen and solems knocking down trees.

The sunrise starts to peek over the horizon as Lea returns the now empty cake wrapper into her pocket, finishing off the night watch. For once, she is thankful she has her own carriage to sleep in.

Lea slips into her makeshift cot and curls underneath her blanket.

Soon they will be at the Bridge of Eden and back off to Glashmere.

Where I will be able to get more cake. Lea smiles, drifting away to sleep.

Chapter 7

Month of Dragons
Day 16

It feels like a dream. A dream where the dreamer is no longer needed. The lush green plains of Ifer mourn as the sun slowly crawls its way up. Its shining rays penetrate the dark sky, clawing the evening like a rabid bear.

Lisha wakes up, startled.

"I guess these stupid things created a barrier for me to rest without interruption," Lisha says, glaring at the rising sun.

She has been asleep for almost a day. *The town has been eerily quiet,* she thinks. The birds sing their songs as the dew of the morning greeted the morning.

"A new day to mourn and lavish the deaths of the pitiful." Lisha yawns, hopping up and walking toward the apple stand again. By this time, the apples have begun to rot.

"I guess no breakfast for me." Lisha scoffs. "I think the screams of the townspeople would be enough to keep me satisfied."

The solems trail slowly behind Lisha as they walk toward the walls of Glashmere.

A wolfen runs up to Lisha.

"I thought all of you died," the wolfen says. "I went back for reinforcements, my lady. I brought a hundred more wolfmen to join the fight."

"That was not needed," Lisha replies. "But I do thank you for that."

"I will join my ranks now, my lady," he says before running back to Lisha's army.

More troops can never hurt, she thinks with a shrug.

Lisha walks toward the castle walls and knocks quietly, anticipating an answer.

"Is anyone home?" Lisha asks.

"Scurry off, foul witch!" a voice yells from behind the walls.

"Well, well. That's not very nice," Lisha replies.

Lisha snaps her fingers, signaling someone behind her. She steps out of the way as solems shoulder through the walls, tearing them down.

"These people truly take time to delay their death," she says.

With little resistance, the pathway opens. The demon army bursts into the town, creating havoc and killing the townspeople.

"They really had too much faith in their army," Lisha says mockingly. "They sent the whole army, even the lookouts, to repel us. The rumors were true that their economy has been struck. It's quite pathetic actually."

Lisha strolls through the town of Glashmere, her army leaving a trail of bloodshed behind her. By the time evening has set in, Lisha, weary from fighting, sits down with the castle in view.

Just a bit more, she thinks. *And we will have toppled this kingdom.*

None of her troops perish. Resistance is futile. The townspeople have no answer to the overwhelming force of the demon army. Lisha pulls out a bottle full of water and slowly drinks it, before jumping in to help with the massacre.

Night has fallen by the time Lisha reaches the castle entrance. She steps aside as two solems slam into the steel doors.

"These are going to take a bit more than a little push, my darlings," Lisha says. "Pull out those trees and ram them against the gates. We need to take this castle by morning."

The solems uproot the nearby trees and use them as battering rams. After a few minutes of endless bashing, the large reinforced doors finally crack, allowing them to breach the castle.

* * *

"My king," a knight says, rushing into the throne room, out of breath. "The demon army has broken in! They will reach the throne room in a matter of minutes."

King Martin, a man in his sixties, strapped in gold armor, sits up from his chair. With his sword in hand, he walks toward his elite knights.

"My men," he says calmly. "I believe we are all that is left of our kingdom. My heart mourns the cries of our people. We must not let these wretched demons prevail. They will soon come into this room, with their snarled fangs and clenched fists. There is no greater honor than fighting alongside you. We must hold this castle until help arrives. We were able to send a messenger to the Southern Kingdom, but it will take some time."

* * *

The front doors of the castle burst open, and two knights fall back from the impact. Shaken with fear, the knights collapse without putting up a fight. The solems smash through the steel doors, breaking them underneath their tremendous force.

Lisha leads the solems into the castle.

It's like a ghost town in here. She moves forward cautiously, knowing a sneak attack could be imminent, and manifests her scythe.

Lisha leads her army up the flights of stairs and past the kitchen. *This place isn't bad looking.*

She starts to imagine all the fun she and Gareth will have after her mission is complete. "Oh, to be held in his arms, how wonderful it is. But our love is more than physical," she whispers. "It's spiritual as well."

Gareth will become so much more powerful after this. Their conquest will change the land of Esteria for centuries to come, making demons above all the other races.

Two large doors stand in front of the demon army. The solems, upon Lisha's command, charge onward and ram against the doors. Their tremendous size and weight easily break the steel locks. Splinters fly out as the dust settles. A single door is all that separates them from the king and his knights, anticipating the fight for their lives.

* * *

Inside the chamber, the knights bring their shields up, forming a wall surrounding the king.

"Shield Protect," commands one of the knights. "Now!"

King Martin, surrounded by his knights, stands tall with his sword in hand. A faded yellow light surrounds them as he raises his sword. A moment of silence passes before they hear the trampling noise of heavy steps, beating down the doors leading to the inner chamber.

The door cracks as more splinters break off and the metal bends. They can see the solems crashing their fists on the wooden entrance, ready to charge in and fight them.

"The doors will not hold," whispers one of the knights. "Can we withstand this assault? Did our messenger make it to the neighboring kingdom? Will they come to rescue us?"

Another knight licks his lips in anticipation, looking at the door almost about to crack, bending under pressure.

Everything falls still, the silence before the storm, as if a heavenly opera is about to start. Then the door breaks, exploding into a fine cloud of wooden dust. The knights keep their sight on the cloud, awaiting whatever monstrosities will come out.

"You're not going to live to see the morning sun!" a voice calls out from the cloud.

"Show yourself, you vile monster. No evil can instill fear in the hearts of the righteous. Thou art damned to taste my steel," King Martin calls out.

"Bow to me, pathetic king, and I will spare you and your pathetic knights. Resist and my solems will rip you from limb to limb."

"We will never bow to evil!" King Martin proclaims. "For glory and honor, we will fight until our last breath. We are the shining light of the Eastern Kingdom of Sol. As long as our hearts beat, they beat to the drums of justice. Our hearts resonate with the cries of the innocents you have murdered. Your evil ends here."

"You welch are all the same," the voice replies, almost uninterested.

"So be it. Cling to your worthless ideas and die deaths befitting of your pathetic honor."

The dust finally settles. King Martin looks in disbelief as ten solems pour into the room. They approach the knights with their hands held high, prepared to strike.

"Goddess Astra," King Martin calls out. "Give us the strength to last until we feel the kiss of your beautiful morning. My knights, tonight we fight for honor and glory. Die a hero's death if you must, but do not let fear overwhelm your heart. If no help comes, I will fight with you until the bitter end."

A solem charges forward and punches the shield surrounding the king and his knights at full force. The yellow shield of protection cracks as the solem winds up his fist for a second punch.

"Lower the shield on my go," King Martin commands.

"Yes, my king," a knight replies.

The solem then thrusts his body in, his fist flying out.

"Now!"

The shield vanishes right before the solem's fist connects, sending it flying toward King Martin. He quickly steps to the side, narrowly dodging the punch. He then grips his sword and plunges the blade deep into the exposed neck of the solem.

"Parry this, you bastard."

He lifts his sword up and slices down, decapitating the solem in one swift stroke. He kicks its body, and it topples in front of the other solems.

"Age has not made our king lose his finesse. Let his speed guide our sword hand," a knight exclaims.

"Show no fear, for these monsters can be defeated," King Martin assures them. "Hold your ground. It looks like they're about to charge."

The other solems charge in with their shoulders, forming a wedged battering ram. Their charge breaks through the physical shield wall, causing many of the knights to break their position and fly away. One of the solems grabs a knight and rips off his arms. The knight screams in agony as blood pours out from his body.

"Stand true, my warriors!" King Martin says as his men are grabbed and ripped apart by the solems' brute power.

King Martin runs toward one of the solem and slides down between its legs. He manages to slice its thighs before the solem can grab him. The solem screams in pain and buckles down. From behind, King Martin raises his sword and plunges it into the solem's neck, killing it instantly.

"Do not let these monsters grab you, men! Strike them where they cannot reach you."

"My king! My sword is for you—"

One knight screams before a solem crushes his head underneath its foot. King Martin stares at his knights' bodies as they are all crushed one by one, feeling powerless to help them escape the death that awaits them.

"Paradise awaits on the other side," King Martin whispers.

He jumps onto the back of the solem and thrusts his sword into its neck, delivering the killing blow.

"For the glory of Goddess Astra and the kingdom of Sol—"

Out of nowhere, a solem punches King Martin behind, sending him flying into the wall at a dangerous speed.

"Argh!" King Martin grunts.

He puts one hand to the ground and kneels, spitting out blood.

That punch almost finished me. Thankfully, he only managed to dent my armor and—

A sharp pain fills his chest. He has broken some of his ribs. He pants as his breathing becomes heavy. He coughs out blood one more time before he tries to stand up.

In the midst of the chaos, the king stands and looks at the blood and death surrounding him. In his mind, he remembers his children, the ballroom dances, and banquets that once painted the majestic room with joy and wonder.

My kingdom has fallen. I have failed my people. With this cracked rib, I am not going to last much longer. He looks down at his sword. *I have one attack left in me. I will not die like a dog.*

"My sword, lend me your strength," King Martin whispers, blood dripping from his mouth.

He looks at the solems walking toward him, ready to deliver their final blow to the battered king. He puts his sword up into the air as the blade cackles with electricity.

"Lighting Blade Final Cut!"

The sword glows yellow and lets out a brilliant light as King Martin runs toward the solems at triple the speed of a normal human. He slashes one solem in half vertically and cuts the arm off another.

"And the wicked shall be smitten by the righteous hand of light. The blood that I will spill will be used to atone for the atrocities you have committed. No evil shall prevail as long as the righteous beat their hearts to the tune of justice."

King Martin prepares for another strike. He lifts his sword hand up, gripping the hilt with all of his strength.

BOOOOM!

A loud, deafening blast meets his ears. Two hands clapped together with great force cause his armor to vibrate violently against his skin. Blood flows out of his torso. King Martin falls to the ground, bleeding from his wounds. His armor crushed into his skin.

"Oh, what a pity," a familiar voice calls out.

"Show yourself, wretched coward. I am still alive and I will keep fighting 'til my last breath."

"Sure you will, sweetheart. But first, let's see you get out of your own armor." The voice mocks him. "A dishonorable end for a pathetic monarch. Your irony is nothing but a jester's cry to be taken seriously."

"Coward!" King Martin calls out, coughing up blood. "Only a thug would dare not bring their face into battle."

"Very well, Your Majesty. I will grant you the final pleasure of viewing my body."

Lisha levitates down from the ceiling, her dark purple dress wrapped around her seductive body. She smiles at the king, licking her lips seductively.

"Beautiful, aren't I?" she says.

King Martin slowly crawls toward Lisha, clawing his way as blood pours from his skin.

"Oh, poor baby." Lisha leans down and strokes King Martin's head. "Did my big boys play too rough with you?"

"Don't you dare mock me, witch," he snaps. "What is your name so that I may curse you with my last living breath!"

"A witch? My, oh my. I expected a much more refined and sophisticated vocabulary from a king such as yourself," Lisha says, slamming her foot on King Martin's head. "Very well, human, I will give you the glory of hearing my name. I am Lisha, one of the three generals in the Demon Lord's army. The most beautiful and charming as well."

"Why did you attack our people?" King Martin grunts. "Have you no honor?"

Lisha digs her heels deeper into King Martin's head, causing him more pain as he coughs out blood and saliva. "I do have one question for you. Have you seen a woman who looks like me before?"

"No! If I did and they were as evil as you, I would sentence them to death," he mutters.

Eyes narrowing, Lisha manifests her scythe, angling it toward King Martin's neck.

"Goddess Astra, receive my soul into your presence," he mumbles.

"I have no need for honor, Your Majesty." She smiles. "What we do to your kind only matters to us. You will die as a witness to our power."

With a swift stroke of her scythe, King Martin's head flies forward. His crown, bloodied, breaks apart as it lands in front of Lisha. She crushes it with her boots, causing the decorated jewels to fly out in all directions.

To hell with humanity. The world forgot about us, but we will no longer be an afterthought. Anyone who gets in our way will die. I guess he didn't know anything.

Lisha turns around and jumps out of the window, her wings lifting her high above the castle into the distant sunrise.

Chapter 8

Month of Dragons
Day 17

The rolling hills of the Eastern Kingdom make traveling to Glashmere immensely difficult.

"I fear I am too late," a man says to himself as he rides on horseback furiously toward the city gates. It is mid-morning and the sky, normally painted in bright blue, is muddled with dark gray smoke.

The young man, Chrono, is clad in a blue tunic and worn brown leather boots. His silver hair glimmers in the wind, held back from his face by a blue piece of fabric. His thirty years of age barely show in his lean build.

Princess Sarah, please be okay. His mind frantically paces between fear and hope.

He races toward the once golden city of Glashmere, now on fire from a demon assault, as fast as he can on his trusty steed, the spotted Annabelle.

Goddess Astra, give me speed.

"Forward, Annabelle!" Chrono yelps.

Annabelle's legs go one in front of the other, galloping at an intense pace. She has been with Chrono since he was a young boy, just like his broadsword, Gladius.

He made it his mission to seek out what evil plagues his hometown.

The wind whips across Chrono's face as he leans forward, embracing the chaos that awaits him.

"Not much longer until we reach the capital!" he tells Annabelle. "Make haste, my girl!" Annabelle neighs upon Chrono's instruction and trots faster.

The capital city is in his sight, but Ifer lies right before it, where demonic activity has been at an all-time high.

At that moment, an arrow skims over Annabelle's head.

"Halt, sweet girl!" Chrono stands on top of Annabelle's back and jumps off, flipping in midair and landing on the ground. She whinnies as if she is preparing to fight with him.

"Foul beast, show yourself!" he yells at the top of his lungs.

A fifteen-foot cyclops with blood splattered over its body with a giant club emerges from the tree line. If this monster was roaming around Ifer, the villagers didn't stand a chance.

Thankfully this is one of the smaller ones, thinks the silver-haired fighter. *But...wait, that was an arrow thrown at Annabelle's head. That means someone else is here.*

A beat passes and another arrow whizzes past Chrono's face, grazing his cheek.

Where in the Goddess's holy name is that coming from?

Chrono surveys his surroundings, awaiting the next attack. He then whips his attention to Annabelle and tells her to run and she complies, running back toward the path they came from.

The giant monster ambles toward Chrono, swinging its fists with intense force. Chrono puts Gladius up to block the attack.

What force! he thinks to himself as the blow pushes him back ten feet. Chrono steps to the right and slashes his sword at one of the cyclops's legs. The cyclops dodges back, avoiding the attack.

That thing sure is fast despite its lackluster demeanor.

Chrono takes out a small knife and throws it at the cyclops's eye. The cyclops drops his club and puts his hand to his eye, screaming in pain.

"Take that, you foul beast!" Chrono shouts. *Time to end this.*

He runs behind the beast and slices each heel with his blade. The cyclops falls to the ground, stomach first, with an enormous thud.

Off to Hell's Kitchen with you!

Chrono jumps on the cyclops's back and slams his sword into the beast's neck. A grotesque yell wails from the cyclops before silence looms across the way.

"Where did that archer go?" Chrono murmurs to himself as he looks around the forest trees, trying to ascertain if another attack is imminent.

When he's sure no one else is there, he whistles for Annabelle to come back.

Chrono is sure something or someone ordered that cyclops to attack him.

He puts his sword back into his scabbard as Annabelle gallops toward him, neighing in relief. "That's a good girl, Annabelle." Chrono coos, patting her head.

He then inspects her body to ensure she isn't injured before mounting her again.

"Let's go, girl!"

As they reach the city of Ifer, Chrono catches sight of the street, and his eyes widen.

Is that a body?

Annabelle slows down as Chrono runs his hand through her mane. He climbs off her back and walks toward the body lying in the middle of the road. A woman.

He places his fingers on her neck but feels no pulse.

Looking down the road, Chrono beckons to his horse. "Come, Annabelle."

She slowly trots beside him as they enter the town of Ifer, finding bodies thrown along the edge of the forest and lying in the streets. The town sign is torn in two, half-broken and strewn on the ground.

"This is horrible." He sighs and frowns at Annabelle for approval.

Annabelle puts her nose on Chrono's ear, breathing heavily and snorting.

"I don't know if that's the answer I was looking for, but thank you anyway, my girl," he says, scratching the back of his neck as they move along.

Chrono walks up to several bodies, touching their neck to see if any life is left. It appalls him to see that the demons even killed some children.

Chrono puts his head down, his eyes swelling with tears. How he wishes he could drop a tear for every loss of life.

He failed his people. They were not ready to face this kind of attack. Not without him there.

The demons knew that their kingdom was falling into a recession, and they took advantage of that weakness.

I wonder if the king is still alive.

Chrono continues to walk through the town, on the lookout for any survivors.

"Help!" a soft voice cries in the distance. "Help me, please!"

Chrono looks around frantically, trying to locate the source of the sound.

"Over here, by the shop!" the voice yells, fading quietly.

Chrono sees an abandoned shop with a shield painted on it and a hand stretched out on the floor by the door.

I hope this isn't a trap.

Chrono walks over to the door and nudges it open carefully, sword in hand.

A young girl comes into sight, splayed out on the floor, breathing heavily, with her legs torn to shreds.

"Please…help me," the young girl pleads.

Chrono sits down by her and gently puts the young girl's head in his lap. "It's okay, young one. I'll do my best." He looks at her leg and hushes her.

She has lost too much blood.

"My m-momma…a-and my papa are d-dead." She coughs and winces in pain. "The solems ate them. And then they s-smashed… everyone."

"What is your name, child?" Chrono strokes the young girl's hair, and she calms down a tad.

"A-Amber," she stutters and starts to cry. "It hurts so much!"

Amber clutches Chrono's arm and he curses, silently praying to Goddess Astra to take the pain away from this child as soon as she can. He knows there is no hope left for this young girl.

He pulls out a vial with a blue liquid inside of it. "This is going to sting, child," Chrono says.

Amber braces herself for the pain, and he pours the numbing elixir on the wound. She huffs and finally stops shaking, lying quietly back in Chrono's lap.

"Am I going to die?" she asks with wide eyes.

He can't tell whether she is asking him or the Goddess, but he answers anyway.

"You are going to live forever," Chrono says with vigor.

Amber stares past him, and she slowly stops breathing.

She is definitely in a better place now, he thinks to himself. *With her parents and the Goddess and all her children.*

Chrono sits quietly as the sun gleams through the small window in the shop. After a few moments, he shuts her eyes. Standing, he carries Amber's body out the door toward the wooded area behind the shop.

He sets her by Annabelle for a moment before grabbing a shovel to dig a shallow grave.

When he's finished, Chrono picks her up and lowers her body into the ground. Tears of sorrow threaten to fall from his eyes.

A death like this should not be so.

The world is supposed to let the old die before the young. Goddess Astra had their lives perfectly timed out until the demon swarms got to them.

The people of Ifer did not deserve cruel deaths.

Chrono used to walk these streets as a young child, getting pastries from the bakery down the road. He remembers how bright and lively everyone was to him, even as he got older.

The people of Ifer deserved to live, and so they shall in Chrono's heart and in the Heavens above.

Chrono says his last prayer for little Amber and then mounts Annabelle's back. *I hope Glashmere isn't as bad as Ifer was,* he thinks as they race east toward the capital city.

The castle walls soon come into view. The brass and wood gates are crushed, lying in pieces on the ground, along with the lifeless bodies of demons and humans alike.

Some of the bodies are torn in half; others still twitch involuntarily in death. They must have died not long ago.

"Come, Annabelle, let's hurry!" Chrono wails.

Annabelle huffs furiously as they leap over bodies and move up the brick road leading to the castle.

"I hope the king is still alive, my girl," he whispers to her.

As they reach the castle walls, Chrono spots a small purple-skinned, spiky demon eating a human body.

"Off with you, foul beast!" Chrono pulls out his sword and slashes the creature across the chest, killing it. Then he gallops toward the castle doors.

Chrono pulls his horse to a stop, hops off her back, and ties her to a column.

"You stay here, girl," Chrono coos before leaving her at the castle entrance.

The vast castle of Glashmere is no small place to explore, especially in the midst of a solem attack. It stands high above the city, towering over the other buildings. Once a beacon of accomplishment for its people, now Castle Glashmere has become an early grave for its subjects.

Chrono walks into the castle, sword drawn. He steps over the body of one of the maids in the first hallway. A heavy scent of blood permeates the corridors.

He is thankful that the curtains on the tall windows are open so he can see, but Chrono knows he may need to use the torch in his satchel soon, as the sun is beginning to set.

He heads up the red-carpeted stairs to the second floor of the castle. *The servants had quarters up here.* Chrono squints as he climbs up.

At the fork in the stairs, a giant picture of King Martin hangs on the wall. Before Chrono, more bodies litter the floor, many with familiar faces, including a maid who took a liking to him.

"Meredith!" Chrono gasps, running over to her.

The paleness of her skin shows signs her life source has been sucked out of her. Chrono fights back the urge to yell in rage, devastated to know her soul did not know peace at the end.

He closes her eyes and lays his hand on her head, thinking of what could have been if he had made it back here sooner.

"My dear friend, I am so sorry," he mumbles, choking on the lump of emotion in his throat.

Swallowing his sorrow, Chrono stands up and continues down the hallway, still on guard.

The throne room is just one more floor away. Goddess, please let them be all right.

He passes by the kitchens up the stairs and makes his way toward the throne room, like he used to. He has the path memorized, having climbed up the same way to see King Martin countless times.

The once twenty-foot-tall doors are a memory, broken on the floor in front of him.

"Goddess, n-no…" Chrono sobs and drops to his knees, looking out across the throne room.

Many of the king's guard, his old friends, are thrown across the room like rag dolls, either torn to shreds or crushed from the sheer force of the attackers. Some are young like him; some are old; some weren't guards at all, but loyal court members to the king.

What type of enemy is even capable of all this destruction?

Chrono sniffs and lifts himself off the floor, hand by his mouth, holding in a scream when his eyes catch what seems like half of the great King Martin.

He looks upon the savagery of the death that befell the king in utter horror. *Does the enemy have no honor at all?* To separate his head from his body was beyond cruel and personal.

"What in Astra's name is going on?" Chrono mumbles in disbelief.

Walking over to the nearest royal blue curtain, he cuts a large piece off to cover the king's head and body, as he deserves.

"Chrono? Is that you?" a familiar voice calls out.

He whips his head around to see the trapdoor behind the throne room flipped open, revealing a womanly shape.

The sweet Princess Sarah straightens to her full height six feet tall, with long purple hair and glimmering, pale skin. Just as Chrono remembers.

She emerges from the shadow of the throne and adjusts the sliver of a pink pearl crown weaving through her hair.

"Your Highness," Chrono murmurs, lowering to one knee in respect. His heart skips a beat as he holds back a smile.

Sarah smiles softly. "Rise, good warrior."

As he stands, Chrono notices the dried blood matted to the princess's dusty rose skirt. She shrugs her coat off her shoulders and wipes down her dress at the bodice.

"Has the kingdom fallen?" Sarah whispers, more to herself than Chrono. "I was visiting my father and in the next moment, he commanded me to hide."

"Yes, Princess," Chrono answers with sadness. "The kingdom is gone, and so are the surrounding towns."

Sarah nods at this information and walks toward her father's throne. "Do go on, Chrono."

"And King Martin…" He gulps, gesturing toward the other end of the room where he covered the good man. "He has perished as well."

"I…I figured." Sarah clutches the throne as she blinks back tears. "I heard the commotion. My father told me to escape through the tunnels, but I decided to peek out from behind the trapdoor."

Princess Sarah is truly her mother's daughter, Chrono thinks, *patient and resilient. Almost too much so.*

Tears start to fall down Sarah's pretty face. "Oh, Chrono, my father was the bravest man I knew."

"I agree wholeheartedly, Your Highness." Chrono goes to sit by the throne steps.

"I was looking through the crack in the door and saw the assault coming through our throne room." Sarah gulps as she continues, "Our knights stood no chance, even with the protective barrier around my father. He was yelling for them to run to safety, but they refused to leave his side."

Chrono bows his head sadly. "His Majesty always cared for his people, even at the end of his life."

The princess nods in agreement, wiping her eyes. "That trait sure earned him a lot of hate amongst the elite but respect among the common man, which was a double-edged sword. He asked the knights to lower the barrier. Then, the knights tried to attack the solems, but…they were brutally murdered. My skills would not have mattered at all in that slaughter."

Chrono shivers at the princess's account. It is unimaginable how much loss she witnessed, but she seems unscathed.

Sarah looks off into the distance and sighs. "Only my father was left then. With several demons closing in on him. He was completely overwhelmed, only killing one out of the dozen that crowded around him."

"What happened next, Your Highness?" Chrono is almost afraid to ask but needs to know.

"At that point," Sarah stares at Chrono directly, "I saw a scantily-dressed woman appear and finish my father off. Like it was her sole purpose for coming."

"Did you recognize this woman?" he asks, suddenly overwhelmed with the urge to find the monster and make her pay.

"No…not at all." The princess looks spent. "She looked right in my direction before flying out of the damned castle. I could have sworn she saw me, but if she did, I probably would be dead, too."

Chrono looks at Sarah with disbelief, shaking his head. "At least we have an idea of what we're dealing with here."

"The solems were cheering her name, but I couldn't hear it," Sarah says as she finally sits on her father's throne. "I will never forget, though, what that woman looks like."

Chrono stood then. "We will get revenge. I swear to you, Princess Sarah. On my life."

Princess Sarah smiles softly at the best War Master of Glashmere, her heart full knowing that Chrono remains loyal to the throne and her father even after all the devastation.

"I wonder about the queen, Your Highness," Chrono says. "Was she a victim of the attack as well?"

"My mother went to warn the townspeople before the solems arrived," Sarah answered. "I do fear the worst may have happened to her, though. Did you see her out there?"

Chrono looks at the ground and sighs. "I did not see Her Majesty nor her body."

"I see…"

The silence grows deafening between the princess and the War Master. No words of comfort line his lips. Chrono shifts in his place by Princess Sarah.

She clasps her hands together. "Well, I believe we should have a proper burial for my father, and then we must seek help from the Southern Kingdom."

"That would be a good idea, Princess." *Is she in shock?* he wonders.

"Is the Bridge of Eden still in operation?" she asks.

"Yes, Your Highness. The Bridge of Eden would be the only way to get there. Queen Charlotte is an honorable woman, I hear. I believe she may take your audience."

"Do you think she will take us in?" Sarah asks.

"I believe Queen Charlotte has a soft spot for King Martin, despite having to rule over the oceanic portion of the kingdoms." Chrono clears his throat and carries on for the princess. "She has a large fleet that could help us against the enemy."

"You are right, Chrono. That would be most helpful." Princess Sarah looks impressed. "I hope she will be willing to hear our case."

Chrono nods in approval as he walks over to the door of the throne room. He bows and says, "I am going to find something to…transport the king's body in."

Sarah nods, mostly to herself, and breathes in deeply.

* * *

After Chrono leaves, Sarah looks around, alone in the throne room.

Her family and her people suffered so much loss and pain, and she hid behind a door while it was going on. The guilt starts to grow in Sarah's heart. She learned how to fight when she was a girl, insisting on accompanying her father and his kings guard during training. Her father would always say that she was his best pupil.

It brings tears to her eyes, but she holds them back and tries to calm down.

Sarah stands from her father's throne and walks over to her father's body, covered by the curtain Chrono placed on top of him. She bends down over him and puts her hand on his body. Chills from his corpse creep up her arm.

"Father, I know you're here with me." Sarah's voice starts to shake. "I promise you I will do right by you and be the queen that the people need me to be, even if I…I know I'm not ready."

Sarah awaits any kind of response, but of course, nothing comes. She bites her quivering lip. The Great King of Glashmere is truly gone.

A moment later, Chrono returns to carry the king's wrapped body onto a spare wagon. Sarah blinks back tears as they make their way down from the throne room and through the terribly silent castle. Everything seems to move in slow motion as they move through the hallowed halls toward the basement, wheeling the dead king alongside them.

Chrono glances at Sarah every now and then, and the princess's face is frozen in sadness.

The duo emerges from the catacombs, the sun shining brightly on them. They turn the wagon and head toward the main road.

Sarah looks around at the bodies everywhere, holding back sobs at the sight of so many people who died without hope.

"I had absolutely no idea our people were going through all of this," she mumbles in shock.

"You know the rumors were spreading," Chrono says, looking at the princess. "You know which ones I am talking about, right?"

"Yes, I know the ones." Sarah nods slowly. "Many of the people in our city and countryside said my father was weak, lacking the spine to push back against the other kingdoms, especially when trading goods."

"Do you think there was some truth to that?" Chrono asks as they continue through the capital. He did not want to believe the king was managing resources wastefully.

Sarah visibly struggles to find words. "I mean, my father was a loving man, and he was strong, but… Obviously, he did the best he could."

She looks down at the wagon holding her father's body. Some chatter emerges from behind them.

"It's the princess!" a voice exclaims.

"Is that a survivor?" Chrono turns around to find a man standing about fifty feet from them.

Sarah runs toward him, and he bows slightly at the sight of the princess.

"Are you hurt?" Sarah grabs his hand.

"Your Highness, I am okay! Just a scratch or two." The man smiles. "We were able to hide at least fifty people underneath our restaurant."

Chrono pulls the wagon over to them.

"Good sir," Chrono says, "kindly gather those survivors. The Great King has fallen."

The man sighs, his eyes red from crying. "I cannot believe it. We all must pay our respects."

Sarah puts her hand on his shoulder. "I am the leader of the kingdom now, but this city is no longer safe. I am sure there are enemies nearby. After my father's funeral, we will travel to the capital of the Southern Kingdom, Lafare."

The man runs to gather the people as Chrono and Sarah go down to the forest area outside the city gates.

Chrono pulls out his shovel and starts to dig a grave for the king.

Two men blowing trumpets lead the townspeople walking out of the castle gates towards Sarah. She greets the man from earlier and offers a wave to the remaining townspeople. They look fearful and distraught. They murmur among themselves at the sight of the princess and the wagon that holds their former king.

The trumpets stop, and the townspeople line up in front of the deep hole in the ground.

Sarah walks in front of Chrono and the people with teary eyes.

"What is a king?" She gulps as she continues, with full emotion. "The Great King was a man of the people. My father loved our kingdom with all of his heart. He lived a life of victory, love, and trust. He was a fair and just man who wanted the best for all of us. There was so much you didn't see that he did for us as a kingdom. In his death, he fought the demon army with all of his strength. He died a noble death befitting of a leader. My father is a hero, and his memory will live on forever. We will rise above this grief!"

Sarah raises her fist in the air, and the townspeople do the same, in honor of the king.

Chrono takes the king's body, wrapped in curtain cloth, and lays it in the ground. The dirt piles on the body of King Martin as he heaves more dirt into the hole.

Sarah walks over to assist Chrono, and they pile more dirt onto the grave together. The two work in silence as they finish the burial of King Martin. The townspeople are silent, too, some of the women in the crowd dabbing at their eyes with handkerchiefs.

Sarah, with tears streaming down her face, turns and hugs Chrono. He wraps his arms around her; their embrace lasts for minutes.

Princess Sarah composes herself and turns toward the townspeople.

"Please," she says to her people. "Make haste and find any wagons and weapons you can. Do not overpack. We must travel swiftly. We leave in ten minutes."

"Look at you giving orders." Chrono chuckles, not used to Princess Sarah in this position.

"I am all they have now, Chrono," Sarah says softly. "We have no idea if my mother is alive or not. Until then, I am the queen or at least acting queen."

Chrono looks at Sarah, proud of the woman she has become. *When thrust into difficult situations, we become who we were meant to be*, he thinks to himself. *I hope that she can lead these people. Who else do they have?*

He looks at the townspeople running into town. He walks towards Annabelle, who gives him a big kiss and whinnies for the queen.

"I will lead the pack, Queen Sarah," Chrono tells her, and she nods in approval.

The townspeople return with ten wagons, not burned down by the fires, and twenty horses.

"That was more than I thought we would find," Sarah says in relief.

Chrono walks up and down the line of wagons, seeing the worry in the eyes of the townspeople.

Show no fear, only conviction. "We are going to be okay," he shouts to everyone. "We need lookouts to take post at the back of the caravan."

Two men immediately take up the position. The women and children hurry into wagons as men take the horses and tie them to the wagons.

"We make way for Lafare, the capital of the Southern Kingdom!" Chrono yells for everyone behind him to hear. "Let us depart!"

Annabelle stands on her two hind legs proudly as Chrono rides to the front of the caravan.

"May the Goddess protect us!" Sarah cries as she rides alongside him on a white horse.

Chrono looks out at the sun sinking down over the hills in the distance. The sunset is beautiful. But he feels the heavy responsibility of caring for these souls.

Will my sword be enough to keep them safe?

All he can do for now is lean forward into the wind as Annabelle carries him and what is left of Glashmere toward an unknown destiny.

Chapter 9

Month of Dragons
Day 18

Despite it being summer, there is still snow on the ground in the Northern Kingdom. The capital, Salazar, sits emotionally isolated from its people by its cruel ruler. The lands around the kingdom are not fertile; the people rely on trade and commerce with the other kingdoms for important resources. Various pelts, especially that of the two-tailed equine, the mormah, have proven to be the most valuable.

King Leo, a tall, pale bald man in his late forties with a large handlebar mustache, sits on his throne, looking out into the blue sky. He wears an unusual crown on his head, one fashioned with the skeleton of a bear he killed in his youth.

"King Leo." A knight rushes in, bowing before the king. "A messenger from the Eastern Kingdom awaits an audience before you."

"Send him in," King Leo replies, stroking his moustache with curiosity.

Another man hurries into the throne room, panting and sweating.

"Your Majesty," the man says. "I bring unfortunate news from the Eastern Kingdom. We have been attacked by the minions of the Demonic Realm. They have besieged our castle. King Martin humbly requests for your help, for he fears that once they are finished with the Eastern Kingdom, they will set their eyes upon yours."

"What happens to your tree-hugging people is none of our concern, knave."

"But Your Majesty—"

"Enough!" King Leo snaps. "You come to me bearing bad news and a plea for help. We are not mongrels like you to succumb to these demons. You think we don't stand a chance against those who encroach on our lands? Off to the dungeon with you."

"My lord," one of the guards replies. "Is this not an open declaration of war, should we harm their messenger?"

"We do not take insults lightly here. None shall know of his disappearance."

Prince Maxim, a short and stout man, looks on as the knight is dragged away screaming. He shakes his head, running his hand through his short, brown, frizzy hair.

"Father," Prince Maxim says. "You deem it wise to turn your back to the people who send us aid during the harsh winter snow?"

"It is either kill or be killed, son," replies King Leo. "We cannot besmirch the needs of our people for those who have already lost. We need to see to ourselves first." He looks over at his son, who wears his own bear cloak. A small crown made of dragon bones adorns his head. *There is nothing redeeming about that boy. Will he ever make me proud?*

Maxim nods at his fathers. In his mind, he believes a different action could have been taken. But he knows better than to challenge his father.

Leaving the throne room, Prince Maxim walks back to his chambers, pondering the day's events and what will become of the Eastern Empire.

I *need to do something to right this wrong. That man was a messenger trying to help his people. My father was wrong for what he did. I must not alarm him, though. I will find a way to get a message to the other kingdoms without raising a ruckus.*

Inside his chamber, Maxim writes a letter and tucks it away in his coat pocket.

* * *

Out in the plains of the Eastern Kingdom, the new queen's convoy comes to a halt. Giant green slime blocks their path. Chrono hops off his horse and walks up to the slime, noticing that it is slumbering.

"Is there any way around it?" Sarah asks, coming up beside Chrono.

"It seems to be resting," Chrono replies. "Things like these are usually locomotive, especially in the day. I should warn you not to walk too near to it, for it may suck you up in its slime."

Sarah looks curiously at the beast. "It does not look threatening in the slightest. It is just blocking the way. I wonder if any music would cause it to move. Do we have anyone with a small harp in the convoy?"

She rummages through the wagons, searching for an instrument of some kind. Chrono looks back, watching Sarah search for something to play. *She's always had a knack for finding the solution*, thinks Chrono. Sarah runs back up to him with a small stringed instrument.

"It's no harp, but it will do," she says to Chrono.

Sarah plays the stringed instrument with precision despite its weathered appearance. The melody does the trick. The slime, around ten to fifteen feet tall, wakes up with a droopy smile on its face.

Chrono stands at the ready with his sword. The slime looks down at Chrono, still smiling, and moves toward him.

"That will be close enough, beast," Chrono warns.

Before he knows what's happening, the slime licks him on the face.

"Ugh, disgusting," Chrono complains, wiping the sticky liquid off his face, looking embarrassed.

"It likes you." Sarah giggles.

"I thought I was fast. That thing moved quickly despite being so large."

The slime, awakened by the music, moves out of their way and into the woods—knocking trees down as it slugs along out of sight.

"I knew we would find some odd things on our journey but that will be a memory to remember." Chrono shakes his head, wiping the slime off his tabard.

Sarah giggles again, watching him desperately trying to remove the slime from his clothes.

"We don't have time to stop, Princess Sarah—erm. I mean Your Majesty," says Chrono. "You should return to your wagon and let us be off with haste."

"I think we should rest," Sarah suggests. "We have you, the War Master, at our side. The townspeople are scared and tired. They need to rest."

Sarah turns away and walks back to her wagon. On her way, she hears several cutting complaints about Chrono.

"Why didn't he come back sooner?"

"He could have saved us all."

"Lazy bum got my family killed. I don't get why we're still following him."

Sarah puts her head down in disgust. *If only they knew the man he is, then they would not throw such stones at him verbally.* She clenches her fist and jumps back into her wagon. *Without him, we wouldn't have made it this far.*

She lies underneath a blanket, looking up at the sky. The gentle breeze blows through the rear of the wagon. She closes her eyes to rest, having stayed up all night.

* * *

Chrono walks over to Annabelle and leads her to sit down. He sets his sword beside him, leaning against her.

"Well, girl, you have been with me this whole time," he murmurs. "We barely made it back to save a few people. Did we really save them?"

Fifty people from Glashmere are in his care, including Sarah. The rest didn't survive the slaughter.

He runs his fingers through his hair, thinking about their childhood. *It's been a long time since I've felt truly challenged. Fighting has always naturally to me. Ever since I was a young lad, I had a wooden sword in my hand. I had to teach myself control because I was always pushing forward ahead without a care. For these people, I need to remember to be cautious. Even though I am one of the strongest in the Eastern Kingdom, I need to be careful not to let ego get the best of me.*

Chrono stays awake for a long time, knowing they could be attacked at any moment. But at last, he allows himself to drift off to sleep.

* * *

Midafternoon comes without a care as Chrono yawns awake. To his surprise, Sarah is curled up beside him, leaning on his chest.

"Sarah!" He shoots up, blushing. "Erm, Your Highness, I don't want people getting the wrong idea."

Annabelle looks puzzled at Chrono. Not knowing whether to stand up or continue resting.

"You are going to scare the poor beast." Sarah yawns.

"Last I saw you, you were heading to your wagon," he says.

"Well, I couldn't sleep in the blasted thing, so I came here to the front of the caravan to find you resting on Annabelle. You worked so hard I felt like it would be a shame to leave you alone." Sarah smiles, her hair waving in the wind.

Chrono, gaining his composure, moves back to Sarah.

"We are friends. I appreciate the concern, but please be careful, as rumors can spread fast amongst the townsfolk."

Sarah blinks slowly, staring at Chrono, before nodding her head.

"That will not stop me from showing you affection, War Master. You are still Chrono, a human who needs warmth and affection. I wanted to give the War Master side of you some rest, but I do have some bad news. We lost one wagon and two horses. A family decided they would rather head to the Western Kingdom instead of the south. They have family in the Western Kingdom in the city of Somal."

Chrono frowns. "Who gave them the authority to do so?"

"They left when everyone was sleeping. One family overheard them say back at the funeral that they didn't trust you. They said horrible things about your leadership and how you would drive us to death. 'How can one warrior protect us all?' they mocked." She shakes her head, pressing her lips together.

"They have the right to feel this way," Chrono replies. "I let down the kingdom by going on vacation to rest. The people died as I slumbered."

"Do not beat yourself up too much. You saved me and the rest of these people as well. We would all be dead if you had not shown up. We had nowhere to go. Who knows what would have happened to us? The land is lost, but the kingdom is still here. The kingdom is the people and I as their leader."

"I trust that you lead us well, Your Majesty."

"No, Chrono," Sarah says, putting a hand on his shoulder. "I place my trust in you to lead our people to safety. One family leaving means nothing. They endanger themselves by not traveling with us. What idiots they are not to follow you. I've always looked up to you, Chrono. Do not dare let the words of a few small-minded people corrupt your character."

Chrono's eyes widen as if seeing the world for the first time anew. "You have my word, Princess." Placing his hand on her shoulder, he says, "I am going to talk to everyone."

Chrono stands up. "Listen here and listen clear!" he calls out.

Everyone brings their attention to Chrono. The townspeople gather in front of the caravan.

"There have been rumors that I am not fit to lead you to our new home." Chrono pauses as the townsfolk glare at him. Some in shock from the king's death and other with faces of doubt.

"You didn't care about us," a man yells.

"Please listen to me." Chrono claps his hands together. "I am a warrior sworn to protect our kingdom. I am sincerely sorry that I was not there for you in the chaos that happened."

"What if there are more of those demons out there?" a woman asks.

"Many of you lost family and friends who cannot be replaced. Our new queen has placed her trust in me, and I plead that you do the same. Put your trust in me, and I will guide us to safety."

"Can you promise us that?" a woman solemnly asks, pointing at Chrono.

Chrono stutters, looking down at the ground, then back at the woman. "Sadly, I cannot," he says softly. "But I will fight with all my might if any threat comes toward us," he continues in a louder voice. We will reach the Bridge of Eden soon and pass into Southern Kingdom territory. Once there, we can finally escape the clutches of danger. Lend me your hand, and I will guide you."

"How can we trust you?" one of the townsfolk asks. "You were not there when we needed you."

"What is important is that I am here now with you. We fall divided if we do not stand united. We are all we have."

Some of the townsfolk nod, agreeing, while others mumble under their breath. Chrono knows it will take a lot more to gain their trust back, but he is confident in himself.

"Once we have a meal, we will head out to the Bridge of Eden. It should be one more day until they reach it. Until then, please be on alert."

Chrono walks back to Sarah, grinning.

"See? I can be a leader when needed," he says. "Thank you for believing in me."

Sarah smiles and walks towards the townsfolk.

"Pray with me," Sarah commands. "Pray so that we may find the light at the end of this darkness."

Sarah takes the hands of two townspeople and leads them in the Holy Prayer of Astra.

Give us light

Let us love

Shine your Glory

From Above

Chapter 10

Month of Dragons

Day 19

The sun rises in Jerut. A week has passed as the party of three prepared for the next leg of their journey.

Slash awakens to a thud outside the door.

"Oh, no!" Sodina shoots awake. "Someone must have touched the doorknob."

Sodina walks over the door, her hair in a mess, and opens the door.

On the floor lies Bridget, stiff as a nail with a pained expression on her face.

"I am so sorry, Bridget!" Sodina says as she kneels down and puts her hand on Bridget to release the spell.

"You could have killed me, woman," Bridget yells as she gets free. "What were you thinking bewitching the door with a paralyzing spell?"

"Well," Sodina chuckles, "Slash was apprehensive staying in a place like this and wanted to feel safe."

"He should feel safe with me across the hall," Bridget grumbles. "I told him I am his shield, so he better believe it."

Bridget slams her fist on the door and wakes Slash. "We leave in thirty minutes for the town of Rinkar, lovebirds."

Slash sits up, wiping his eyes slowly, sending Bridget a small smile before she turns around, heading down toward the first floor of the inn. *My own fear hurt Bridget. This anxiety is getting out of control. I need to figure out something soon.*

Slash rolls out of bed and goes to Sodina. "Good morning my love," he says, walking up behind her and wrapping his arms around her waist.

"Good morning, honey." Sodina turns around slowly, her lips touching his. "We better get going." She changes into her green dress.

Once they're both dressed, Sodina and Slash get their things together and head down for breakfast. Bridget is already sitting at a table, sipping on some coffee, when the two walk in holding hands.

"I told you guys thirty minutes, but you took thirty-five. The bacon is already eaten. I left some toast and eggs for you."

"Calm down, we are not in a rush," Sodina says. "Either way, I am still cursed. Let's take our time and enjoy breakfast."

Sodina sits down at the table with Slash. He picks up his fork to take a bite of the salty eggs.

"These things have a bit too much spice on them," he says with his mouth full.

Bridget laughs, spitting out some of her coffee. Sodina giggles along with her.

"You think that's salty? Come on, Slash," she says. "You need to expand your palate a bit, buddy."

Sodina cuts into her eggs, takes a bite, and frowns. "These are a little salty."

"I guess I will let you guys get your own food next time." Bridget grins. "Talk about ungrateful."

Slash looks at Bridget, unamused.

"Just kidding." She laughs again. "Can't you take a joke?"

"It's still early, you know. I don't usually wake until around late morning."

Slash leans his head on the table, acting like he's falling asleep.

"Sleepyhead, wake up." Sodina smacks him on the back of his head. "You need your food to be big and robust."

Bridget smiles, looking at the happy couple.

Hopefully, one day, I can have a husband like that, she thinks as she watches their exchange. *Or maybe if Sodina passes one day, I can still marry Slash.*

The thought has occasionally crossed her mind that Slash would make a great husband. Reliable, kind, and respectful. And absolutely not bad looking.

"What are you day-dreaming about, Bridget?" Sodina asks curiously.

"Nothing," Bridget replies in a beat. "Just thinking about the next leg of our journey. I will get the horses ready. Met you guys outside in a few minutes."

Bridget walks up, putting her cloak on, heading out the door.

"She's in some kind of mood today," Sodina mumbles as she takes another bite of her eggs.

I wonder if we will find a cure for this poison, she thinks sadly.

Sodina hasn't yet let Slash know that her arm has started to flash a number occasionally. Some days, it flashes 999, while others, it flashes 68. She doesn't have the faintest idea what it means, but Sodina is confident of one thing.

She does not want a number in the single digits.

Anything below ten could indicate I'm near death. Sodina continues to drown in her thoughts.

Is it some sort of trick to make her anxious? Her head spins.

Sodina wants answers even more than Slash knows, but she will not let him see her shaken. Eventually, this poison will kill her.

Hopefully, the Tears of Ella elixir she has will be enough to combat the curse until they find a cure.

Slash looks over at his wife and notices she is still chewing on the same eggs from a few minutes ago.

"Baby," he says lovingly. "It would do you well to swallow that already."

"Oh, yes." Sodina giggles in reply, almost choking on the rest of the eggs in her mouth. "I meant to do that."

"What were you thinking about, my love?"

"I...was thinking about Amanda and Lorenz," Sodina answers

quietly. "I wish they were here to go on all these adventures with us. There is so much of the world they didn't get to see."

Slash kisses Sodina on the cheek. "My love, we have yet to understand the intentions of that attack."

Sodina nods, finding relief in the words of her dear husband.

"I swear to you that we will," Slash continues on. "That is a promise I made to myself that day and every day I live. I will find their killer and bring them to justice."

His body trembles slightly. The grief of the horrible moment when they lost their two friends is still with him.

"We will make it all right one day," Sodina whispers.

She grabs his hand, and they leave to find Bridget.

* * *

Outside, the sunlight beams brilliantly over the town of Jerut.

It's still ugly, though, Slash thinks to himself. He is immensely happy the sun is shining after the rainfall the other day.

Bridget walks up to Slash and Sodina, waving two full leather satchels at them.

"I was able to purchase some items for our journey," Bridget exclaims proudly. "We have at least three days of supplies. It should be a one-day trip on horseback."

"What did you get?" Sodina asks the warrior woman curiously.

"We have some potions, herbs, bread, and apples! Let's make haste and get to Rinkar. The individual I know there is a seer."

The trio jumps on their horses and trots toward the town's entrance.

"It's a shame we can't get the horses going until we get out of the gates." Bridget sighs.

"I know. It's a stupid rule," Slash says. "But I'd rather not end up in jail today, especially since time is of the essence."

The trio reaches the gate and spurs their horses on.

"Come on, girl, let's go!" Bridget yells.

Before them lies the border of the Northern Kingdom, which they will not cross over. The snow-capped mountains send a chill throughout the entire valley.

Bridget throws Slash and Sodina thick coats. "We may run into some winter weather on our way to Rinkar. Put those on!"

"We have yet to visit there," Slash yells up to Bridget. "I heard their king punched a bear and rode it back to their castle," he says. "He then proceeded to keep the bear as a pet."

"But who knows what's fact or fiction?" Sodina laughs, her words not reaching Slash's ears. "I think I may need to speak louder next time."

Hours pass as the trio pushes through the cold wind until they enter the forest line.

"We should take a break now," Bridget says, jumping down from her horse. "With the cold air, the horses are working twice as hard."

Bridget opens her pack and pulls out a piece of bread.

"It's cinnamon," she says, handing it to Slash.

Slash takes a bite of bread. "It's terrific, thanks." He smiles at Bridget. His black hair is covered in snowfall and leaves from the journey.

Sodina watches the exchange from her place near her husband and tilts her head, wondering what will happen next.

"You need to clean out your hair." Bridget laughs. She comes close to Slash and pulls out the debris, being sure to get extra close.

Slash blushes slightly but thanks Bridget. He tears off half of the cinnamon roll and offers it to his wife.

Sodina looks at Bridget peculiarly but sits down to take the bread from Slash.

"Tell me about this seer, Bridget," Slash asks. "Can she truly see the future?"

"Well, she can see different pathways," Bridget replies. "Because the future's not set in stone, lots of factors can still affect it. I am hoping she can at least give us some insight as to what direction to take next. You guys have been searching for the last five years, and nothing has happened. It wasn't by chance that you happened to stumble upon me."

The couple ponders the new information, and Sodina reaches for Slash's hand. He gives her a small kiss on her cheek from his new spot seated next to her.

"Your savior is here!" Bridget stands up, striking a goofy pose to lighten the mood. "In all seriousness, I hope we get some answers. She owes me a huge favor."

"You know a lot of people," Sodina says, and Slash chimes in, "And a lot of people owe you."

"Well, it comes with being a traveler," Bridget responds with a shrug. "You meet all sorts of people on your merry way. How about you two? I'm sure you've met a couple interesting characters!"

"We've traveled to a few cities, yes, but we were people of the wilderness," Slash explains. "Our hometown of Ifer was a small farming town outside the capital of Glashmere. We provided almost all of the food to the kingdom."

Sodina blushes at the memory of her and Slash sharing their first kiss while foraging for berries during one of the winters back home.

"While we are exiled from Ifer for the death of the mayor's children, we still would like to revisit Glashmere." Slash sighs. "I wonder if they still have that bakery with the sweet rolls."

"The icing was so sweet your teeth would rot on sight!" Sodina says. "But boy, was it good. We grew up always getting free rolls from the old bakery."

"Have you guys known each other for a long time?" Bridget asks, trying to hide her jealousy.

"Yes, since childhood," Slash says. "Sodina and I finally got married after the trip when we lost Amanda and Lorenz. Our ceremony was small in Glashmere. We even have our initials on a tree right outside the city."

"S and S, our initials," Sodina says dreamily. "I wonder if they're still there."

Slash pats his wife's hand as he reminisces. "Some people from our town joined us in the capital. We had just enough money to rent out the chapel there. Right after we got married, we started our journey to find a cure for Sodina. Since then, we've had no luck. We were at our wit's end when we met you."

"You practically saved us." Sodina sighs.

"I bet you're a strong warrior, though," says Bridget, cocking an eyebrow at Slash.

"Swordsmanship came naturally to me at a young age," he replies. "The problem was my stamina. I was born with a weakened immune system. I was a frail child. It took years of eating correctly to grow into the man I am today. Long, prolonged fights make it difficult to take on high-profile quests. But Sodina, here, is proficient at magic. With her magic skills and my ability to find the weak points of our enemies, w've always made enough money to get by."

"That's why I never heard of you!" Bridget laughs.

"I'm serious," Slash answers.

Bridget smiles at the lovebirds. "Of course."

"We are thankful to be in your company," Sodina adds. "We really are."

"I am thankful to be in your company, too!"

Bridget runs over to Slash and puts him in a headlock, much to Sodina's dismay.

"You're cute when you're being sensitive." Bridget giggles.

Her bosoms are too close, Slash thinks to himself. *I need to get out of this headlock.*

Before he knows it, Bridget flips him over onto his back.

"You need to be on your guard at all times!" Bridget exclaims. "We are going to work on your stamina right now!"

Bridget takes off her cloak and assumes a fighting stance. Slash is winded from her random flip and immediately regrets opening himself up to someone other than his wife.

"Sodina, you can join in, too! What if your magic runs out? You need to be able to defend yourself."

Sodina looks away from the warrior woman shyly. "I'm okay for now, Bridget," she replies.

"Suit yourself, tiny." Bridget shrugs and turns her attention back to Slash.

"Do I even get a say in this?" he asks his opponent.

In a flash, Bridget punches toward Slash's face. He ducks and throws his fist at her shoulder before she jumps back to land a kick straight in Slash's stomach.

Sodina watches with a mix of awe at Bridget's brute strength and horror for her husband, who is losing terribly.

"You're going to make me throw up that bread I just ate, lady!" Slash screams.

"Then dodge my attack, Sir Lack-of-Endurance!"

Slash leans forward and runs to Bridget's right side. "Just because I don't train with my fists doesn't mean I don't know how to fight." He grunts as he lands a fist in Bridget's right cheek and delivers a roundhouse kick to her chest.

"Ugh!" Bridget jumps away. "Good hits, man, but now I'm serious."

She takes off her boots and runs at Slash. Grabbing his arm, she pulls him down to the ground.

It's time for the double clap.

She puts both of her hands on his ribs and tickles him. Slash tries to get out of the dreaded tickle hold but to no avail.

Knowing he might die from laughing, he taps out the ground.

"How did you know I was ticklish there?"

"I didn't." Bridget grins triumphantly. "But there was a great chance you were! That was a good session."

Bridget slaps Slash on the back, knocking the air out of him again.

Slash, not wanting to appear weak in front of Sodina, acts like the hit didn't hurt.

Sodina laughs at the finale of the entire spectacle. Bridget bows playfully and tips an imaginary hat.

"That was definitely something," Sodina says to both of them. Slash puts a hand on her shoulder, trying to catch his breath but giving her his best smile.

Bridget eyes the two lovers and flips her hair back.

"Where did you learn to fight like that?" Slash asks, breathing heavily.

Bridget smiles looking out into the distance. "In the Northern Kingdom, they have grappling schools. There many places where a person can learn to fight like that. There are masters of different styles. Some masters specialize in kick and punching, while others focus on taking your opponent down quickly. I trained in several different styles, but the one that made the most sense to me was taking someone down quickly. My size helps as well. The greatest thing to remember is that size can also be a crutch. I learned that several times from my master up there, who made me squat for hours on end."

"That sounds horrible," Sodina says, giggling.

"Don't laugh at my pain." Bridget says, pointing at her. "You two can take a nap." She stretches her hands. "I'll stand watch. We can leave in the next two hours."

Slash and Sodina thank her and curl up beside their horses and fall asleep.

Bridget looks up at the sun and squints at its brightness.

The two lovers near her are fast asleep, and it paints a pretty picture for the lone warrior watching over them. They look so in love and at peace, even in their sleep. Bridget shifts uncomfortably before deciding to sit under a huge oak tree near them.

Who would have thought my purpose in life was to help these two on their journey?

On her last trip to Rinkar, Bridget saw the old seer and had her fortune told. The seer proclaimed that she would meet a young couple on the road to recovery. It made no sense to her at the time, but Bridget sees now that the seer wasn't a phony.

It's refreshing for Bridget to be on a journey with companions for once. Genuine, kind-hearted ones such as Slash and Sodina. It is so hard to come by those kinds of people in Esteria, and she usually has to have her guard up.

Bridget stretches out, still lost in her own thoughts. She tries her best to be as silent as possible, but every step she takes seems too loud.

These are the first genuine people I've met in this world other than Anna. Goddess Astra, please give me the wisdom to make the right decisions.

After a moment, Bridget snickers to herself. *Look at me being religious.*

* * *

The two hours pass in silence as Bridget watches over Slash and Sodina.

"Wake up, lovebirds!" Bridget splashes water from her canteen onto their faces.

"That's cold!" Slash yells, dripping with a lot more water than his beautiful wife, who giggles beside him.

"Well, it wouldn't be hot in this tundra, would it?" says Bridget.

Slash and Sodina pack up their bags quickly and jump on their horses. Bridget looks back at the lovebirds and starts speeding through the thick forest.

"I hate hearing all of the sounds the woods can make," Sodina yells as they continue on. "You never know what might jump out at you."

Riding on their horses, the trio pass by merchants and traveling families, taking care not to run into anyone.

"It's quite busy for this time of year," Bridget says. "We should be getting to a big clearing here in a few minutes."

Not long after, the forest gives way to a large field where a settlement of at least five hundred people are making camp.

This is amazing, Slash thinks to himself.

The sun says its goodbyes as the night sky starts to show its glory.

They dismount from their horses and walk into camp. Bridget pays the lead merchant.

"This place is a popular tourist attraction," she explains as she leads the couple through the crowds. "Just had to pay for our stay here. The Eastern Kingdom provides the best security for all who visit."

"Oh, look, it's a traveling circus." Sodina smiles. "I wonder where they're off to."

"Probably to the Northern Kingdom, my love," Slash notes. "Even though it's snowing most of the year, they still need their entertainment."

Slash follows Bridget to the spot designated on the slip of paper they were given by the lead merchant. While it isn't the most massive spot, it's more than enough room to pitch a few tents and make a fire.

"Here's to home for the night." Bridget yawns. "We will arrive in Rinkar tomorrow."

The trio put their horses into the temporary stables nearby.

"With all the merchants and tents, we need to grab something to eat,"

Bridget says with vigor.

The company of three walks down the rows of merchants selling wares.

"Sweet buns, pancakes, large steaks—there is so much to choose from!" Sodina says dreamily.

Her face lights up with excitement, and she pulls Slash toward a stand with jumbo shrimp.

"Sodina! It's my favorite food!" Slash's eyes widen as the shrimp sticks dance in his mind saying, *Eat me!*

"Go ahead, get something, dear." Sodina pats her husband's arm.

"May I have four large shrimp on a stick with hot seasoning, please?" he asks.

"Coming right up!" the merchant answers, wrapping the shrimp for Slash. "Four gold coins, kind sir."

Slash reaches inside his pack and removes three gold coins confidently.

The merchant squints at him and says, "I said four."

"Well, I only have three and you've already finished my order."

The merchant sighs and frowns at Slash, shoving his food at him. "You are getting a deal today." He grumbles. "But do not expect to get another deal tomorrow if you are still here."

The merchant waves off Slash and Sodina.

Bridget walks up with two large steaks, eating one of them in mere minutes.

"This thing really hits the spot, Sodina." Bridget smiles. "Women like us have to keep up their figures."

Sodina's eyes fix on the steak in Bridget's hand. She floats up a few inches above the ground and toward the giant-bosomed woman. "I'd like to taste that, please."

"Hands off, girl, you get your own!" Bridget bellows. "Though, I'm not that cruel."

Bridget takes off a small piece of the steak and throws it into Sodina's mouth. Slash watches in delight.

"Where is the establishment you got this from, Bridget?"

Bridget points toward the east part of the camp, and Sodina floats away quickly toward the steak.

"I didn't know Sodina could fly." Bridget claps with joy.

"She can't," Slash says, his smile turning to a frown.

Both of them look at each other and they chime in unison, "That's odd."

Slash stares after his floating wife, and he just knows something amazing happened before their eyes.

On the other side of the camp, Sodina's feet hit the ground as she stares intently at the merchant.

"Do you have the steak you sold the giant woman a few minutes ago?" she asks sweetly.

"We are all sold out," the merchant replies as he arranges someone else's order.

Sodina falls to the ground slowly, the people around her looking at her weirdly. She lifts herself up off the ground, looking at the man.

"What do you have then, sir?"

"We only have lamb's meat, miss."

Sodina slams her fist on his serving table. "I will take some of that with the seasoning from the steak you made."

The man grins. "It will cost an extra gold coin."

She groans as puts the coin on the table.

A few minutes later, Sodina's lamb is ready and the merchant hands it over.

"Thank you, sir! I will be back for your specialty meat tomorrow. I will definitely be the first in line."

Sodina gleams as she walks back to Slash and Bridget with meat in hand.

"Did you get what you were looking for, love?" Slash asks his wife, who is now chomping through the leg of lamb.

"No, they didn't have it, but the seasoning on this poor man's lamb is enough for me!"

Bridget strokes her chin, looking at Sodina with puzzled eyes.

"You sure are a strange woman when you're hungry." Bridget laughs and the couple follows along.

The trio heads back to their plot of land for the night and settles into their sleeping bags around the fire. Bridget is the first to go, snoring loudly and very unladylike. Sodina follows soon after, cuddled against her husband, who is struggling to keep his eyes closed.

* * *

The nightmare hits Slash about five minutes into rest. He rolls around in his sleep as the horrible dream unfolds.

He sees his dear friends, Amanda and Lorenz. Slash tries to reach out to them and call out their names, but they can't hear him.

A demon woman's voice laughs maniacally and taunts Slash's ears.

"You're too weak!" it shrieks, and Slash covers his ears, screaming. "They died because you were not enough!"

Before him, Amanda is impaled by the sharp longspear that took her life. Beside her, Slash watches in horror as a scythe chops Lorenz into pieces.

Over and over again, the nightmare replays in Slash's subconscious.

His eyes shoot open as his friends fall, and he breathes heavily. Slash checks his surroundings to make sure it was just a dream. He sighs to himself, nuzzling his wife.

Damn it all, he thinks. *If Astra does exist, why didn't she do something? How come Ella did not know there were enemies nearby? Was Ella in on it? Were we betrayed and doomed from the very start?*

Slash tries to fall asleep despite the thoughts and doubts littering his mind, and he ends up passing out.

* * *

In the trees above the sleeping trio, a masked figure looks over Slash while he is sleeping, ready to slit his throat with a knife hidden by his sleeve.

"Wake up! Please!" a man yells in the distance. The sun is starting to rise.

Nagi jumps away into the shadows on top of a wagon before Slash shoots up with sweat on his forehead, reaching for his sword.

"The capital Glashmere has fallen!" The man continues yelling, riding through the camp on horseback, clanging a bell. "Meet at the camp entrance for more information!"

The words ring through his ears, and Sodina slowly wakes up at his side.

Bridget sits up and rubs her eyes. "What's with all the commotion, man?"

"The Eastern Kingdom has fallen," he repeats.

Slash stands up abruptly and starts to feel dizzy. He is about to faint when Bridget catches him at the last moment and helps him sits on a nearby bench.

"Whoa there, friend, take a seat first!" she says to the poor lad, fanning him. Sodina joins him on the bench and rubs his hands to calm him down.

"Keep it together." Bridget looks at Slash and slaps him lightly in the face. "We'll get more information in a few minutes."

"Yes, sweetheart," says Sodina. "You wouldn't want to be knocked out in front of the other campers. Let's get going. We need to figure out what is going on."

The trio heads to the front of the camp toward a voice speaking about the current situation.

The yelling man says his name is Sam, and he's a knight from the Western Kingdom. He claims they received a message from the Eastern Kingdom knighthood, and the trio listens intently.

"I have come a long way to get this message to you," Sam shouts so everyone around him can hear. "The knight from the Eastern Kingdom collapsed and died after giving us this message."

Sam pulls out a scroll and reads the words on the manuscript.

"The Eastern Kingdom has been invaded by the demonic empire. Many towns around the realm have fallen, including Dalton and Ifer. It is unknown at this time if the king, queen, and princess are dead or alive.

"Everyone traveling through the empire must exercise extreme caution. Checkpoints connecting the four kingdoms are currently beefing up security. It would be foolish to move through the Eastern Kingdom without being able to protect yourself. Those who do so will be inviting death. 'Til then, pray to Astra and be aware of your surroundings."

Sam finishes solemnly, and the crowd erupts with questions for him, swamping the poor lad.

"Ifer has fallen." Sodina gasps, falling to the ground. "Our friends are all dead."

"He didn't say that…" says Bridget, but her face is grave.

"There is no way they could have survived if they were attacked without warning."

"These are the people who exiled you, are they not?" Bridget asks.

"Yes, they are, but we still care about them," Slash says.

"I just…" Sodina struggles to find the words. "I cannot believe it. If Ifer fell so easy…Astra knows what happened to Glashmere."

"What would provoke the demonic empire to make a move now?" Slash mutters to himself as Sodina and Bridget talk next to him. His anxiety drowns out all of the noise around him.

He shakes his head and listens as Sodina goes on.

"There was an uptick in attacks from those traveling into the Great Forest," his wife says uneasily. "Maybe those were warnings that something was about to happen."

"Who could have seen this coming, my love?" Slash answers with another question. "If they have taken the capital, then that means all the knights are dead and the king…"

"We don't know that," says Bridget. "We need to travel to Rinkar to know the truth. Going through the night could be dangerous, since we are still in the Eastern Kingdom, but there have been no reports of demonic activity around these parts."

"We must make haste to Rinkar, then, before we're held up here." Sodina tugs Slash after her to begin packing up their makeshift camp.

The trio runs back to their horses and quickens their pace.

"We should be there by dawn, right, Bridget?" Slash asks and yawns slightly.

"Don't worry, I have some coffee candies we can take to keep us awake." Bridget throws a bag of candies to each of them. "Take about five.

That should pep you up."

The couple and Bridget take their candies and walk their horses to the gate.

The man opens the gate for them to exit. They mount their horses and take a right, heading toward the fork in the road up ahead.

Bridget leans up on her horse and leads them right at the fork. The cold air blows past them as the horses gather speed going into the forest.

A spider falls straight into Slash's mouth as they race past a spiderweb, and he spits it out, causing laughter to erupt from the two women riding alongside him.

The hills twist and turn for hours as they continue on their journey, passing by more people on the route.

"Rinkar! Over there!" Bridget exclaims.

She spurs her horse on as they gallop up the last hill toward the town of Rinkar.

A light snow starts to fall as they enter the city. Sodina pulls out her gloves and puts them on, starting to get a bit chilly. Slash smiles softly at his strong wife, and they follow Bridget on to park their horses by the entrance of the city.

Walking underneath the town sign, an old man welcomes them to Rinkar.

"Cause no trouble," the old man coughs, "and the knights will show no aggression."

The old man waves goodbye to the trio as they continue on their way.

"It's so cold!" Sodina shivers.

"Welcome to the coldest city in the Northern Kingdom, sister." Bridget smiles. "You know I am from the Northern Kingdom, right?"

The couple looks at each other and back at the warrior woman in confusion.

"No." Slash scratches the back of his neck. "We didn't know that."

"Well, I am, but I do not claim this kingdom," Bridget explains. "The people are emotionally distant here and I am not."

"It's probably the weather." Sodina giggles.

Bridget looks at Sodina, shaking her head. "Besides, my foster parents who loved me still sent me away to that academy. I have sweet memories of my time up there, but I am a traveler. My heart is with those I spend my time with."

The morning sun rises above them, showing the glorious splendor of the Rinkar Mountains, for which the city was named.

"If you guys are not too tired, we can get some breakfast first before going to the seer?" Bridget offers. "What do you think?"

Sodina grabs her arm as the number 53 flashes by her wrist. She quickly covers it and walks toward Slash. But she barely takes a step before she stumbles and falls to the ground.

"Sodina!" Slash runs to her and flips her over onto her back, laying her down.

Bridget appears at his side as they look at her with concern.

"It's okay," Sodina whispers. "Just the poison kicking in."

"She needs some water," Slash says, and Bridget puts her water canteen up to Sodina's mouth.

Sodina sits up slowly and gets to her feet.

"I'm all right now, thank you, my love." Sodina pats Slash's hand and turns to Bridget. "We need to get to the seer. We need to know what is happening to our people and how to heal me right away. Breakfast can wait."

The trio moves on, grabbing breakfast to go along their way to Bridget's mysterious friend.

"What is her name?" Slash asks as they head farther down the main road of Rinkar.

"Why not leave a little mystery?" Bridget winks at him and skips forward.

Heading down the street, Sodina notices that the brick tiles littered across the city make Rinkar feel more exquisite than it actually is.

"I wish they would have spent a bit more on the buildings," Slash says as if reading his wife's mind. "This brick is rather pretty, but it does not equate to the shoddy building colors. Everything is brown here. It makes my mind feel quite dull."

The couple continues to survey the city as they walk down the street.

A colorful building with a large circle top comes into view in front of them. Bridget zooms forward to the large double doors as Slash and Sodina follow closely behind her.

"Hello? Dearest and greatest seer in the region?" Bridget shouts as she knocks on the door.

A deep female voice comes from the other side and bellows, "What is the password?"

Bridget knocks twice, pauses, then knocks three times rapidly. Her companions watch in amusement at the dramatic affair of opening the entrance.

"Bridget!" the voice hoots as the doors swing open to reveal a woman dressed in a royal blue robe with stars embroidered at its hem.

"Stella," Bridget says with a grin. "A pleasure as always."

"Come in, my sweet. And your friends, too. It has been some time since I last saw you. Who are they?" Stella asks as she approaches the hesitant couple.

Bridget explains their situation to Stella with only her eyes, and Sodina is impressed by the woman's ability to read her large friend.

"Oh, I see," Stella states. "Well, of course I can tell your fortune, and I do owe a favor to Bridget."

The petite old woman walks over to a table with a golden cloth and crystals scattered in the middle. "Walk over here by me, my sweeties." She beckons to the trio to follow her inside. The double doors shut behind them.

Sodina looks around the home. Only a few candles offer light to the room. *It feels more like a dungeon than a house.*

Stella opens her wrinkled hands to the pair. "Close your eyes, dears, and think of the most tragic thing that could happen to you," the seer says.

Slash and Sodina sink into the two chairs before her. Opening their hands, they put them into Stella's. Bridget watches nervously.

Stella shakes and sits back in her chair.

"Oh, my…" she utters with emotion. "I see something horrible! Something that cannot be explained. I see a dragon, a spear, and a small child. I also see a great war with loss. Such a significant loss for you and your friends. I see freckles and vengeance. A man with a secret. Hidden love for those taken by fate. I see a woman baring her burden on her own."

Stella lifts off her hands from the couple and turns her attention to Slash.

"You are burdened with guilt." She meets his gaze, as he swallows hard. "Remember your anger will be your undoing."

She turns slowly to Sodina. Tears are already welling up in the young woman's eyes. "And you, dear Sodina, need to enjoy life, for you will die soon with regrets."

Sodina starts to cry silently in her seat.

Slash stands up abruptly. "What do you mean, old woman?" he yells, panic ringing through his voice. Bridget puts a hand on his shoulder to calm him down, but he pushes it away.

"Your wife will die due to your anger, Slash," Stella retorts. "You sought something that was sealed away. You already lost something dear to you. Your actions have consequences, son. Was it worth it?"

The mood in the room shifts; it is as quiet as a funeral. Bridget could drop a pin and everyone could hear it.

"I'm going to die soon… Well, we all are, but…" Sodina looks at the ground. "What do you know about my death, Stella?"

Bridget slowly lowers her head as a single tear streams down her cheek. *To think this would be the outcome.* She desperately wishes she could change the news her friends received. But Stella has correctly predicted ninety-eight percent of individual's fortunes.

"I've made it this far due to my ability to persevere," Sodina exclaims. "I carry a heavy burden for our family. Slash has never left me for another woman, nor will he. He will find a way to save me from this fate. I have trust in my loving husband, Bridget, and Goddess Astra. We will not be overcome by the darkness of this world. My destiny is my own."

She stands then and holds Stella's wrinkly hand. "I respect you and your vision, but if the Goddess wills it, we will find a way. Goddess Astra loves her children."

"Poor child." Stella squeezes her hand tightly. "You will tempt fate."

Stella shakes violently as she closes her eyes. "If you want to tempt fate, I have but one thing to tell you. To the south lies your answer."

"You mean the Southern Kingdom?" Slash asks.

"I only have that for you, son," says Stella. "The rest is up to you to decide."

The seer lets go of Sodina's hand and turns away from the trio, ducking through a beaded curtain and disappearing farther into her humble home.

The trio walks outside, and the breeze from the mountains chills their bones. Slash pulls out his gloves to finally put on. Sodina throws on a heavier coat.

"The sun is out, but it doesn't feel like it is." Bridget sighs sadly.

Sodina walks over to a nearby bench and sits down as the other two follow.

"I know I told you we would receive guidance, but I never expected it to be this upsetting," Bridget huffs and crosses her arms. "Stella is the best, I know, but it seems she saw two paths for how your lives can unfold."

"Right..." Sodina mutters. Slash is still stunned into silence beside his wife.

"The paths are nearly identical in everything, but with you dying in one and the other...being an unknown future." Bridget wraps her arm around Sodina before continuing. "We do not know if this trip to the south will be in vain, but it's worth a shot. If the Eastern Kingdom has genuinely fallen, we need to make our way around using the back roads. Eventually, we will reach the Bridge of Eden. The bridge has checkpoints, and with the increased demonic activity, I'm sure they will be more stringent on who they let through."

"We should be fine as long as we do not appear to be a threat," says Slash, finally recovering from his shock.

Sodina starts weeping silently again and sniffs into the sleeve of her coat. Slash rubs her back gently.

"Adventurers are good for commerce, so it shouldn't be a problem if we try to get through the checkpoint," Bridget says. "We won't know unless we try."

"We have to try." Slash looks into his wife's eyes. "You were right, Sodina. We will choose our own destiny, I swear it."

"Though the future may be bleak, at least we have each other," Bridget says passionately. "Let's rest for tonight and head out in the morning. We will be skirting the desert on our way to the Southern Kingdom. I believe their capital is Lafare. We will probably face a lot of monsters and bandits along the way."

"With chaos erupting in the Eastern Kingdom and a lack of leadership, we should be prepared for anything," Slash adds.

"You know what, Sodina? I am going to carry you to the inn so you don't tire," Bridget offers with a proud smile.

Slash looks at Bridget but doesn't say anything. He turns away, walking ahead of Bridget as she takes Sodina into her arms.

Bridget is wise beyond her years, really, Slash thinks to himself. *Coming to my wife's comfort while I'm here...unable to utter a word.*

Stella's words echo in his head. Sodina will die because of his anger.

His fist clenches. *I swore to protect her and that is what I will do. What the seer said is not for sure. I will twist fate, Goddess Astra knows!*

The trio heads to the nearest inn. They can only rent one room, since there is little vacancy after the events that transpired at the camp.

"Well, we should all head to bed," Bridget says, yawning.

She walks into the shadowed corner of the room and strips down to her night garments.

"No peeking, Slash." She chuckles.

"Why would I?" he replies. "I'm happily married!"

Sodina blushes and gives him a chaste kiss.

"Don't worry, I will sleep on the floor," Bridget says and immediately falls asleep as she lies down in her cot.

Sodina and Slash lie in bed, snuggled together. The flames from the fireplace warm them from the Rinkar cold.

Slash peers into the fire before closing his eyes. The fire of revenge burns intensely in his soul. *Do not lose control.*

Chapter 11

Month of Dragons
Day 20

The morning sun glistens over the city of Glashmere. The streets are painted red from the blood of the massacre earlier. The stench of death and decay fills the city as the anguished cries of terror still echo in the streets.

Gareth walks up the street toward the castle. His eyes show satisfaction. He takes a deep breath to relish another victory.

"This will do," Gareth says, smiling. "A fortress which we will build our city in. We will solidify our army here."

He raises his hand and signals his generals to come closer.

"Generals," he says. "Have the wolfen work on setting up the catapults. Lay down traps around the city walls if you must. I am sure they are going to stage an assault to retake the city. Now that the Great Forest and Glashmere are ours, we can continue our invasion in the weeks to come. Rest only when you need to."

"Now can we have a moment alone to spend some time together?" Lisha says, caressing Gareth from behind. "How I crave you, my lord. After claiming a castle for you and killing the pathetic humans, I should be rewarded."

"I gave an order to fortify the city. I must oversee the defenses, and you must help as well."

"Oh, my lord." Lisha gives him a seductive smile. "I'm tired from all my work. The other generals are more capable of handling that task than me. My body is suited for a more specialized task. Would you like it if I changed into something more revealing?"

Lisha snaps her finger, stripping her fair-skinned body of its clothes.

"Lust after me, Gareth."

"Time is of the essence." Gareth pushes Lisha away. "A day full of love will come, my dear. Humans are persistent creatures. They are like rats in a colony. Let one live and they'll be back in greater numbers. We should strike them in one swift stroke. Their numbers mean nothing compared to our demonic might."

Lisha snaps her finger again, now fully clothed.

"So be it," Lisha says with a sigh of disappointment. "I will ensure the walls are rebuilt. I will get some of our solems to do the bidding. Since there are so many of them, it should be done in no time."

Gareth grins, lifting Lisha's face into his view. "Soon, darling, we will have the whole of Esteria as our playground."

"Seriously, woman, you should keep your clothes on," Neron says, slinking up to them from behind. "Only the weak crave the carnal temptations of the flesh. Now, get the solems to work. I am going down to the town of Ifer to lead the wolfen there in fortifying the village."

"Hmph. Be off then," Lisha replies. "Don't forget to take that ugly face of yours."

Lisha signals two solems and points at the door of a nearby house. She orders the two to prop up the door as she puts a magical enchantment on the handle, keeping it in place.

"Oh, how the wonders of demonic magic are put to good use." Lisha winks at the solems, who continue to do their work.

A knight who stayed hidden during the assault peers around the corner of the house where Lisha is repairing the door. *That's the witch who took my friends. She is going to pay.* He narrows his eyes at her, clutching the blade in his hand and pulling out a vial of holy water from his pocket. *If I can just get over to her unnoticed, I can make something happen.*

A twig snaps behind him.

What was that? He jumps, looking around. *Where did she go?*

"Looking for me, dearie? Lisha says, appearing behind the man.

"By the light!" He swings his knife around, aimed at Lisha's neck.

In a flash, Lisha grabs his arm and breaks it in half.

"Augh!" He screams in pain as the knife falls to the ground and his arm spews blood.

"You're not worth my time, insect." Lisha pulls the man onto her bosom and strokes his head. "Oh, poor thing. The least I can do to you is give a little tease before you burn in hell.

She snaps the knight's neck. His body falls to the ground, lifeless.

"Pity. I had to get my hands dirty." Lisha wipes the sweat off her bosoms and kicks the knight's body away from her.

A troublesome lot, she thinks. *That holy water could present a huge danger to us. That is the water of the Goddess.* She frowns. *If they find some way to create a weapon with that, then this whole conquest won't be as much fun as it is now. Good thing for us, few humans know of that legend and how to manifest holy water into weapons.*

Lisha walks up the pathway leading to the castle, signaling a few solems to follow her. *We should be safe. Lord Gareth will defeat them before they gain the upper hand.*

She walks into the castle, searching for Gareth, but bumps into Nagi.

"I thought you were on a mission," she says.

"I do not report to you, temptress." Nagi hisses before disappearing into the city streets.

"Always rude, that one," Lisha mutters.

Lisha finds Gareth in the dining room of the castle, drinking a glass of wine. She walks up to him and plops into the seat beside him.

"What news did Nagi bring you?"

"He thinks he may know where our daughter is," says Gareth.

Lisha jumps up in excitement, her fists clenched together.

"Our little demon will not be so small when we find her," Lisha exclaims. "Our dear daughter."

"We are not entirely sure if this woman is our daughter. She did emit a purple aura that was demon-like. It could be a fluke or a real lead. He is going to keep an eye on her. This woman resides in Artemis, a town near the border of the Southern Kingdom."

"Send me there, Gareth," Lisha commands.

"Absolutely not. You are needed here on the front lines. I need all of my generals here until we are ready to invade the Southern Kingdom. Nagi and the Dark Order will continue their mission to find her."

Lisha calms herself down, understanding the position of their end. She shakes her head and picks up a glass of wine for herself.

"My apologies, my lord." Lisha bows. "How about a toast to our newfound kingdom?"

"A toast to our milestone." Gareth smiles. "We have better weather here and the locational advantage to make our empire genuinely expansive. If the humans try to attack from the Great Forest, there will be no entry, and a frontal assault is out of the question. Either way, it is certain death for them. We can build here and wait for our prey to come. Our kingdom will just open its mouth and let the prey go in. We have them at a checkmate."

"Walk with me, my dear."

Gareth takes Lisha's hand as they stroll through the castle, looking at art and the massive library.

"While we do hate the humans, the history of the demons and the humans are intertwined. Both were created by the Goddess Astra, and were meant to live in harmony with all of the creatures in the land."

They stop in front of a tall painting depicting a woman holding an apple as lightning strikes the mountains behind her.

"Look at this art. We have the same ability to create something amazing. Humans always thought they were better than us, and racial tensions increased amongst the populous, leading to the incident known as the Great War. We lost that war because the Goddess sided with the humans and then left the land to mourn the deaths of her children. You may know that as the Legend of the Tears. The holy city of Arcadia. None have seen it for years. Legends say it floats over us invisible to our eyes. Astra must pay! That is what Helion wants! That is the reason we read the Gospel of Helion in the Uncharted Lands and gained these powers."

Gareth leads Lisha into the castle's back room, where Ella is being held in a demonic locked cage.

"This pathetic goddess is of great use to us," Gareth says, biting

Lisha tenderly on the ear. "I kept this process a secret from you. I created truly amazing creatures by draining her life force."

Lisha's eyes widen in awe. She inspects the cage closer.

"Only you know this, my love," Gareth says, pinching her butt.

"Oh, you are quite the tease." Lisha blushes.

"I have been conducting experiments like this, which successfully have created the wolfen you see today. It works by taking in the essence, the consciousness, and the logical power of the human brain and fusing it with the body of a wolf. I have successfully created a powerful and intelligent creature. It is no simple task and must be done with caution. This room is where I will create our army. The solems are easy enough to bewitch, but we need creatures that possess reasoning. I want a well-built army feared for both their intellect and strength. "

Lisha grabs hold of Gareth and kisses him deeply.

"You are a genius, my dear. Esteria will be ours in no time." Lisha says, caressing Gareth's face. "Perhaps after we are done with Esteria, we can set our eyes beyond the sea? To the lands far from here where we can spread our empire."

"The sea sounds like a beautiful idea, my love." Gareth locks eyes with Lisha and kisses her passionately.

Chapter 12

Month of Dragons
Day 21

Chrono looks back with a sigh of relief, pleased they made it this far with only one incident to speak of. The morning sun peeks through the clouds, lining the sky as the caravan travels forward toward the Bridge of Eden.

The Bridge of Eden is a massive structure built by the best builders from the Eastern and Southern Kingdoms. This bridge is vital to the trade routes for all four kingdoms.

The bridge hangs over one hundred feet above the river. Certain death awaits any who fall from its height.

Sarah speaks to the children in the back of her wagon, telling them about the structure they will soon see.

"Tell us one more, please!" a child begs.

"Well, any more and it would spoil it for you." Sarah smiles softly and pats the child's small head. "We should be there soon." She gestures out of her wagon, and Chrono follows her eye.

Chrono looks out into the distance and sees a large tower—likely an outpost.

"We should be coming up on the bridge anytime!" he shouts toward the people on horseback following him.

Chrono leads the convoy up past the watchtower. No one appears to be inside of it, but Chrono knows he has to be cautious.

"Stop right there," a voice says. "Give us all of your money, and we will spare you."

Chrono looks out in front of him and sees a man in brown clothing.

"We far outnumber you, boy!"

Chrono stands on top of Anabelle and flips off her back, drawing his sword in mid-air and landing on the ground.

"I highly doubt you will be doing anything of the sort!" he says. "Do you know who you are speaking with, ruffian?"

He points his sword at the thief daringly.

"You have a brazen mouth for a young man," the thief says.

"Save it!" Chrono yells and barrels toward him.

Midway through his run, Chrono feels an arrow strike his shoulder.

"Augh!" Chrono stops and runs to the left behind a large rock.

Where did that arrow come from? Chrono wonders.

"Give it up, boy." The thief snickers. "Again, we far outnumber you. Now, give up your wares, or you will meet Astra in the afterlife."

That's it, they were using the guard towers! Chrono thinks to himself. *They took out the guards from the Southern Kingdom and placed their own. I was a fool not to prepare for that.*

"Stay away from me!" a townswoman yells. One of the thief's cronies is trying to drag her off.

"You get away from her!" Sarah proclaims, leaping out of the caravan.

"Well, well, well, what do we have here?" the thief says. "Is that Princess Sarah of Glashmere? Oh, boys, come on out. We have a special guest with us today. The princess herself has made an entrance."

Another group of cronies emerges from the trees as Princess Sarah is surrounded, protecting the townswoman behind her.

"I heard the kingdom fell. So, it's true," he says.

Sarah walks up to the captain of the thieves. "What is your name?"

"It's Wes, Your Highness," he spits. "There are twenty of us and only one trained warrior in your group."

Chrono looks past the rock, but a volley of arrows keeps him pinned down from moving.

"Well, Wes, I ask you to let us pass," Sarah replies in confidence. "We are on a journey to the Southern Kingdom. You appear to be from Glashmere but have chosen a path of wickedness."

"This is our calling, lady." Wes leans in. "You nobles know nothing of what it takes to survive in the real world."

Sarah smells the odorous breath coming from Wes. "You would do well not to get too close to me, sir," she says.

Chrono clenches his fist and tries to move again, but another arrow whizzing past his head stops him.

"Don't try anything stupid, War Master," Wes shouts at him. "That's right! I know who you are. You're fast, but can you dodge ten arrows coming at you?!"

Wes grabs Sarah and licks her neck. She yelps and pushes him away.

He slurps his words. "Well, I will let you go if you give me a piece of that royal buffet."

Wes winks at Sarah, who throws a slap in his face.

"Not in your life, you creep!" Sarah shrieks.

"You shouldn't have done that, you harlot!" He snarls and grabs Sarah by the neck.

Sarah squeals in discomfort, and Chrono springs into action.

"Come out without your weapon, or I will put a knife right through the princess's neck," Wes taunts.

"Actually, it's Queen Sarah to you." *Damn, is there no way out of this?* Chrono grips his sword, then places it on the ground in front of him. Standing up, he walks slowly from around the large boulder toward the thief. "I would surrender now if I were you."

"You're one to talk." Wes sneers. "Get on your knees, rodent!"

"I will never bow to you," Chrono says. He stands his ground and looks Sarah in the eye.

A trumpet blast comes from about a hundred feet away, and Chrono turns around.

Is that the flag of Glashmere? It can't be!

"You need to duck now!" a young woman yells as she storms in on horseback.

Two mages yell incinerating spells as fireballs fly toward the thieves, catching five of them on fire. The remaining thieves scatter into the woods.

The lone woman in front of the pack stands on the back of her horse. "You dare touch the princess!" she yells, and Chrono is frozen in shock and awe.

The woman releases one arrow from her crossbow. It hits Wes directly in the middle of the head.

Wes's body goes limp and slumps to the ground.

Sarah runs toward Chrono, hugging him tightly. "I was so scared, Chrono!" She clutches his tunic as tears stream from her face.

"It's all right, we're all right." Chrono strokes her hair gently to calm the princess down.

"We were saved by our townsfolk," Sarah mumbles into his chest. "I can't believe it!"

The caravan pulling Duke Matthew stops in front of the War Master and princess in an embrace.

Matthew leaves his wagon and walks over to Sarah.

"Princess Sarah." He drops to his knees, bowing his head.

"It's acting queen now, Duke," Sarah says. "We have yet to locate my mother. We are under the assumption that she is dead."

Matthew raises his head to meet the princess's eyes.

"You may stand," Sarah proclaims. "Where are you coming from exactly?"

"After our successful trade with the nobility on the coast, we are coming from the town of Lir in the Southern Kingdom," Duke Matthew says proudly.

"You have not heard, then!" Sarah gasps. "Glashmere has fallen, and the king is dead."

"Be careful with your words, Your Highness," Matthew says.

"I would not lie about such things," Sarah cries as she continues. "I saw my father die. It was by the hands of a demon woman of some sort. She was wicked and powerful, but I did not catch her name."

The woman who struck the thief with her crossbow walks up to hear the final part of the conversation. "Are you saying we have no home to go back to, Your Majesty?"

Sarah looks at her. "You're an archer, aren't you? That patch you bear, you are part of the Glashmere archery corps."

"The best one there is," Matthew says. "This is Lea."

"Save your false flattery, sir," Lea says, rolling her eyes at Matthew.

"We were in quite the situation, Lady Lea," Chrono says. "Thank you for saving us. My strength alone was not enough to keep the princess safe. I mean the queen. I am indebted to you."

"No need to bow, sir. I'm no one of significance. Just Lea will do," she answers nonchalantly. "I was just saving the queen from that man."

"What are the next steps for us, then?" Matthew asks the new queen.

"We are headed to the Southern Kingdom to seek refuge there and request an audience with Queen Charlotte," Sarah replies, almost hesitantly.

Chrono catches the apprehension in her voice and realizes that Sarah is nervous. And rightfully so. For a monarch to kneel to another is a huge feat.

"Are you sure she will see you, Your Majesty?" the duke ponders aloud.

"We have nowhere to go," Sarah admits as she looks toward the remaining people of Glashmere, who stopped with them to rest after the events with the thieves.

"Why not head north to seek refuge with King Leo? We can plan a meeting with him instead," Matthew offers.

"There is no time!" Chrono says sternly. "You will fall in line, Duke Matthew, and follow her orders."

"Just who do you think you are, warrior?" Matthew snarls at Chrono.

"That's enough, Duke Matthew," Sarah snaps, giving him a stern glare. "Chrono speaks for me. He is my knight and anything he says I will back with full intent."

Sarah nods in approval to Chrono. Matthew looks upset but doesn't argue.

"Let us make way now for Lafare, the capital of the Southern

Kingdom." Chrono looks at Lea and holds out his hand. "Since you are the strongest warrior, I would like your help in leading the caravan."

Lea shakes Chrono's hand firmly and smiles. "I wouldn't mind leading the charge with you." She puts her hands on her hips. "Strongest warrior is kind of a stretch, though," she says in a joking manner.

"We will make camp here tonight," Chrono commands the gaggle of people. "Everyone is still reeling from the stressful situation, so it will be best if we wait for a new day."

"I think we should have some sort of service for those needing comfort, no?" Sarah says. "Anyone who needs relief, please come over here. We will say a prayer for the fallen and for our safety."

Sarah leads fifteen townsfolk over near a tree, and they hold hands, standing in silence. Lea looks over at them curiously.

"I didn't know there were followers here," Lea mumbles to herself.

She walks over to join them and puts her hands over them as well. They welcome her into the circle.

Sarah exclaims, "If anyone would like to pray, please do."

"I would like to sing a song, if I may, Your Majesty," Lea gulps. The queen and townspeople arrange for her to be in the middle of their prayer circle to begin her song.

Flying high in the sky
Where sorrows fade
My soul in care
No guilt or pain
For Astra's love
Covers shame

Lea twirls in circles as her angelic voice rings throughout the camp.

Chrono looks on Sarah and the others. Their faith and resilience gives him the confidence to move on. *Maybe one day, I will have faith that can move mountains*, he thinks as Lea continues her song. His eyes lock on Sarah, singing along with her eyes closed.

'Til then, my blade will be the gospel, and I will kill all who try to harm Sarah. That is my mission in life and purpose now.

Sarah gives each of the individuals in the circle a hug, overwhelmed with emotion.

"I didn't know you could sing like that," Sarah says to Lea.

"Yeah, you know it's a hidden talent." Lea looks away from the queen to hide her blush.

"You seem really quiet to me."

"I am, but I do love spending time with people. I tend to observe before leaping into any situation," the small archer woman admits to the queen, who listens intently.

* * *

Evening sets in as fish is served for dinner. Chrono and some of the townsfolk are able to get enough fish for everyone in the company, even with the addition of Lea and Duke Matthew's men. Everyone looks happy as the moon shows its glimmer over the traveling party.

Lea leans back, rubbing her belly. "I could not bear to eat anymore. That was a wonderful dish, and I rarely eat fish."

Chrono gives Lea a puzzled look. "Fish is excellent for any long journey! And so accessible. It doesn't take much to cook it properly and make it delicious."

Sarah giggles at Chrono's intensity about health. "I do know that those abs do not lie. Chrono works really hard to maintain his physique. Please forgive his outbursts, Lea."

Chrono blushes, and Lea looks at the two with a huge grin.

The War Master of Glashmere is dense, Lea thinks. Obviously, the queen is flirting with him, and all he can do is act like a schoolboy.

Sarah laughs loudly, looking at Chrono's expression. "Silly man, you are. Getting all hyped up over aquatic life."

The group of three laughs and continues to make conversation late into the night.

"I am going to turn in now," Lea says. "I haven't had this much fun in a long time. Good night, you two!"

Lea takes her bow and walks over to a blanket on the ground. "Sleeping underneath the stars is good for the soul," she whispers, and soon falls asleep.

Chrono looks deeply at the glistening moon, thinking about the upcoming journey. Sarah clears her throat to catch the War Master's attention.

"Yes, Your Majesty?" he asks her.

Sarah scoots closer to him and looks directly in his eyes. "You're truly a wonderful man, Chrono.

"Oh, I wouldn't go so far as to say that, Your Majesty..."

"And maybe...one day...something more." Sarah leans in to nibble on his ear.

Chrono jumps up from his seat on the tree trunk, thinking about Sarah being his wife. He never even considered he could marry her even if he adores her greatly. She is way out of his league. *Why did I immediately think of that? She is the acting Queen of Glashmere, for Astra's sake!*

"I think being called a War Master's wife would be much more fulfilling than queen," she says, blushing as Chrono stares back in disbelief. "I have been thinking of you a lot lately... Did you know they say the best marriages are between those who have known each other a long time?"

"Sarah...I mean, my queen." Chrono fumbles over his words, staring into the depths of her eyes.

Sarah takes his hand and holds it firmly in hers. Chrono's palms are sweaty and Sarah notices, giggling.

"I'm in absolutely no rush to marry, by the way," Sarah says.

Chrono is still at a loss for words as Sarah lets go of his hand to walk back toward her wagon. His eyes follow her hips. *Her walk is enchanting.* He shakes his head, panicking. He has never looked at the queen like that before.

Chrono wants to sleep but feels a heavy responsibility to watch the entire caravan.

Sleep, Chrono, sleep, he thinks to himself. Chrono leans on Annabelle and closes his eyes, falling asleep underneath the stars.

* * *

The next day, Lea wakes up with dried drool on her face and laughs at herself. She stands and walks over to a bucket to wash her face with cold water.

It is showtime, and Lea knows they absolutely need to make it to the Southern Kingdom today.

The caravan packs up from yesterday's events. Lea mounts her horse, catching up to the front of the company to lead the way.

Chrono rides over to Sarah's wagon on his horse and greets her with a, "Good morning," through the wagon opening. Sarah rubs the sleep from her eyes and smiles brightly.

"Let's get moving, everyone!"

Chrono and Lea lead the pack as they proceed toward the Bridge of Eden.

The caravan comes up to the bridge, a hundred feet wide and stretching as far as the eye can see from where they were.

This is genuinely amazing, Sarah thinks as she looks over the edge of the bridge at the river below.

The Glashmere children gasp and peer out over their wagons, starting a little commotion about how beautiful the sight is. Sarah can see their mothers hushing them and making sure they won't fall overboard.

She smiles sadly, missing her own mother and father very much.

Chrono and Lea continue to lead the caravan over the bridge.

"I think our meeting with Queen Charlotte will go well," Chrono yells over to Lea at his side.

"This bridge is a vital connection between our kingdoms," Lea answers. "It represents our unity."

Chrono nods in agreement and pats Annabelle's head as she continues to trot.

"Once we get over this bridge, we should be in Mala, yes?" Chrono says. "We may need to rest there to up the morale of the caravan."

Lea frowns. "You have to remember time is of the essence. We have no idea how many demons are on the move or where they will strike. We do not know if Queen Charlotte has heard our kingdom has fallen."

"Sarah said her father sent messengers to each kingdom asking for help. No help came. All we can hope for is that Queen Charlotte will hear us out," Chrono replies quietly as he looks over the edge of the water.

"If our hearts are pure, she will see our reflection," he mutters.

"And if she thinks they're not, Chrono?"

"Then we will probably be sentenced to hard labor."

Lea blinks at Chrono. "Straight to the dungeons would be a little far-fetched. You are the War Master, after all. Your name is known throughout the land, so it should carry some weight."

As Chrono gets lost in his thoughts, the end of the bridge finally comes into sight. The Southern Kingdom is known for all of its cutting-edge safeguards to protect the kingdom.

"State your business, travelers!" a southern knight bellows from his position high up in the watchtower.

"We seek an audience with Queen Charlotte, sir!"

"Who might you be?"

"I am the War Master, Chrono, and we carry Queen Sarah of Glashmere. Our kingdom has fallen and we are refugees. The Great King Martin has fallen as well."

The knight climbs down from his spot and squints at Chrono. "I have heard of the Glashmere War Master but never seen him before."

Sarah gets up out of her wagon and reaches for the knight.

"Kind knight, I am Queen Sarah. What Chrono speaks is true. We are displaced from our home with nowhere to go. The Southern Kingdom is closest to us and we seek an audience with Queen Charlotte."

The knight looks at Sarah. "Oh! You really need a bit more sun, Your Highness," he says in a laughing manner. "Word was that you were pale, but this is surprising! It's true!"

The knight whistles, and a few other guards emerge from the watchtower to join him. They all bow in respect for Queen Sarah of Glashmere.

"We will let you pass," the first knight says. "You are now in the Southern Kingdom. Behave yourself, and I hope you find what you're looking for."

"Thank you, kind knight," Sarah says, bowing her head before turning back toward her wagon.

"I forgot how much darker-skinned the people in the Southern Kingdom are," Chrono says as they lead the caravan forward past the Southern gates.

"It's all of the sun, sir," Lea explains. "Really, you shouldn't say those things out loud. People may take offense to that."

"I apologize. You're right, Lea."

"Being right by the ocean has its perks. You get sun, lots of different fish, and the ability to go out to sea."

"Sounds like a traveler's paradise, indeed!" Chrono exclaims.

Lea chuckles at his innocent expression. "You really need to travel more, War Master."

The convoy passes through the checkpoint, making its way toward Mala. Lea and Chrono scout ahead to ensure the roads will be easy to traverse for the wagons.

"This sand is something else," Lea shouts over to Chrono. "Thankfully, the passageway to the city is paved with bricks, so there shouldn't be any problems with us getting there."

"We may want to encourage the townsfolk to stay there while we head to Lafare," Chrono says. "It isn't too far from Mala."

"Yes, that seems smart," replies Lea as they push their horses to the max, traveling quickly.

The beach finally comes into sight as the caravan makes its way into the fishing town of Mala. Chrono jumps off his horse and walks into the town, with Lea following him.

"I will head to the city's lord and explain our situation," Chrono says to his new friend.

Lea nods in approval as she walks over to where Sarah's wagon is parked.

Sarah looks out of the cart at Lea. "What is it, dear?"

"Chrono is heading to the mayor's house, wherever that may be. Apparently, he knows the mayor here from a long time ago."

"Well, that's Chrono for you, the War Master himself using his title wisely."

Sarah and Lea giggle, and Lea heads back to the front of the caravan. She pulls out the Gospel of Astra and recites to herself quietly.

Those who are seeking a reason for their existence look to the stars.

There you will find the infinite glory of Astra.

She created each one with loving-kindness.

When you feel as if you cannot go on

Remember the stars

You are worth so much more than them

Lea rarely cries, but her tears flow as she reads the chapter over and over again. Her life feels as if it's changing before her eyes. Only Astra knows the grand adventure set in stone for her. She reminds herself that she needs to keep her skills on par with Chrono's to defend the people properly.

Though she does not have the War Master's ability, she does have her crossbow.

Lea used to be an elite archer with the Glashmere Archery Corps, who proclaimed they were the shining light of the kingdom. And while that title does not mean much now, she decides to wear it with pride from this day on.

I am the shining light of the Eastern Kingdom.

Lea closes the gospel, her eyes red from tears.

All right, no one needs to see you cry, Miss Shining Light.

She puts the book away and sits down beside her horse, awaiting Chrono's return.

* * *

Several hours pass, and the sun sets on the small company of Glashmere folk who are now settling in for dinner.

Chrono appears before Lea, and she springs up from her seat by her horse immediately.

"How did it go, Chrono?"

"Well, my hair was longer years ago, but I showed him my sword and he knew I was telling the truth. He says our people can stay here, but they need to make their own way. He will provide tools for us to build temporary homes and fishing gear. The rest is up to us."

Chrono walks down each wagon in the caravan, explaining the plan to the townsfolk. Lea follows after him.

Sarah, getting out of her wagon, heads to the two of them.

"You, me, and Lea are heading to Lafare in the morning to seek an audience with Queen Charlotte," the queen says to Chromo. "A messenger has been sent to let her know of our arrival."

"Until then, we'll have to sleep underneath the stars," Chrono replies. "There are bathhouses nearby if you'd like to explore town. Since I am the War Master taking refuge, it gives the mayor assurance that no thieves will try to enter."

"So, we have a home in exchange for security, then." Sarah giggles at Chrono.

Sarah and Chrono's eyes lock for a moment, and Chrono looks away in a flash. Lea raises her eyebrow at the mighty War Master. Seeing him weak for the queen like this is really entertaining. She hopes he'll keep pining for Sarah so she can watch him unravel.

After supervising the Glashmere people setting up their tents, and one hearty meal later, Sarah trails through the forest, Chrono on her tail as her guard.

She sways with the wind and her gown ruffles through the grass. Chrono is over the moon that the princess queen is finally letting loose after a stressful few days.

Through the brush and past their camp, Sarah comes to a patch of beach. The waves quietly crash against the shore. It is a magnificent sight for Sarah, as she barely got to leave her old kingdom before this journey.

She takes her sandals off and starts to run around the sand. Chrono looks on, hands behind his back, trying to keep his composure.

"I think I need a shower, War Master!" Sarah exclaims. "The ocean sounds great! The water should be warm this evening, I think."

Sarah runs toward the sea, removing her robes and her day gown in the process. Chrono gasps and follows her.

"Princess, I mean, Queen Sarah!" Chrono panics. "The water may be cold this evening!" His face turns beet red as he runs toward her.

Out in the distance, ignoring Chrono's words, Sarah jumps into the ocean.

"Too late!" She screams and laughs, splashing around like a child.

Chrono walks up, shielding his eyes from the beauty of Sarah's body. Her undergarments cling to her body, lit by the moonlight. Never in his wildest dreams did he imagine seeing her like this.

Sarah looks over at Chrono. "Oh, don't be shy, silly! Come join me."

"I—I…"

"It's just me but only in my underdress. You have done such hard work leading us. You deserve the fun!"

Sarah runs out of the water and drags Chrono in with all of his clothes on. He can't fight a queen's orders, so he throws his soaking wet jacket and shirt into the sand.

He dives in and they swims for a little while. The two chat about sweet nothings. Sarah keeps her eyes on the War Master the whole time, stealing a look at his bare, toned chest whenever she can.

He is so handsome, she thinks as he floats on his back next to her, his eyes closed to feel the moment.

Sarah joins him and sighs happily, reaching for his hand. His eyes shoot open, and he squeezes her hand back. It seems so strange that it fits perfectly in his.

Their fingers intertwine and they stand up in the shallow pool of water, eyes on each other.

Sarah inches closer to him until they are nose to nose. She can feel him breathing heavily. He smells of pine and mint.

He stares, at a loss for words, at the beautiful woman in front of him. She smells like vanilla and roses, even if they are playing around in the salt of the ocean.

Before he knows what she's doing, Sarah closes the gap between them and kisses him gently on the lips. Chrono kisses her back passionately, pressing her closer to his body.

Sarah moans and tangles her hands in his hair as the kiss deepens. He snaps out of his dreamlike state at the sound, turning away from her. The water is cold, but he feels the heat emanating between them; it makes him sweat.

"That…" Sarah starts. "That was long overdue, I think."

She winks at Chrono, who is still frozen in place, and wipes her mouth. Sarah splashes water at him playfully and swims away back to shore.

"I have no idea what just happened," Chrono mumbles.

Sarah's lips tasted of the sweetest honey. Maybe I do need to let myself go a little.

The moon shines over the ocean as Chrono stands there, grinning. He has come a mighty long way with her. He swears to himself in that instant one day he will marry Sarah. He will be the man she deserves to have by her side.

* * *

Lea walks up to the beach to find Sarah and Chrono sitting on the sand by their wet clothes, talking.

Those two are so silly, she thinks as she approaches the water, giving the queen and the War Master their privacy.

Lea takes off her trusty leather boots and socks to put her feet into the ocean. Tomorrow, they will be heading to Lafare to seek an audience with Queen Charlotte. *What if the queen doesn't believe us, and the mayor's word isn't enough?* she wonders.

The queen should know the War Master, though. All four kingdoms participate in the tournament that he wins every year, after all.

Lea's mind wanders as she strolls along the shoreline silently. *The moon is beautiful tonight. She* smiles and closes her eyes to feel the ocean breeze.

"Not so fast!" a voice yells.

Lea feels her body fly into the air as Sarah puts her into a headlock.

"Never let your guard down." She laughs, dropping Lea out of her hold.

"Who knew you were so strong?" Lea smiles shyly.

"Remember, I am an elite warrior princess! Now a queen." Sarah smirks.

Lea puts a game face on and suplexes Sarah into the water with force.

Chrono runs to them frantically, looking at Lea with a slight frown. "You don't have to do it so hard." He eyes Sarah, who is laughing in the shallow water.

"Oh, Chrono, I can take it!" Sarah stands and throws a handful of sand at Lea. "Though, I am worn out now. We should really turn in for the night."

The trio heads to the camp, putting their clothes out to dry over the tropical tree branches. They slip into their nightclothes and sit by the fire, leaning on their horses.

Chrono puts his sword beside him, looking at Sarah and Lea. "We should leave early in the morning. The townsfolk will be safe here underneath the mayor. He will be looking after us and providing what we need to build our homes."

"That's good," Sarah says. "I'd rather not leave them, but I have a duty as their queen to see this through."

"Goodnight, all," Chrono says, pulling a woolen blanket over his body and falling asleep right away.

Sarah and Lea speak about the upcoming journey before falling asleep by the fire. The moonlight shines brightly over them as if Astra herself is smiling, watching her children rest.

Chapter 13

Month of Dragons
Day 22

The cold wind makes Salazar its home. The brisk evening air rushes through the underground pathway of King Leo's castle.

Prince Maxim hobbles along, dragging his meaty legs, carrying him as fast as he can go. He approaches a knight, sliding something into his hand.

"Do not let my father know about this," he says quietly, giving the letter to his trusted knight of eighteen years.

"Yes, my lord," he replies. "What if the king finds out?"

"He won't because he thinks nothing of me. I am not fit nor intelligent in his eyes. He does not expect his son would do any cunning plotting behind his back. Get that letter to the Southern Kingdom then to the Eastern Kingdom. After that, head to the Western Kingdom. We need to ensure our neighboring kingdoms know that my father could be joining the demonic empire. After what he did to the envoy from the Eastern Kingdom, I fear this could be his next move."

"Yes, my lord." The knight bows. "I will make haste!"

Prince Maxim looks down the stairs covered in snow, praying his letter of hope will make it in time without fail.

* * *

Bridget yawns, waking up from the hard floor.

"Nothing like a good night's rest to keep the body moving," she jokes. "Wish I could sleep somewhere better."

Slash rolls out of his bed and heads for the room where breakfast is being served, leaving the two women behind.

"Is Slash all right?" Bridget asks. "He looks like a corpse that rose from a thousand-year slumber."

"He was restless most of the night," Sodina explains, biting her lip. "Something must be bothering him. He didn't even say good morning to me. Maybe he's in a rush to get to our destination."

"Up and at 'em, your husband is." Bridget laughs.

Sodina changes into her brown pants and a green tunic top for the day and heads downstairs to the lobby.

Slash sits at a table, staring at his coffee, slumped forward and letting the heat of the drink warm his face.

"Honey," Sodina says. "Are you okay?"

Slash looks at her with tired eyes and blinks slowly.

"Erm," Slash mutters. "The realization that our home is gone is too much to bear. Even though they exiled us, my heart aches. My mind is weary of these travels, and with the future unknown, my optimism is at an all-time low. I have doubts that I am going to save you. And please don't start that we-are-all-in-this-together, feel-good sermon. I would rather not hear it now."

Slash shakes his head, rubbing his hand on the warm cup.

"The realization that we have no idea where to go or what to do terrifies me. I'd rather have the assurance of death here than head into a fate that cannot be undone. I could not save Amanda and Lorenz." Slash lets out a short, dry laugh, looking at Bridget, who has just come downstairs. "What if something were to happen to you, Bridget? I have no doubt about your martial abilities, but there's always a bigger fish."

Bridget walks over to Slash and slaps him on the face.

"Ouch." His brow furrows, and he rubs his cheek. "What was that for?"

"You speak as if you have never been in a battle, Slash. I'd rather not call you a boy, but you sure are acting like one," Bridget complains. "You're married, right?"

Slash nods.

"You can fight right?" Bridget asks.

"Yes. But—" Slash lowers his head.

"Uncertainty is a burden to the whole group. You'll be nothing but dead weight if you continue like this. I'll tell you this: We are heading to the town of Artemis next. They have a library that may contain information about an extremely potent elixir. I was talking to a merchant the other day in the camp. They say that the ingredients are found in hard-to-reach places. There is a rumor that a great priest in Lafare knows of the trials passed down from generations. It's a challenge, yes, but it's the best lead we have," Bridget explains.

Slash grins for a moment, but then he shakes his head.

"So, we go to Artemis and find some books with clues in it. That is supposed to save Sodina. What if this priest is dead when we get there? What if the information is outdated?"

"Like I said, Slash, uncertainty is a burden. We have to hope and we have to try. Sodina has yet to give up; I haven't given up. And I am sure we have thoughts that have yet to be expressed, but losing faith does nothing for our journey. Buckle up, drink that coffee, and go change. Cry but rise above the darkness." Her eyes flashing with resilience, Bridget sits down.

Slash stands up and pats Sodina on the shoulder before heading upstairs.

"You were a bit hard on him," Sodina says to Bridget. "He suffers greatly from anxiety, so I give him grace."

"He needs to know what is going on," says Bridget firmly. "If you lack the wisdom to see where his uncertainty can lead us, then he will never grow into the man who will save you."

Bridget sits back in her chair, looking at Sodina with a wry smile.

"A little tough love never killed anyone, dear. With our small pep talk, he will either rise above or sink into a more profound depression. If that's the case, just lie with him to get his focus back." Bridget laughs.

Sodina blushes. "You said that out loud, you know."

"I know." Bridget chuckles. "But it will work itself out.

The two of them finish their breakfast and head out of the inn to fetch their horses.

* * *

Up in their room, Slash glares at his sword. *Who do they think they are? I will chart out my destiny and slay those who have twisted fate. If the demonic empire has taken our home, I will take it back no matter what.*

Slash shakes his head, deep in thought. *And I will get some answers.*

After changing into new clothes, he jumps out the back window. He needs to get to the stables, but he doesn't want to be seen. So he climbs up to the roof and jumps to a nearby building. He continues jumping across the rooftops until he reaches the edge of town, making sure he stays out of sight of Sodina and Bridget.

Slash jumps down toward the northern stables and requests a horse. While this horse is not as healthy-looking as the last one, it will do.

"You're going to Glashmere?" asks the man. "It's a few days of travel to Glashmere. You do know it is overridden with monsters?"

Slash nods. "That is why I am going to make sure those monsters do not cross the Southern Kingdom's border. The answers I seek for those I love may be there," he tells the stable owner.

He mounts his horse with a few days' supply of meals and potions and leaves Rinkar, riding on the path en route to Glashmere.

* * *

Bridget and Sodina walk toward the southern stables to gather their horses.

"Where is Slash's horse?" Sodina asks, her eyes widening. "It's gone."

Bridget goes to talk to the stable owner and soon comes back. "He says another gentleman took his horse."

"But who?" Sodina shakes her head. "We'd better go find Slash."

Sodina and Bridget mount their horses, ride back to the hotel, and check their room.

"He's not here!" Sodina cries.

"Huh. That fool. Did he head out on his own to Artemis?" says Bridget. "What has gotten into that boy of yours, Sodina?"

"Oh, Slash, where have you gone?" Sodina whispers, putting a hand over her mouth.

"If he left just now, then he's about an hour ahead of us. Let us make haste, Sodina."

The two of them get on their horses and ride out of town toward the city of Artemis.

Sodina leans on her horse as the cold wind brushes over her face. The sun shining down offers little warmth as the two of them weave their way through the forest, heading down toward the coastline.

"The climate should be changing in a day or two," says Bridget.

"We have yet to see Slash."

"We are riding our horses a bit hard. We need to take a break and tend to them."

Bridget and Sodina stop by a nearby creek and sit down. Their horses drink their fair share of water.

"You don't think Slash headed back to Glashmere, do you, Bridget?" Sodina asks, letting a tear drop while she's looking down at the grass, the wind blowing her hair into her face.

Bridget sits close to Sodina, reaching for her hand.

"If he did, he's an idiot." Bridget grunts in disappointment. "If we were to follow him, it would surely be our end—the three of us versus the whole demon army. We would lose in a flash, but not without taking out at least a few hundred of those creatures."

She slams her foot down on the ground as she starts kicking the dirt around. *Where is he? How could he leave his wife? What about me?*

"Damn it all! We will know the truth once when we reach Artemis," Bridget snaps.

Sodina reaches into their sack, pulls out a piece of bread, and takes a bite.

"Ugh, this is pumpkin bread." She sighs. "I hate pumpkin bread."

Even so, she takes another bite, not wanting to waste it.

Bridget stands up and walks toward a tree and cuts it down with her axe. The loud fall disrupts the area. A couple of birds fly up as the two hear something rustling in the bushes near them.

"Well, I should have expected that."

Bridget turns around to see two wolfen, teeth snarling, ready to pounce.

"Sodina, I've got this."

Sodina stays seated, eating her pumpkin bread.

"You will make an excellent meal, human," one of the wolfens warns.

"I'd like to see you try." Bridget smiles and charges at the wolfen.

With a quick swing of her axe, Bridget cuts one of the wolfen's arms off and kicks the other in the chest.

"You insect!" The wolfen snarls, howling.

He claws at Bridget's face but misses his mark.

"A little to slow there, buddy," Bridget mocks.

The other wolfen lies on the ground holding his chest, gasping for air. Bridget stomps over to him and slams her axe into his neck.

"Go back to the netherworld where you belong, demon spawn."

Turning from them, Bridget goes back over the creek and washes her hands.

"What about the other one?" Sodina asks.

"Poor fellow had his lung crushed by my kick. He shouldn't be much of a problem," says Bridget, putting her axe on the ground. "Even if he charges us, I'm sure you will roast him with a fire spell or something."

Bridget smiles as she finishes cleaning her hands and sits down beside Sodina.

"That was a great warm-up, although, I am going to need the rest of my energy to punch Slash when I see him." Bridget shakes her head. "That man. Seriously. What is he thinking going out there on his own by himself? He needs to bulk up a bit. I'd train him if I could."

They sit in silence for an hour, both thinking about what the future holds.

"Let's get going," says Bridget at last.

The two of them jump onto their horses, pushing toward the distant horizon. The sun continues to flow across the sky as dusk sets in.

"We need to get to another safer spot soon," Sodina says, pointing at an open field in the distance. "I'd rather not stay in the woods where spiders and other creepy creatures can get us."

"Can't you just put a barrier or something to protect us?" Bridget says, mimicking a shield with her hands.

"A barrier uses a lot of magical energy," Sodina responds. "I can't keep it up that long. I'd rather not waste a lot of magical energy, especially as my life force is being drained as we speak."

She feels dizzy as she tries to focus her strength on keeping herself on her horse. *I cannot let Bridget know I am struggling this much*, she thinks to herself. *If she knew I would end up being a burden to her. Bridget is strong, but she has her limits as well.*

Sodina looks at the moon, making its entrance into the sky as a small cabin comes into view.

"Do you think that is worth checking out?" Bridget asks.

Sodina nods in approval.

The two speed toward the cabin. Bridget slows down as they both bring their horses to a slow trot. No lights come through the cabin windows.

"Looks empty, but let's make sure," Bridget says in a hushed voice.

Bridget draws her axe as Sodina chants, preparing a paralytic spell. Bridget kicks the door in to reveal an empty bed and pitch-black room. Sodina snaps her finger, and a small spark flies out of her finger, illuminating the room.

"No one here," Sodina says. "The place is ours."

"No one yet, at least." Bridget chuckles. "Close the door quickly and put a spell on it."

Sodina runs over the door to secure the bolts with a magical lock.

"In the name of the Goddess, Astra, protect this building with your love."

Sodina uses another spell to enchant the door and repair it, so it no longer shows any sign of Bridget's break-in.

"If anyone is to come, the horses will alarm us, but hopefully that won't be the case," says Sodina.

They find candles in the cabin and light them.

"You know, if Slash is headed to Glashmere, he might still find some way to survive," says Sodina heavily. "I want to believe that, but if the demons have taken over the whole region up to the Bridge of Eden, there is no telling what will happen to him."

Bridget yawns. "I want to believe that, Sodina, I do. But your husband could be walking right into a death trap. I am trying to be real with you on this one. "

Sodina curls up in a ball underneath her traveling blanket, crying softly.

I miss him. He is my shield, lover, and warrior. To be apart from him is truly heartbreaking. We have known each other since childhood. We embody that those who grow up together eventually marry. Yes, he was always last in our races as children, and he never made it to knighthood. But he is excellent with a sword, and one day I will bear his children.

Bridget smiles at Sodina, knowing full well what they have to do. "Hey, Sodina."

"Huh?"

"We are going to save you and find Slash, but we have to do it wisely. Okay?" Bridget reassures her. "Goodnight, Sodina."

Bridget falls asleep, snoring wildly.

Sodina sits awake for a while, looking out the small window toward the stars. She catches a glimpse of what looks like a pair of wings and a body she can't quite make out. *I must be tired, but that looked like an angel of sorts.*

Slumping back into the bed, she soon falls asleep despite Bridget's snoring.

* * *

Slash pushes through the tree line opening, entering a field filled with slimes. The sun starts to rise over the hills of the Eastern Kingdom.

"Get out of my way, slime bags." Slash leans forward on his horse, pushing through the one-foot-tall slimes on the ground. Green goo oozes through the grass as the horse tramples over hundreds of slimes in the open field.

The horse, exhausted, falls over at the end of the meadow.

"Get up, you weak animal!" Slash yells, punching the ground as the horse lies exhausted, panting for air.

What are you doing? he thinks to himself. He falls over on the horse, exhausted from traveling all night.

I am no good to anyone if I cannot get there.

Slash pulls out his map, trying to make sense of where he is.

I followed the signs, so I should be on the outskirts of the vast forest right now. I can cut through the Great Forest to get a look at the situation. If I charge right in, then I'll probably die.

"Think rationally, Slash," he says to himself.

The rational thing to do would have been to stay with Bridget and Sodina, but I needed to do something.

Slash pulls out a bottle of water and leans the horse's neck on his lap.

"I am sorry, ole girl. I pushed you too hard." He pours the water into the horse's mouth and lets it rest.

Getting to his feet, he builds a small tent and then pulls out a piece of pumpkin bread to eat.

"Thank goodness I brought a few of these," he says. "It might be enough to last me 'til the upcoming battle."

The dew of the morning brings peace to his growing anxiety.

I have no idea what I'm heading into. He sighs. *I could be walking right into my death.*

Slash rests for some time, ensuring his horse recovers its strength for the next hours of travel.

"Calm mind equals precise action," Slash says to himself, mounting his horse.

He sets off toward the edge of the Great Forest, anxious to see what awaits him.

"You shouldn't be here," a voice whispers as he pats the horse on its side.

"Who goes there?" he asks, looking around.

A fairy flies over to Slash and reveals herself to him.

"My name is Tori, human, and you're making a grave mistake."

"A fairy?" Slash says, his brows lifting in surprise. "I thought all of you were wiped out."

"There are still a few of us left living high above the trees, but our hometown in the forest is destroyed," she explains. "If you seek to stop the demonic army, you will fail. I tried to stop them from destroying Glashmere, but my powers were not enough. I am still hurting from that fight. If you wish to throw your life away, be my guest."

"I have a personal stake in this fight," Slash responds. "My wife's life is in danger! She is heading to the south to find a cure, but I need to end this now. I appreciate your concern, Tori, but I must destroy them. This is my home, and I will assassinate their leader. Cut the head off and the rest will scatter like vermin."

The sweat from Slash's hair drips to the ground. Tori knows full well that he is nervous and not willing to show it.

"The forest is mostly empty of these demons," she says. "Most of them have made the passage through the woods to Ifer. I will help you to the forest border, but no farther than that."

Slash nods, appreciating the help.

"Lead the way, fairy," he says.

"It's Tori."

"Lead the way, Tori."

The dew of the morning pours into the forest, leaving a sweet smell brushing through the trees.

"You need to watch for the demon generals," Tori tells Slash. "They specialize in combat and are incredibly durable. Even my fairy magic stood no chance against them. There is a daunting witch with them who is quite strong. She uses this powerful weapon to fight up close or strike at a range. She loves to fight but also lets her minions do most of the work."

"What is her name?" Slash asks.

"I can't remember. They knocked me unconscious. All I remember is that I was powerless to stop them. By the time I woke up, they had taken control of Ifer and Glashmere. Their influence is probably spreading toward the Bridge of Eden. They have solems, wolfen, and all other sorts of demons under their control."

"We probably have more than you can count!" a voice threatens, clawing toward Tori.

A wolfen ambushes them from behind.

Tori leans back, avoiding the attack, her wings glittering in the daylight piercing through the trees.

Slash draws his sword as the wolfen stands between him and Tori.

"That was close."

Slash charges toward the wolfen, swinging his sword at its chest, missing the mark. The wolfen gets on all fours and runs toward Slash.

"Windstorm!"

Tori puts her hands out as a large gust of wind plows through the forest, pinning the wolfen against a tree.

"You forget, demon spawn, these forests still call to us fairies," Tori shouts. "Though you have defiled this place with your wicked ways, judgment will come. Your corruption will never prosper!"

Slash runs forward again and drives his sword through the chest of the wolfen, killing it instantly.

Tori puts her hand down, breathing heavily.

"I have yet to recover fully from my battle, but I have enough to best these foul beasts." She wipes the sweat off her head, the morning heat from the trees taking its toll on her. "Let's keep moving, shall we?"

Slash keeps his sword at the ready as the two quietly walk through the lush forest.

"Why didn't you guys take action sooner if you knew the demons would launch an attack?" Slash asks.

His mouth twitches as he looks over at Tori, awaiting an answer. But several minutes pass without any word from her.

"We didn't have time to do anything," Tori responds at last. "It was a typical day, and apparently, the demons had the power to break the seal on the magical barrier that prevented them from getting through. They caught us by surprise. It was easy for them. They destroyed the village and wiped out almost all of our people. Only a handful of us survived. I have yet to understand where they could have gotten the power to make a move like that. You see, we had no idea this attack would happen. It was swift, decisive, and overwhelming," Tori explains quietly to Slash.

Tori continues to fly forward, leading Slash toward the city of Ifer. Hours pass leading into the late afternoon, and several more times on their journey, a wolfen or two appears. Slash always responds with a quick stroke of his sword. He focuses on his mission, smiling often at Tori, letting her know he is thankful for the assistance.

Soon the destroyed town of Ifer comes into view through the trees.

"Those bastards couldn't have..." Slash clenches the handle of his sword, looking at the mass grave outside the town. "Wait until I get my hands on them."

Tori puts her hand on Slash's shoulder.

"You need to sleep, dear child." She touches Slash's head, causing him to fall into a deep sleep. "My child, you will need to rest for the upcoming battle."

Tori places a magical barrier around Slash and puts the blanket from his sack around him.

He mentioned that his wife was headed south. I pray that she does not come this way. I need to get back to watching over the forest to ensure no humans try to enter who are not capable of taking care of themselves, Tori thinks, as she floats above the now unconscious Slash.

* * *

Bridget and Sodina walk into the town of Artemis as the soaring buildings trace the evening skyline.

"These buildings are almost as large as ones in Glashmere," Sodina observes. People line up in the streets, selling wares of all sorts. "We need to ask the guards if they have seen Slash."

Bridget and Sodina walk over to the welcome center of the town and ask their question, describing Slash as best they can. The guard responds with a shake of his head.

"He may not be here." Sodina weeps quietly.

"We do not know if he passed by the town. He could have traveled toward the Bridge of Eden and completely passed by Artemis," Bridget explains, trying to reassure her. "You know Slash, he likes to take it to the extreme despite not having the endurance to do so."

Sodina nods, wiping her tears, hoping Bridget is right.

"Let's find an inn before we get exploring. I just need to rest a little and adjust my armor—"

"It's Bridget!" a young girl screams.

"Bridget the busty warrior," a man says.

Bridget blushes and speaks quietly under her breath. "Only common folk call me that."

A small crowd of people gathers around Bridget.

"You are famous around here for taking out those bandits a few years ago," a man says.

"Can you kiss me?" another man asks, leaning in for a kiss as Bridget edges away from the group.

"I think not, but I appreciate the kindness." Bridget shakes a few hands and walks back to Sodina.

"You are popular, Bridget." Sodina giggles.

Bridget gives her a nervous smile. "I have built a reputation for solving problems. Along the way, I may have made a few fans, but so has any adventurer, you know," she says with a shrug. "There is Marth the Great, who slew ten bears with his bare hands. He lives in the Northern Kingdom, sitting on the money he made in the War Master tournament. There is a woman whom men are in awe of called Elena. She is a mage who learned sword skills. She used spells that make her sword skills as fast as lightning and took down many famed swordsmen. A lot of men are jealous of her. I think she lives in the Southern Kingdom."

"Have you ever entered the tournament?" Sodina asks.

"Not yet—flashy matches are not my style—but maybe someday," Bridget says. "Anyway, I'm famished. Before we go investigate, let's get something to eat."

The two of them check into their hotel, grabbing a few beef kabobs from a local merchant stand on the way to the local library.

"Look at the size of the library!" Sodina's mouth drops open as they walk into the library with their kabobs.

"No food in here, young ladies." A stern voice speaks behind.

A young female with glasses and a tight dress walks up to them.

"The waste can is over there. We close in two hours, so make it snappy."

She walks back to the desk. Bridget clenches her fists, clearly annoyed.

"So, we have two hours to search," Sodina says. "If we cannot find the answer tonight, we need to come back tomorrow."

Bridget and Sodina grab all the books they can on medicine and alchemy, going back to the table with at least twenty books in hand.

"Oh, my goodness, this is going to take a bit of time."

Sodina opens one book and reads the pages slowly and intently.

"You know, reading that slow is not going to help us in any way," Bridget says. "We need to enlist some help."

Bridget leaves Sodina, walking toward a group of young scholars.

"Hey, boys," Bridget says seductively, leaning down on the table. "I need some help finding something here. Any of you strong young men care to lend me a hand?" She winks.

One of the young men jumps up. "You're Bridget! I have heard of your tales of legend. You defeated one of the elite dragons and wear its scales as your cloak."

Bridget's cheeks turn rather pink. "Well, I did do that some years ago."

"My name is Peter," he says. "I will help you until the library closes."

Bridget nods as the young man follows her to the table where Sodina is sitting.

"I got us some help, Sodina."

Sodina looks up without saying a word, her eyes wide, but cracks a small smile before quickly going back to reading.

"Is she okay?" Peter asks.

"Mhmm, she is just focused," Bridget replies. "Let's get to it, young man."

Bridget slaps Peter on the back, almost making him trip. He holds his chest as he catches his balance.

"Sorry about that, Peter, I've got strong hands." Bridget chuckles. "So, we're looking to find an antidote to a certain poison and disease that we're unsure of. Do you think we can find anything that could help us with that?"

Peter sits down and starts to browse the books.

"This one seems interesting," he says. "*Traditional Medicine for Poisons and Venoms.*"

The trio browses the books for some time, finding some valuable items.

"Sodina, look!" Bridget yells.

"SHHHHHHH!" The librarian reprimands her from her desk.

"Oh, sorry." Bridget apologizes before sitting down.

In a lower voice, she continues, "There is a story about a legendary potion that can cure any ailment. The book says it could contain some sort of plant or root from the heavenly city of Arcadia. Scholars do not know for sure. It seems this potion was last seen around the time of the First Great War."

Sodina looks over at Bridget and Peter, twisting her mouth.

"If it's been that many years, then the ingredients may be difficult or near impossible to find. There are experts in the Southern Kingdom who know of what could have happened to these items or locations," Peter explains. "This book is a hundred years old, so those who contributed to it might be dead. It's a long shot for you guys, but I think you should go for it. Please do be careful, though. Searching for items like these has led many to an early grave. I've read accounts of horrible deaths. Seeking the supernatural can either be a great discovery or lead to fear beyond imagination."

Peter looks down at the ground then back up at the two women. "I need to get back to my friends, but I am thankful to have met you." He shakes Bridget's hand and heads back across the library.

Sodina walks over to the counter and checks out the book. She and Bridget leave the library and find a hotel room, discussing the events of the evening.

"This book has a lot I want to read. I will stay up all night, finding out everything about these historians and whom to look for in the Southern Kingdom. Hopefully, they are not dead." Sodina looks down at the book.

Bridget and Sodina settle in for the night and look over the book.

"It says here that there are many priests in Lafare who have traditionally made this potion. They could still be able to produce it or at least know more," Sodina says. "The book mentions that each of the items are in a specific place, but the landscape of our world has changed since the war. We now have four kingdoms instead of one, and the demon realm is taking the rest of the Eastern Kingdom."

She frowns. "What if it is impossible to get to some of these locations?" She looks down at the book, wondering if this will truly help them, but they have nothing else to go on. This is the only route they can take. To cure herself, they will have to go off the wisdom of an old book—to a town she's never been to.

Slash, I hope you found this information as well, Sodina thinks to herself. She hopes he found his way in this direction, but a faint sense of doubt lingers in her mind.

"We will head to the library tomorrow and see if we can find any more information," says Bridget. "We can return the book in the morning and head out toward the Bridge of Eden, if you are okay with making a night trip, that is."

Sodina nods at Bridget, knowing they may make up some time and catch up to Slash.

"Hopefully, Slash is there or he's waiting for us to cross into the Southern Kingdom together."

The two of them lie down in their respective beds and close their eyes for the night.

Chapter 14

Month of Dragons
Day 23

The humidity is unbearable that morning in Mala.

Already drenched in sweat, Sarah pulls up her sleeves as she puts the saddle on her horse. Preparing for the trip took longer than expected. It took a day to gather the supplies needed for the journey to Lafare.

Sarah looks over to the townspeople, who have everything they need to get through the next few weeks. Leaving them with more than enough is important to Sarah, Lea, and Chrono. They gave up all of their supplies to the people and went and purchased new supplies for their journey. Though Chrono was a bit perturbed about this, he knew it was vital to get them ready.

"We are moving out soon," Chrono says to his horse. "I feel like we wasted too much time, my girl."

Chrono sits there, tapping his finger on Annabelle, as Lea and Sarah climb up on their horses. The people wave goodbye as the trio moves out.

Sarah waves back along with Lea and Chrono as they trot off toward the edge of Mala.

"What a beautiful day!" Lea sings. "I am so ready to get going on this adventure."

Who knows what will happen? I never imagined this would be my life after signing up to escort Duke Matthew on his mission.

Sarah looks back at Lea, smiling. "We have much, much more to do. There is a lot we have to negotiate for and a kingdom to take back. It is all overwhelming."

"Adventurers, hold on!" someone yells. A middle-aged man runs up to Chrono. "The mayor said to give you this for your journey. It's not much, but he said there is no way he could send you on your way without something."

The man hands Chrono a pouch with about a hundred gold coins.

"This is too generous of the mayor. What a blessing." Chrono thanks the man as well.

"The mayor says it is okay to take it without question, sir!"

Chrono nods. It sounds very much like his old friend, indeed.

"Let's get moving," Chrono yells.

The trio gains speed going out of the city of Mala, heading east toward Lafare, the capital of the Southern Kingdom. Lafare is an eight-hour journey away.

Lea starts to enjoy the setting in the Southern Kingdom. The people are exotic, and their life is different from what she knew back in Glashmere. She adores the open nature of their landscape instead of the claustrophobic forest trails in the Eastern Kingdom. The green grass-covered hills of the Southern Kingdom lead the party to several cliffs showing the fantastic view of the ocean.

Sarah gallops past Chrono, smiling. "Try to catch me, serious War Master!" She pushes forward with the wind blowing her purple hair furiously.

The sweet smell of her hair hits Chrono's face.

"I never back down from a challenge, Your Majesty!" Chrono pats Annabelle on the head as she speeds forward, leaving Sarah in the dust.

"No fair!" Sarah yells from behind Chrono. "You've had that horse for years, and she responds better. I have yet to build a bond with the horse I just got from the stables."

Chrono slows down and pulls up beside Sarah, chuckling. "I will never lose when I have to rise to a challenge even against you, dear queen."

Sarah makes a pouty face as she nears Chrono. "You know, I am coming of an age where I want to search for love."

Chrono's confident demeanor cracks and he gulps nervously, listening on as Sarah continues.

"I hope you know how I feel..." she says. "I know that kiss meant something to the both of us. I truly care not who sees my affection toward you."

Sarah looks over into Chrono's eyes, her purple hair shining brilliantly in the wind.

"I need you in my life, Chrono. If you would have me."

Chrono blushes at the thought and smiles shyly. "Please give me time, dear Sarah. I do not want to decide in haste."

He has an urge to wed her right this moment. He has known Sarah for almost all of his life. She has seen his journey and walked with him throughout his growth. She has been there for every win he made in the War Master tournaments. But if he is going to wed the queen, he wants to contribute to the relationship. *Adventuring would take me away from her for months.*

These thoughts swirl in his mind as he gazes into Sarah's big beautiful eyes.

Lea looks at the two talking but cannot hear their conversation. She figures it would be better to leave them to their privacy again.

She really appreciates how honest and genuine the new queen is. Opposite her, though, the War Master looks like a bumbling idiot, not knowing how to respond to whatever the queen is telling him.

Lea wonders if anyone will ever look at her the way Chrono looks at Sarah in such a private moment.

To her left, a ten-foot slime with a wicked smile appears over the horizon.

"What a huge boy!" she exclaims, riding in front of the couple protectively.

Chrono nods at Lea. "We need not engage. The open plains give us the advantage."

The slime looks as if it might pounce for a moment, but then turns away and slinks off over the hills.

Sarah puts her hand over her chest in relief. "Whew, I thought it was going to charge. I have heard that some slimes can jump in the air if evil mages have magically enchanted them."

"Thankfully for us, we can continue without a battle," Chrono adds.

Sarah glances at her hip, where a small knife is tucked away just in case they are called to action. She really hopes she won't have to use her knife-throwing skills just yet.

The trio travels for hours as the sun reaches its peak, beating down on them. They decide to rest by a large group of banana trees, as the horses seem tired from the whole day's ride.

Chrono, Lea, and Sarah jump down from their horses, enjoying some shade.

Lea wipes the sweat off her forehead. "The humidity here is otherworldly. I'm afraid I may need to strip down and take off my jacket."

"You can show some skin, Lea." Sarah smiles.

"I would rather not pass out in front of you, Your Majesty," Lea says. "If I need to show a little skin to make sure I survive, then those monsters will have to look at me."

Lea undoes her jacket and rests it on her shoulders to reveal her toned upper body. Sarah whistles and Chrono hesitates slightly, glancing at Lea.

"Oh, Chrono, it's okay, feel free to look." Lea raises a brow at Chrono, wondering how this man will ever marry Sarah.

The two women laugh out loud at the situation, and Chrono hurries to arrange a packed lunch for the three of them to change the subject.

The Glashmere townsfolk packed a few pieces of fried fish, bean stew, and several pieces of bread for their meal. It makes Sarah smile to think that her people are still thinking about their welfare. The burden of keeping them safe weighs down on her a little more.

"We have about four hours of traveling left by the way the sun goes, sir." Lea speaks to Chrono directly. "We should get there soon, judging by your mayor friend's map."

Chrono stretches, yawning slightly. "While Annabelle is comfortable enough, four more hours of traveling will be taxing. I could use a nap. Even us elite warriors have to rest up. But oh, well, it'll have to wait." He stands up, walking toward Annabelle. "Come on, then, ladies. We should get moving."

The trio cleans up their wares and boards their horses for the second leg of the exhausting journey.

* * *

The beautiful hills near the ocean give way to the broad plains leading to the city of Lafare. Lea looks sadly back as the big blue sea disappears from view.

"Do not worry, Lea," the queen says, looking forward to the open field. "When all of this over, we can visit the sea again."

Chrono speeds ahead of the two, taking the lead. It appears that the trail they are following goes through an endless plain.

The trio passes by small settlements and cabins selling wares, until they reach a dense patch of tropical forest.

"This was not on the map," Chrono admits as the path becomes difficult for the horses to traverse. "We need to cut through this dense grass."

The trio dismounts from their horses and pulls them along as they walk behind each other in a straight line.

Chrono pulls out his sword, chopping the abundant grass with intense swipes. "Stay close, please, because anything could be lurking in this grass."

Lea pulls her horse behind her in one hand and brandishes a large knife in the other.

The stillness of this tropical forest is only awoken by a slight hiss every minute.

Sarah, trembling, whispers to Chrono, "How much longer until we get through this to some clearing of sorts?"

Chrono looks back quickly as he chops more grass in front of them. "I apologize, Your Majesty, I can't say."

The trio continues through the grass, and their horses start to whiny and fuss about. Lea keeps watch in every direction behind Queen Sarah and Chrono, making sure nothing is about to spring at them.

"Eek! What was that?" Sarah squeals, feeling something slither by her feet.

Chrono moves forward quicker. "It should be nothing, Your Majesty. I think I can see a clearing up ahead. Let's move!"

He chops quickly, trying desperately to reach the opening with the two ladies behind him. He feels as if something is hunting them and he can't shake the fear.

The hissing around them grows louder and louder, until it's right beside them, and then it stops.

The trio barely catches their breath as a large tail smacks Sarah into a tree.

The horses scatter, running in different directions.

"Sarah!" Chrono yelps.

An incredibly large snake slithers out of a hole in the ground. It has slimy scales, and its length stretches as far as the eye can see, double the size of Glashmere's tallest warrior, who is seven feet.

Before Annabelle can get away, the snake wraps around her, choking the horse tightly. Chrono cries out for the poor animal but makes his way toward the unconscious Sarah by the tree. Lea whips out her bow, aiming for the creature while defending the queen.

"You humans always think you will get the upper hand!" the snake hisses in a sly voice.

The snake stretches up, towering over Lea and Chrono.

Lea checks on Sarah and finds a pulse. "She's alive, Chrono!"

"You let Annabelle down this instant, or I will cut to shreds!" Chrono yells.

"How rude of you!" The snake scoffs. "You didn't even ask for my name and you're already making demands."

"What is your name then, beast?"

"My name is Basil, one of the members of the Dark Order," he hisses proudly.

Chrono squints. "The Dark Order, you say? Never heard of it."

Basil tightens his grip around Annabelle. "Oh, you'll wish you did, sir."

The horse shakes and trembles underneath the pressure of Basil's strength.

Chrono lunges at Basil with his sword drawn.

"Tsk, tsk." Basil slinks around smoothly. "So quick to anger, War Master."

"So, you've heard of me," Chrono spits. "Let. My. Horse. Go."

"Fine, here you go."

Basil hurls the horse toward Chrono. He ducks as Annabelle flies towards him, and she slams into a tree, shrieking in pain.

His thoughts swirl between rage and grief, but he knows he had to focus on getting to safety before he can check on his horse.

Chrono runs toward Basil, swinging his sword at the snake's tail, but Basil slips underground in an instant. The ground rumbles and shakes underneath their legs.

"We are dead if we stay here, Chrono!" Lea yells. "We need to go!"

Chrono looks back at Lea. She is right, but there is nowhere to go. The way forward is still full of thick brush, and going back the way they came is not an option. They can't be sure when the beast will strike next. Their legs tremble with fear.

Basil's tail pops up out of the grass, smacking Chrono around and sending him ten feet into the air.

Chrono hits the ground with a loud thud and groans.

Lea shoots an arrow from her crossbow, but it misses its mark as Basil's tail goes back underground.

"Damn it!" Lea says in frustration. "Chrono, I can't get a bearing on him!"

She runs to Chrono, lifting him up. Sarah is across from them, slowly coming to her senses but still wincing in pain.
"Do you have any extra potions to help us in this situation, War Master?" Lea asks.

Chrono points at Annabelle. "They may be all crushed now, but I do keep them cushioned with wool in my sack."

Lea runs over to Annabelle as fast as she can.

Basil's head pops up again. Lea dodges him, swiftly delivering two arrows into the snake's neck.

"Persistent human!" Basil yells, slithering back underground.

Chrono stands still in the center of the small clearing they've made, focusing on where the next attack might come from. His eyes lock on Sarah's slumped form, still having difficulty regaining her senses.

Basil jumps out of the hole and hits Chrono in the chest before he can react, knocking him backwards.

"Now for the finish!" Basil's hisses and bares his fangs before lunging.

Chrono swings his sword just in time and chips one of Basil's teeth. Basil wails and jumps back underground.

Lea rummages through Chrono's bag, searching for any potion that will help them in battle. "There's nothing here, sir!"

"No need to panic, Lea." Chrono coughs, trying to get to his feet. "We need to call for the horses and proceed forward at all costs. I'll carry Sarah—"

Basil springs up again and pushes Chrono into the air. His fangs shine in the sunlight.

"Humans, meet your demise!" Basil yells.

Chrono, filled with adrenaline, backflips in the air, landing on his feet. Basil seems surprised by the quick movement, but grunts and springs toward the War Master anyway.

"It is you who will meet your demise, Basil Monster!" Chrono twists his body into a downward circular motion as he cuts Basil clean in half with his sword.

Basil's body hits the ground with a thud. The trees and grass around the group disappear in a flash.

Was it all Basil's illusion? Chrono wonders in surprise.

Chrono runs over to Annabelle.

"Sweet girl, are you okay?" Chrono pets her as the horse whimpers softly. "You've done so well, my faithful steed."

The memories flow through his mind back to his younger years when King Martin gave him Annabelle as a present. *The king saw it fit to bless me with you. I have failed the king and also the steed he entrusted me with. What type of warrior am I? What type of man loses two things he is meant to protect?*

Chrono puts out his hands, stretching his body over Annabelle's.

"You will not die alone! I will ensure those who are responsible will pay for their evil. You have my word."

Annabelle's breath weakens, and her chest stops moving.

"No!" Chrono screams as he leans on his horse, weeping uncontrollably. "Annabelle!"

Sarah sits up slowly from the ground.

"What happened?" she asks faintly. "Lea?"

Lea bows her head at the queen, not saying a word. Her eyes start to swell with moisture from the sound of Chrono's screams. The archer helps the queen up and pats her arm.

"Chrono?" Sarah catches sight of him in the corner of her eye. "Chrono!"

Sarah runs over to him, almost stumbling as she gets close to him. Chrono continues to weep into his horse's chest.

"Oh, no," Sarah whispers. "Annabelle… She's not… Is she…?"

Chrono does not respond to Sarah, but turns to her with tears streaming down his face.

Sarah leans down behind him and hugs him tightly. She strokes his hair to soothe him.

"Annabelle was one of our own." Chrono chokes on his words. "We practically raised her since birth. She has been with me since my early teens."

Lea walks over to the two and puts her hands behind her back.

"Your Majesty, I found something in the beast's body," she says as Chrono sniffs, and Sarah urges her to go on. "It looks like a seed of some sort. It appears that he was able to create this vast tropical forest by putting demonic energy into the ground and using this seed as the catalyst."

"That's insane." Sarah shakes her head and turns her attention back to her weeping War Master.

Lea bows and whistles, hoping the horses that ran off will make their way back.

Chrono straightens, wiping his eyes, and Sarah reaches for his hand, squeezing it tightly.

"I'm here for you, Chrono," she whispers in his ear. "It's okay to be vulnerable right now."

Sarah kisses his head gently, and Chrono's body becomes putty in her arms.

"Cry, my dear War Master."

"It's not fair, Sarah," he mumbles into her chest.

"I know, my love, I know."

"Did you just call me 'love'?" Chrono tries to compose himself and eyes the queen.

"I did, Chrono." Sarah chuckles lightly. "Because I love you. I…have always loved you. I can't deny that anymore."

From her spot a few feet away, Lea can hear the exchange between the queen and the War Master, and she smirks.

Finally, she thinks. *Of course, the queen would be the first to admit her feelings. I really admire her for that.*

Chrono nods and gently asks Sarah to let him go for a moment so he can catch his breath. Sarah doesn't leave his side, as he is still silent after her confession.

"Sarah…" Chrono moves closer to her. "I want you to know something."

"Yes, Chrono?"

"I…love you, too."

Sarah immediately lifts him up and tackles him, kissing him passionately.

Lea looks away in disgust. She doesn't need to see that after their eventful afternoon. Public displays of affection always make her sick.

"I…" Chrono clears his throat as Sarah pulls away from him slowly. "I just wanted to be honest… I do intend to marry you, Sarah. One day."

Sarah's eyes widen. "Yes, of course, I will marry you. A million times over. As soon as you're ready."

Sarah hugs him tightly again, and Chrono coughs, laughing lightly.

"Be careful now, I am still a little sore."

Chrono reaches for a stray rope from his pocket and ties it around Sarah's ring finger.

"A promise, dear one." He kisses her hand, and Sarah's eyes well up with tears.

Lea turns around, seeing the proposal, and jumps in the air happily.

"You two are going to make a fantastic couple!" Lea grabs both of them by the hands and smiles. "I can't wait to see the life you build together."

"Eventually," the couple chimes in unison.

Sarah, overwhelmed by all of the emotion, gets to her feet. "We need to do something about Annabelle's body, you two."

Together, they clear a large grave for Annabelle and say a prayer for her.

"She was a beautiful steed, black as night and fast as they come," Chrono says quietly. "I will miss her deeply. The king always told his warriors this phrase." He pulls his sword from its sheath, pointing it toward the sky, and yells, "We are the Shining Light of the Eastern Kingdom! I vow before I leave this world, I will destroy the Dark Order and all of those who stand with them."

* * *

The trio walks away from the grave with nothing but their backpacks as the evening sky starts to appear.

Rounding the corner of the now-empty patch of land, a large city comes into view.

"We've arrived," says Lea, exhaling in relief. Chrono and Sarah hold hands and walk on.

I wonder if Queen Charlotte will see us even though it's late in the evening, Lea wonders.

A group of knights comes towards the trio.

"What happened to the forest that was here?" the tallest knight asks as they approach.

"There was a demon spawn that created the woods," Chrono explains. "And we killed it."

Lea pulls out the demon seed and hands it over to the smallest knight. The three Lafarians look at it curiously.

"Men, it's the War Master Chrono!" the first knight says in surprise. "You need to get to the castle quickly."

The knights guide them into the capital with haste. They escort the trio into the castle where Queen Charlotte awaits.

An announcement trumpet sounds off, and the three are led into the Lafare throne room through its huge iron double doors.

"Queen Charlotte, we bring the travelers from the Eastern Kingdom!" the tall knight announces.

The beautiful Queen Charlotte stands from her throne and walks down the red carpet to them. She is adorned in jewels and necklaces of gold. Her crown sits elegantly atop her elaborate updo, and her dress is a striking wine red that complements her dark skin perfectly.

"Sweet Sarah," she says in a soft voice.

Chrono and Lea bow as Sarah holds her head high. She tried her best to keep upright, even if she is covered in dirt and still weary from the previous hour of fighting.

Queen Charlotte looks deeply into Sarah's eyes. Sarah peers back intently, awaiting her next words.

"Princess, or should I say Queen Sarah. I have heard of the tragedy in your home. We heard of your situation long before the War Master here spoke with the mayor of Mala. Please join me in my receiving quarters."

Charlotte leads the group to a room with golden chairs and a large round table.

Ten knights come into the room with them but stand tall behind Queen Charlotte, not saying a word. Lea is intimidated by their number, but makes sure to keep a straight face, representing the tough Glashmere spirit.

"Forgive me for appearing rude, but I find it hard to believe that King Martin is dead. He was a trusted ally and friend. Our partnership was growing at a rapid pace, but the demons took him before his time." The queen's calm yet stern voice resonates with Sarah as she continues.

"Since we do not know what happened to your mother, you are the leader of your people," Charlotte says. "To bear that burden has to be exhausting for a lady as young as yourself."

Sarah nods in agreement. "I want to introduce you to Sir Chrono and Lady Lea."

"I've heard of the War Master." Charlotte nods and turns her attention to Lea. "It's a pleasure to meet you, Lea."

"The pleasure is mine, Your Majesty." Lea bows with a serious face.

Charlotte acknowledges her greeting and looks back at Sarah.

"What is it that you need from me exactly?" She sits down at the head of the table, and they all sit as well.

"We have come to request aid to retake our homeland," Chrono responds.

"Why should I put the full force of my kingdom behind you?" Charlotte stares at Chrono.

"You said it yourself, Your Majesty," Lea interjects. "That King Martin was a trusted ally and friend."

"That is the case, but I also have my own borders to protect, and you only have fifty people from what I hear."

Sarah nods sadly. "Please continue."

"I cannot lend you any troops, but I am not heartless. I have sent letters to the other kingdoms to have a summit to discuss the matters at hand. We do not know how large the demonic army is, nor how vast their influence may be."

Chrono crosses his arms in frustration, listening to the Southern Queen.

"To head out now without knowing those variables would bring about unnecessary loss." Charlotte waves her hands around to show the gravity of her words. "I must ask you to be patient until the summit meets in a few days. Oh, dear Captain Robert, please go on for me."

Captain Robert steps forward, and Lea notices that he is the same small knight they encountered earlier.

"We received an alarming notice," Robert says. "Just this morning, King Leo of the Northern Kingdom killed a messenger from the Eastern Kingdom."

"HE WHAT?" Chrono yells, and Sarah hushes him. She sits still and silent in shock. Queen Charlotte pinches the bridge of her nose, sighing.

"That is a declaration of war," Chrono says, putting out his hands and gesturing wildly.

"Are you sure this report is accurate?" Lea asks.

"The letter came from Prince Maxim himself," Charlotte says.

"I heard the prince up there is spineless and useless."

Robert laughed. "I believed so as well. But apparently, he did have enough spunk to sneak a letter past his hard father."

"I know that King Leo is hard," Sarah says, "but a traitor and a murderer? I couldn't have imagined."

Chrono sighs beside her and tries to calm himself down.

"We do not know if he has sided with the demons or acted on his own accord," Charlotte explains, looking down at the table.

"Unfortunately, we must prepare for the worst-case scenario—a joint attack from the demonic empire and northern kingdom," Robert continues for the queen.

"That is the precise reason why I cannot lend you any troops, but I am committed to helping you," Charlotte adds. "It is late, though, and if you will excuse me, I must get some rest. Robert, you know my orders. Goodnight, all."

Robert comes up to the trio. "You will be our guests here at the castle. My men will show you to your quarters. The summit will convene in three days. Feel free to explore, but please do get some rest."

Captain Robert and Queen Charlotte leave the room together, but not before Charlotte offers a small smile to them.

"This way," Tall Knight bellows, leading the trio to their quarters for the evening. "The bathhouse is down the hallway. Men are on the left and women on the right."

The knight bows and walks away, leaving them to their rooms.

"I guess we each get our own room." Lea shrugs.

"I am thankful for the kindness we are being shown." Sarah sighs.

Chrono sits down in the hallway, leaning into the comfy chair by the door of his quarters. "Ladies, please go ahead. I am going to rest for a moment."

Sarah slinks over to Chrono and kisses him on the cheek. "Goodnight, my love."

Chrono blushes and answers, "Goodnight."

Lea and Sarah head to the bathhouse together to wash off the dirt from their journey.

Chrono walks into his room and lies down on his bed. His ribs are killing him after the earlier against the stupid Basil creature.

He slips into nightclothes laid out from Queen Charlotte's brood and puts on some ointment to soothe the ache in his ribs. His eyes slip closed for a moment and then open again as the pain resonates throughout his body.

Just relax, Chrono. He imagines the voice of his beloved Sarah, and Chrono slowly falls asleep, thoughts of the upcoming war against the demons running through his mind.

Chapter 15

Month of Dragons
Day 24

Rain pours over Glashmere, hitting the castle like a thousand needles. Gareth, exhausted from planning their next move, walks into his room. *I never get tired of seeing the king's room. That fool had it good. Little did he know that everything he loved would be taken from him.* The Exalted One chuckles to himself.

He walks over to a shelf in the corner and pushes it to the left, revealing a stairwell. He proceeds downs the stairs into a dimly lit room with a large bookcase. A small orb, perched on a golden statue of a hand, sits on a circular table. *There are still secrets I must keep from those I love.* Gareth walks over to the bookcase, pulling out a small book.

"This will do." He puts the book down on the table. The words *Soul Stealing* are written in small black lettering on the tattered brown cover. Gareth opens the book and begins to read the ancient language of his ancestors. He places his right hand on the orb.

A mist appears in the orb, swirling between dark purple and pitch black. A brooding, mysterious voice speaks into the consciousness of Gareth.

"Let us begin."

Gareth closes his eyes, his arm shaking violent as he tries to keep his balance.

"What have you done with the power I gave you?"

Gareth stutters, trying to get the words out of his mouth. "I have destroyed the Eastern Kingdom and taken their castle."

"Why have you not killed every last human on Esteria?" the voice yells.

"My lord, this power you gave me is wreaking havoc on my body. I cannot take it."

"Silence!" the voice yells. "You found the Orb of Prye in the Uncharted Lands, did you not?"

"Yes, my lord," Gareth says, trying to stand. Sweat pours from his body as the overwhelming energy from the orb funnels throughout him.

The voice goes from angry to calming as Gareth takes a heavy breath and steadies himself.

"I have come to expect too much from you. You do have seething anger inside of you. That woman you love does she know about this place?"

"No, my lord! I did as you instructed to. I am only revealing those things you have told me." Gareth is relieved that the pain in his body has subsided.

"We will see," the voice says in a calming manner. "You must finish what I started. Some of my memories and power are trapped in this orb. It pains me to not be able to leave this prison."

The voice pauses for a moment. The colors of the orb swirl, revealing a brilliant city.

"Do not tell me that is what I think it is." Gareth mouth drops wide open as he glares into the orb.

"Yes!" the voice says in a menacing tone. "The heavenly city of Arcadia. This is where we will lay our gifts in front of Astra. When I was still in my physical body, there was no other place I wanted to be."

"My lord Heli—" Gareth starts to utter his master's name.

The voice rises in an anger once more, causing Gareth to shake violently. "You have not earned the right to say my name."

The magical energy swells throughout his body. His bones feel like they are going to shatter. "Please, my lord," he mutters, nearly passing out.

The energy calms as Gareth falls to the ground, his hand sliding off the orb.

I must tolerate the pain. Gareth stands up, putting his hand back on the orb. "What is it that you wish me to do?"

"You are your own man. I do respect that. There is one way you can crush any rebellion you face. Destroy the world tree, Elysium. That will cut off the magical strength of any of your adversaries."

"How do I do that?" Gareth looks deeply into the orb, seeing an image of the world tree appear before him.

"Read the ancient text. I sealed away my memories in cursed items throughout Esteria. Find them and you will find the way forward."

Gareth lets go of the orb again, and it returns to its former transparent appearance. *More cursed items and destroying the world tree. All who pursue the world tree die tragic deaths. How am I supposed to get there?*

Gareth sits down on the brown leather chair in the corner of the room.

One thing I know for certain. I must not fail my master.

Month of Dragons

Day 24

The whistle of the wind rustles the leaves over the motionless body of Slash as he jolts up, looking into the night sky.

The last thing I remember was Tori, and then everything went black. Slash looks around and the area seems empty of enemies. *Nighttime is a perfect time for me to sneak in.* He drinks some water and takes a bite out of his pumpkin bread. He then follows the tree line, heading towards the outer wall of Ifer. *There is no one around, or if they are, they may be asleep.*

Slash looks up at the night sky. It felt like the heavens were aligning for him, showing the path he was walking was a noble one. Slash climbs a tree and jumps over the stone wall, landing into the town of Ifer.

The smell of blood and death was thick as smoke as Slash hugged the stone wall, sneaking his way past a sleeping wolfen and solems standing guard.

They took over the whole town. Slash kept his profile low trying not to draw attention to himself. At that moment, he runs right into a wolfen.

"It's a h-h-h-human!" the wolfen tries to sputter.

Slash grabs the arm and the neck and the wolfen and slams him into the wall. Concussed by the blow, the wolfen stumbles back. Slash pulls out his sword and thrust it into the back of the wolfen, killing him. He catches the body before it hits the ground and lays it down softly. *Those things weigh a lot. Hopefully, that did not alarm anyone.*

Slash moves through the rest of the town - through the main gates open to the city of Glashmere. He sees two wolfen and solems standing guard at the main entrance.

I need to find a way around them. I know this city better than anyone. I Slash remembers a place he used to hide as a child during hide and seek. *I hope that area has not been replaced yet.*

Slash crawls in the grass, keeping away from the wolfen's sight.

"Do you smell something?" The wolfen asks.

Slash pauses, glaring at the wolfen from the tall grass.

"It's probably human flesh from the mass grave," the other wolfen responds. "Nothing to be alarmed about."

Slash continues to crawl towards a section of the stone wall a few yards up the road. "Okay, I made it." He crawled over to the wall and pushed into the stones. *It is still weak.* Slash carefully pulls out each stone to reveal a pathway into the city of Glashmere. He puts each stone back, covering his tracks, making sure no one follows him.

Slash sees a body in the middle of the street. *Oh my goodness, that's the owner of the bakery I used to go to.* Slash runs over to the body, knowing that he was long dead. *What horror.*

"So nice of you to join us." A voice says from above.

Slash looks up to see a woman in a purple dress fly down slowly in front of him.

"I knew it was only a matter of time before some fool would try to sneak into the castle. You must have some skills to make it past the solems and wolfen."

Slash stands and takes a step back, his hand firmly on the handle of his sword.

"I would think twice before attacking, boy," she says.

"Who are you?" Slash asks.

"I should be the one asking you that question, insect. But since these may be your final moments, I'll tell you. I am Lisha, one of the three generals underneath the Exalted One, Gareth. I will make your death quick and painless underneath this beautiful night sky." Lisha chuckles. "Here I wanted to spend a night with my love."

Lisha sighs. She manifests her scythe, preparing for battle.

"That scythe!" Slash freezes, his mind racing back all those years ago with Amanda and Lorenz. *That is the scythe that cut my friends out of my life.* Slash grips his sword, drawing it quickly. *I'll finally get my revenge. This is for you Amanda and Lorenz.*

Slash speeds forward, swinging his sword, aiming towards Lisha's neck. Lisha jumps back, avoiding the attack.

"Another feisty and stubborn little human," Lisha mocks. "You want to play games? Let's play, insect."

"You witch! You have no idea the pain you have caused my family and me." Slash runs at Lisha and swings his blade upward towards her neck. Lisha blocks the attack with her scythe, the noise ringing in her ears. Slash puts his sword away and delivers a palm strike to Lisha's chin followed by a double clap on her ears. Lisha stumbles back, composing herself.

"What did you do to me, human? I can't stop this ringing in my ears."

Slash runs behind Lisha and puts her in a headlock, increasing the grip.

"How dare you touch me!" Lisha bellows.

Lisha jumps into the air and lands back first onto the ground, slamming Slash into the concrete. Slash's body hits the ground and he spits out blood from the impact. Lisha picks up Slash and punches him in the chest. Slash's body flies back, crashing ten feet away, rolling on the ground.

"Augh." Slash breathes heavily, reaching into his pocket. Pressing the bottle to his mouth he gulps down a pain-numbing potion. *I need to keep going.*

Slash stands up, feeling his legs shake but continues to concentrate on maintaining his balance.

"Oh, I remember you." Lisha saunters towards Slash. "You were in the cave with the goddess. I remember now. Yes, wrong place wrong time.

You shouldn't have gotten away, but that minor goddess saved you. What a pity. I could've killed you those years ago if it wasn't for that meddling little thing. I did enjoy snuffing out your poor friends existence."

Lisha licks her lips before she throws the bottom end of her scythe against Slash's chest. She lifts her hand and the back end of the scythe flips up, knocking Slash in the chin. Slash falls on his back, breathing heavily.

"I cannot give up," Slash mutters. He leans over and grabs his sword off the ground. Before he can compose his thoughts, Lisha stands over him.

"As expected. You were a coward before, but now you're just pathetic. Such a pity that is all you can muster."

Lisha grabs Slash's neck and lifts his body into the air. She takes Slash and slams him into the ground his head bouncing off the concrete.

Slash lays on the ground, looking up at the stars. *I couldn't avenge you, Amanda and Lorenz. I couldn't save you, Sodina. My body won't move.* Slash tries to muster the strength to stand up, but his body remains motionless. *I guess feeling no pain is not a bad way to go out.*

Lisha picks Slash up and levitates into the air heading towards the castle. "I was going to kill you, but I have a better idea," Lisha tells him.

Slash looks down at the town, flying fifty feet in the air. His vision dims out until he loses consciousness.

"Gareth, I found a human trying to sneak into the castle." Lisha, holding Slash's body, walks toward Gareth.

"Isn't that the young boy from all those years ago? I remember seeing him before we took that pathetic goddess into captivity. The young boy thought he could escape, but here he is crawling back to us now."

Gareth grins, stroking his chin. "Perhaps we could use another human for a little experiment. We can use him as a bait. I am sure someone will try to come for him. Put him in there with her."

Lisha walks behind Gareth and puts Slash into the room with Ella. Lisha chains up Slash and leaves him there.

"Is that-" Ella gasps. "No, it can't be."

Ella looks over at Slash's beaten-down body and cries.

"What did they do to you, child of Astra?"

Ella reaches out her hands and sends a small ball of light that covers Slash's body.

"That should heal most of the wounds." Ella gasps heavily. "I still have some of my magical strength. They've been draining me ever since the captured me." Ella clenches her fist, panting, before passing out. *This is all I can do to help, Slash. Take my strength and I hope that yours wouldn't falter.*

Several Hours Later

The morning sun shines as Bridget and Sodina wake up after their second day of studying.

"Let's get a move on," Bridget says.

Sodina sits up from her slumber, stretching out her arms and yawning wildly.

"I think we should take it easy, Bridget. I cannot take this exhaustive pace. You may have the endurance to do so, but I cannot. I still have this poison to deal with."

Sodina looks down at her arm, one of her veins visibly glowing purple before going back to normal.

Bridget looks at Sodina with concern and nods. "We can take it easy. We have rushed this far and have yet to find Slash. All we can do is pray and hope he slows down so we can catch up."

Both women get dressed and head out of the inn after paying their dues for the past few days.

The cloudy sky dims the beauty of Artemis.

"I'd rather not travel in the rain, but we have no choice," Sodina sighs.

The pellets start to fall as Sodina and Bridget reach the stables. A masked figure trails behind them at a forty-foot distance, watching their movements.

Bridget jumps on her horse followed by Sodina.

"Okay, our next stop is the Bridge of Eden, but there is a traveler's market along the way. The size of it depends on how many merchants are on the road at the time. I want to pick up a new outfit since we are going to Lafare. These clothes will be torn by then."

"That sounds like fun," Sodina exclaims, her eyes closing slightly before she snaps herself back, focusing the journey ahead. *I need to focus because this poison will not beat me. Slash, you always comfort me that we will find a cure. Thankfully, the tears from Ella are still working against the poison in my body. But I wonder for how long?*

Bridget and Sodina head onto the road heading south towards the Bridge of Eden. The forest of the Eastern Kingdom starts to fade away as Bridget and Sodina ride their horses towards the border.

"The roads are busy today," Bridget says to Sodina, pulling her horse back closer to Sodina.

"I enjoy this pace a bit better." Sodina smiles. "I agree with you, there are a lot of people traveling today despite the rain."

"I am thankful that the rain is not impeding that much on our journey. This is light rain and somewhat peaceful, but this type of weather does lead to rivers being flooded, and we need to watch out for that, especially when crossing small creeks."

Sodina looks up at the sky. *Where are you, my dear? I hope you are well and not pushing yourself too hard. Even if you get in a pinch, you have some potions to help you. I am worried about your wellbeing and your anxiety. For you to leave me like that is shocking, especially with the current state of our family and kingdom.* A tear streams down Sodina's cheek, blending with the rain.

"Thinking about Slash again?" Bridget elbows Sodina.

"You almost knocked me off my horse!" Sodina yells. "This rain makes the saddle especially slippery."

Sodina slides to the left and right, trying to align herself back to the center of the seat.

"You know a little humor will help the journey go by quicker," Bridget laughs. Sodina giggles, her mind still wondering about Slash and his journey.

The two of them trot slowly, making their way through the rain and eventually coming into view of the Bridge of Eden.

"Did you see the stone bridge?" Sodina gasps. "It's huge!" Bridget looks at Sodina.

"Definitely. She's a beauty, one of the most fabulous creations of our time."

The rain clears as the afternoon sky starts to show its light.

"This rain finally let up." Bridget removes her hood. "All of that rain has me soaked, but look, we are almost to the bazaar."

A large group of tents can be seen in the distance the aroma of meat lingering in the air. Bridget and Sodina pass by families in wagons and other merchants carrying their goods. Sodina smells something eerily familiar.

"That's the meat vendor from near Jerut!" Sodina exclaims, smiling in excitement.

She pushes her horse to gallop quickly towards the camp. *I know that smell from anywhere.* Sodina thinks to herself.

"Hey, wait up!" Bridget leans down and her horse gathers speed to try to catch up with Sodina. That woman smells meat, and she transforms into another person. Bridget laughs as Sodina reaches the camp before her and checks into the stables. "I have yet to catch up to her." Bridget rushes into camp, slowing her speed to get to the stables. "Okay, now to find Sodina."

A masked figure sneaks around, blending in with the people, trying to follow Bridget.

Sodina follows her nose, leading her on a magical journey.

I know you're here. Sodina thinks to herself.

A few feet away, Sodina sees a familiar man.

"That's him!" Sodina runs towards the stand, her hair flying in the wind as she appears before the man winded and hungry. "I want two of your dragon meat specials with extra salt and your signature sauce."

The man looks at Sodina oddly then smiles.

"I remember you, lassie." The man says. "You are in luck. I just started to make this evening's batch of meat. I will have it ready for you in a jiffy."

Sodina sits down at a bench nearby the man's makeshift shop. *I'm ready for meat, yes, I am, I am ready for meat, I need it now. So luscious and meaty, it's time for me to feast.* She sings in her head, leaning left and right.

"Did you hear that people have been storming the Eastern Kingdom?" A man walks by, speaking to another merchant.

Sodina looks up at the two men walking by. *People are storming the castle?* She thinks. *That is suicide. If the entire might of the Eastern Kingdom cannot beat the demon empire, what do a few people think they can do?* It sounded heartless, but as Sodina thinks of any way to get back home the only way she could think of is gaining the help of the other kingdoms.

I'm a girl from a small town trying to stop something much bigger than me. Sodina's thoughts swirl between the meat and everything that has happened. *Goddess Astra, I pray that I have the strength to get through.*

"Lassie, you are deep in thought over there," the man says.

Sodina's head pops up as she smiles. "Is my meat ready?"

"You bet," he says.

Sodina floats an inch above the ground, towards the man as her feet hit the ground.

"Thank you for this delicious treat." Sodina giggles, taking a large bite out of her dinner. She walks back towards the makeshift stables at the front of the camp.

"Hey, Bridget," she says. "Don't worry. I got some for you too."

Bridget uncrosses her legs. She half expected to receive nothing for the troubles of making sure Sodina paid for her horse being kept at the front of the camp.

"There are at least five thousand people here," Bridget explains. "We have a place to pitch our tents. And get this! Our spot is right next to the bathhouse. We do not have to walk far. Apparently it's a permanent fixture because this area is always busy with traveling merchants, families, and minor nobles."

Bridget and Sodina sit on the bench watching people pass by, enjoying their meal. Sodina leans on Bridget, stuffed from eating all of the dragon meat.

"I cannot move. You are going to have to carry me," Sodina says.

Bridget looks at Sodina and smiles.

"You know that was way too much food." She laughs. "Okay, young lady, I can carry you." The stars were in the sky by the time Sodina and Bridget reached their reserved spot.

"Down you go, dearie. I hope you are feeling better now." Bridget smiled, putting Sodina in front of the tent.

"I'm so tired I don't even feel like bathing," Sodina says. "I am going to head to bed. I will take a shower in the morning." Sodina starts to build their tent for the night.

Bridget grabs her clothes and some soap before heading to the bathhouse. "Since it's late at night there should be hardly anyone in there."

Bridget changes and walks into the bathhouse, still wearing her cloak for protection. *I know these women will think it weird I am wearing a cloak to the bathhouse, but this cloak protects me at all times.*

Nothing but my birthday suit and cape. Bridget smiles, jumping into the bath.

"Hey!" Another woman yells. "This isn't your private pool."

"Get over it lady, I've been traveling all day. If I want to splash in the water, I will do so," Bridget responds sharply.

The lady makes a disapproving look at Bridget and gets out of the pool. The other woman follows suit, disturbed by Bridget's actions.

What a bunch of stuck ups, she thinks to herself, sinking underneath the water. Bridget closes her eyes, floating face down into the water, letting the warmth cover her.

Before she could realize it was happening, a hand is wrapped around the back of her neck, pushing her deeper into the water. Bridget tries to yell but the grip becomes tighter.

Who is this attacking me? The thought of drowning clouds her mind as she tries to push up from the bottom of the bath. Using all her strength, she pushes herself up from certain death, knocking her assailant off her back.

The masked man jumps back, waist-deep in the water. Bridget regains her composure, her eyes glow purple with rage as she notices the familiar face.

"You're the creep who attacked us in Jerut."

Nagi steps back, observing the glow coming from Bridget's eyes.

Oh, I see, he thinks to himself.

Nagi runs out of the bathhouse disappearing from Bridget's sight. "Come back here," Bridget yells. Still naked, Bridget runs towards the exit of the bathhouse. She sees the bodies of the two women that stormed out in the hallway lying face down with stab marks in their necks.

I wished no ill will towards those women. She runs past their bodies. Bridget, outside of the bathhouse, looks left and right, but the man was nowhere to be found.

"I hope Sodina's not in danger." Bridget runs back into the bathhouse to grab her clothes.

Two knights traveling from the Northern Kingdom walk into the bathhouse.

"We may have some questions for you," one knight says.

Bridget, now fully clothed, walks past them without a second glance and heads back to the plot of land where their tent was. Sodina, half-awake, looks at Bridget.

"What happened?" She asks.

"You remember that masked man who attacked us in Jerut? He appeared again and tried to drown me in the bathhouse. I let my guard down. He killed two women as well and wanted to add me to the body count. I shouldn't have been so relaxed. We need to get that man before he attacks again," Bridget says sharply. "The next time I see him, my ax will cut through his spine."

Sodina looks up at Bridget with a smile. "I will back you up next time. I'm sorry I was not there to help you."

Bridget lays down beside Sodina and closes her eyes to rest. Bridget has a flashback to her academy days, where some of the professors would drag her by the neck for not doing certain things.

I am so angry, she thinks to herself. Bridget feels these emotions in her dreams while she tosses and turns throughout the night. Sodina, awoken by the erratic movements of Bridget, puts her hand out and emits a healing aura from her hands to soothe her. Bridget stops tossing as her body relaxes.

Rest my friend, and let us continue our journey tomorrow. Sodina closes her eyes to go back to sleep, hoping that Bridget would rest well for the remainder of the night.

Bridget rises awake with the sun already in the middle of the sky. "Oh my goodness, we overslept!" Bridget pushed Sodina slightly to wake her up.

"Uh." Sodina groans and sits up, slobber leaking from her mouth. "What happened? Where are we?"

"We are in the same tent," Bridget laughs. "But we are behind schedule."

"Everything happens for a reason," Sodina replies, wiping the slobber from her lips.

"Let's get a move on." Sodina and Bridget pack up their goods and head for the front of the camp to gather their horses.

"Oh, I almost forgot to get that combat dress I wanted," Bridget says.

"I will go get the horses," Sodina says.

"Sounds good." Bridget smiles. "I will be right back."

Bridget runs looking for a specific vendor she had seen some years back. "I hope they are still traveling around."

A large tent a little way away comes into her line of sight.

"I think that's it!" Bridget exclaims, looking at the shield at the top of the tent. Walking in, Bridget sees several vendors selling sexy combat ware.

"Get your steel bikinis right here! Perfect for training!" Another man yells.

"You need a bra? This one is perfect for preventing baddies and cutthroats from copping a feel," another man says.

"This place is like a pervert's paradis,." Bridget mutters. "But thankfully everyone seems modest here."

That's the dress. Bridget walks over to a man selling chain mail dresses.

"For you, Lassie, it will be 20 gold coins."

"That's steep," Bridget mumbled.

"This is the most elegant chain mail fitted to be a dress for protection and flexibility," the man explains. "I had it woven in the city of Somal in the Western Kingdom. As you know, they are known for their exotic weaving techniques. The chain mail is infused with pieces of dragon skin, so it's sexy and lightweight. Perfect for fighting those baddies."

Bridget tapped her index finger on the wooden stool in front of her. "I will give you 18 gold coins and a hug."

"You got a deal, lassie."

Bridget pays the man but only delivers an intense fist bump.

"Way to get a man riled up, but no worries, I will take my money happily. But next time I see you, I expect that hug."

Bridget smirks and walks towards a small enclosure where she can change. Slipping off her garments, Bridget slips on the chain mail dress with black leggings. *This fits so well.* Bridget smiles, punching and kicking to test the flexibility of the material. *It hugs my hips just right too. I wonder what Slash will think about this dress. Bridget, that's not right.* She thinks in her mind. *He's taken and I don't feel like that.*

Bridget looks down at the ground, thinking about her past sorrows of professors who assaulted her back at the academy. *I am not my past.* Bridget cries, slightly muffling her tears in her arm. *Okay, one day, I will find that man who loves me for me, including these large hips.*

Bridget smacks her thighs and walks out of the door to leave the tent. Bridget walks back to the front of the camp, skipping along and enjoying the feeling of her new dress.

"You look happy," Sodina says, leaning on the horse outside the campgrounds.

Bridget bends down with a smile. *A new set of clothing will always do the trick.* She winks.

"I have some leftover pumpkin bread that is still good," Bridget says, waving a piece at Sodina.

"I think I am over pumpkin bread at the moment." Sodina puts up her hand, grumbling slightly.

"The Bridge of Eden is not too far off from here. Let's get a move on," Bridget says, jumping on her horse and trotting out of the camp.

Sodina follows slowly, feeling somewhat tired.

"You do not look too good," Bridget says to Sodina. "It is probably all of that worry. Let's travel a bit slower. Slash is probably fine and taking care of business. He can be focused at times and probably did what he did to help us. Trust in him, okay?" Bridget speaks candidly, looking at Sodina with care.

Sodina looks down at her horse, the sun beating on her.

"I understand what you are saying, Bridget. Let's keep moving."

She looks down at her arm the poison making it presence known. Looking forward, she follows Bridget as they gallop towards the Bridge of Eden.

"I can smell the ocean from here!" Bridget shouts. She leans her head back, breathing the air rushing past them as the Bridge of Eden comes into view.

"I have never seen something this fantastic," Sodina says, looking in awe at the structure.

Bridget smilea widely. "This is one of the most famous landmarks of our time connecting the Southern and Eastern Kingdoms."

Sodina looks down as the horse walks across the bridge at a slow pace to view the fantastic structure and water underneath.

"Do not look over too far, Sodina, you could fall in," Bridget jokes.

Sodina continues to peek over the edge, making sure to stay firmly planted on the saddle.

Up ahead, two large groups of knights patrol the end of the bridge.

Two guards come to check on Sodina and Bridget as they come to the end of the bridge.

"What is your business in the Southern Kingdom?" One knight inquires.

"We are travelers, and we are seeking knowledge," Bridget explains.

"We are on high alert because of the recent invasion of the Eastern Kingdom," the knight says with a cautious voice. "Cause no trouble on your visit. If you do, there will be swift repercussions."

The knight steps aside to allow Bridget and Sodina to pass.

"I am thankful they are taking the threat seriously," Sodina states.

Bridget and Sodina gain speed heading down the hills that lead from the steep cliffs down to the beach.

"This view is something out of heaven," Sodina says. "I hope Slash was able to see this."

Sodina looks towards the ocean, her face gasping in awe as they ride towards a town in the distance.

"The sun is setting, and as much as I want to get to the next town, this should be our resting place for tonight."

An old man greets Sodina and Bridget as they come towards the gates.

"Welcome to Mala, young ladies. We close the city gates in twenty minutes."

"Thank you," the two women reply before they walk through the gates.

"Is that an Eastern Kingdom flag?" Sodina looks left as she sees two small houses and several tents.

"Sodina, is that you?" A familiar voice calls out. "Sodina!"

An old woman runs as fast as she can towards Sodina.

"You are the baker's wife from Ifer. You're Margaret. I remember you." Sodina waves, jumping off her horse.

"It's a shame you were exiled." Margaret holds Sodina's hand.

"What happened to you?" Sodina asks.

"We were attacked by the demonic empire. I was visiting Glashmere, getting goods when everything broke loose. All our people were slaughtered. A man in the nearby restaurant called for me, and I ran as fast as I could to the door. He had a trap door in his restaurant, and there were about fifty of us underneath. We heard the screams of all the people, then silence. After the chaos, the queen is nowhere to be found and the king is dead. We buried him."

Sodina lowers her head, shaking violently.

"So the rumors were true. We heard of this tragedy on our journey."

"Who is your friend?" Margaret asks.

"This is Bridget," Sodina smiles.

"Nice to meet you, young one."

Margaret grabs both of Bridget's hands and kisses them.

Bridget nods in approval and stays silent.

"Have you seen Slash?" Sodina canvases. "We fear something terrible has happened to him."

"I have yet to see your husband," she responds. "Knowing Slash, he is probably fine. That kid always had a knack for adventure, but not much for endurance. He was always the last one to finish races that you all had as kids."

Sodina blushes. "Slash is special," she says. "He has a heart like no other and follows his passions with unwavering confidence."

Margaret looks at Sodina and smiles.

"Young ones, you must come and eat with us. You must be famished from your journey."

Bridget and Sodina tie up their horses. They walk with Margaret to a large fish fry happening around the camp.

"Everyone listen up!" Margaret claps her hands, rounding up the townspeople. "This is Sodina, our sister from the Eastern Kingdom. She is from Ifer. Some of you know her as the exiled one. This woman is no exile, but our family. Treat her with care."

Most of the town's people cheer, accepting the two to their group.

"Eat your fill, young ladies," Margaret smiles. "There is something else you must know," she says, looking at the two of them.

"The War Master, Queen Sarah, and an archer named Lea went to Lafare to seek information from Queen Charlotte. I think it would serve you well to travel there and seek an audience with her."

Bridget finishes a piece of fish and nods.

"We were headed there to find some information. If the queen is available, I think that is a great idea." Sodina smiles, finishing a small piece of shrimp.

Hours pass as Sodina and Bridget enjoy their fill of food.

"You must stay in the cabins."

Margaret leads Sodina and Bridget to her cabin and to two beds inside.

"You must stay here in my cabin. I can sleep outside on a horse or elsewhere. You are our guest, so please make yourself at home."

"We can't take—" Sodina started.

"Be quiet child, and accept our blessing. Okay?" Margaret closes the door.

"This sort of kindness is way too much" Bridget says. "But I won't turn it down."

Bridget looks out the window towards the sky, hoping their trip was not in vain.

"I think that we should head for the queen first, she might know where to find the old sages who know where to get the item we are looking for. I feel as if we are getting close," Sodina says.

"I think you're right," Bridget replies. "Let's roll out early in the morning and make a good time for Lafare. Hopefully, the queen will have time to meet with us."

Sodina closes her eyes to rest, and Bridget lays down as well.

The sun rises as Bridget and Sodina pack up and head out of their cabin. Margaret walks up to Sodina with a small package.

"Take this fish, and please do eat it quickly," she says. "No one would want to be around you with stinky fish in your pack."

Sodina giggles and nods, knowing that fish is probably not the best food to take on a journey, but since Lafare was not too far away, she felt okay taking it.

"Thank you for your kindness," Bridget says.

Bridget shakes hands with Margaret before they head off on horseback towards the Lafare.

"Thank you for your kindness!" Sodina yells, waving back as they gallop away.

"I heard a rumor there was a thick forest that appeared out of nowhere," Sodina says, looking over at Bridget.

"Some of the knights stationed here checked it out, but when they arrived, there was nothing there," Sodina says. "With the darkness growing in our land, there are probably going to be more strange occurrences. We need to keep our guard up. If something like that is happening in the Southern Kingdom, that means the demon empire has already made their move."

Bridget looks out at the winding road leading to a fork. "It looks like Lafare is this way. Let's keep pushing forward."

Sodina and Bridget keep a steady pace so as to not wear out their horses as the hours pass by like the gentle ocean breeze.

"I find it odd that the capital of the Southern Kingdom is more inland than by the coast," Bridget says. "They say the naval fleet is down towards the most southern tip. The town is called Ferrymore. Apparently, they trade a lot with the continent of Endrea. That voyage is several weeks at best.

You could say the Southern Kingdom is never wanting for anything. They are a pivotal hub for shipping goods. If another war were to happen, I would put my money on them."

"I didn't know that," Sodina says. "I think that living next to the ocean is Astra's way of blessing her people. They have food, fun, and a way to escape if something horrible were to happen. Plus, they all have great skin living in the sun like this. I'd like a little chocolate skin sometime."

Sodina winks, thinking about Slash's lovely smile.

"What is that up there?" Bridget points.

Bridget and Sodina trot past by what looks like a royal carriage.

"That must be a diplomat of some sort, especially with that type of gear. They must be from the Northern Kingdom."

Bridget catches the eye of one of the knights but quickly turns away.

"Let's move on, Sodina."

Bridget and Sodina travel through dense groups of tropical trees as the city of Lafare comes into view.

"There it is." Sodina smiles. "I am so tired. We only stopped once, and for a day trip, those hills had to be hard on the horses."

"Let's hurry into town and see if the queen is available!" Bridget yells.

The two of them push their horses to continue as they draw near the gates of the town before the sun starts to go down.

"What a majestic city," Sodina gasps, looking at the building structures.

Checking their horses into the stable, Sodina and Bridget then rush their way to the castle.

"We are here to seek an audience with the queen," Bridget explains to the knight.

"You are cutting it close," says the knight. "But the queen is still seeing people. What is your request?"

"We seek the queen's wisdom in finding a way to retake the Eastern Kingdom and for finding a legendary item that can cure poison."

"Please wait here," he says.

The knight walks into the throne room and returns ten minutes later.

"You may enter. Please be respectful to the queen."

I wonder what she is like. Sodina put her index finger on her chin.

Bridget and Sodina walk into the throne room to find Queen Charlotte dressed in a white dress, awaiting their presence.

"I hear that you are from the Eastern Kingdom." Queen Charlotte speaks in a stern but comforting voice.

Both Bridget and Sodina bow.

"Yes, Queen. We seek the power to retake my home," Sodina replies. "This is my friend Bridget who hails from the Northern Kingdom. She has joined my husband and me on our travels. I have been cursed by the demon army, and we also seek an item to heal me. We did some research in Artemis. This research led us here in front of you. We seek to find the healing relic, and any guidance would be helpful."

Sodina and Bridget lift their heads.

"You may stand," Charlotte says. "What you seek is noble. I have heard of the destruction of the Eastern Kingdom and the death of the king. Others seek the same thing. I would like to help you. There is an important meeting happening tomorrow to decide what action to take. Since you, Sodina, hail from the Eastern Kingdom, you have a personal stake in the matter. We do have one guest quarter available. I would give you better than that, but the leaders of the other Kingdoms are coming in for the summit. This will be a closed summit, but I am permitting you special access in the overflow section. There will be others there that have a personal stake in the matter. You are to speak nothing of this event except with the people who are participating."

Queen Charlotte snaps her fingers. "One of my knights will show you to your sleeping quarters. The summit will start mid-day tomorrow after a breakfast feast in the morning. Do not be late. Good night." Charlotte waves as she leaves her chair, heading towards her quarters.

"This way, please," a knight says, guiding Sodina and Bridget out of the throne room and up a flight of stairs.

"The royal breakfast will start in the morning when the bell rings. Please be on time wearing something... more presentable."

Sodina looks down at her pants and boots, caked with mud from the journey.

"Okay," Sodina says quietly.

Lea walks out of her room, looking down the hallway. *We have guests.* Lea walks towards Chrono's room, where he and Sarah are talking.

people in the room down the hall." Lea whispers. "One of them looks really tough and is tall. She is wearing a sexy chainmail dress. So she has some money."

"You are a cautious one, Lea," Sarah giggles.

"They are probably here for the summit as well," Chrono explains. "Well, it's almost bath time, so I would think we can meet them there."

"See you tomorrow," Sarah giggles, kissing Chrono on the cheek.

"It sounds too good to be true," Chrono says, blushing while sharpening his sword.

Lea and Sarah grab their clothes and head for the bath at the end of the hallway.

"I saw someone down the hall," Sodina says. "She looked at you with a weird face like she was trying to figure out if we were here to cause trouble."

"Well, we can't please them all." Bridget winks. "Let's get out of these clothes and get a bath in."

Bridget and Sodina walk towards the bathroom at the end of the hallway. Walking in, Bridget and Sodina sit at the edge of the warm bath with towels wrapped around them.

Sodina looks over to Sarah.

"Aren't you the princess?" Sodina asks.

"Yes, and you are?" Sarah responds.

"I am Sodina from the city of Ifer, near Glashmere."

"You hail from the Eastern Kingdom as well. That makes us sisters." Sarah walks over to Sodina and gives her a big hug.

"We are here to find a plan to take back our home," Sodina explains.

"Sorry, but I can't help but join in the conversation," a woman says, waving to both of them. "Hi. I'm Lea. I was part of the archery corps, but those are no more. I am now an adventurer with Queen Sarah."

"The queen is dead. Or so we assume. We have yet to find my mother, so until then, I am in charge of my people," Sarah says, looking into the bathwater.

"What brings you to Lafare?" Sarah asks.

"There were three of us, but my husband is gone," Sodina explains. "We have no idea where he went. I fear that he went to fight off the demon empire alone. I don't know what got to him, but I pray every day that he is safe."

Sarah bows, saying a silent prayer.

"Well. We will take our home back, I am sure. We have hope, and soon with the Southern Kingdom wanting to back us we will rid our land of the demons," Sarah assures Sodina with a reaffirming smile.

The four ladies share stories of their journeys thus far, hopes, dreams, and fears. Hours pass until their skin gets clammy.

"I am going to need to get some lotion," Bridget giggles.

"Good night to you too. It has been a pleasure talking with you," Sarah waves, exiting the bath.

"We look forward to seeing you in the morning." Bridget and Sodina wave before getting dressed and returning to their respective rooms.

"Who knew the queen was that amazing person?" Bridget elbowed Sodina slowly.

"She is humble for sure," Sodina says. "To be put into a position of leadership that young would rattle some people, but we only have fifty people in our kingdom, so that's a great start."

"Start small and grow your way up." Bridget sighed. "That seems so far away."

Once they enter their room, they are surprised to see a couple of women inside.

"What is all of this?" Bridget stood there her mouth agape.

"I have been waiting here for hours," a woman bellowed. "We need to get you two fitted."

The two women rip off the clothes the others are wearing and start measuring their bodies.

"This dress will not do. You need to look your best for the queen." One of the maids shuffled around, turning Sodina in a circle.

"Get another one from the pile," the other woman yells.

"Just wait!" Bridget giggled, trying not to laugh. "I'm ticklish there."

Sodina gives in to the woman tugging her all about.

"Just don't pinch me on the butt cheeks," Sodina says, trying to resist laughing.

"Don't worry," the woman says. "We are almost done. Here we are. For you, dear, this dress will do."

Sodina is given a blue dress with white buttons down the back and white heels. Bridget is given a yellow dress with purple stripes.

The taller woman shuffled towards the door. "You two are going to look lovely in the morning. Don't be late!"

The women take their rolling closets and slam the door behind them.

"Oh, my goodness," Sodina gasps. "I feel violated. She rubbed every curve on my body."

"I must say, the dress does fit quite well even though it's a little snug around the bosoms." Bridget gave a quick twirl. "I like it though. I love how it makes me look curvier than ever."

"We need to get some rest." Sodina says.

"I wonder if the queen and Lea had to go through the same thing. If so, why did they not warn us? I will make sure they know of this tomorrow," Bridget says.

"Good night, my dear friend."

Bridget smiles, coming over to fist bump Sodina. Bridget falls asleep, immediately hitting the bed. *Is Slash dead? How come we cannot find any trace of him on this route? Please be okay.* Sodina closes her eyes for the night, tears streaming down her rosy cheeks.

Chapter 16

Month of Dragons
Day 25

Gareth walks down the long hallway leading to his prisoners' cells.

He puts his hand on the door and releases the magical seal, granting him entry.

"Wake up, human!" Gareth walks up to Slash, glaring down at him. Pulling his leg back, he barreled his foot into Slash's chest.

"Don't hurt him," Ella wails.

"Shut up, pest," Gareth snickers. "You are going on an adventure with me this morning, boy."

Slash groans as he is lifted into Gareth's arms.

"Hold on tight!" Gareth walks out of the room and flies out a window as the sun rises. How beautiful it was. *One thing I adore about living in this new castle is that I get to see the sunrise.*

Slash fades in and out of consciousness as they travel over the trees at least a hundred feet into the air.

Where is my wife? Slash tried to muster some amount of strength for a counterattack.

He knew if he did break Gareth's grip he would surely fall to his death. All he could do was to wait and see where Gareth was taking him. Trying to compose his thoughts, Slash passes out.

"We are here," Gareth says wickedly. "The Bridge of Eden."

Gareth pulls Slash's hair, yanking his neck back to wake him up. "This is one of your cultural landmarks, is it not?"

Slash pressed his lips closed, refusing to answer the Demon Lord.

"Answer me, boy," Gareth snarls, pulling Slash's hair back further.

Slash screams in pain. "Yes, it is!"

"Today, you get to witness my power. It is an honor to see my work, boy." Gareth holds out his free hand and chants slowly. "Dark matter!"

A purple ball of energy five feet in width leaves Gareth's hands and hits the center of the Bridge of Eden, causing a massive explosion. Slash heard the horrified screams of the people on the bridge who were trying to cross.

"You murderer!" Slash clenches his fist. "There were innocent people on that bridge!"

"Tsk, none of that matters." Gareth smacks Slash on the head. "Be a good human and watch death unfold. So beautiful, no?"

Gareth smiles, looking down at the chaos. The middle of the bridge collapses, leading hundreds of people to their deaths in the river below.

Slash thinks about squirming, but knows that more pain would come his way if he did.

"If the fire wasn't lit, it is now," Gareth says quietly. He turns around, leaving a hole of destruction in his wake and heading back towards Glashmere.

"I hope you enjoyed that display of power, boy," Gareth says to Slash, who is weak in his hands. "I will bathe this world in darkness. The Goddess does not care at all for you humans, yet you worship her blindly. This world will be mine before you know it. You can build bridges, castles, and anything you want. Nothing can stop my power."

Slash was silent as they flew over the forest. Gareth kept yapping away.

"If the angels and goddesses are still around, I will find the city of Arcadia if it still exists. If it does, I will find it and bring those angels down to our realm. I will take the city for my own and slay every heavenly thing. All shall bow beneath my heel. How do you like that, boy?" Gareth looks down at Slash, awaiting a response.

Slash ignores the question completely.

"You don't have to answer that," says Gareth, "But just know anyone who tries to rescue you will die a miserable death. Your existence will prove useful because, apparently, someone loves you. You would not be fighting so hard to make it if it was not. You will be back to your cage soon, boy." Gareth speeds back toward Glashmere, the wind ripping around them.

* * *

Back in the Lafare palace, the morning breakfast was quiet and full of tension. A room full of royalty and commonfolk sat around the table.

Queen Charlotte walks towards the front of the table. "Please eat your fill because this food was made with love."

The Queen, noticing the tension in the room, tries to calm everyone's hearts with her words but everyone was left unphased.

"I, for one, will not turn down a good meal, Your Majesty," Bridget says before digging into her plate of french toast and coffee.

King Leo glares down the table disapprovingly.

"You peasants," King Leo says under his breath.

"Now, King Leo, do not dishonor my guests," Queen Charlotte says sternly.

"I would never, Your Highness," Leo says, cutting his eyes toward both Charlotte and Queen Victoria from the Western Kingdom.

Queen Victoria, who's shade of brown was darker than Queen Charlotte's, leans over to grab a banana from the bowl of fruits in front of her. Her flowing silk white dress magnified her beauty tenfold. A large diamond ring decorates her right index finger. "You know this is the first time the leadership has met like this in a long while. I assume you are well, Princess Sarah."

"It's Queen Sarah now," Charlotte responded.

"We have yet to locate the queen," Sarah says quietly.

"You leave a child in charge," Leo says sharply. "No wonder the kingdom is in disarray. I would have stormed the gates already."

"I am not a child, Your Majesty," Sarah spits. "I am a completely capable noble woman. You will do well to watch your mouth."

Chrono, who is beside her, slips his hand over hers under the table to calm her down. King Leo scoffs and takes a turkey leg to chomp down on, adverting his eyes from her gaze.

Breakfast passed quickly and everyone enjoyed the meal, small chatter lighting up the room to Queen Charlotte's delight.

With tension still in the room, everyone heads to the Royal Court Room to discuss more pressing matters at hand.

Charlotte leads everyone as she thinks to herself. *If we were to take Leo prisoner today, that would be a declaration of war. But a declaration of war was already at hand due to him killing the Eastern Kingdom messenger.*

Only Queen Sarah and I know that. I have yet to inform Queen Victoria, but she may already know.

Charlotte walks up to a chair that is slightly elevated above the others. She thought she would play it by ear as there was a sizable audience.

Charlotte stands to address the group. "As you know, the situation in our land has become dire. There is great turmoil with the Eastern Kingdom falling. Princess Sarah has become a queen, and there are few survivors from this tragedy. We have also learned that the demonic empire is progressing, destroying the smaller towns in the Eastern Kingdom. It will be only a matter of time before they launch an all-out assault on the other kingdoms. The Southern Kingdom is the closest to this situation. The mountains and the desert separate the Northern and Western Kingdoms."

"What will you have us do in this situation, dear Charlotte?" Victoria asks.

"I believe all the kingdoms should unite and take out the threat quickly before they have the chance to bolster their forces," Charlotte responds with no hesitation. "Your help would be much needed during this time."

Leo coughs, "While what happened to Glashmere was a horrible tragedy, why should I risk my kingdom's lives to help you?"

The Northern King eyes Sarah. "Your father was soft, thus he was killed."

"Wait just a minute," Chrono stands up. "You have always been abrasive, King Leo. We should work together and listen first instead of creating strife."

"War Master is a term given to a meathead that can only fight," Leo scoffs. "You are no strategic mastermind, Chrono. You are a young knight who is only good at fighting."

"Hold your tongue now, Leo," Charlotte snaps at him.

"We will lend you no forces," Leo says, "But I will give you a small offering of five thousand gold coins from our reserves. Use them however you like."

Leo leans back in his chair, losing interest in this meeting every second.

"Thank you," Sarah says, offering her best royal smile to Leo, even if he was an annoying git.

Leo ignores her gaze as he continues. "I only contribute to preventing all-out war."

"That is gracious of you, King Leo," Charlotte explains. "What say you, dear Victoria?"

"I will give you five thousand of my best soldiers and ten thousand gold coins, but it will take some time to gather the necessary forces," Victoria says. "Please give me time to build this up for you. I need to ensure that our borders are protected as well. I have a duty to my people."

"Thank you so much," Sarah says, and chatter erupts at the table in awe of the Western Queen's generous gift. Queen Victoria smiles and nods.

"Though," Victoria starts, eyeing Leo from her seat, "I have heard a rumor lately. There may be a traitor in—"

"Queen Charlotte!" A knight runs in, yelling at the top of his lungs. "The Bridge… The Bridge of Eden has been attacked. The whole bridge has all but collapsed!"

"What?!" Charlotte runs past the chairs and table where everyone was sitting.

Everyone looks at the knight, awaiting answers.

"Do we know who did it? How many deaths?" Charlotte asks frantically. The whole room grew tense again with anticipation.

The knight bows his head sadly. "Some eyewitnesses say they saw a man floating above and shooting purple rays towards the middle of the bridge, Your Majesty. It could be... hundreds of souls lost."

"Astra, have mercy!" Victoria gasps.

Leo smirks slightly and Birdget catches his grin.

He knew this was going to happen somehow. Bridget crossed her arms, cutting her eyes at the muscle-bound king.

"This summit is done for today," Charlotte says. "Feel free to stay here, esteemed leaders. Queen Victoria, you have the most extended trip home. I would get to your people quickly. We will be sending messengers to each kingdom."

"King Leo, I need passage through the mountains if that is possible," Victoria asks.

"Do as you see fit, you will have safe passage through the kingdom," Leo responds, not meeting her gaze.

"Everyone, be on high alert and watch for any out of the ordinary activity!" Charlotte orders her men as they scatter away. "As of right now, we are at war with whoever destroyed our bridge!"

"Any act of aggression will be met with swift action, boys," Charlotte says. "I pray Astra protects us all."

Charlotte walks out with Captain Robert hurriedly, already zipping out orders.

Leo gets up to leave, but Victoria grabs his arm and pulls him in close.

"If you are sleeping with the demonic empire Leo, I will kill you myself the next time I see you," Victoria says quietly yet intently.

"Is that a threat, Vicky? Careful with your words," Leo pulls his arm away and heads out the room, throwing his coat over his shoulders arrogantly.

Bridget walks up to Queen Victoria who is left scowling at the door with Sodina close behind her.

"I think he is up to something," Bridget tells her. "He cracked a smile when he heard the bridge collapsed."

Victoria takes a deep breath before answering. "I believe that he is up to something, but all we have is a letter from his son stating he murdered an Eastern Kingdom envoy. I wanted to gut him where he stood, but that would cause more harm than good."

"That's right, Your Majesty," Bridget replies.

Victoria sighs at Bridget. "I really must get going. Please watch over yourselves."

Bridget watches as Victoria walks away with five of her knights to depart for the Western Kingdom.

Sarah walks over to Bridget, Sodina, Lea, and Chrono.

"I cannot help but think of all of those innocent people who lost their lives," the young queen says.

Silence falls between the five of them. Sodina whispers a small prayer to Goddess Astra, the events of the meeting feeling heavy over her shoulders.

"I believe that fate has brought us all together," Chrono says. "We must unite and take down this evil. We need to find Charlotte and ask her about those legendary items you spoke of last night."

"We have no idea what the thing does, Chrono," Lea says. "It could be a sword, plant, or there could be nothing there at all."

They head to the hallway to find Charlotte thinking intently.

"Queen Charlotte, we have something to ask you," Sodina says.

"What is it, dear?" Charlotte looks at them.

"We are seeking an item that could help us sway the battle in our favor," Chrono says. "When Bridget and I were in Artemis…"

"There was a legend of an item that could heal poison or give strength," Bridget explains. "We figure the individuals that wrote the books have long since passed. The text was old, but if there is any hope to help us on our journey we would appreciate your guidance."

Charlotte pinches the bridge of her nose and sighs. "You are speaking of what we call the Trials of Heroes. Legend has it that there are specific landmarks that present those that pass the trial with what they desire most. It is said that only the strongest in strength and mind can complete these trials. In the Age of Heroes, there was a dark lord named Helion that was able to complete the trails due to his immense strength. He used the items granted from the trails to plunge humanity into the First Great War. Ever since Helion was defeated, the trails have been attempted, but none have returned. According to history books, there is the Valley of Sorrows, the Cave of Remedy, and the Tree of Woe. Legend has it that each one is guarded by one of the legendary hero's comrades. Only fools would attempt these trials. If you genuinely want to go, then I cannot stop you. Your first stop should be the Valley of Sorrows, which is north of here. Hopefully, you will find what you are looking for."

"Thank you, Queen Charlotte." Sodina shakes her hand.

"Please be careful, young ones," Charlotte says, walking away.

"The queen is really quite amazing," Sodina says to her group.

"We have our destination. If it's a fight the demonic army wants, it will be a fight they get," Bridget exclaims and puts her fist in the air.

"I hope we find the item needed to heal me," Sodina whispers quietly.

"Maybe this trial will give us multiple items, Sodina," Chrono smiles.

"We won't know until we try," Bridget adds, patting her friend on the back gently.

Sarah looks intensely at Chrono. "My love, this is a dangerous journey. I think it may be best that I head back to Mala and be with our people."

Chrono reaches to stroke her cheek and says, "I believe that it is best as well. We should head out to the Valley of Sorrows tomorrow then."

Sarah leans into his touch and smiles. Sodina watches them with a little pang of jealousy. She missed her husband so much in that moment. *Slash, you are fool at times. How could you leave me?*

"I think we take today to grieve those that were lost," Lea says.

The group of five nod in unison and walk out of the palace, towards the front of the castle.

"The sun is shining brightly today, but it's raining," Sarah says, looking up at the sky. The tears start flowing from her cheeks. Chrono hugs her from behind.

Sodina starts to cry too, thinking about Slash and where he might be.

My dear husband, I miss you deeply, she thinks to herself.

"Okay, let's go get some supplies and rest," Bridget states to cut the moment. "We have an intense journey ahead of us."

The group of five go out to various shops around town and buy the appropriate items needed. The hours pass quickly from shopping and spending time together.

The sun goes down, bringing the evening stars into view.

"We are perfectly prepared for the trip tomorrow!" Bridget smiles as they all meet up in front of the castle.

"Guys, I am going to sit out here and admire the stars for a bit," Lea says. "See you in a bit, okay?"

Lea pulls out her copy of the Gospel of Astra and sits on a nearby bench. Sodina sees and nears her shyly.

"May I join you, Lea?" Sodina asks. "We don't have to talk or anything…"

"I would like that, Lady Sodina," Lea says, and pats the empty seat next to her. Sodina bows and joins her, praying her own spontaneous prayer alongside the young archer.

The rest of the group walks up to their rooms.

Chrono walks into his room and starts to close his door when Sarah puts a hand out to stop him.

"Chrono," Sarah says quietly, "Do you have a moment, love?"

"Of course, Sarah," Chrono replies, "Please come in."

Sarah walks into Chrono's room and closes the door behind her. Chrono stands by the edge of his bed, waiting for the Queen's next move.

"I want to make something clear to you," Sarah approaches him, pointing a finger at his chest. "Do not go dying on me, Chrono, do you hear me?"

Chrono takes her hand and pulls her in for a tight hug.

She sniffs, hugging him tighter and says, "I want you to promise me that you will not die on me. I would not be able to bear it."

"I promise, my love." Chrono kisses her hair and pulls away from her slowly. "We need to get some rest. I need to take you to Mala in the morning."

"No need to," Sarah says. "I already made arrangements to be escorted by two of Queen Charlotte's finest knights."

Chrono shakes his head. "Of course you did."

He turns away from her to pack his small leather bag with clothes. He keeps his sword by his bed. Sarah watches him quietly and starts to remove her gown and strips off her undergarments.

The War Master turns towards her again to find Sarah completely bare for him. His jaw drops a little and she throws her head back in laughter.

Chrono keeps his gaze up at her face, "S-Sarah, I—"

"Oh, hush, my love," Sarah slinks up to Chrono and wraps her arms around him. He immediately slips his hands down to feel her soft skin.

Sarah kisses Chrono, her lips pressing firmly against his. "We will make love until dawn War Master, and that's an order from your queen."

Chrono answers without hesitation. "Your wish is my command, Your Majesty."

* * *

Outside, Lea looks up to the sky, looking silently at the stars.

I wonder if we are going to make it, the young archer thinks to herself.

Sodina looks at Lea, wondering what she was thinking.

"I think we should not stay out here too long," Sodina says to her friend beside her.

"You know, Lady Sodina," Lea sighs. "I am scared. I have no magic like you. I never could learn it. I can only shoot arrows and I have tremendous agility."

"That is what makes a great knight and assassin," Sodina moves to comfort Lea.

"This quest where we could be in real danger to take down an unknown enemy..." Lea crosses her arms. "Do we have what it takes?"

"I—"

"And your husband is missing! Are you mad at him? He could with another woman!" Lea waves her arms around. "If I were you, Sodina, I would be looking for him, not worrying about some trial."

"He could be doing all sorts of things." The thought never crossed her mind that Slash was tired of caring for her. "The thing is, I am not strong enough on my own. I am becoming weaker each day," Sodina explains. "I miss him, but I have a feeling that we will cross paths soon. I trust him with my whole heart."

Lea opens the Gospel of Astra and turns to the first page of the second chapter, beginning to recite. "When facing trials, it is essential to remember your faith. In the darkest of moments look to the stars…"

"And Astra will fill you with joy," Sodina finishes for Lea. "She is with us always."

"Don't look at me," Lea says quietly. "I am an ugly crier."

Sodina slides closer to Lea and leans on her.

"Keep the faith, my friend," Sodina says to the young woman next to her. "We'll get through this together."

"Together," Lea repeats. "I like that."

The two women stand and hold hands as they make their way back to their rooms in the palace to rest before their long journey.

Chapter 17

Month of Dragons
Day 26

The moon glistened as Gareth stood on the balcony of the former king's room. The lush purple chair invited him as he sat and opened the Gospel of Astra.

"The Gospel of Filth should be a more fitting title," Gareth scoffs. "To think my ancestors worshiped that joke of a goddess."

"Hello there." Lisha walks in and rubs Gareth back.

"Not now, Lisha. I am thinking about what the next move shall be for us. We have taken almost all of the Eastern Kingdom. Besides, I have destroyed the primary connection between the Southern and Eastern Kingdoms. Everything is going according to plan."

"Why not take some time and spend it with me?" Lisha winks.

"I have another mission for you. There is a legendary tree called the Tree of Woe that sits near the border of the Southern Kingdom. There exists a path that is dangerous for most humans. I would like you to guard that area in the near future."

"You want me to defend a stupid tree?" Lisha sighs. "Well, I have no idea why, but I will do what you say. I want to be rewarded for this. I want you and nothing else."

"If there is time, yes, we will be together for a while." Gareth smiles.

"Well, I will be on my way." Lisha walks up and kisses Gareth on the cheek before walking out of the room.

I wonder if he truly cares for me or the mission at hand. It's probably nothing. Lisha stretches walking out of the castle, and flies into the sky heading towards the Tree of Woe.

* * *

Charlotte walks down the stairwell towards the kitchen. "I guess I am late." Charlotte looks at everyone who is setting out on the journey to the Valley of Sorrows. "I do have news for all of you. A thick purple fog has been spotted near the Bridge of Eden. We do not know if the fog will cross over the gap and proceed near Mala. Until then, I would steer clear."

"What about the Tree of Woe?" Lea asks. "We need to get there immediately."

"I hope that you will find a way," Charlotte replies. "As of right now, it seems all but impossible to get there."

"Something will come up," Chrono adds.

"I trust that Astra will guide us," Lea assures.

Charlotte nods and smiles.

"I must be off. Please do take care. You have our full backing. Once our army is ready, we will launch a full assault on the demonic empire." Charlotte smiles, walking away.

The group finishes their breakfast and heads out the castle.

Queen Sarah grips Chrono's face, kissing him on the cheek.

"I will see you soon, Chrono," she says. "Please be safe until we see each other again."

"Queen Sarah, if you will, kindly follow us," a knight says.

One of the knights put Sarah on the back of his horse.

"Please do watch after her," Chrono requests.

"You worry too much, silly." Sarah winks.

"Do not worry, War Master," the knight replies. "The queen is safe with us."

The knight nods as they go off into the distance. The group waves until Sarah disappears from their sight.

"We should get a move on," Chrono says.

Lea looks over at Chrono. "I know you miss her, Chrono. Though I have only known you for a short time, this much is true. Annabelle was close to you. That horse was with you since you could ride. You have to keep moving forward. You have a special someone you must get back to, so journey with us and focus on the task ahead." *Does anyone want me? This journey to help Sodina may help me to find my place in this world. My true calling.* Lea fixed her eyes on the ground, questioning if this was the best choice for her.

Chrono nods, looking at the sky. "Let us ride!"

The group rides their horses and head towards the north.

The Valley of Sorrows, Bridget thinks to herself. *I wonder what is in store for us.*

"Time is of the essence, friends," Chrono says, riding from the front and leading them towards the cliffs and paths ahead.

The cliffs and ledges lead the group up and down for hours until they reach a hill leading down into what appears to be a thick fog.

"Where did this fog come from?" Lea says. "I can't see a thing."

"I think it would be wise if we stopped for a bit" Bridget suggests.

The group gets off their horses, trying to ascertain their location.

"The map shows that we could be closing in on the valley any moment, but I think we should stop, Chrono," Bridget says. "This is getting a bit eerie."

"Who dares walks on this hallowed ground?" A loud deep voice bellows.

Chrono draws his sword, scanning the area.

"You would be wise to leave this place. All who enter shall fade to nothingness," the voice threatens.

"Show yourself, fiend. We fear nothing, not even death!" Chrono yells.

The voice leaves all of their ears and silence once again envelops them.

"I'm tired after riding all day," Lea sighs.

After the group gets off their horses, the horses turn around and run away.

"Wait, come back!" Chrono yells. "Ahh, dang it. They got away."

"We have no idea what time of day it is since the fog is so thick," Sodina explains. "Judging by how long we have been travelling, it must be near evening or so. It feels as almost if we are in a timeless void."

The group of four sit around, resting for a bit.

"I will take the first shift," Chrono offers. "You three get some rest."

Chrono scans intently into the fog, his sword right in front of him, ready to strike anything that would come at them.

An hour passed and all that is heard are the quiet snores of his companions.

"You will never be enough for her," an eerie female voice whispers into his ear.

"Wicked monster, you will never break me." Chrono closes his eyes to focus.

"Oh, but I will," the voice says. "What will happen if the demons make it to Mala, and you are not there to protect her? The monsters will have their way with her and rip her from limb to limb. Her screams will fill their ears with glee. You will be able to do nothing about it."

"Enough with this trickery, foul beast," Chrono says, standing.

An image of Sarah appears before Chrono, being killed gruesomely by a solem.

"You fiend, don't touch her!" Chrono runs towards the solem, but it disappears.

Looking back, Chrono sees nothing but fog.

"Wait, oh shoot." Chrono sighs. *I lost them. I let my emotions get the best of me. I guess there is nothing left to do than press forward.*

"Why did you kill me?" A child appears before Chrono. "Why did you kill me?" The child asks again.

Chrono stands stunned, looking at the child. "This cannot be. What trickery is this?"

"Why did you k—" The boy screams, interrupted by a loud ringing.

"You were a threat to his Majesty, the king!" Chrono bellows. "We received intel that the group of bandits would be using a child to attack the king. The king was always kind to his people, being in close contact with them. You had a knife and were going to stab the king."

"That is no reason," the child yells. "You are a murderer, Chrono. You think so highly of yourself but you're nothing but a cold-blooded murderer."

"Stop it," Chrono demands. "I am no murderer!"

MURDERER MURDERER MURDERER

KILL YOURSELF KILL YOURSELF KILL YOURSELF

"Stop! Please stop!" Chrono feels his legs tremble, shaking wildly.

MURDERER MURDERER MURDERER

KILL YOURSELF KILL YOURSELF KILL YOURSELF

Chrono steps back, tripping over a skeleton. He stumbles on the ground as he tries to look for his sword in the fog. The voice continues to blast him, now with a louder echo.

KILL YOURSELF CHRONO

FALL UPON YOUR SWORD

MURDERER MURDERER

YOUR BLOOD FOR MINE

Chrono runs away from the child, covering his ears and screaming.

"Get away from me!" Chrono screams. "Get out of my head!" Chrono kneels, panting as he violently rolls around on the floor, screaming for the voices to stop. *I am the most wicked of them all. How can I call myself a War Master if I have innocent blood on my hands?*

Sarah appears before Chrono, kneeling in front of him.

"Come on, love. Kill yourself and the pain will stop," Sarah says.

Chrono felt his eyes water. "But— I can't— I-I-I can't—"

"You killed a young boy and had relations with me. You think I could love a man like that? You are filth, Chrono, I'd want to see you dead rather than alive," Sarah laughs. "What makes you think a royal like me would lie with a lowly person like you? You are filth! Dung! The ground where I wipe my heels. No one will ever love you, Chrono. Kill yourself now and save us all the trouble."

Chrono looks at Sarah with tears in his eyes.

"Do you really think that of me?" Chrono bows his head, taking out his sword and raising it in the air.

"Kill yourself, insect. You are worth nothing."

"Very well." Chrono raises his sword up in the air. "Farwell, sweet world. I go to Astra's bosom."

"Yes, yes, yes. Hurry up already!" Sarah eyes glowed dark red.

"I will, my love," Chrono screams. "I will!"

"Did you hear that?" Bridget shoots up. "Where is Chrono? Wake up, you two!"

"What happened?" Sodina asks, wiping her eyes.

"Chrono is gone, and I heard a scream," Bridget explains. "Chrono, can you hear me? I swear I just heard him just now. Come grab your belongings and look for him. He might be in trouble."

"What is that smell?" Lea asks. "It smells like old garbage left out in the sun."

"Keep your wits about you," Bridget proclaims. "The fog can hide creatures of any size."

The trio walks ahead, slowing watching their step.

"Did you hear that rustle?" Lea whispers. "What was that?"

"Weapons out ladies!" Bridget commands. "Looks like we have company."

The three of them take out their weapons, circling around each other's back.

The silence fills the air as the group moves forward at a steady pace.

"You are worthless," a bellowing voice snickered.

"What was that?" Bridget asks.

The voice spoke again. "Shut up, whore. You know yourself that you're nothing but a man's plaything, nothing more."

"I am not worthless," Bridget yells, pointing her axe to the fog. "You take that back, lest you feel the tip of my axe on your neck."

"You don't even know what you're fighting for, whore. I know your past and you will never escape that," the voice echoed softly.

Bridget snickered, "You know nothing."

"You feel dirty! You wear that chainmail dress to feel sexy. Deep down, you are a wounded child stuck in your adolescence."

"Stop it," Bridget mutters.

DIRTY WHORE DIRTY WHORE

KILL YOURSELF KILL YOURSELF

Bridget puts her hands to her ears and cries. The voice continues to echo the painful memories from Bridget's past.

"You have to fight it, Bridget," says Lea. "I think the voice is attacking us from different angles, trying to distort our thinking us. Resist everyone."

The voice spoke softly into Sodina's ears. "Your husband is dead, and I know it for sure."

"Huh?" Sodina felt a chill come over her body.

Sodina looks out into the distance and sees Slash with his neck snapped and a sword impaled on his back.

"Do not say such things," Sodina commands, pushing her hands out. "Illuminate!" A ray of light pierces through the fog, revealing a path lined by dead tropical trees. "This way!"

Lea and Sodina run towards the path.

"Bridget, what are you doing?" Lea yells.

Bridget kneels on the ground and takes out her ax, lifting it above her head, ready to strike it down on herself.

"Don't do it!" Lea yells. "You are loved!"

Lea pulls out her crossbow and shoots it at Bridget, deflecting the axe before it hits her.

"Leave me alone!" Bridget yells, lifting her ax again to finish the deed.

Lea runs, shooting another arrow, stopping the attack.

"Snap out of it!" Lea yells, slapping Bridget in the face. Bridget's face turns bright red from the sharp slap and tears stream down her face. She drops her ax.

"I am nothing more than a whore," Bridget sobs. "Why won't you let me atone?"

Bridget looks up at Lea.

"Let me atone!" Bridget yells at the top of her lungs. Bridget looks down and grabs her ax. "If you don't let me atone, then you will pay the price."

Bridget stands up and swings her ax towards Lea. Lea dodges swiftly to the left. Bridget swings upward, aimed at Lea's neck. Lea steps back, does a backflip and lands on the ground. Lea shoots two arrows towards Bridget. Bridget cuts one of the arrows in midair and takes another to her shoulder.

Bridget pulls out the arrow from the chainmail. "You will pay for that!"

Sodina runs back towards Bridget.

"Please stop, Bridget. Goddess Astra, give me strength." Sodina starts to chant a spell but feels dizzy and leans against a tree. "Not now, please. I need the strength."

Sodina looks out to see Slash's body being beaten by a giant troll, crushed by his club.

"No, don't kill him," Sodina whispers. "We have yet to have any children."

Sodina falls to the ground, passing out as her vision grows dim.

"Sodina!" Lea looks over at Sodina on the ground. "Bridget, you big breasted maniac, stop fighting me."

Bridget throws her ax towards Lea. Lea ducks down as the ax hits a tree. Bridget barrels towards Lea, her fist clenched.

The voice speaks in her head. "Yes, kill her. She hates you and everything about you."

Lea throws her bow to the ground and puts her arm up to block the blow but is pushed backwards into a tree.

"I'm surprised you took one of my punches." Bridget leaned back shifting her body to the left. Bridget dashes towards Lea and knees her in the chest before lifting her by the neck.

"Hearing your neck snap will do my heart well, worthless wench," Bridget says with a twisted smile, her eyes glowing purple.

Lea tries to lift her arm to punch but loses strength. *Sodina, please wake up.* Lea closes her eyes as she feels her body growing cold.

Bridge smiled, licking her lips. "Time to die—"

A wooden sword hits Bridget in the back, knocking the breath out of her.

"Augh," Bridget yells, letting go of on Lea.

Bridget turns around to see Chrono standing, sword in hand.

"Lea tends to Sodina," Chrono says.

Lea runs behind Chrono toward Sodina lying on the ground.

"I will knock some sense back into you," Chrono says. "This beast, or whatever is hidden in the fog, is taking our weaknesses and turning us against ourselves and each other. Wake up, Bridget!"

Bridget looks at Chrono and smiles.

"I am awake, Chrono. I see that you are no different from Lea in your decision making," she says, running towards Chrono.

"You leave me no choice then." Chrono stands with one leg in front of the other, ready for her attack.

Bridget punches towards his head. Chrono blocks with his sword and smacks her in the gut.

"Aghh," Bridget grunts.

Bridget shakes it off, delivering two rapid punches at Chrono stomach. Chrono jumps back and hits Bridget twice in each knee with force.

Bridget wobbles a bit and gains her composure.

"War Dance!" Chrono breathes in rapidly, increasing his speed and runs towards Bridget. He slams his sword's hilt between her eyes, knocking her out.

Chrono quickly turns and catches her before she falls to the ground.

"I know that voice was hard to resist," Chrono whispers. "Rest now, friend."

Chrono lifts Bridget on his back. "Oh boy, she is heavy."

Sodina sits up after minutes of Lea shaking her to wake up.

"Thank goodness you're okay," Lea smiles.

"Is the path still open?" Sodina mutters.

"Yes, your magic was powerful enough to dispel the fog blocking the way," Lea says cheerfully.

"We should rest there before proceeding," Chrono says.

The group of four continues into the passage cutting through the trees.

Upon further inspection it appears to be a bridge of some sort, but without the water, Lea looks up at the stone above them. Chrono lays Bridget on the ground.

"I will keep her company," Sodina walks over to Bridget and puts her head in her lap.

"I never knew you had two swords on you, Chrono," Lea says to Chrono.

"I keep a wooden sword on me for training and non-lethal attacks. I am thankful I had it on me."

"They must be guarding something of high value here." Chrono scratches his chin.

"They almost had us there. I had virtually no will power to resist." Lea looks at Chrono.

"I did not have it as bad as you. I think because I studied the Gospel of Astra, I was shielded from the demon's attacks. Not saying you are a terrible person, but I have read the Gospel of Astra and prepared my mind mentally for any trial. I am glad all of that reading came in handy," Lea smirks.

Chrono looks at Lea, puzzled and shaking his head, keeping his mouth shut.

"You think you have won?" The voice beckons. "But you are nothing but spiders waiting to be squished!"

"I'll kill you!" Bridget shoots up, almost hitting Sodina. "Oh, I am so sorry, Chrono and Lea."

Bridget sits up and pats Chrono on the back and goes to hug Lea. "I had no control over myself. That voice spoke into the depths of my soul with conviction. It wanted me to enjoy killing. It was awful. The voice preyed on my emotions and memories."

Chrono nods in agreement. "Yes, whatever and whoever this evil force is, it can see into the hearts of man."

Sodina stands up. "We should be on our way."

The group takes a moment to drink some water and walk towards the end of the bridge.

"Careful now," Chrono says, walking with his sword held upfront.

The fogs start to clear as a dual stone stairway appears. The group walks up the stairs cautiousl, into a lair made of stone. Three chests appear out of thin air in front of them.

"I am Serena!" A voice calls to them. "The Great Healer from the Age of Heroes. My friends and I defeated the Dark Lord Helion. Your reward awaits, brave adventures."

"Reward?" Bridget asks. "You mean—"

"Please choose a chest, and I will escort you out of the Valley of Sorrows."

"Not on your life," Bridget says. "We have no idea what you say is accurate. For all that we know, these chests could kill us or transport us to another area."

"HAHAHA!" The voice laughs. "Foolish children of Astra, you are too damn smart for your own good."

A black dragon, ten feet tall with a book in his hand, flies down out of the fog.

"This will not do. You did not fall for my enchantment. I have orders to kill all of those who would interfere with Gareth's plans. Prepare to face the wrath of Finos, The Black Nightmare, and one of the Seven Sentinels of the Dark Order."

Finos spreads out his wings and hovers above the ground. His yellow eyes are pierced with hate as he glances at the heroes before him.

"He can fly, he'll be difficult to fight," Lea whispers.

Sodina closes her eyes and starts to chant.

"I have twenty arrows left and some elemental ones as well, but I'd rather not use those. I suggest an all-out attack," Chrono says, winking at Bridget.

Bridget lifts Chrono on her back, pushing off her shoulders he leaps towards Fino's sword in hand. Chrono swings his sword at Finos's face, but he blocks with his claw and grabs Chrono by the neck.

"Die, human," Finos roars, leaning towards Chrono.

Lea shoots an arrow into Fino's wing, narrowly missing as Finos dodges and drops Chrono. Bridget catches Chrono before he crashes on the ground.

"I got you there, buddy."

She runs towards Finos and throws her ax like a boomerang towards his neck. Finos dodges the ax and dives towards Lea.

Lea shoots Finos, hitting his left eye. Finos bucks wildly, staying put on the ground. Lea jumps in his face, takes the arrow out and stabs him again.

"Persistent little bug." Finos violently shakes his head, tossing Lea into the rock wall.

Lea stands up, slowly surveying the situation. Breathing heavily, she pulls out an enchanted ice arrow. Lea focuses, draws her bow, and lets the arrow go.

Finos, seeing the arrow, dodges to the left. The arrow hits the wall, creating a jagged area of ice.

"Tricky, human," Finos says. "Only a fool would fall for that trick."

Lea falls to her knees, breathing heavily. Bridget jumps towards Finos, swings her axe down, cutting off his tail.

"You witch!" He yells, turning around, swiping his claws at Bridget.

Bridget puts up her ax, deflecting one blow as the other strike hits her in the chest. Bridget is pushed back ten feet as blood drips from her wound.

"Ugh." Bridget breaths heavily as she feels the deep cut. Bridget licks the blood from her finger and smiles. "It's been a while since I've killed a dragon."

"Dare not t think I am just any regular dragon, arrogant witch." Finos smiles. "Now prepare yourself!"

Finos flaps his wings and flies towards Chrono, grabbing him, dragging him across the ground and crashing into the wall. Chrono spits up blood from the attack. Finos then punches Chrono the chest, lifts him in the air, and slams him down.

Bridget runs towards Finos and punches him in the face. Finos flies up in the air and dives towards Bridget. Bridget dodges to the left and punches Finos again. Finos flinches and flies back.

"I've heard about you. Woman," Finos says, wiping the blood from his mouth. "I heard you killed a dragon for your cloak."

"That's right," Bridget says. "It wasn't easy, but it was definitely worth it."

"Wipe that smile off your face," Finos yells. "I will burn all of you, sending your souls to Astra this very instant."

"Caperous Aiera!" Sodina shouts, pointing her staff toward the air above her.

Finos flies towards the top of the lair but suddenly slams into an invisible barrier, knocking him off balance. The beast tries to flap his wings, but he flails around.

"What was that?"

Lea looks at her three friends. "Take this!"

Lea sits up and shoots an ice arrow towards Finoss' torso.

"No one can defeat me!" Finos opens his mouth, cackling with fiery embers.

POOF

He tries to breath out fire, but it fizzles.

"What the—" Finos's upper body starts to freeze as he tries to move about.

"Time to end this." Sodina runs toward Fino. "Goddess Hammer!"

A hammer of light manifests from her staff and slams into Finos's chest, shattering his body in a thousand pieces.

Chrono stands up, holding his arm as Lea, Sodina, and Bridget walk towards him. They all hug and smile.

"We did it, everyone." Exhausted, Sodina smiles, falling to the ground.

Lea runs over to Sodina. She sits down, laying Sodina's head in her lap. "I knew we could." Lea looks up. "Thank you, Astra."

"You did well, Children of Astra," a female voice calmly speaks.

A ball of light descends from the sky, floating above them.

"This used to be a shrine dedicated to me, Serena, but Gareth and his dark magic twisted this place and put that wicked dragon in charge. My soul could not depart entirely to the other side without knowing this place was safe. I did not have enough power to do anything. All I could do was watch as countless humans killed themselves, trying to get to a false treasure. It was one of the worst things to endure. You, dear children, have done it. I sense a sincere desire for healing among one of you. Please step forward." Sodina sits up looking nervous, but steps forward.

"You, child, carry a heavy burden." Serena says.

Sodina nods.

"I know what you seek, and maybe this will help you."

Out of thin air, a small seed appears.

"This seed is called Light's bane. It is a seed from long ago, with healing properties even mysterious to us. Use it well."

Lea looks at the ball of light. "I have a question."

"Dear child, my time is up, but all your questions will be answered soon enough. Extinguish the darkness," Serena whispers.

A brilliant light surrounds the group.

Bridget wakes up, lying on the ground, to see a beautiful lake lying in front of her with a stone walkway leading to a monument.

"Where did the valley go?" She asks.

The rest of the group sits up and, to their amazement, see the same sight.

"What happened?" Chrono wonders.

"I think that that lake is where the valley is," Lea says.

The morning sun shines brilliantly as birds start to chirp. Sodina pulls out the seed from her pocket.

"Today we gain some ground back for the human race. Wherever you are Slash, I am going to find you. We are going to kill this poison within me together!"

The group sits up laughing about how they barely made it alive, and they start to walk towards the stone monument.

"Thank you, Serena!" The group yells, as they head back.

"We have no horses, so it's going to be a long way back to Lafare."

Sodina lets out a whistle but none of the horses appear before them.

The group saunters back towards the town of Lafare where not a soul is in sight. Chrono looks out towards the sky.

"I cannot walk anymore. We need to rest," Chrono complains, panting. "We are still not 100 percent from that fight."

Chrono falls to the ground on his face. Sodina stops and pulls out some water and puts the bottle towards his mouth.

"Hopefully, someone will come by soon. Walking all the way back injured is no way to travel."

Bridget looks out as the sun starts to go down.

"It looks like we are sleeping underneath the stars."

Bridget wraps her cloak around herself as the four huddle on the ground together for warmth.

"Even though we are in the Southern Kingdom, it can still get a little chilly at night," Lea says.

The group tries to cover themselves underneath Bridget's coat, just barely fitting.

"Good night, everyone," Chrono says, falling asleep.

"I don't find this awkward at all," Lea whispers to herself as she falls asleep.

Sodina starts to fall asleep but hears a voice in her mind. *Dear child, you are destined for greater things than you know.* Sodina smiles, feeling as if she was spoken to by an angel or Astra herself.

"Thank you," Sodina whispers before falling asleep.

Chapter 18

Month of Dragons
Day 27

The darkness of the room was pierced by a sliver of moonlight as Slash fixed his gaze on the large but lackluster goddess sitting across from him.

"You are from all of those years ago." Slash pulls his arms up in anger but is chained to the ground. "What good would it do anyway?"

Ella is silent and doesn't turn her attention to Slash as he continues.

"I assume it was you who gave me some sort of refuge with your healing…" Slash grumbles. "I have a question. Why didn't you sense the presence of evil when we were about to leave?"

Ella looks at Slash pointedly. "I let my guard down. Apparently, the demonic army found a way to get into that holy sanctuary though otherworldly means. All I could do was get you two to safety and hold them off."

The goddess continues as Slash shifts in his position.

"As you can see, they captured me and have been draining my power ever since. I am a shell of my former self. What is a force for good that has been twisted and made into something evil? While I am not immortal, I can withstand a tremendous amount of pain and draining of energy. Alas, even I have my limits."

Slash scoffs.

Ella sighs. "I am sorry I could not save your friends, but you really need to find some way to get out of here. You have a wife to get back to."

Slash looks around the room, feeling dejected. "I am a fool. I thought I could change the future by coming here. I felt that if I took down those that captured our home, I could undo the curse put on Sodina. I saw his power. He is beyond anything I can ever hope to be. If only there was some way to find his weakness and to beat him."

"You speak as if you want a death sentence, son," Ella answers Slash with confusion. "You cannot hope to beat him."

Slash looks up at the ceiling and lets out a laugh. "I have to at least try."

The hours pass as Ella and Slash grow closer, talking about life and any possible way to get out of their situation.

"I assume they are going to be in here any moment to drain more power from me. It would be best if we tried to get some sleep," Ella says as she lies on the cold, hard ground, turned away from her new friend.

Slash looks over to Ella. Though a shell of her former self, she was still a sight to behold.

"I promise we are going to get out of here," Slash whispers to her before falling asleep himself.

* * *

"Hello, wake up! Wake up!" A young boy exclaims and pokes Bridget's face with a stick.

Bridget sits up quickly, ready to strike, but the boy topples over and cries out for his parents.

"Oh, Astra, I'm so sorry!" Bridget says. The boy runs back to his mother and father who have approached the group.

"We were travelling through this area and found all of you lying here. My name is Pieter," the father explained as the boy looked at Bridget from behind his leg.

The rest of the group wakes up and sits up, looking up at the morning sun. Bridget stands to introduce herself to the mother and father of the small boy.

"I am the Warrior Bridget of the North." She bows at the family. "I am with the War Master Chrono and Lady Lea of Glashmere."

"My name is Pollock," the small boy mumbles to Bridget, and she smiles.

"What are you doing out in the middle of nowhere, War Master?" Pieter asks. "I recognized your face as soon as I saw it."

"It's a long story," Chrono responds.

"Though, Pieter," Bridget notes. "If it is not too much trouble, can we get a ride to Ferrymore?"

"Why Ferrymore, Bridget?" Lea asks.
"That should be where the next trail is, I hope," Bridget continues. "I studied a map and saw several islands. If this Cave of Remedy is what we are looking for, our best bet is to head to the largest harbor in all of the Southern Kingdom."

"We will pay you for your time, kind sir," Bridget says.

Pieter nods. "Sure, we can take you to Ferrymore. Delena, my wife, and I had business there in a few weeks anyway. I can make some money with all my wares down there sooner." The man smiles as he lets the group of four on the second wagon.

"Delena will guide the way for you. All you have to do is rest."

The woman sits in the seat while they all pile into the back.

She smiles at them and says, "It is a three-day journey from here, young ones. We will be stopping periodically to ensure our horses get enough rest. All I ask is that you be respectful and help out where you are needed."

Pollock runs and sits next to Bridget, hugging her arm. Bridget laughs at the child and pats his small head.

"No problem at all, madam," Sodina answers for the group. "We appreciate your kindness."

The woman nods as they start to make their way on the long journey south, leading to Ferrymore.

Sodina sits up towards the front near Delena.

"Is it okay if I sit up here?" Sodina asks.

Delena has her eyes on the road as they trot on. "Where do you hail from, Lady Sodina?"

"I... am from the Eastern Kingdom."

"Such a shame what happened to Glashmere," Delena frowned.

"How did you know I was from around there? Sodina asks.

"Your reaction when I ask the questions,"Delena winks. "When you get older, you naturally pick up on things."

Sodina chuckles and the two women start up a conversation about Delena and the rest of her family. Sodina learns that Delena and Pieter are parents of many children who had grown up and started their own families. Their youngest was Pollock and he was a miracle child, as he was born when Delena turned fifty.

Chrono looked up from sharpening his sword and caught Lea's eyes.

"You seem impatient. I can tell. It must make you a little upset, Chrono," Lea says. "You want to press on so quickly to get back to Queen Sarah, but maybe it is the will of Astra that we have this time to rest. No one forced you to come. We are in no shape or form to get to the next trial."

Lea rubs her shoulder and Chrono frowns at the girl. She stares up at them. "That must hurt."

Leo sighs. "It does, but at least we're alive."

"You're right, Lea," Chrono admits.

Little Pollock curls up into a ball by Bridget's leg and snores lightly. Bridget leans back against the wagon, closing her eyes.

I need more sleep like this little man. Bridget falls asleep in an instant, snoring loudly next to the child.

"Ha, she is already out!" Lea whispers and chuckles lightly.

Sodina looks back and sees Bridget sleeping next to Pollock.

That woman is something else. You can't blame her either, we just fought a battle, Sodina thinks to herself.

Hours pass as the group stops right before the junction leading back towards Lafare.

"It feels good to see people on the road, right, Lady Delena?" Chrono says.

She nods as they take the road south, heading toward Ferrymore. "We will stop here for the night."

The carriage in front of them stops as Delena jumps down, walking towards her husband.

"They are causing no trouble, Pieter dear," she says to her husband.

"I didn't think they would, my darling," he replies, getting down from his wagon to carry little Pollock out of the guests' wagon.

Pieter walks back towards the wagon and addresses the group, "You guys can sleep in there if you would like. I will get started on dinner."

He pulls out a pot from their pack and starts to make a fire. Delena and Pollock cut up vegetables to put in the stew as it starts to boil.

The aroma begins to fill the area as Sodina walks to sit by the fire, everyone else following closely.

"I assume by the way your party is dressed, War Master, you are on an adventure," Pieter notes. "I apologize I don't know any of your companions."

"We are on a quest to take back our home, sir," Chrono explains. "But I fear we are being engaged in a much larger crisis. There are monsters appearing in places never seen before and whole habitats are changing. There are dark forces at work."

Delena nodded beside her husband. "They say a purple mist has started to surround the Eastern Kingdom. No one has any idea what it does or if it is just dark energy beginning to plague the land."

"We heard about it in the other towns we visited." Pieter shakes his head. "If there are any people trapped there still, I feel bad for them. They do not deserve that fate. To be slaughtered, tortured, or enslaved by the demons."

"Is it true that they say that demons have yet to invade Jerut or Rinkar?" Lea butts in.

The old couple look at each other and then at the young woman and nod. Delena answers, "Since those towns are farther towards the Northern Kingdom, they have not been compromised."

"That is good news," Bridget says and Sodina fidgets by her.

"It's unbelievable," Sodina adds sadly. "It's like we were just there."

"There are those that have fled, of course," Pieter continues. "So the economy in those towns are not good. I feel as if there is a significant change coming to the land of Esteria."

Delena looks at her husband with kind eyes as all of them enjoy the stew he boiled up. "You young ones should get to bed. We have a full day of travel tomorrow."

Pieter stands up with his wife and Pollock follows as the family heads to their wagon for rest.

Lea turns her attention over to the War Master.

"Are you alright?" She asks as Sodina and Bridget chat over the rest of the stew opposite of them.

Chrono answers, "Yes, I am doing well, but worried. I feel as if the more time we take, the more people die. At times I feel as if I am only a War Master in title, but not action. I want to end the suffering in this world, but I am only one man."

Lea puts her hand on his shoulder. "Cheer up, Chrono. We will take care of this evil and help people at the same time. These things take time. If you lack faith, look to the stars."

Lea turns around, her emerald pigtails fluffy in the wind, twirling about as she lays down beside the wagon in a sleeping bag.

"See you all in the morning!" Bridget jumps in the wagon and falls asleep quickly.

Chrono looks at Sodina still by the fire. He walks up to sit beside her on the tree trunk. "You know, from what I have heard about your husband," he starts, "he sounds like an exceptional swordsman. I bet he is hacking up any challenge that lies in front of him."

Sodina sits in silence for a beat before saying a quiet "thank you," to the kind War Master.

"It's time we get some rest, Lady Sodina. See you in the morning." Chrono leaves her to her thoughts as Sodina looks into the fire, her heart burning with passion.

I must get stronger. I need to be healthy for Slash. I will not let this poison win.

Sodina looks down at her arm, her veins glowing purple and back to normal. She lets out a small cry as the pain from her wrists shoot up her arms.

The pain was starting to become unbearable for the woman.

Sodina puts her hand on her arm and tries to heal her pain, but nothing happens. She lies by the fire and thinks of her husband until sleep overwhelms her.

The morning comes as the group packs and heads out for the next two days' journey. The tropical trees and breeze make for a pleasant trip for the group.

Pollock has once again stuck beside Bridget, and they start to play with his small set of marbles.

Sodina sits in front with Delena as a large city comes into view.

Before them at the bottom of the hill was the city of Ferrymore. Sodina heard that it was a large city by the ocean with a massive naval fleet, but she never thought she would see it. She wished Slash was with her to see it too.

"You know, milady," Delena interrupts her thoughts. "They house the Naval Academy here."

"I did not realize that," Sodina responds.

"There are times where we hold joint training," says Lea, coming up behind them. "While the Southern Kingdom does focus more on naval operations, they have their ground troops as well. Their maritime fleet is a major hub of commerce with the continent across the ocean."

"What is over there across the sea, milady?" asks Sodina.

"The continent of Endrea," Delena replies. "Some say they could wipe us out in an instant. Other states are savages who eat each other. Those are tales that we heard as children. Most people do not know about Endrea or what goods we get from them. Much of that is kept at the higher levels of government. From my knowledge, the two continents have lived at peace."

"I guess it's mutually beneficial not to cause a war," Chrono states.

"Young ones, we are almost there," Delena states.

She follows her husband's wagon of goods as they go down the hill towards the town of Ferrymore.

The stone road is littered with traffic as the group rides closer to the city.

"Look at all of this activity! It is good to see cities that are not affected by the demonic empire," Lea says.

"Welcome to our city!" An elderly local woman says, waving as they enter the city gates.

Pieter stops his carriage near the front of the city.

"Young ones, it is time for you all to be on your way," he says. "You do not have to pay us anything for the journey. We are happy to be able to assist those who are trying to stop the evil from taking over."

The group shakes hands with the family as they go off in the distance.

"Now we have to find a boat of some sort," Chrono says, putting his hands in the air to stretch from the long journey.

"I guess the best place is to head for the docks." Sodina watches the townspeople all busy in their own activities. "This town is massive."

The hustle of the day creates crowded streets for the group to navigate.

"Excuse us," says Lea, the smallest of the group, having trouble pushing her way through the crowds.

Bridget chuckles and bellows, "Coming through, people! Please get out of the way!"

Bridget's shouts clear the way in front of them and Lea blushes, thanking the giant woman.

The four of them make it towards a back street.

"I think it will be easier for us to get down to the docks this way, away from all of that foot traffic," Lea explains. "I have a tremendous sense of smell so I can get us there quickly."

She walks forward, leading the group around the outer parts of the city down to the docks.

Men and women walk by standing upright with the most precision in suits with naval badges on them.

"Look how regal they are," Sodina whispers.

Lea looks back at Sodina, grinning. "Yeah, they are some sharp individuals. The Southern Kingdom is classy when it comes to their naval fleet. They are the best of the best. Their academy brings individuals from all over Esteria to study and train."

"They're extremely radiant," Bridget notes. "Sadly, there are those in the Northern Kingdom that are racist toward them because of their darker skin."

Lea continues, "When you look at the geography of our continent, you have the Eastern and Northern Kingdoms that have fairer skin due to the climate. The Southern Kingdom is slightly darker because of the amount of sunlight they receive. The Western Kingdom is desert, so they are darker than the Southern Kingdom. It's just a product of the climate, really."

"Such racism should not be tolerated," Sodina agrees with her two friends.

Chrono looks out toward the docks at two young people arguing. "What is going on over there?"

The group looks over and sees two people pacing back and forth on a medium-sized boat.

The girl yells in frustration, "You never let me do anything with you!"

"I do not want you to get hurt!" The boy shouts in reply.

"You are so selfish! That is exactly why no one will sail with you!"

"They can't handle my intensity! And you can't either!"

Chrono walks up to the boat first. "Kind people of Ferrymore, do you have a moment?"

The two teenagers look at Chrono and frown.

"What do you want?" They ask the War Master in unison.

"We wanted to get safe passage to an island," Chrono explains. "Some people call it the Cave of Remedy. Are you familiar?"

"You sure you wanna go there, sir?" The girl raises her brow at him while the boy crosses his arms.

The boy whispers to the girl and they have a small, hushed conversation in front of the group. Sodina smiled and was reminded of her old friends who would argue but always consult one another about anything.

"It's going to cost you," the boy huffs. "Name your price."

"Will twenty gold coins whet your appetite, young man?" Bridget walks up and shows a sack of money.

"That's perfect!" The boy's eyes light up as he jumps down from the boat. "My name is Malik, and that gremlin is my twin sister Maria."

Maria punches Malik's shoulder before gleaming at the group. "Nice to meet you! We transport people to the islands for tourism and such. Dangerous island adventures are not our forte, but we can make it happen for ya!"

"You seem a bit young to be sailing a ship," Lea says jokingly.

"Our parents died in a storm a few years ago, and we inherited this ship, ma'am," says Maria. "To make money we take people out on this boat. My brother has a stubborn attitude and cannot entertain. We are down on our luck at the moment."

"Thank you for the funds, ma'am," Malik winks at Bridget.

Chrono put up his hand. "We didn't even tell you our terms yet."

"No matter! It's a done deal!" Malik quickly takes the money from Bridget, smiling. "Well, are you ready to go? Hop aboard the Diamond Stallion. The mightiest commercial vessel in Ferrymore."

Maria holds out her hand to let the group board their boat. "I personally do not think this ship is that mighty, but welcome anyway."

Bridget giggles at the girl, trying to keep a straight face. "I like your spunk, kid."

The group of four walks onto the boat's deck.
"So…" Malik begins. "We do not have a crew at the moment so you will be the crew on your journey!"

"Follow me, please," Maria says. Maria shows each of the group how to hoist the sails and guide the boat.

After about two hours of training, it was time for them to depart from the shores.

Malik turns the ship around, facing the wind. "It's a two-day journey to the Cave of Remedy and quite honestly, I would rather not sail there, but money talks. I see all of you are tired, but it's time to depart," Malik says. "I am sure Maria trained you well."

Sodina leans over the side of the boat, exhausted.

"I need to rest, Malik," she breathes heavily.

"Well, you can relax after we get the sails going, ma'am." Malik steers the medium-size ship out of the harbor.

"Let's go!" He yells as his makeshift crew hurries to follow his commands.

The Diamond Stallion starts to catch the wind as it hits the gentle waves gliding it away from the shore.

"Everyone, take a rest!" Malik yells. "The sails are set, and all I have to do is set the course." Malik looks down at the compass in front of him. "We sail north towards the Cave of Remedy." Maria looks over at Malik and his bald head.

"I wish you would grow some of your hair back," Maria says. "It was nice and curly like mine."

"I swore I wouldn't when our parents passed, sister," Malik says sternly. "You remember."

Maria nods and pats him on the back. "Yeah, I know, but—"

"It would do you some good to look at your past now and then and not forget where you came from. Do you think we will run into any trouble, sis?"

"I believe that we should be fine," Maria answers her brother calmly. "If we do run into trouble, then we have our clients to lean back on. They look like they can handle themselves."

"You got that right," Malik replies and smiles, keeping the boat heading north.

Chrono walks towards the middle of the boat and sits down. Bridget sits down behind him.

"Hey, War Master, how are you feeling?" Bridget looks at him suspiciously.

"I miss Sarah!" Chrono says. "I miss her embrace and I am trying to keep my mind focused on the task at hand. I was hoping I would get some sort of weapon or armor but we had no time. We have no idea how many demons we will be facing. We have no idea of their power. If this is the resurgence of the Demonic Empire? What are we going to do with a seed? I want something that can be used to help us gain ground."

Bridget sits there in silence as Chrono continues to ramble.

"Are you jealous of Sodina?" Chrono pauses to let the giant warrior woman reply.

"I think Serena wasted a chance to give us what we truly needed," Bridget replies quietly.

"She looked in each of our hearts and saw something in Sodina. I care for her as a friend, but as a warrior, I would like to be prepared." Chrono shakes his head. "I am so worried that I will lose you guys. We are bonded as warriors, and I feel as if I am the leader. As a leader, I have to protect those I care for."

"We all fight for noble reasons," Bridget sighs.

The boat rocks slightly to the left but regains its stability in the waves.

"What Sodina is after is healing, as you know. I, such as yourself, do not devote my full flesh to following Goddess Astra," Bridget says. "I want to have the ability to twist fate, change the future, and walk my path. She is on a mission that is greater than all of us. It combines her healing journey with the passion for taking her home back. Also, she wants to find her husband. As we complete the trials, who knows what we may find?"

Bridget sits by Chrono as they stare up at the sunny sky.

"I think I'm going to be sick," Chrono says, running over to the end of the boat and releasing his breakfast into the sea.

"Ugh, that is not fun," Lea looks over, quickly handing her canteen over to the poor War Master who is obviously not a Master of the Sea like the twins.

Chrono drinks his water and sits towards the edge of the boat. The ship continues to sail as the town of Ferrymore disappears from their eyesight.

Malik looks out into the ocean and Maria sniffs the salty sea air.

"I think we should be hitting some calm waters soon," he tells the group. "I had no idea the wind would be picking up so quickly."

Malik grabs the steering wheel of the boat and stands firm.

Maria says, "Hang on, everyone! It's going to be rough for a while."

Rain starts to fall as the ship shakes violently with the crashing waves.

Maria runs up to Malik and the twins are completely soaked. The group of adventurers they had as clients were shielding themselves with their coats.

"Are we going to make it, Mal?" Maria asks over the storm.

Malik looks at Maria and smiles. "We have been in worse storms."

Sodina puts out her hand and chants, "Goddess Astra, protect us!"

A shield of green light protects the group from the rain.

Sodina smiles, wiping the sweat off her head. "That should give us time to get down under!"

The group runs as the boat still shakes, but no rainwater hits them as they run below deck.

Bridget sits on the wooden floor. "This was unexpected. All of this to save the world, huh?"

Chrono laughs, "It wouldn't be an adventure without a lot of struggle!"

Lea quietly sits down on a box near the wall of the boat, opening the book of Astra.

"Goddess, help me to stay calm," Lea softly chants over and over.

"This doesn't seem normal!" Malik says, looking out into the ocean.

A bump is heard from underneath the boat and Malik tries to steer the boat away from the rumbling in the distance.

"Oh, great, the last thing we need is something attacking us!" Malik yells. "Maria, we need our clients' help! NOW!"

Maria runs down towards the stairs leading underneath the deck. "Everyone, we need you! There's something in the water!"

Chrono pulls out his sword and runs up the stairs first, the ladies following him. Looking at the rain clouds, a giant tentacle slams into the barrier, shaking the ship violently.

"Astra, help us," Malik groans and turns the ship to the right as the waves hit the boat again.

"We have a guest!" Chrono shouts. "A sea creature of some sort is attacking the boat. It has massive tentacles."

The boat comes to a violent halt as two massive tentacles slam into the barrier, breaking it and hitting the boat.

"It's going to pull us under," Malik says. "In these waves, we do not stand a chance. Do something!" Malik tries to hold the boat steady in the waves as it shakes violently.

Lea pulls out her bow and shoots one of the tentacles to no effect.

Bridget runs up with her axe and slams it into one of the tentacles, cutting it in half.

The tentacle flops on the deck. "Help me get it off!" The warrior woman roars.

Bridget, Lea, and Sodina lift the tentacle, throwing it off the deck as the giant creature retracts its injured tentacle into the water.

Another tentacle slashes violently across the deck, smashing into one of the wooden masts and sinking back into the sea.

Malik looks out, trying to steer the ship free of the creature's grip.

The wind blows the ship as they continue to sail through the storm.

Sodina looks up at the rain trying to concentrate, but her arm was pulsating with pain. She grabs her arm, letting loose a healing spell to help the pain. *Not now, body, do not act up on me. My friends need me!*

Sodina weeps quietly. Lea comes over to Sodina and puts her hand on her shoulders. "We are going to make it, milady, we will!"

Another two tentacles crash around the rear of the boat, shaking it wildly.

"Whoa," Malik yells, looking back. "Uh, guys, that thing is trying to flip us backwards now."

Maria runs up with a knife in each hand and stabs the tentacles rapidly, doing no damage.

The creature smacks Maria into the air, her body hitting the middle mast of the ship and falling hard onto the deck.

"MARIA!" Malik wails but continues to hold the steering wheel.

Chrono runs up the stairs and cuts the two tentacles off the beast. A loud screech is heard underneath the boat as the water becomes black as night.

Malik looks out in fear, knowing that this could be it for him. *I have never seen such evil*, Malik thinks to himself. *This creature seeks to send us to an early grave.*

Malik grips the steering wheel as he continues to push through the waves, his compass guiding the way through the storm.

Lea lifts Maria and sits her near the middle mast. "Wake up, sweetie!" Maria's body slumps over. Lea wipes water out of her eyes. "She is still alive and I feel a pulse!" She yells to Malik.

"Please take care of her, miss!" Malik answers, still struggling to control the wheel.

Lea grabs Maria's body and carries her down the stairs below the deck.

"You humans think you are so smart," a voice echoes from the waves. "The age of darkness is upon you, and there is nothing you can do to stop it."

The pounding rain eased as the the sea creature wraps the rest of its tentacles around the boat and sits its face near the front of the ship.

"We don't give a damn about your darkness!" Malik screams. "Let go of my damn boat! I have money to make!"

Malik struggles to get the ship out of the creature's grip to no avail. Chrono and Bridget were at his side, trying to help hold the wheel.

"Silence, puny human, I am Nautica of the Dark Order!" The creature spits. "I am here to see that you will die. You may have killed one of our comrades on your way to Ferrymore, but I will prove to be your death and undoing. You will not hinder Lord Gareth's plans to bathe this world in darkness."

"How does he know about that?" Bridget whispers to Chrono.

"I can hear you, big-bosomed human," Nautica chuckles darkly. "Do not look so surprised, dear. That idiot, Basil, was nowhere near as strong as I."

Bridget runs towards Nautica, slamming her ax into his mouth. "Not as chatty either!"

"Oh, dear, that will not do. You injured my beautiful face," he yells.

Nautica throws ink out of his mouth onto the deck, making it extremely slippery for the group. "Now... how shall I kill you? Ah, yes, I will let the sea take you as not to dirty my tentacles with your filthy bodies!"

Nautica starts to crush the boat, wrapping it with his tentacles.

"Do something, please!" Malik yells. Chrono tries to get his footing and Sodina is on the other side, holding onto the boat with dear life. She cries in pain, for she was too weak to use her powers to help defeat Nautica.

The boat shakes as wood can be heard splitting in half. Malik tries to steer away, but his efforts created no action.

The boat snaps in half as it starts to sink.

Malik stands there in tears, looking at the other half of his ship beginning to sink into the ocean. Lea runs up the second half quickly, carrying Maria.

"It's going under rapidly, Malik!" Lea shouts.

"To the escape boat, now," Malik answers immediately.

Malik runs towards the back of the ship. Sodina grabs onto Chrono as they push up toward the end of the ship, the rain beginning to hit them harder than ever.

Sodina puts her hand out. "Windstorm!" A gust of wind shoots out of her hand as it propels them to the upper deck, where Malik was already in the boat.

Lea throws Maria in as everyone else stumbles into the boat. Malik lowers the boat into the stormy waters and cuts the ropes from the larger ship.

Chrono rows the boat with Malik as the storm waters rock the little boat profoundly.

Sodina whispers quickly. "Be still, waters, please, in the name of Goddess Astra."

"Waters be still," Lea mutters along with Sodina as they put their hands together.

"WATERS, BE STILL!" They scream in unison.

The waters start to calm as sunlight breaks through the clouds.

Chrono clenches his sword, looking out into the calm waves of the sea. *How did we survive that, and why didn't the beast give chase?*

Malik rests his unconscious sister in his lap and tries to take deep breaths to calm down as he looks back at his family's ship sinking in the distance.

Lea falls into Sodina's lap, crying like a baby. "The Goddess heard our prayers," Lea sniffles. "I thought we were done for."

"That was terrifying," Bridget admits beside them as she continues to row.

Maria shoots awake, looking around at everyone in the boat. Malik sighs in relief and sniffs, patting his sister's hand.

"W-what happened?" She asks quietly, trying to find her voice.

"The ship is no more, sis," Malik says. "We almost died."

Malik hugs Maria who was starting to cry.

"What are we to do now, Mal?" Maria asks through her tears.

"We are now with this group of brave warriors," he says proudly. "They tried to fight off the beast, but nothing worked. If it had not been for them, we surely would have died."

The twins shared a quick embrace and the adults of the group watched lovingly.

Malik pulls out his compass. "Well, if we continue this direction, we should hit the island by sundown."

"You think you are getting away from me, humans?" A voice yells, rocking the boat. A tentacle smashes into the ship, sending everyone into the air.

Nautica slams his tentacles into the water, making a whirlpool for the humans.

Chrono looks over to his friends in the air, and blacks out.

Sodina looks up at the sky, putting her hand towards the sun. *Please, someone help us.*

A ball of yellow light surrounds the group and Sodina blacks out.

"You shall not take them from this world, you foul beast!" A female voice says commandingly. A beam of light shines brightly across the ocean as Nautica retreats underneath the water.

"Children, sleep well and rest your bodies. Go forth towards the future," the voice says softly.

Sodina wakes up, coughing hard. "What was that?! Where are we?"

Sodina looks to her left and sees Lea and Bridget, and to her right Malik, Maria, and Chrono. The group was scattered across the shore of a secluded beach lit by the moonlight and stars above them.

Lea sits up and brushes sand off her face. "The last thing I remember was being flung into the air with such force."

Sodina looks down at her hand and sees two pendants, one in each hand. Sodina puts the necklaces around her neck, wondering what their use would be.

Chrono stands up, looking up at the night sky. "How long have we been asleep on this beach?"

Malik and Maria look around. "I thought we were dead," they say in unison.

"I thought we were done for too, kids," Bridget says and leans back, looking at the stars. "Thank goodness someone saved us, or it was sheer luck we got out of it."

"I think it was the Goddess that saved us," Lea responds.

"Think what you like, little one," Bridget smiles. "I believe that we were just lucky, and that was it."

Sodina looks down at the pendants at her neck, one green and the other red.

There was something about the pendants that made Sodina feel at peace. They seemed to glow softly just for her.

Bridget gets up and walks over to the trees and starts cutting wood for a bonfire.

Sodina sits by the ocean, looking out into the waves. "How will we get back?" She whispers to herself. "We are so far from civilization."

"There may be some commercial fishing vessels that pass by, but this island is out of the way," Malik says. "Most people who come here are adventurers seeking an early grave. I have hope that we will be rescued. As long as we keep a fire going, everything will be okay."

Sodina smiles sweetly. "Thank you for taking us on. You had no idea this would happen, but you still fought courageously to save us from that monster."

Malik blushes and turns away. "It's no problem at all."

He laughs and walks away, putting his feet into the ocean.

"Never mind him, ma'am," Maria says, walking up to sit by Sodina. "He always blushes when pretty women talk with him."

Chrono and Bridget come back with wood and start to build a fire.

"Man, I am famished," Chrono says.

"Is there anything to eat around here?" Bridget yells. Lea laughs at the giant woman's display of hunger. The twins start to explore with her.

Bridget walks back over to the forest line. She climbs a tree and finds fruit growing from its branches.

"Hey, everyone, I found some food!" Bridget pulls down a bunch of bananas.

Malik sprints towards Bridget and takes a banana, peeling it quickly.

"We do not know if it's poisonous," Sodina says.

Malik eats the banana with a huge smile. "I am not dead, am I? Oh, this is ripe!"

"If he's not dead, it should be fine, Sodina!" Bridget laughs.

Bridget hands the bunch of bananas to Sodina and goes back up the tree for another bunch.

"Will you guys go exploring tomorrow for what you came looking for?" Malik asks.

"Yes, of course," Chrono says confidently. "Did you want to come, kid?"

"I'd rather stay here and try to signal for a boat," Malik shrugs.

"Suit yourself," Chrono says, laughing.

Sodina thought of her dear husband again and how much he would've loved to be on this adventure with them. Lea saw her friend sigh sadly and she went over to her to give her a quick embrace before they set up their packs to sleep.

After resting, the party starts to wake up from their slumber. Chrono was the first awake, so he headed to the tree line to fetch more bananas.

"I was able to get a few bunches for us as we travel," Chrono says, handing Lea, Sodina, and Bridget a batch each.

The three ladies sit up slowly, putting the food in their packs.

"We are off, kids! See you later!" Bridget pats Malik on the back with full strength and he starts to cough wildly. Maria laughs and waves at them as they disappear into the trees.

Chrono walks in front of the group, leading the way through the sandy tree line. Lea pulls out her bow to keep it at the ready.

"We have no idea what we may come against," Lea says. "I will be prepared to put an arrow in our enemies' eyes."

Bridget looks back at Lea, nodding in approval and pulling her axe from her back.

Sodina, at the group's request, keeps a look back as the sun beats down in-between the trees.

It was so hot that Lea had already taken off her overshirt and tied it around her waist. *I'm not built for tropical weather,* she thought.

Chrono continues forward with his sword drawn as he sees a cave in the distance. Chrono walks forward into the foot-deep water up towards a door.

"Be on your guard, everyone," Chrono whispers.

Chrono steps down into the cave and slips on a step, sliding to the bottom. The ladies gasp.

"Are you okay, Chrono?" Bridget shouts.

"I am!" Chrono says, "But watch your step, it's slick."

The rest of the group walks down the flight of stone stairs into the cave's depths.

"Though this is underwater, it seems protected from being flooded," Lea notes.

The group walks up towards an opening where they see lit torches.

"I wonder if those are for someone else, or is this by happenstance?" Chrono says.

"I have a bad feeling about this," Lea mutters.

"Look up there," Sodina points.

A massive mural behind the torches comes into view as the group gets closer. Sodina looks closely at the wall.

"It seems like the pathways of water pressure here lead to different areas, like a maze of sorts," Bridget says as she squints at the mural. "At the top of the mural is a... boat? Or something."

Chrono examines the picture closely, "It does look like a boat, but I wonder why a trial like this would reward someone with a boat."

"There are two paths." he says. "One to the left and one to the right."

"Why don't we split up?" Lea offers and Bridget scoffs next to her.

"I think that is a lousy idea," Bridget answers the little archer. "We have no idea what we might be facing."

"Each path does seem to lead to the boat at the end. How hard can it be?" Sodina asks the group.

"If we survived fighting that dragon, I'm sure a little water won't kill us," Bridget smiles. "Plus, my bosoms are floating devices, don't you think? Short stuff, you are with me." Bridget pushes Lea towards the right door.

Chrono nods at Bridget.

"Let's go, Sodina," Chrono says, walking towards the left door.

"Please be safe, you two," Sodina says while walking with Chrono.

Bridget puts up her thumb as they disappear into the darkness. Sodina walks behind Chrono as they make their way through a narrow set of stairs heading deeper into the cave.

"The humidity is too much down here," Chrono says.

Chrono takes the top of his tunic off and wraps it around his waist.

Sodina looks at Chrono's back and sees jagged scars from his previous battles. She wonders if they were scars from War Master tournaments or scars from fights he'd been in to protect Glashmere. She shivered a little, thinking about it.

The pair walks down the stairs for five minutes before they come upon a pool of water with a sign in front of it that tells them to jump in.

Chrono looks around the small room looking for clues, but nothing pops out to him.

"I think we have to go into this pool of water like the mural says." Sodina pinches her nose and jumps in without hesitation.

"Wait!" Chrono shakes his head and jumps into the pool after her.

Sodina, barely able to keep her eyes open, feels her body being pulled in different directions for what seems like forever as she lands in another room similar to the first one.

Sodina coughs up water and gasps for air.

Chrono appears out of the hole.

"Please don't do that again, Lady Sodina!" He gasps for air.

Sitting up, he looks around the room. Chrono huffs while wringing his shirt of the excess water from the jump.

"Torches are here to keep the room lit. How convenient."

Sodina looks around the room.

"Illuminate," she says as a bright light surrounds the room from her staff. Sodina winces in pain as she loses balance, slumping against the wall.

"Sodina!" Chrono runs to her aid, catching her before she hits the ground.

"I'm okay." She wipes her head before taking a sip of water from her bottle.

Chrono nods with a look of concern in his eyes. "Let's go, I do not think there is anything here to help us." Chrono walks in front of Sodina as they head up a flight of stairs.

"This makes no sense going up and down like this," Sodina says. "How do we know which way we are even going?"
"This is madness, I agree," Chrono says as he walks up to another clearing. He looks at another mural with a man standing in front of aboat, pointing towards something unknown.

"This mural is different from the last, and it got smaller it seems." Sodina examines the mural and sees the man holding something in his hand.

"I am soaked," Sodina laughs.

"I know the feeling," Chrono takes off his boots and empties the water out of them.

"Queen Sarah is going to find this journey surprising once you get back to her."

"I know," Chrono smiles. "She'll be insanely jealous." He rakes his hand in through his hair. "We should go."

Sodina giggles, covering her smile. "Right."

Chrono slips his boots back on and they make their way through small hallways. The corridors were so narrow that they had to walk carefully on the wall's edge. Certain death was the alternative if they fell into the pit filled with spikes made of rocks.

Chrono leads the way to another set of stairs as they find another small pool of water.

"I could pass out from all of this humidity," Chrono breathes. "It's almost unbearable." Chrono pulls out a bottle of water and takes a swig. He offers some to Sodina and she gladly takes a large gulp.

"I need a nice, long bath after this," Sodina says in a tired voice.

"Are you ready?" Chrono looks back at the lady. Sodina nods and they both take a very deep breath.

The pair jumps into the small pool of water as their bodies are carried through a series of tunnels full of water.

Sodina closes her eyes and passes out from the pressure of the pool.

Chrono emerges from another pool of water holding his heart.

"This pressure almost killed me that time," he says. "The pathway was much longer."

Sodina's body was pushed up by the water pressure with a large splash.

"Sodina!" Chrono yells as he runs over to her.

She is cold from the water but the War Master feels a slow pulse at her wrist.

"Please wake up," Chrono says as he picks up her body and lays it on her side to pat her back with some force. He notices her shoulder is dark purple.

Sodina's body lay still for a moment before she wakes, coughing up water and a little blood.

Chrono notices the blood but does not mention it. It could have been from the pressure of their jump.

Sodina sits up, feeling woozy. Chrono pulls out another bottle of water and puts it to her mouth. Sodina gulps the water slowly.

"Thank you," she says.

Chrono nods as he helps Sodina to her feet.

"Come on," he says quietly. Chrono walks forward, putting her arm around his waist to hold herself up.

"You have done well to make it this far." A male voice echoes in the dimly lit hallway. "Where three or more are gathered, destiny awaits you."

Chrono looks around, but sees no one.

"We are getting close," Sodina whispers. "We have to keep going, Chrono."

Sodina's eyes close for a moment, then reopen as she sees an image of Slash smiling in the distance. It was only an illusion, but it was enough to give her strength to move forward. She missed his smile, loving nature, and never-say-die attitude. *I miss his hugs. He gives the best hugs.*

Chrono looks over to Sodina, her face clammy from all the water. *Poor thing*, he thinks as they walk on.

Chrono and Sodina pass another mural that is smaller than the last.

"Oh, War Master," Sodina's voice shakes from her growing weakness. "Another one of those pressure waterways and my head is going to explode. I don't know if I'll make it…"

"We must," Chrono soothes her. "This trial is not for the faint of heart. We need to know what lies at the end."

Chrono looks down at Sodina with a steadfast look in his eyes. "We must master this trial. Your husband is waiting for you."

"You're right. I can do it for him. For us."

Sodina lets loose a small smile and walks with Chrono who is still supporting her.

They walk to the door on the left and into a small pool of water. A small sign is lit with the word "Elite."

"Here is what we are going to do," Chrono instructs. "I will hug you as we go into the water. I will hold your nose and vice versa. That way, you do not have to take in as much water."

Sodina nods, holding Chrono tightly. "Alright, the sooner we get this over with, the better."

The pair jumps into the water, preparing themselves mentally.

The water buffets their bodies as they keep their eyes closed and they go through several tunnels being pulled left, right, then left twice, and right once before they emerge from a large pool in front of a large door.

Chrono and Sodina gasp for air as they crawl into the open space in the large room.

Sodina turns on her back, breathing slowly.

"We made it," she whispers. "We made it, Chrono."
Sodina turns to her left and holds out her hand for Chrono, who lays exhausted on the ground breathing heavily. He takes her hand and squeezes it lightly before turning and closing his eyes to rest.

All they had to do now was wait to see if Bridget and Lea made their way to them.

* * *

In a cavern far from Chrono and Sodina, Bridget and Lea walk into a narrow corridor filled with deep water.

"It looks like we are swimming, little one," Bridget observes.

Lea and Bridget put their boots in their sacks before stepping into the water and paddling towards the door at the end of the hallway.

"I cannot swim well," Lea says to Bridget as they swim forward.

"Damn, that is going to be a problem because there is going to be a lot of swimming, it seems." Bridget huffed trying to catch her breath.

Bridget and Lea get to the end of the doorway and stand up, dripping with water.

"Whew, the humidity is on another level," Lea breathes heavily.

Bridget groans, running her hands through her hair, "Ugh, I want to get my hair fixed as soon as we get out of here."

Lea looks from the corner of her eye towards the water as a fin of some sort appears, then disappears.

I must be seeing things, Lea thinks, shaking her head as they head through the next door. "More water," Lea says with a sigh.

"Yep," Bridget smiles apologetically. "This room is different. It appears to be a maze of sorts. I cannot see a door at all."

Bridget dives into the water, followed by Lea as they swim through the maze.

"Something just grazed my foot!" Lea yells to Bridget.

Bridget looks back at Lea. "Swim faster!"

Lea grunts as they swim through the maze and come out the other side in front of a door.

Lea leans over, exhausted. "How many more rooms of this stuff, Lady Bridget?"

"Not one more," a voice says as a trident narrowly misses Lea's head.

Bridget ducks as the trident hits the stone door by them.

"We are at a disadvantage here," Bridget yells. "RUN!"

Bridget grabs Lea's hand as they go through another door, seeing a long narrow stretch of deep water ahead.

"Hang onto my back," Bridget yells at Lea. Bridget jumps in the water as Lea grips her back and swims at an intense pace towards the next door.

Another trident flies past Lea's face.

Lea pulls out her bow with one hand and expertly shoots one arrow into the water.

"Can you go any faster?" Lea yells to Bridget.

"I'm... Urgh... Trying!" Bridget snaps back as she struggles to go faster with her full pack and a human on her.

A fin appears above the water as another trident flies towards Lea.

Lea ducks and shoots two arrows into the fin. "Got ya!"

A pool of blood starts to form as tridents cease flying.

Bridget climbs onto the stone stairs as Lea jumps off her back. Bridget gasps for air. "Whew, I have not swum that fast in a long time. Those people who talk about aging were not kidding about the late twenties kicking your butt."

"You okay?" Lea asks.

"Do I look okay, short stuff?" Bridget shouts. "I am exhausted. That swim took a lot out of me."

"Thank you for doing that for me, Lady Bridget."

Bridget crossed her arms, nodding. "No problem, little one."

Bridget stands up and walks through the next door with Lea to reveal another door right after it and a deep pool of water.

"Now what?" Bridget sighs, scrubbing her hand on her face.

"That is the only way down, it seems," Lea says, "Look at the water bubbling up from the hole in the ground."

"Let's take the plunge then." Bridget holds her nose, jumping into the water as Lea follows.

The water pushes them down a slide as they twirl in circles for several minutes before falling into a room and hitting the ground hard.

Bridget looks up, trying to concentrate as she sees two figures in front of her.

"Chrono and Sodina!" Lea squeals.

Chrono looks over at her.

"Lea! Bridget!" He says, running over and high fiving them.

"We made it," Bridget says, standing up slowly. "Man, is my body beat."

The giant warrior woman leans over, stretching her back.

Lea sits up on and shakes her head.

"Ugh, I am so dizzy," she says. "I never want to see another pool of water again."

Sodina sits up and walks over to the group of three.

"I am so thankful we are all here in one piece," She gleams as she sees her friend group complete.

"I had to swim away from some damn creature with Lea hanging onto my back!"

Lea smiles at Chrono and Sodina. "I owe Lady Bridget my life now."

The group erupts in happy chatter, telling each other the tales of their adventure through the cave.

Above them, the cave rumbles and they all stop to hear a voice echoing around them.

"You have done well, Children of Astra," the voice bellows. "You have made it this far. You should be radiant with pride."

"That is the same voice from earlier," Chrono tells the ladies. "Did you guys hear it?"

The three of them shake their heads.

"Chrono, are you pulling a joke on us?" Lea asks, concerned that the War Master was trying to fool them.

"I don't hear anything!" Bridget exclaims and Sodina nods in agreement.

"Sorry, Chrono," Sodina says, "Nothing for me either."

Chrono hushes them and listens to the voice again.

It tells him, "Walk through this door where your treasure awaits."

A door appeared on the wall in front of them and the sight startled the ladies.

"It's telling us to enter," Chrono says. "I believe we should."

"Lead the way," Lea gulps as she gets behind Bridget and Sodina.

The group of four walks towards the door, exhausted but with their weapons drawn.

"Be on your guard," Chrono says sternly.

Chrono opens the door. They see a strange contraption and a large, burgundy chest inside.

"What you seek, you will find…" The ladies finally hear the voice and Lea readies her bow in defense.

"Who are you?" Lea shouts at nothing. "If you're another creature of the Dark Order, we will take you out! Immediately!"

"I am not of the Dark Order, Children of Astra," the voice responds. "I am the spirit of Adonis, the speedy right hand of the ancient hero, Dalvar. I am sure you have met Serena. We are the heroes of old who destroyed the Dark Lord, Helion. I do sense evil is afoot. Though you are a ragtag group of individuals, your hearts are pure. Trust in each other and the path before you will shine brighter than ever."

A ball of light appears before them and begins to float upwards. The light reveals a wooden ship docked at the edge of a pool of water that wasn't there before.

"What is that, O Spirit of Adonis?" Sodina asks.

"Use your heart to make the way," Adonis says intently as the ball floats out of their eyes' reach.

"That makes no sense," Bridget snaps. "All of these riddles are making my brain hurt."

Sodina walks up to the chest and opens it slowly. She reaches down to pull out a small bottle of oil with one piece of green grass in it.

"It is labelled Astral Root," Sodina says.

"That is extremely rare, Sodina!" Chrono sprints over to her to examine the bottle. "That will be critical in curing your poison. Keep it safe."

"We should rest before figuring out our next steps, team," Bridget says and yawns, stretching out her long limbs. "I am too beat to think."

The rest of the group agreed and made a small camp of the cave ground.

An hour or two passes with the group of four lying on their backs resting, trying to catch their breath.

Sodina stands up and walks towards the wooden-looking ship. "It looks like a ship but without a rudder," she whispers to herself. *I wonder what it's doing here,* whe thinks as she steps in. As she boards, one of the pendants on her chest emits a bright light.

"Oh my!" Sodina yells to her friends. "Everyone, climb aboard!"

The team scrambles to pack their things and Bridget yells, "We better get on that thing fast!"

The ceiling above starts to shake as the rocks come apart, revealing the night sky.

Sodina looks up and beams, "It's for us!"

The boat starts to lift off the ground as Lea runs towards the front of the ship where the wheel sits. "I think we need to lift it more, Lady Sodina!"

Sodina walks over to Lea and looks around to see a small hole, perfectly shaped for one of her pendants.

"Go on, milady," Chrono says behind her. "We have nothing to lose."

Sodina puts the necklace in place as the ship shoots through the hole in the rocks and out into the sky at a furious speed.

"Hold on, everyone!" Lea screams, gripping the steering wheel. "It's going to be a wild ride!"

Sodina, Chrono, and Bridget put their hands on the center mast of the ship, and they come to a stop in the sky, fifty feet above the ground.

"I cannot believe it..." Bridget stares around them at the stars and holds her hand out to feel the breeze of a cloud floating past them.

Lea's eyes twinkle with delight, holding the wheel of the ship.

A voice echoes in everyone's ears.

"This is the flying ship of old that we used to assault the Citadel of Fear all those years ago," Adonis explains. "We defeated the wretched Helion and celebrated on this very deck."

Chrono's eyes widen in disbelief as the voice continues.

"Use it well," Adonis says as the voice fades out of their ears.

"So is this how we use this thing?" Lea turns the wheel and the ship turns quickly to the right.

"Careful, Lea!" Chrono yells. "You could throw us all overboard!"

Lea lets go of the wheel, walking away with her hands in the air.

"Well, the pendant is the source of its power so it must help somehow," Sodina says.

She walks over the wheel and tilts it slowly towards the ground as the ship gracefully flies down towards the beach.

"What in Astra's name is that?" Malik looks up to see a large boat flying down towards the beach.

"Maria!" He screams. "Maria, wake up! Look at that."

Maria's eyes open slowly and then widen in amazement.

"That's just a flying ship, Mal," Maria yawns before freezing. "Wait. A flying ship?!"

The twins look closer and see the group of adventurers who had left them days ago on board, waving from the deck.

They look at each other in amazement before running up to them as the ship landed straight on the sand.

"How was that even possible?" Malik touched the ship's smooth surface in awe. "Where did this beauty come from?"

"We found it in the Cave of Remedy after the water trials we faced, kid," Chrono explains. "It was an experience I would rather not go through again."

"You got that right, War Master," Bridget bellows as she jumps off the boat's edge. Lea walks off the boat behind her, laughing at her friend who was now shaking herself dry like a dog.

"We are so tired after all of that," Sodina tells the twins.

Maria embraces her tightly and says, "We're glad you all made it out safe. We were afraid something had happened to you when you didn't come back after the second day."

"We were gone for days?" Chrono strokes his chin. "It felt more like hours in there."

"Must be magical after all," Lea sang as she passed him. "We are wet and need to dry our clothes."

Lea takes off her top and pants and puts them around the fire. "I will keep my undergarments on. I'd rather not strip down naked in front of everyone. Ha." Malik blushes slightly at Lea who is revealing some of her skin before looking away.

"Well, I am not shy." Bridget walks behind the boat and takes off her chainmail dress and cloak. "Well, are you guys ready for a show?"

"Wait, we do not need to see all of that!" Chrono yells. Bridget walks back around from the boat with her cloak wrapped around her. "Just kidding," Bridget chirps.

Sodina falls to the ground laughing. "I thought you were going to let your prized possessions feel the wind tonight," she says. "I'd rather not," Bridget says quietly. "I am saving those for someone special."

Malik turns around quickly, not wanting to look at all of the beautiful women sitting around the fire trying to dry off.

"It's been rather quiet the past day, or two," Malik explains.

"I lost track, honestly," Maria says. "We were trying to flag down boats, but none dared come this way. They know of the danger of this island. I'm sure they saw the fire, but none came to our aid."

"But now that we have that ship, we can get back home," Malik reaches for his sister's shoulder and gives it a loving squeeze.

"You all should rest," Maria offers. "We'll be happy to watch over you for the rest of the night."

"Fine by me. Thank you, kids." Chrono lays down by the fire, still in full gear, and falls asleep right away with his sword by his side.

The rest of the adventurers follow to dreamland and the twins add more driftwood to the bonfire.

"I want to take a look at that ship," Malik turns to Maria. "Do you wanna come with me?"

Maria shrugs and they walk over to the ship to look at the wood and the craftsmanship.

"It could use some fixing up," he says. "Some... more modern touches, no?"

Maria rolls her eyes at her brother and crosses her arms. "Mal, it's a magical ship. It looks perfectly fine to me."

The twins board the ship and near the steering wheel that was glowing in the night.

"Whoa, what is this pendant here?" Malik says as he puts his hands on the steering wheel. The wheel zaps him and he jumps back in pain.

Maria laughs hard at him. "I think the ship got offended, Mal."

"Ouch," Malik grunts. "The pendant lets off light and the wheel returns to a standard color when I come near it."

"I mean, you weren't there with them, Mal," Maria responds. "You probably don't have the power to fly the thing."

"Even though I have the most experience with ships," Malik grumbles.

"Oh, silly, you need to give it a rest." Maria pats her brother on the back. "It's just not meant for us. We are just along for the ride, you know. It could be a grand adventure if we stick around."

"You're right, sis." Malik guides his sister off the boat. She rubs her arms as the ocean breeze makes her shiver a bit.

"We have no fighting skills whatsoever and would only slow them down," Maria says sadly as they near their camp again.

"I know, but these people are really unique, sis," Malik states. "They are an odd bunch, but I believe they've accepted us already. What's a set of twins in a team of a noble, warriors, and a peasant witch?"

"Wow, I can't believe you made that up yourself," Maria giggles. "There's actually a brain in there!"

"Oh, be quiet, you." Malik smiles. "I can be the smart twin if I wanted to. But I'll stay the dashingly handsome one."

Maria smacks him on the back of his head and they burst out laughing quietly, trying not to wake up their new friends.

Malik lays down beside the fire and falls asleep as Maria watches out to protect them through the night.

* * *

"Rise and shine, everyone!" Maria yells at the top of her lungs.

Bridget shoots awake and jumps up, ax in hand.

"You did not have to scream so loud, kid!" Bridget answers in a pouty voice.

Sodina rubs her eyes, sitting up, not letting Maria's voice shock her into starting her day.

"I could've used some more sleep, dear Maria," Sodina says.

"Sorry," Maria replies shyly. "We made you breakfast and didn't want it to get cold."

"That's very sweet of you." Sodina patted Maria's cheek before getting up to stretch.

"At least our clothes are dry now." Lea yawns as she puts on her overshirt.

Sodina walks over to put on her boots and Malik zooms in proudly.

"We grabbed some fish with our bare hands in the shallow water and cooked them up for you!" Malik says vibrantly.

Chrono and Lea were the last to wake to the smell of fried fish and stewed greens.

"Thank you, Malik," the War Master says as he nears the boy. "It looks great."

The group finishes up their breakfast and pack their things.

"Now, there is a world that needs saving." Chrono looks back at everyone as he walks onto the ship. "Ferrymore is back south, so we can use my compass to get us back home."

The group walks on the boat and closes the door behind them.

Lea walks up to the wheel. "I am going to give this thing another go." She lifts the wheel and the ship shoots straight up into the air.

Everyone hangs on to dear life and Bridget yells, "Lea, relax!"

"I'm sorry! I want to go higher," Lea says. "Hold on, everyone!"

Lea leans the wheel back as the boat climbs two hundred feet into the air.

Maria groans next to Sodina. "I think I would rather be on the sea. I absolutely dread heights."

Lea looks down at the pendant as an N appears on it and she bites her lip, turning the ship around as the pendant shows an S on it.

"Okay, now we are good," she smiles. "En route to Ferrymore."

"This wouldn't be so hard if I was steering the boat," Malik grumbles under his breath.

"I heard that," Lea answers sharply.

Lea dips the ship slightly as everyone bounces around.

"I get it," Malik says. "Please do not make everyone suffer for my sake."

"Do not critique my navigation skills, kid," Lea huffs. "This is a flying ship, not a regular one. No one knows how to do this."

Malik's face wrinkles with annoyance and gives up. "I know, I apologize. Go ahead, Captain Lea."

"That's more like it," Lea smiles. She pushes the wheel forward as the boat sails gracefully in the clouds.

"I guess I'm just useless now." Malik frowns and walks over to his sister, hanging his head in shame.

"Oh, stop being so dramatic, Mal!" Maria chuckles. "Lighten up! We're on a flying ship!"

"Where to next, Captain?" Chrono grins.

"Let's get Malik and Maria home." Lea smiles to her band of friends.

For the first time in a long time, Lea felt useful. No longer was she an orphan begging for scraps. She felt at peace, guiding the ship through the blue skies of the Ocia Isles. She had precious cargo and finally felt for once that she could manifest the love in her heart by transporting them safely.

Lea smiles, looking into blue skies as she guides the ship towards the town of Ferrymore.

Chapter 19

Month of Dragons
Day 28

Slash spits up blood as he lies on the ground writhing in pain.

Gareth punches him again before kicking him down.

"Your purpose will soon be clear," Gareth tells Slash before walking away, closing the door.

"Slash, are you okay?" Ella asks.

Slash holds his stomach and rolls on his back.

"Can't he just kill me right now rather than go through this? This Gareth knows he could kill me any moment, but he lets me suffer. I wonder if dying now would be better, and I can see Sodina in paradise after all of this is said and done. I want to have hope. This talk of destiny and slaying demons seems much for us. All I wanted to do was go on an adventure with our friends. Now I am a pawn in his sinister plan.

"I want to see Sodina smile. Damn it. I want to see her smile!" Slash clenches his fist, slamming it into the stone floor, his knuckles bleeding.

Ella looks at Slash, trying to find some way to comfort him.

"I know a way you can escape," Ella whispers to Slash. "It will not guarantee you will be able flee from this place, but it will give you a fighting chance."

Slash looks over at Ella, his eyes wide.

"My body has taken all it can. I cannot stand by to let them take any more of my power. They can hold me here, but they cannot stop me from giving up my spirit to help others in need."

Ella closes her eyes as her body fades away, forming into a small ball of light and floating over to Slash.

"You can use me to help you." Ella's voice echoes in Slash's head as the ball of light turns into a saber.

"This is the Sword of Discernment. Pick it up," Ella says.

Slash crawls over to the sword and puts his hand around its hilt. Slash immediately sits up as the power of Ella fills his soul.

"I feel incredible!" Slash jumps up and does a backflip into the air. "I can run for miles with this power."

"Please know this power will not make you invincible, Slash," she says. "You are still human, but this sword has what little strength I had left put into it. With this power, you have a chance of escaping this forsaken place."

"It is a heavenly sword that gives the user a Supreme Art called Perfect Vision."

"Those types of skills are only heard in legends, Slash."

"What does that do?" Slash asks.

"Once a day, you can use a skill that lets you see the enemy's next move in battle. Be wise using this as it could prove fundamental in turning the tide of battle. I will be here with you. I am your servant. It is the very least I could do. After all, I could not save your friends all those years ago."

Slash cries, gripping the sword. "You have given me a fighting chance, and for that Ella, I owe you."

Slash stares at the door with a magical seal on it. *That arrow with a sword going through horizontally brings back a distant memory from my travels. I cant place it.* "I could break that, but it might set off an alarm."

Slash looks up at the window with the moon shining through. Slash jumps up on the wall and grabs on the metal bars. He pulls out his sword and cuts the bars off, slowly catching the metal as not to cause a ruckus.

"That's about ten feet down."

Slash looks over at a tree below him in the distance. "I can make that." Slash jumps out, landing on the branch of the tree and grabbing another branch. "Ouch!" He says, pulling out a tiny piece of wood from his palm. *That was nothing but a small splinter.* Slash jumps down towards the ground, scanning the area.

The night is as beautiful as ever. Slash leans low to the ground and runs towards the front of the castle, hiding amongst the bushes. *Sodina, I am coming for you. I'm so sorry for leaving. What a fool I am. Bridget will probably punch me in the face when she sees me. I left on her bad side.* Slash walks near the edge of the bridge, trying to figure out the best way to make it across without alerting the wolfen guard.

"I am beat after all of that training," a voice says.

A ten-foot-tall woman in a bright blue dress and purple wings approaches the two wolfen.

"Madam Claudia." The wolfen bows.

"No need for pleasantries," Claudia says. "I am the same as you. We are all on the same team."

Slash looks at the immense appearance of the demon before him. He knew that power emitting from her would overwhelm him. He was in the haven of the Demonic Empire and one mistake would cost him his life.

The wolfen howl as they bow at Claudia, who walks past them.

"I wouldn't mind licking her face," one of the wolfen says.

" I heard that," Claudia bellows.

The wolfen turns his head and smiles.

My only approach is direct on and taking them out. Slash pulls out his sword and walks out the bush as one of the wolfen turns around.

"It's time to close the gate for the night."

The other wolfen bow as they walk into the castle, closing the gates behind them.

That was close. He runs down the hill towards the town of Glashmere, keeping himself hidden on the side streets. *Just a bit more.* The edge of the city came into view. There were several wolfen sleeping in the streets.

He sneaks his way around, eventually reaching the castle shortcut in the stone wall he went through previously. Slash moves the rocks quietly before he runs towards the tree line outside the town of Glashmere.

I should have never left you, Sodina. Slash sits behind a tree catching his breath. *I have not run that hard since I proposed to Sodina all those years ago in the open fields of Ifer.* The chilly night breezes ruffles his hair as the moonlight shines between the trees. *Sodina, I am coming for you. Just wait for me.*

Slash stays by the tree line as he travels past the town of Ifer and into the vast forests of the Eastern Kingdom.

Well, there is no way to get to the Southern Kingdom now that the Bridge of Eden is destroyed. Who knows, they could have rebuilt it? Slash ponders. A wolfen comes into view in the woods. He sneaks near him and slices his neck from behind, silently killing him. Slash takes the sack off the wolfen's back and finds potions and fish.

"This was a great steal. Thank you, Goddess Astra."

"It was the goddess that gave you the power to escape," Ella says, giggling.

"I know." Slash sighs, running through the tree lines. "I think this is far enough. The town of Ifer is out of view."

Slash sits behind a tree exhausted from his clean sprint from his imprisonment.

"I need to sleep."

Slash lays down, covering himself with branches and leaves. *Hopefully, they will not find me here.* Slash closes his eyes, dreaming of Sodina as he drifts off to sleep.

...

"I see it!" Maria yells. "I see the lights of Ferrymore. It was just about a day's journey instead of several days like on a ship."

"We are fortunate," Malik says.

Chrono looks over at the end of the vessel, still several hundred feet in the air.

"I wonder why we are called Children of Light. I am a warrior, but this purpose that was put on us seems so much larger than we can achieve. Who are we even fighting? The demons are the only threats here. I know that the Eastern Kingdom needs to be taken back, but who is the real enemy? I wish to strike them down with my sword." Chrono sighs.

Bridget looks over at Chrono with a face of care, but says nothing.

"Queen Charlotte is building the army to take back the Eastern Kingdom," Chrono explains.

"I know that you seek the strength to destroy our enemies, Chrono." Sodina says, putting her hand on Chrono's shoulder. "I wonder why Goddess Astra has not given you a weapon of sorts. Maybe you already have everything you need."

Chrono stares off into the sky, thinking. *I wonder what Sarah would do?* Chrono thinks to himself.

"Hold on everyone." Lea steers the ships down towards the dock of Ferrymore.

The boat dives sharply towards the water as Lea pulls the wheel back, and the boat hits the water gracefully.

"What in Astra's name is that?" A man asks.

"It's a flying ship," Malik says, jumping onto the stone dock.

The man stands there, his mouth wide, unable to say a word. Maria walks onto the docks.

"Thank you for bringing us home." Maria smiles.

"What are you going to do now?" Lea asks the twins.

"We wanted to come with you, but we know there is no room for us on your journey." Malik grins nervously.

Bridget nods in approval.

"We will find our way." Maria smiles.

"You have shown us we can survive something like that. We can do anything." Malik smirks.

"Thank you for everything," the twins say in unison.

Malik and Maria run off into the city.

"Without them, we would have had no chance to make it this far," Lea whispers. "I will miss their banter."

"They were instrumental in our journey," Sodina adds. "Do we have any money left over from all of that?"

"We lost a lot in the storm," Bridget nods. "But fear not, we can make some up or pander a bit. You have the fearless adventurer, Bridget, and the War Master, Chrono, at your service."

"Our names must mean something in this area of Esteria," Chrono nods. "I fought with a few warriors here in the War Master tournament some years ago. One of them was an older man by the name of Leon Fankhauser. He owns an inn and spa here in Ferrymore. We could offer to do some work for him. I think his inn is called Broken Tooth Inn."

"It sounds like a place where people with no teeth go," Lea jokes.

Chrono looks back in disapproval at Lea but walks off the boat. "I know the way, follow me." He walks off the ship into the city as ladies follow in line.

"The town is lovely at night," Sodina giggles, wandering throughout the city.

"I love the coastal breeze on my face," Lea smiles, walking behind Chrono.

"I smell bad. I could use a shower right now." Bridget frowns, walking in front of Chrono. "When are we going to get there, Chrono? I am ravenous."

Chrono leads the group up a hill, passing by a corner and reaching a remarkable three-story building. Chrono opens the door and walks into the inn.

"Welcome to the Broken- By the Goddess, is that you, Chrono?" Leon walks towards Chrono and smacks him on the face. "I still have a sore spot on my ribs from when you punched me. Dear boy, come here. Let me look at you."

Leon, a slightly dark man in his sixties, bald with a small well-trimmed mustache, puts his hands on Chrono's face. "You still look good," he says.

"Good to see you too, Leon." Chrono smiles, putting his hands on Leon's shoulders. "We require a room for the night."

"My boy, anything for you." Leon smiles.

"Can we at least do the dishes for you?" Chrono asks.

"No, that will not be necessary at all." Leon gestures towards the stairs. "Sasha, come here, please, honey."

An older woman with short, spiky hair walks over to Leon.

"Please show them to the twin executive suite with the private bath, please."

Sasha nods, smiling, leading the group up the stairs.

"Here is your room. Try not to have too much fun." Sasha smiles, winking at Chrono.

"What is that supposed to mean?" Bridget asks.

Sasha says nothing as she heads back.

Bridget opens the door with the key and walks in. Lush purple and red linens line the room with bright red coppery curtains and a covered balcony bath tucked into the corner.

"Oh, my weary bones." Lea walks over and falls on the sofa.

"Guys, you need to bathe before sitting down on any of this luxurious furniture," Sodina reprimands.

Chrono walks into the room and sees a door. "I guess my suite is there. You ladies have a good night."

Chrono walks into the partner suite and closes the door.

"I guess he must be tired. I am going to the bath right now," Bridget yells.

Bridget strips down and runs toward the balcony, almost tripping. She sees a handle and pulls it down as water falls from piping above.

"Oh, I see. They must heat the water from the rooftop and put soapy water in it," Bridget says excitedly. "I like it! It's just the right temperature."

Bridget sits in the water as it spills over her body.

"Ladies, come on in, the water is excellent!" Bridget puts bubbles in her hair as she dips underneath the water and back up again.

Sodina and Lea walk in and step into the bath.

"You sure are passionate tonight, Bridget," Lea says.

"I want to feel clean and sexy for the next part of our adventure. You never know who we will meet."

Lea looks down at her body, not as robust as Bridget and frowns. *I wonder if a man will ever want me,* she wonders. Lea sits down in the water and washes.

"While we're here, I think we can plan out our next direction, ladies. We have a problematic next leg of our journey. Our plan tomorrow is to head to the Tree of Woe in the Eastern kingdom."

Our home. We have been away for so long, I wonder what has become of our home? Sodina sinks into the water, slumping.

Lea looks saddened by the thought of heading back.

"Cheer up, ladies. We're on the home stretch now. We have passed two of the three trials, and I am sure we are getting closer to finding a cure for you, Sodina."

"Hmmm. You have been looking paler than usual, Sodina," Lea says, looking at Sodina with concern.

"It's nothing I can't overcome," Sodina assures them. "I have to overcome it."

Underneath the bubbly water, Sodina's wrist shakes violently. *Keep it under control,* Sodina thinks to herself, trying to calm her trembling.

Bridget cuts her eyes towards Sodina but says nothing.

"Anyway, we need prep by buying some food for the journey," Bridget explains.

"I wonder how fast that flying ship can go?" She says. "If we go too fast, everyone will be thrown out." Lea sighs.

"Why don't we buy some rope and create a belt of sorts for higher speeds?' Bridget smiles. "We can wrap it around the mast so we can travel faster."

"That's brilliant idea." Lea sits up, splashing water everywhere. "I think that will work. I can push the limits. I am a wild child! Watch out demons, you won't know what hit you when Lea comes charging in," Lea exclaims, pointing at the stars.

"I will smile brightly and push the limits of my mind and body!"

"Where did all of that come from?" Bridget smiles.

"I have been quite depressed lately, trying to find my place in our journey. I feel I have little to offer in battle now. I have to admit, I'm out of elemental arrows. I'm just an archer and nothing more."

"You saved us in that water cave, don't think of yourself so little," Bridget says happily.

"I agree," Sodina smiles.

"Well, ladies, my skin is getting clammy. I will turn in for the night." Bridget walks out of the bath to dry off.

"Do not worry, Sodina. I know you are in pain. There is no need to hide it." Lea observes the large purple area around her friend's right shoulder. "There is more got to be more than this pain in your shoulder."

"You are intuitive as ever, Lea."

Lea walks over to Sodina and puts her arms around her.

"I will be with you, my friend. You have my bow and quickness to aid you in your healing journey. Rest well, knowing there are those you can share your burdens with."

"Thank you," Sodina says, leaning in and wrapping her arms around Lea. Lea turns around, her pigtails wet with water, as she grabs a towel from the cabinet.

"Good night, Sodina." Lea closes the door as she dries off.

Slash, if you are out there, my sweet husband, please come back to me. We are joined and my heart aches not knowing you are here fighting this battle with me. Sodina blows a kiss towards the moon before she steps out the bath to head to bed.

The morning sun cracks through the curtains as Bridget turns over on her bed. *Just let me sleep more.* Bridget rolls off the bed drooling, she wipes her mouth, crawling back into the bed. Sodina looks around, her hair curly and puffed. She falls back into her pillow.

Chrono knocks on the door. "You ladies need to wake up."

Chrono knocks loudly. Lea walks up to the door, opening it.

"Go away," Lea groans before closing the door.

Chrono looks puzzled, shrugs, walks back to the reception area.

Leon waves at Chrono as he walks out the door.

I have some money, just enough gold coins to buy a few things. I guess those women need their beauty sleep. Chrono pulls out two gold coins from his pocket as he walks up the street to a vendor. *Why waste money when I can work?* Chrono runs towards the docks to find some fishermen having trouble lifting crates of fish.

"Excellent day, gentleman." Chrono waves.

"Good morning, what do you need?" One of the men asks.

"If I help you, could you give me some of that extra rope you have on board?"

"As long as you are not asking for money, have at it." The man pointed at the dock.

Chrono helps another fisherman lift a large crate into the harbor towards a stand.

The man smiled. "You help cut the fish, we throw in some fish for you after."

Chrono nods, putting the crate down. "Why not?"

Another man shows Chrono how to cut the fish and prepare it for packaging.

Chrono takes the knife and slices up several fish, being careful to cut out the bones as requested by the fishermen.

Four hours pass. Chrono wipes his head, beating with sweat.

"Job well done, young man. You work hard, unlike the other scallywags here." The captain of the boat smiles with delight.

I feel like I did most of the work, Chrono thinks.

"One crate of fish that should last you a week, and here is some rope for your troubles. Thank you once again." Chrono takes the fish and carries it back to the flying ship.

"All in a day's work." Chrono takes the rope and cuts parts of it off to make restraints, and ties them all to the center mast of the boat. He sits down, drinking some water from his bottle as Lea, Bridget, and Sodina approach him.

"We felt sorry you did all that work. We went shopping for potions and food. We got you something." Lea pulls out a small cupcake with white frosting.

"Eat up, you! We got it for you because it was sweet of you to do this for us." Sodina smiles.

Chrono, famished from his work, chows down on the cupcake, eating it in three bites.

"That hit the spot." Chrono lays back on the boat as he looks up at the sky.

"Well, you can rest on the journey. Captain Lea will guide us to our next destination." Lea taps Chrono on the head before she heads up to the steering wheel.

"I believe we will need to head Northwest, dear," Bridget says to Lea.

"The Tree of Woe," Lea says. "I wonder what horrors await us there."

Lea drives the ship into the air as it leaves the water, steadily flying up. "I will push it a bit, everyone."

The group wraps the rope around their bodies, securing themselves.

"Hey everyone, we didn't open that door over there," Bridget points.

"There is no need for the rope when we can go under the deck," Lea says.

"We were so tired we didn't even notice the bottom half of the boat." Chrono sighs. "All of that fish cutting for nothing."

Bridget walks over to the hatch, opens the door and walks down into the boat.

"It wasn't for nothing. We still have a lot of food to fuel us for this journey." She smiles.

Bridget observes the area underneath to find four beds and a sofa. "It smells rough down there, but it's been hundreds of years since anyone has ridden this thing." She opens a small chest to find a few hundred gold coins. "Hey, everyone! W-we are rich!" She stutters in shock.

Chrono goes down the steps and checks.

"Oh, my—" Chrono looks at the coins. "Is this currency even relevant anymore?"

"Gold is gold." Bridget winks. "Any fool would want some of it. We have enough here to get whatever we want for food and weapons—no need to work hard when we can use these coins."

"If they are not as useful, we could sell them to a historian as well." Chrono nods at Bridget.

"Hold on to your nearest buddy because we're about to have a little fun now." Lea smiles before she pushes the ship to go faster through the clouds.

Sodina lies flat on the floor of the boat as the wind pushes through her hair.

"I am alive!" Lea yells, as she goes up into the clouds several hundred more feet.

"Lea, can I at least go under the deck?!" Sodina yells. "I am feeling sick."

Sodina's body lifts into the air, floating up past the mast as a barrier prevents her from flying off the boat.

"Oh! The ship has its own magical barrier so we can never fall off—"

Sodina slams into the floor.

"Ugh, still, it does nothing to soften the blow." Sodina sits up, catching her breath.

"Did you know that, Lea?" Sodina yells over to her.

"I might have tested it while everyone was away," Lea winks.

"You did not bother to tell us, you know. All that work, Chrono did to get the rope."

"What is life without a little joy? Plus, you always tell me to smile more." She looks down at Sodina. "I feel useful and alive."

Sodina walks up to the wheel where Lea is standing. "Let me fly the ship for a bit. You go rest, friend." She takes the wheel and her arms feel weak. *Must not let them know I am hurting.* Sodina smiles, grabbing the wheel. She steers the ship down steadily below the clouds, two hundred feet in the air, as Lea sits down on the deck floor.

"You know Sodina, you are strong. Fighting poison and fighting demons. I admire you." Lea smiles looking up at Sodina.

"You know, I used to be the weakest one in our group. Healing spells is all I could muster growing up. Some individuals, as you know, have an affinity towards magic while others are drawn more to weapons. Some do neither and focus on supporting professions like potion-making and blacksmithing. I was told to focus more on potions, but I enjoyed the sense of adventure."

Sodina smiles, feeling nostalgic.

"Growing up with Slash and our friends, we always would run around town acting like we were going on adventures. Slash was the leader even though he lacks endurance. He could only last in a fight for a few minutes. His courage is something I admired. Even though he would be down and out, he always pulls out the battle at the last minute. He is a master strategist in battle. He'd rather run from a fight he knows he will not win. Some people call that cowardice. I find it endearing that he has the wisdom to know when to attack or not. That is a characteristic of a genuine leader."

Lea smiles as she pats Sodina on the shoulder. "I will stay with you up here as we journey to our next destination."

Hours pass as Sodina and Lea switch places traveling through the Southern Kingdom.

"The wind is fierce up here," Sodina whispers as she puts on a coat she found underneath the deck.

Chrono walks up towards the deck, his hair messed up from lying on the bed.

"That is the most comfortable bed I have ever slept on. I guess the heroes of old had class as well to choose such fine linens. It may need a good cleaning, but we all get dirty anyway."

Bridget walks up, stretching as she looks out through the clouds and into the stars.

"We are making great time. We have already passed by Lafare, and we're somewhere near Mala I think. We are still heading northwest, so we should cross into the Eastern Kingdom soon. Be at the ready."

Sodina guides the ship as it continues to fly past the town of Mala. The tropical trees disappear as the dense forest of the Eastern Kingdom come into view.

A purple fog manifests as the ship crosses the border into the Eastern Kingdom.

"Oh, my goodness," Sodina gasps, putting her hands over her mouth.

"Is that?" Sodina mutters.

"It is." Chrono clenches his fist. "That is what is left of the Bridge of Eden. Those downright, undercutting, no-good-for-nothing heathens did that."

"All of those people they killed." Lea bows her head in sorrow. "Goddess Astra, keep my bow steady as we go back into our home."

"I can smell it," Sodina cries. "The demon stench that permeates the kingdom. They have taken it all. I feel the pain and suffering."

The ship continues to glide over the gap left by Gareth's attack on the Bridge of Eden.

"My sword will go through the one who did this to our kingdom," Chrono snaps. "The fog is heavy over this area."

Lea slows the ship in surprise as a large branch comes into view. "Hang on!" Lea dips the ship downward, diving towards the enormous tree. "Augh." She pulls the ship's wheel back towards her and the ship hits the ground, grinding on the ground but otherwise still intact.

"That was a bit of a rough landing." Lea stands up, surveying around the area they landed. "It looks like the ship didn't take too much damage."

Chrono opens the door and looks around the boat with Bridgct.

"I agree with you, Lea. It appears to be in good shape still."

"Let us depart," Sodina says confidently.

Lea pulls out her bow as the group walks through the fog towards the path leading to the Tree of Woe.

"Something doesn't feel right. We have yet to hear any voice or run into anyone. Usually we face something. This feels too easy," Lea whispers.

"Maybe the gods above are giving us the chance to have an effortless task this time. They know we are beaten down from the last trial." Chrono smirks. "I am thankful for the effortless march, but let us not forget to keep our guard up." Chrono pulls out his sword, leading the rear of the pack.

"I see a clearing up ahead, and a pathway," Sodina whispers to the group. "Be ready for anything."

The group walks into the clearing slowly, preparing for an attack.

"Oh, it's about time you show up," a voice speaks seductively.

"Show yourself," Chrono yells back.

Lisha appears, blocking the path to the Tree of Woe. She claps her hands as she walks down the steps to greet the group.

"Gareth was right. Someone would try to pull something sneaky here." Lisha snaps her fingers at her purple dress covering her body, tightening the grip around her.

"Good day, filthy humans. I am Lisha, one of the three generals of the Exalted One, Gareth. Will you kindly die for me? Just a little death for dear ol' me? There is no way you are getting past me."

Chrono steps in front of Sodina, pointing his sword towards Lisha.

"Were you the foul beast that blew up the Bridge of Eden?"

"Foul beast? Your words hurt me," Lisha says, laughing. "Would a foul beast have breasts as beautiful as these?"

Lisha pushes up on her chest, perking up for Chrono. "Be in awe, dear human, at my beauty."

"The name is Chrono, the War Master, and you will meet your end."

"Not interested in having fun? You humans are truly the boring lot," Lisha giggles. "In that case, I would give you a free touch before snapping your neck."

"I rather just slay you where you stand. Everyone at the ready!" Chrono looks back at Bridget, Lea, and Sodina.

Lisha runs towards Chrono, jumping in the air and slamming her scythe towards his head. Chrono pulls out his sword and clashes against her mighty weapon.

"Agh." Chrono gets pushed back, parrying the attack.

"Not bad, human." Lisha winks.

Lea runs towards the side of the clearing and shoots three arrows towards Lisha. Lisha jumps back, dodging the arrows and she throws her scythe towards Lea.

Bridget throws her ax toward the scythe, deflecting it.

Lisha looks towards Bridget and grins.

"You have a good pair of bosoms on you, young lady," Lisha smiles. "Almost too good to be killed."

Lisha puts her hand out as her scythe materializes back in front of her.

Bridget runs to pick up her ax back in front of Lea.

"Okay Lea, jump off my back and shoot an arrow at her. I will run in and attack with my ax."

Lea nods.

Sodina jumps back towards the clearing of the entrance, freeing herself from the danger, chanting a spell.

"Hopefully I have time to unleash this." *Everyone, please hold out until then.*

Chrono runs towards Lisha. She swings her scythe, narrowly missing as Chrono ducks to the ground. Chrono swings his sword towards her legs but she jumps over the blade. Chrono jumps up, swinging his sword upward toward Lisha's neck and cutting her on the chin.

Bridget bends down as Lea jumps on off her back, shooting two arrows towards Lisha. Lisha dodges one arrow as the other pins her dress to the ground. Chrono swings his sword towards Lisha's neck as she snaps her fingers and her outfit changes, freeing her from the arrow. Lisha rolls to the left and punches Chrono right in the stomach, sending him flying into the air.

Chrono falls to the ground with a thud.

"Ugh," Chrono grunts, trying to stand up. "Is that the best you got?"

Lisha smiles, running towards Chrono, punching him in the face twice and kicking him across the ground.

"Chrono!" Lea yells, shooting two more arrows.

Lisha runs towards Lea before Bridget jumps in front of her, punching Lisha in the face.

"Stand back, you witch," Bridget warns, her eyes glowing purple with rage.

"You!" Lisha points at Bridget. "Who are you? Your eyes glow like a demon."

Lisha walks up towards Bridget, putting her weapon away. "These bosoms and hips, you have the same body type as me."

Bridget pushes her away before pointing her axe towards Lisha.

"Back off, witch. Don't you dare touch me again."

"Could it be?" Lisha says, distraught. "Could you be my daughter?"

"I am no daughter of yours," Bridget charges.

Lea runs from behind Bridget and shoots an arrow into Lisha's knee.

"Ugh," Lisha grunts. "This is none of your business, insect."

Lisha steps back, shooting a small purple ray and hitting Lea in the shoulder.

"Argh!" Lea screams, her shoulder bloodied. "She got me. I think my bone is broken. I can't draw my bow this way."

Bridget runs towards Lisha, swinging her ax before Lisha swiftly dodges the attack.

"Tsk. Tsk. Your attacks need work, my daughter." Lisha sneaks in a punch on Bridget, hitting her in her stomach before she delivers an uppercut to the chest.

"I will spare you your life, my daughter. You are meant to serve with me and your father. You are the princess to the demonic realm. They stole you from us during a battle twenty-five years ago. Your father and I were not strong enough to fight the hordes of humans then. Surrender now and come with me, lest you want your friends to die a horrible death."

"Shut your mouth! I am from the Northern Kingdom, with loving parents who cared for me." Bridget swings her ax wildly, Lisha dodging each attack. Bridget swings her ax down at her but Lisha grabs on Bridget's limbs, stopping her attack midway. She throws Bridget upwards before manifesting her staff.

Lisha scoffs, licking her lips. "If that's the way you want to play it, then so be it, dear daughter."

Lisha slams the blunt side of her scythe onto Bridget's chest as she falls, slamming it down on her back after she crashes on the ground.

Bridget coughs up blood, trying to push herself up. "I am not your daughter, witch. And even if I was I would never give myself to the likes of you."

Lisha walks up to Bridget slowly, smiling genuinely.

"Come, my daughter, enough with this petty shuffle and fulfill your destiny with us. Your father awaits your presence."

Lea sneaks up on Lisha, stabbing her with a dagger in the back. "Take that, you monster."

"When will you insects learn?" Lisha reaches back and twists Lea's hand, snapping her wrist before throwing her away. Lea hits a tree before crashing on the ground.

"Lea!" Chrono and Bridget yell.

Chrono sits up, catching his breath.

"War Dance!" Chrono doubles his speed by steading his breathing and he dashes towards Lisha, kicking her in the face.

"Pathetic twig." Lisha pulls out her scythe, swinging towards Chrono but he ducks, narrowly missing his scalp.

Bridget stands up, running towards Chrono, helping him stand right back up.

"You ready?" Bridget asks.

Chrono nodded affirming her prompting. "Always."

"Elite Tornado!" They scream in unison.

Chrono and Bridget twirl in a circle as they let go in the air, swinging their weapons in a flurry of attack. Lisha puts up her scythe, blocking each attack. Bridget kicks Lisha's heels, tripping her. Chrono swings his sword down, cutting her hip.

"Enough of this playtime." Lisha jumps back, rubbing her hip. "You will pay for this insurrection, you filthy insects."

"Ice Prison!" Sodina calls out.

Three large pillars of ice suddenly surround Lisha, closing her in. Lisha tries to move, but cannot.

Sodina leaned over breathing heavily. "Thank you for distracting her long enough."

Chrono looks back and nods.

"Time to finish this!" Chrono screams, lunging towards Lisha's head with his sword.

"This isn't over yet." Lisha bows her head before screaming. "Sentence of the Damned!" The ice explodes as two large purple arms appear out of her back, swiping down on Chrono. "Die a horrible death you arrogant waste of flesh!"

Chrono eyes widen as he braces for imminent death. Bridget runs in front of Chrono, pushing him out of the way, turning her back towards the two enormous fists. The twin fist hit Bridget at full force, shattering her dragon cloak and slamming her into the ground.

"Foolish child, you waste your life trying to protect these worthless humans." Lisha laughs. "I thought of you as brainwashed, but never a fool."

Bridget crawls towards Sodina, who is shaking in fear.

"We need to leave," Sodina mouths. "Ray of light!" She yells. A ray of radiant light surrounds the area, blinding Lisha. Sodina runs over to grab Lea and Chrono.

"We need to go!" Bridget pushes herself up, limping away from the blinded Lisha.

The group manages to run as fast as they could back to the ship without Lisha in sight.

"Almost there, but be careful! She could still be around," Chrono warns.

Sodina opens the door quickly and puts Lea softly underneath the deck. Bridget and Chrono run onto the deck and fall on the ground in pain. Sodina runs towards the wheel and lifts the ship off the ground, starting to fly into the air.

"You will not get away!" Lisha yells.

She throws her scythe but only manages to cut the side of the ship, which is 100 feet in the air. They managed to quickly fly away, disappearing into the clouds.

"My daughter," Lisha whispers, looking up. "I will find you and kill those humans you are with. We will live together as a family and I will kill anyone who will stand between us."

Lisha shakes her head, rubbing her hip where her wound counties to bleed. "Damn rats. They got me good. I should report back to Gareth promptly." Lisha slowly floats back to the forest, disappearing in the mist.

"Chrono!" Sodina yells. "Take the ship. I need to heal Lea. Keep the course south, right towards Mala. We need to get out of here as soon as possible."

Bridget sits up on the edge of the boat, caressing her back and spitting up blood. "That witch got me good. I swear, the next time I see her again I'm gonna pop a vein."

Sodina runs downs the stairs quickly towards Lea.

"I am pretty banged up," Lea whispers.

"Let me see it." Sodina puts out her hands as a green light surrounds Lea.

"That should ease the pain. We need to get you to a doctor. Lay here and let my magic soothe you." Sodina closes her eyes. "Rest, dear friend. You did amazing."

Lea closes her eyes, falling asleep on the bed. Sodina puts her hand on Lea's head, smiling and walking towards Bridget.

"Your cloak... I can't believe that she destroyed it," Sodina says to Bridget.

"I took a killer blow to my back, but the cloak took most of the damage. That impact had to break one of my ribs. I am having trouble breathing," she says. Sodina puts her hands on Bridget's right rib and whispers a healing chant.

"That should help a bit. Here, this should help." Sodina hands Bridget a pain-numbing potion. "These were not cheap, you know?"

Bridget gulps the potion down, wiping her mouth. "I will put my ax through her throat when I see her next."

Sodina puts her hand on Bridget's shoulder and walks up to Chrono.

"Here you go, War Master," Sodina offers. "I saw you take a couple of—"

"I am okay, just some pain, but nothing was broken," Chrono interrupts. "We need to save our potions for battles we hope to win. Even though we have all that money, we need to be wise."

Sodina nods in approval. "At least let me do something for you." Sodina puts out her hand before she stumbles slightly. Chrono looks with concern as Sodina waves her hand.

Chrono shook his head. "I am okay. Just felt dizzy."

Sodina lets out a green mist that surrounds Chrono and gives him fresh energy.

"I feel like a million gold coins!" Chrono yells.

"I can only cast that spell once a month, so hopefully, it will serve you well."

Sodina sits down on the steps near the top deck, exhausted from all the action. Bridget walks up to Chrono and Sodina.

"To face someone that powerful." Bridget holds her ribs slightly. "What chance do we have, you know? She was one of the demonic generals. Her power was terrifying, and that speed was something nothing of us could match at our current skill levels. The craziest thing was that she said I was her daughter. Imagine that? What if I am a demon? Does that make me?"

"If you are a demon." Sodina smiles at Bridget. "Then you are still our friend. That is what all that means. We will fight and die beside you on the battlefield."

Chrono nods in approval, looking at Bridget and Sodina.

"I think we should head to Lafare instead of Mala. I know that the journey may take more time, but they have better facilities. I'd rather not face Sarah yet, knowing that she may want me to stay with her. I miss her, but we have to get ready for war. Getting back to Lafare, hopefully, Queen Charlotte has made some headway in gathering an army."

"I hope so as well," Bridget adds. "The immense feeling of dread over the Eastern Kingdom is palpable."

"You two get some rest. I will guide us safely to Lafare," Chrono tells Sodina and Bridget before they return inside.

Chrono let go a smile. "Those ladies work themselves too hard," he mutters. He drives the ship through the clouds slowly as his thoughts trail. An image of Sarah appears in his mind while the gentle breeze blows past him like an angel's kiss.

Chapter 20

Month of Dragons
Day 29

"Master!" Lisha runs into the castle in Glashmere, running toward the throne room to find him sitting pleasantly.

"What is it, Lisha?" Gareth scowls at her. "You're disturbing my quiet time."

"Our daughter," Lisha says as she floats towards him. "I believe we found her. Her name is Bridget."

Gareth was lost in thought. "So, the reports Nagi submitted were correct."

Lisha tried to concentrate the pain searing through her body. "Yes, Dearest One."

"She was strong, right?" Gareth looks down at Lisha.

"Yes, and she travels with a group of humans," she says, cowering at his feet.

"Something is amiss because the boy and the fairy have gone missing." He strokes his chin, the gears turning in his head.

Lisha states, "I sent wolfen to find them, but they have yet to find anything yet."

"No matter," Gareth waves her off. "That pathetic goddess had outlived her purpose. They could not have gotten far."

"Yes, Dearest One." Lisha bows her head as Gareth stands from his throne.

"Since you returned here without our daughter, you need to be punished." Gareth flies towards Lisha and puts his hands on her throat and slams her to the ground.

"How dare you show your face here without our daughter? I sent you there because there were rumors, and all you had to do was kill a few humans!" Gareth yells in rage towards Lisha, and she cowers in fear.

"I tried, Master, I tried," she responds, struggling in his grip.

"Do not utter my name!" Gareth yells in her face.

"You're choking me," Lisha cries out.

Gareth lets go of his grip and walks back up to the throne chair, wringing his hands together.

"I am sorry," Gareth pinches the bridge of his nose. "My emotions overcame me. You are precious to me, Lisha, but do not upset me again or I may not control my rage."

Lisha bows, still shaking from the events and waits for Gareth's next instruction.

"Our army is thirty thousand strong," Gareth bellows throughout the whole throne room. "Half of the sentinels are on covert missions, while some have returned. We will march when I feel ready. I am planning on moving some primary force towards Dalton and more towards the Bridge of Eden for security. I would like you to rest here and not fight, Lisha."

"Yes, my Lord. I hear you loud and clear."

"The humans may have our daughter fighting on their side, but I would not want my lover to come to an unfortunate end." Gareth looks Lisha straight in the eyes.

"Yes, my Lord." Lisha bows again and floats off, leaving the throne room.

Lisha clenches her fists as the throne room doors close behind her. "Who does he think he is to treat me like that?" Lisha mutters to herself. "I'm not even his wife!"

"You should not have upset him," Neron says from behind her.

Lisha punches him in the shoulder as she passes by him on the steps to her sleeping quarters.

"Shut your mouth, Neron. I do not answer to you."

"But you do answer to him, Lisha," Neron retorts and turns away from the woman, making his way down the steps as she goes upward.

Lisha floats to the ground and continues the walk towards her room. She sighs and takes off her robes, lying in bed stomach down.

"Let me be of some comfort, Lady Lisha," a small voice says.

"Oh, Hilda!" Lisha sits up to see her old servant. "You scared me! It is just you."

Hilda walks from behind a curtain at the end of the room and puts her hands on Lisha's back to start massaging.

"Do not let the Master get to you. He is only doing what needs to be done, even if it's done in anger."

"How do you know that, Hilda?" Lisha whispers.

"I know everything that goes on in this castle, Lady Lisha." Hilda continues massaging her with her hands. "I am here to serve everyone in this castle. To recognize their every need and to meet that need in the most perfect way possible."

"I want to ask you to do something for me," Lisha whispers. "Monitor Gareth's emotions and report back to me how he changes. Something is wrong with him."

"Yes, milady." Hilda bows as she walks out of the room.

Lisha puts her hands on her heart and slams her fist into her pillow.

My daughter, I will find you and bring you to your senses. You will not live in ignorance any longer. Stay strong for me, and I will rescue you from those human's clutches.

Lisha curls up in a ball and cries, looking out the window of her room into the black sky of what was once Glashmere.

...

Slash wakes up to find a small fairy flying over him.

"Tori!" Slash sits up in amazement, peering into her eyes.

"Thank Astra, you made it out of that forsaken place," Tori winks at Slash. "And you don't look half bad."

"I... had help." Slash looks down at his sword.

"Yes, I have spoken with Ella already," she says, buzzing around his face. "Us spiritual creatures can communicate telepathically you know, unlike humans. She told me of what you went through and that you stood no chance. With that sword, you can fight back. Do not be foolish and throw your life away."

Tori smacks Slash on the head. "You got a second chance. You were delivered from the darkness by the heavenly realms. Make your way back to your wife."

Slash sits up from underneath the brush and looks around.

"How long was I asleep?" Slash wipes his eyes.

"For at least a day or two," Ella giggles. "I was able to travel through the Eastern Kingdom looking for survivors and have found very few. The towns of Rinkar and Jerut seem to have some normalcy to them. Dalton and Artemis have fallen. Gareth controls everything you see around these parts. From listening in on conversations from wolfen, he has sent two of his seven sentinels to Rinkar and Jerut to overtake them. Instead of killing everyone like in Artemis and Dalton, they will make the people slaves."

"That's horrible," Slash sighs.

"But..." Ella gasps. "That's not all. An enormous force will head down to the Southern Kingdom to wage war with them. I have no knowledge of when that is supposed to happen, but there could be many high-ranking demons amongst those forces."

"I need to get to the Southern Kingdom and warn them. The only way to get there is to fly," Tori says brightly. "I can get there, but it may be too late."

"Could I come with you?" Slash asks, yearning to see his wife.

"You are too heavy for Tori to carry over a large body of water, Slash," Ella laughs. "I would head to Artemis and see if there is any resistance there. With a town that large, there may still be a light of hope."

"I need to find a horse, though," Slash says. "There must be one around here."

"To whistle loudly would draw the attention of our enemies," Ella whispers.

"It may take us a few days to get there on foot, especially if things get nasty, and we have to fight. I'd rather avoid fighting unless need be," Tori smiles.

"I have already put several wolfen to sleep, trying not to kill them," the small fairy continues. "Even though Gareth's minions have killed many of our people, I still have compassion for his creations."

"Those tortured souls lack empathy and only know to kill," Slash agrees. "I do feel sorry for them."

Ella keeps silent on the matter and does not say a word.

"Well, from here we should head southwest. I am ready when you are," Tori says.

Tori high fives Slash and follow behind him.

Slash keeps a low profile while traveling through the forest for several hours, weaving in and out of the line only to take breaks to eat or rest for a moment.

"We are making good time, I think," Tori says, flying behind Slash. "But my wings are getting tired already."

Tori stops by a tree and lands on the ground. "We need to rest, Slash. We are no good to anyone if we cannot fight."

Slash looks back at Tori, nodding in approval but wanting to go on.

Slash sits down back to back with Tori, her wings wrapping around him like a warm hug.

"Do not mind me," Tori whispers. "Putting them around you is just a way to relax them. Is that okay?"

"I see no problem with it," Slash says. "I am tired too, and we are friends even though you knocked me out. I think that was for your own good."

"I knew you needed to rest and I saved you. Be grateful." Tori wraps her wings around Slash tightly, then lets go.

"I get it, believe me," Slash says. "You were instrumental in preparing me, but I still lost. I should have gone back to Sodina, but I was sure I could prevent Gareth from completing his mission."

"They have no idea what is coming." Tori shook her tiny head. "But Queen Charlotte is a wise woman. She will be ready. I only hope that they prepare sooner rather than later."

"I think she will be prepared," Ella pipes up. "The foe they fight is greater than they have ever known."

Slash looks up through the forest to see a horse before him.

"Is that what I think it is? We need it!" Slash jumps up to run towards the horse.

"Sit down," Tori speaks sharply. "You will spook it if you run towards it looking like you just won the prize of your life."

Tori flies over to the horse and puts her hand on its head. "Be at peace, creature of Astra."

The horse sits down on all fours and lays its head on the ground.

Slash walks up to look at the horse that bears the flag of the Eastern Kingdom.

"This was a knight's horse. I thought all of them died protecting the kingdom." Slash looks around the horse for any weapons or notes, but doesn't find any.

"I wonder where the rider is or if he is even still alive," Ella says.

Slash sits down beside the horse and pats it on the head.

"Be good for us, okay, sweet boy?" Tori tells the horse before sitting beside Slash.

"Do you genuinely believe you can liberate Artemis?" She asks him. "What if a powerful enemy awaits you there?"

"I will cut them down," Slash says with confidence.

Fifteen minutes pass as Slash and Tori rest up.

"Let's get going," Slash says confidently, standing up the horse and jumping on its back.

"I have never ridden a horse, so I shall join you!" Tori flies upon the horse's back and wraps her arms around Slash. "Let's go!"

Slash turns the horse around, heading towards the direction of Artemis. The horse gathers full speed and pushes harder than ever before.

"Ready, fire!" A voice shouts as arrows fall from the sky.

"Elemental Barrier!" Tori yells to cast a force field of light to protect them from the arrows.

Slash stops the horse in the middle of the clearing as more than fifty archers on horse come out of the sides of the forest.

"You there!" A man steps forward, jumping off his horse. "What is your name, and what is that creature that accompanies you?"

"My name is Slash from the town of Ifer. You look like Glashmere knights to me!"

"You hail from Ifer." The man gestures for his men to lower their weapons. "We are fellow countrymen, then. My name is Bartholet, a captain of the Glashmere Archery Corps."

Tori flies down towards Bartholet, looking at his brown cloak and muscular figure.

"I am a fairy from the Great Forest, but our people are almost extinct."

Bartholet bows to Tori. "You are creatures that we have yet to understand fully. We ask for your aid in a task, Slash. We were separated from the rest of our group heading to Rinkar, Jerut, and Artemis. These areas are next to be conquered by the forces of evil."

Slash's face lights up as he jumps off the horse. "You can remove the barrier, Tori. These men wish us no harm. We were headed that way, you may accompany us."

"I appreciate that, Sir," Bartholet bows, "But I must be honest. Only one-third of what you see are trained warriors. The rest are survivors dressed in warrior clothing. We are giving the illusion of being well prepared when this is more like a militia than an army. We have spirit, and my trained men have been working with them to improve their marksmanship. They have nowhere to go. This is home, and they will die on this soil if need be. Once again, we thank you, and we are sorry for attacking you."

Slash grins at the captain.

"You know we were in no actual danger." Tori smiles and elbows Slash in the arm. "I would've let you know right away."

Bartholet bows a third time as he turns around to his men. "Listen, all! This man rides with us to Artemis. That is the closest city to where we are now. We will take back our homeland or die trying!"

The men yell in unison, "For Glashmere!"

"Let us be on our way," Bartholet yells as everyone falls in behind him.

Bartholet nods at Slash as he joins the group of men with Tori.

"Nice to meet you," a man says, riding by Slash.

"Nice to meet you, too!" Slash fist bumps the man as they journey together.

"I am from Dalton, which was completely wiped out by the demons. They killed everyone. Only a few of us survived. Their significant power overwhelmed us in an instant. It was like an ant fighting a cyclops. No hope of survival."

Slash shivers, imagining the scene this young man has seen. "What is your name?"

"My name is Marco, sir."

"I am Slash, no need to call me sir."

"It's good to find a friend here," Marco chuckles as they ride along. "Too many of these guys are bent on revenge. I want revenge, but if I let it consume me, I will lose who I am. Meeting someone level-headed like you, Sir—I mean, Slash, is really nice."

"That's funny, Marco," Tori giggles, flying next to Marco. "Slash is the least level-headed human I've met!"

"Whoa." Marco's eyes widen at the sight of her. "You are…"

"A fairy," Tori winks and flies around the head of Marco's horse, causing the light gray animal to whinny. "Get used to it."

"I was going to say… you're beautiful, ma'am." Marco smiles wide at Tori. "I've never seen anyone like you. Fairy, human, or otherwise. It's a pleasure."

Tori turns pink and she squeals with glee. "You're a sweetie, Marco! I like you already!"

Slash lowers his head, trying not to eavesdrop on their connection. He missed Sodina so much watching Tori aimlessly flirt with the Dalton knight.

As soon as the sun hit the middle of the sky above them, it was finally afternoon for the travelling group.

"Cyclops!" Bartholet yells as a fifteen-foot cyclops throws a tree towards the group, barely missing them. "Split formation into the trees and take cover! NOW!"

Half of the group goes into one half of the tree line while the other half takes cover on the opposite side.

"Fire at will, men!" Slash screams.

Tori flies above them, trying to distract the cyclops by spinning around his face.

The men shoot arrows towards the cyclops's eye and it puts up its arm to block the arrows. Bartholet rides toward the cyclops as it punches towards him.

Bartholet jumps on his horse's back and runs up to the arm of the cyclops, taking his arrow and stabbing it in its eye.

Bartholet's horse runs around behind the creature as Bartholet jumps down, landing on two feet and sitting on it.

"Let me lend you a hand, Captain!" Slash shouts. "Or maybe an arm!"

Slash climbs off his horse and runs toward the cyclops, cutting off the right arm of the beast with his sword.

The cyclops stumbles back, waving its left arm violently in the air. The beast roars in pain.

"Now, men!" Bartholet yells.

A second volley of arrows penetrates the monster all over its body.

The cyclops falls to one knee, wailing in pain.

Slash runs back towards the cyclops, pushing his sword into its bleeding eye. The cyclops finally falls on its back and Slash jumps on its body to stab his sword into its heart three times over.

The cyclops stops moving and lies still, still bleeding from its wounds.

"You truly are incredible with that sword, Slash!"

"Years of farm training, Captain Bartholet," Slash smiles. "Let's get out of here. He might have a friend."

Bartholet yells out to everyone in the woods to follow Slash's orders.

Tori brings the horse back around to Slash, lifting him onto it with a levitation spell.

"Those were pretty fancy tactics there, you," Tori whispers to Slash.

"So you've known how to ride a horse this whole time? You're brilliant, Tori. Making me do all the hard work and barely helping us."

"I figure you wanted to get some practice in, and you guys looked like you had it. No need for me to waste my magic on such a low-level monster. You will need it for the future. Also, fairies know how to do everything humans can do easily! We just choose not to." Tori smiles, guiding the horse behind the rear of the group.

"That was amazing," says Marco as he pulls up beside Tori and Slash. "You took that thing out with no problem. I am sure only one of my arrows at least hit it in the arm."

Marco's tanned skin and a small smattering of freckles on his face glistened in the setting sun. Tori noticed how handsome he looked.

"I am sticking with you, my brother in arms," Marco smiles as he keeps pace with Tori.

Bartholet leads the charge through the night and keeps pace as the men follow up behind him.

The next two days of the journey were uneventful, only stopping for a brief rest for an hour or two.

"You humans are pushing it a little too hard, don't you think?" Tori whispers in Slash's ear.

"There are lives at stake, Tori," Slash answers. "So I understand where Bartholet is coming from. The men that are with him feed off of his passion."

Slash turns the corner along with the rest of the group as the gates of Artemis come into view.

"Men, prepare yourselves for battle!" Bartholet yells.

Everyone rushes through the gate on horseback as they look around to find no one in sight.

Where is everyone? Bartholet thinks to himself.

"Stay at the ready, men," Bartholet howls to the group.

The group guides their horses through the streets as they come to the town square where an enormous fountain is overflowing with blood.

"Human blood," Slash gasps, seeing a bone float in the fountain.

"Very intuitive, human." A two-headed wolfen that stood seven feet tall walked from behind a building as fifty more wolfen surrounded the group, their mouths foaming.

"They fled underground but were slaughtered," the wolfen barked, laughing. "We ate most of the humans in this town. Taking this city will surely net me a spot as a sentinel in the Dark Order."

"You speak of killing humans as a sport," Bartholet yells at the large wolfen.

"The name is Xander, human. Gareth created me to destroy scum such as you," Xander spits. "You will die a miserable death here with your fellow humans. Fight if you will, but know this. I will torture you before killing you. Ripping off each limb until there is nothing left but your torso sitting there on the pavement as a bloody stump."

"This does not look good, man." Marco looks over at Slash, clasping his sword.

"Tori, we are going to kill that large wolfen immediately. Can you carry me?" Slash asks.

"Well, I can, but I will have to use all my strength to toss you," Tori huffs.

"Do it!"

"Attack!" Xander yells as the wolfen lunge towards the group of men on their horses. They were being surrounded quickly by the wolfen cubs.

"Fire!" Bartholet yells frantically.

The men on horseback release arrows into incoming Wolfen.

Ten wolfen fall immediately, arrows hitting them in the chest and head.
"Scatter, men use your speed to your advantage!" Bartholet yells.

The remaining men on horseback try to leave the area as all exits are blocked off by wolfen.

"Fire at will and stay alive!" Bartholet screams as he pierces a huge wolfen himself, its black gooey blood splattering everywhere.

The wolfen lunge again, jump, and begin grabbing men off of horseback and clawing them in the neck.

"Any time now!" Slash shouts as he and Marco kill the cubs racing towards them.

"I am gathering all my strength!" Tori yells in reply. "Hold on!"

Tori's wings grow twice in size as she snatches Slash by the back and takes him up into the air.

"Throw me as hard as you can, Tori!" Tori spins five times in the air as she throws Slash toward Xander.

"What do you hope to achieve, human?" Xander looks at Slash, closing in on him.

The wolfen commander growls, jumping into the air toward Slash.

Slash closes his eyes and activates his Perfect Vision trick that he learned from Ella.

A vision of Xander trying to grab his neck in midair flashes into his mind.

Slash turns his body to the right and cuts right through Xander's mouth, slicing the top of his two heads clean off.

Landing on the stone steps, Slash turns around with an intense look on his face.

The wolfen cubs stop and look towards the corpse of Xander, their now-dead leader, not moving.

The cubs howl and leave the area immediately.

"Take the head of the master, and the pawns will leave," Marco utters as the trio nears Bartholet by the fountain of blood.

His arm was bleeding from a wound he received from a wolfen, and Tori was quick to do a healing spell to patch it right up.

"Thank you, kind fairy," Bartholet says.

"How many did you lose, Captain?" Slash asks as they approach.

"Too many." Bartholet bows his head. "At least a third of my men are dead. For them to cause so much suffering is so little time is astounding."

"You were terrific, Slash," Marco says as Bartholet looks away from them to check on the surviving members of his squadron. They wave from the other side of the town square and begin to clean themselves up from all the wolfen blood.

"You were also glowing green in that last moment of Xander's life." Marco scratches his head. "It was something otherworldly. I've seen magic, but that speed was something different."

Bartholet nods, affirming what Marco saw. "I think that is precisely why the wolfen ran, Slash. They did not want any part of what you were about to do next."

"What will you do now?" He asks Slash.

"I need to find some way to get back to the Southern Kingdom," Slash answers.

"Right now, that is impossible, as the bridge is destroyed." Bartholet shakes his head. "Shame, really."

"We heard about that," Slash sighs.

"The best we could do is send word to Rinkar and Jerut and have the townspeople make a trip here," Marco offers the captain. "For this place is cleared of wolfen. It should be safe for refuge."

Bartholet signals ten of his most able men towards him.

"Make haste toward Rinkar and Jerut. Five of you go to one town and five to the other. I know you are tired, but please get there and save those people. Bring them to refuge here! Save as many as you can."

Slash enjoyed watching the Captain bark out orders and get straight back to work even if they just had an incredibly hard battle an hour ago.

"Yes, sir!" The men yell in unison as they leave the town of Artemis, heading northwest toward the outlying cities of the Eastern Kingdom.

"I implore you to stay here with us." Bartholet holds his hand out to Slash. "We could use you to train soldiers to take back the capital."

Tori taps Slash on the shoulder and nods at him. "It wouldn't hurt, Slash."

"Of course, Captain," Slash accepts. "I'm not doing anything else."

Slash shakes hands with Bartholet as they sit down on the steps.

"You know I always wanted to be a knight," Bartholet sighs. "I was never strong enough or got good enough grades to get into any academy. Eventually they needed archers, and I had excellent hand-eye coordination. I just joined the corps and rose the ranks quickly. People were drawn to me because of my leadership capability. I can strike quickly, but hitting hard is a problem. I have been working on my upper body strength."

"I'm sorry, I'm rambling now." Bartholet puts his hands through his hair slowly. "You know, I am so thankful to have met you. You were never in the corps, right?"

"That's right, I taught myself how to use a sword," Slash laughs, piecing together memories of his childhood. "I would practice on slimes and other weak creatures in the forest. Adventuring was always on my heart, and eventually, I went on one. I would say that led me to where we are now."

"Let's kick this damned demon army out of our home," Bartholet nods. "They will not last one day against our might."

"Agreed," Slash sighs.

Marco and Tori were deep in a light conversation when Slash whistled to signal his friend.

"I was in the middle of something, Slash." Tori crosses her arms in frustration. "What did you want?"

"Tori, I... I want you to find my wife. She has to be in the Southern Kingdom," Slash begs. "I ask you, as a friend, to find her. Let her know that we are planning an attack on the empire. Artemis was saved but at a high cost. Could you do that for me?"

Tori's expression turns serious and she nods, flying up, looking down at Slash.

"Till then, stay alive, okay?" Tori says, giving Marco a quick kiss on the cheek before she flies off into the night sky.

Slash looks out after her, wondering if he would ever see Sodina again. *Just wait a little longer for me, my love. I'm coming.*

Chapter 21

Month of Fairy
Day 1

Three days have passed since the group left the Tree of Woe. Chrono, wide awake still, sees the city of Lafare. The sun rises as Chrono looks out to see the lake beside the city. *The perfect place to land.*

Bridget, Sodina, and Lea have been out cold since our battle. We will need to get them checked out. Most of Sodina's right arm is a dark purple now. Chrono steers the ship down toward the lake, landing it softly. He walks down the stairs and wakes up the three ladies.

"We've arrived in Lafare."

"Thank you for bringing us back here safely." Sodina smiles at Chrono as she stands up.

"Let us head to the castle," Chrono says.

"Queen Charlotte should be happy to see us," Bridget says, walking out the boat.

"Bring some gold just in case we need to pay the doctor. If we are asking for the best, then let us treat them well with payment."

Sodina walks over to her pack and grabs 15 gold coins. She puts them in her pocket.

Bridget picks up Lea in her arms. "All right, short stuff, I will carry you to the castle for free."

Lea looks up at Bridget with a sincere smile and closes her eyes to rest more.

As the group walks off the steps, the boat fades away.

"What happened to it? Bridget asks, perplexed.

"Maybe it served its purpose," Chrono speculates. "It got us here, and that is all that matters."

The group of four head to the castle from the lake docks of Lafare.

"The city streets are alive this morning," Chrono says to the group. "Vendors and blacksmiths line the streets of Lafare. I notice an increase in blacksmiths from the last time we were here."

"They have ramped up operations I see," Bridget adds.

Reaching the castle, the group walks into the throne room where Queen Charlotte walks down to greet them.

"Children of Light, I see you have returned. But in what condition, I may ask?"

"We require a doctor," Chrono replies. "Then we will fill you in on what happened. Two of my comrades have broken body parts and dislocated joints."

"Get these women to a doctor now," Charlotte bellows. "Take these women to the healing wing."

"Yes, queen," the knights reply.

Three knights usher Sodina, Bridget, and Lea to the healing wing.

"Now, War Master, follow me to the Generals' quarters. Let us discuss what happened and our current plans."

Sitting down, Charlotte crosses her arms, her dark skin glowing as the sun hits her through the castle windows.

"As you may have noticed, we are building up our army. It will be a while before preparations are ready."

"How many months?" Chrono asks, looking worried.

"At least three months to prepare our troops," Charlotte replies. "Remember, we are a more naval kingdom. Ground warfare is not our forte. You are asking us to fight in a climate we do not train for. To bring in experts to train our troops and prevent unnecessary death is my duty as the queen. I will not send my people to slaughter."

"That is understandable, Queen Charlotte." Chrono gapes at her.

"Now tell me of your journey, now that this is out of the way," Charlotte laughs loudly.

"We have completed two of the three trials. We have faced a dangerous enemy along the way. We also learned the demon army has a hierarchy. Their leader is named Gareth. Underneath him are the generals and the Dark Order. We fought members of the Dark Order, slaying one of the two we encountered.

"The members of the Dark Order are powerful and only working together, we could defeat them. In the ocean off Ferrymore lies a beast in the ocean that threatens our vessels. We were sure that we would meet our end. Something or someone saved us, but we were not able to make out what. Sodina has received an immense amount of favor from the hero of old. Her quest is personal, and the heroes of old knew that. Who am I to judge who they give their blessings upon?"

"Do we know how many are in their army?" Charlotte asks Chrono. "What of spies? Any word of working with the Northern Empire?"

"We know little," Chrono responds. "We know they are powerful, and their general almost killed us. I will never forget her name. Lisha, a she-demon who kills humans for sport. Her appearance was sexy, and she could change her outfit on demand by flipping her finger—such power I have only seen the like at War Master tournaments of old."

"You did well to get out of there alive. You know well to retreat when you can. I trust you, War Master. You were directly under King Martin. He trusted you with his life so that I will trust you. You are one of the strongest warriors in the land. We must double our efforts to prepare for this enemy. We will still march to the Bridge of Eden. There may be some way for us to cross. We will try it and see what happens. "

I remember Sodina telling me something, Chrono recalls.

"When she received the pendants after waking up from the attack on us at the ocean, Sodina said that one of them would make way for us. What she means by that I will never know, but just something to keep in the back of your mind."

Charlotte nods before she walks up.

"Rest up, War Master, I will need you to train my warriors in the art of ground warfare."

Chrono nods.

"If you need me, just ask one of the knights, and I will try to make time for your group. Think of this castle as your home."

Charlotte walks out, heading up to her bedroom to rest.

Chrono walks out and takes a left towards the healing wing. There he saw Bridget sitting on the bed, rubbing her ribs.

"They said it would be a month before I can start training again. Lea would be healing up a month and a half in a cast."

"I'm thankful to be alive," Lea whispers over to Chrono. "I will come back stronger than ever."

Sodina walks over to Chrono and puts her hand on his shoulders.

"What did you hear from the queen?" Sodina asks.

"It will be three months until we can launch an assault on the demon empire."

"Three months?!" Bridget yells.

"Keep your voice down," Sodina quips at Bridget.

"Well, I guess it doesn't matter, because we are no good to anyone at all right now. I am ready to bash some skulls though." Bridget puts her left fist into her right hand, clenching them tightly.

"What else did she say?" Lea whispers to Chrono.

"That we can stay here again at no cost and that we have nothing to worry about. I will rest a few days and then train some new soldiers coming into the army. Until then, we have to rest and prepare our hearts and minds for a fierce battle. Is there anything any of you need at the moment?"

"I would like to speak with the potion master of the castle. I have the Light's Bane and Astra root in my sack. I hope that he has a robust root of some sort I can add to make a powerful potion."

"Were there not three items you needed? Lea asks.

"Yes, but we could not get that one because of Lisha." Sodina looks over at Lea. "We'll have to work with anything we have right now. Anything is better than being in pain."

Sodina's right arm shakes violently, glowing purple. She puts her left hand over it to stop the shaking.

"She has a point," Bridget sighs.

"I'll go see them now," Sodina says. "Stay here." Sodina exits and approaches the nearby knight. "Where is your potion master?"

The man points behind him sternly. "She is up the stairs to the left."

Sodina turns the corner towards an enormous door, knocking on it. "Hello?"

"Hold on one second, dear." A tall dark-skinned woman with greying hair opens the door.

"My name is Cynthia, how may I assist you?"

"I wanted to make a potion to help heal my body," Sodina says, gasping.

Cynthia sighed, hanging her head low. "Poor thing, you do not look well—"

Sodina puts her hand on the door, barging in. In front of her was a room filled with books and potions. "I need it now!" She screams. "I feel as if my head is about to split open." Sodina grabs her head, feeling dizzy for a moment and trying to steady herself.

Cynthia grabs Sodina's hand and sits her in a chair.

"Now you do know that potions take some time to make. I just cannot whip something up. I heard about your group. You should be resting right now. You are in a healing ward outfit, and there is no need to be pushing yourself."

Sodina looks down at the white line robe and shakes her head. "I am ready."

"If you insist," Cynthia says in a deep voice. "What do you have?"

Sodina opened her satchel. "I have Light's Bane and Astral Root."

Cynthia perks up. "You have some rare items there, sweetie. How did you gain those items?"

"Well, it was a lengthy journey through some legendary trails. We frequently almost died. They blessed me with the items by the legendary heroes."

"I have heard." Cynthia smiles. "I have some friends who are historians who speak of those forbidden trials. They say that fools waste their lives, finding what is in there."

"They are not lying." Sodina smiles. "I am thankful we got out of there alive."

"Well, let me see those items." Cynthia gathers them and puts them into a small kettle. "What do you want to achieve with this potion?" Cynthia asks.

"I am poisoned," Sodina whispers. "I have been for some time. I have some angel tears flowing through me."

"Interesting." Cynthia looks back at Sodina, climbing a ladder reaching for a book. "Ah, yes, I think I have some of this on my shelf over here. White Rosia is found in the Northern Kingdom, specifically in the city of Vecher. It's a bitter plant, but has been found helpful in fighting off poison and helping people recover when mixed with other plants. I will put this in there with your two ingredients. See me in three hours, okay?"

Cynthia smiles, grabbing Sodina's hand and walking her out the door. "Get some rest."

Sodina looks at the door closed in front of her. *Potion masters are always weird*, she thinks to herself, walking back down towards the healing ward. *I am barely holding on. Being poisoned this long takes a toll on my body. I am thankful to goddess Astra. I would be long dead if I had not taken those tears when I did.*

Walking down the stairs, Sodina turns the corner to find Bridget and Lea having a cup of tea in their beds.

"You missed it Sodina," Lea smiles, looking her way. "Bridget tried to train and was put in a headlock by a nurse."

Lea busts out laughing.

"Ow, I should not do that," Bridget groans. "All I wanted to do was work on my punches."

"I will do it again if you cause a ruckus," the nurse reprimands. "Your orders are to rest."

"Yes, I understand," Bridget says mockingly, rolling her eyes.

The nurse walks over and smacks Bridget on the head.

"Do not play with me." The nurse bends down and looks Bridget directly in the eye. "Rest up so you will be ready for your next adventure."

Bridget sinks under the sheets, not saying anything.

"Too quiet, Bridget," Sodina giggles. "That is quite a feat."

"It is good to see you smile, Sodina. Are you getting a potion made?"

"Yes, I'll have it in a few hours from now." Sodina smiles. "The attacks are coming more frequently, and my body can barely take it. I hope that this does the trick because I may not last much longer."

Sodina sits on the bed beside Lea.

"We know you are in pain," Bridget says, muffled from under the cover. "We are here for you, friend."

"Fear not because you are not alone." Lea smiles, walking over to Sodina slowly.

"You should not be out of bed," Sodina says sharply.

"I know. Take my hand, friend." Lea bows her head. "Goddess Astra, this soul needs you. In your holy name, we pray that her body finds peace that covers her entire body with your love. Permeate her bloodstream with your healing aura and wipe the existence of poison away from her soul. Thank you for your blessings and for protecting us during this tumultuous time. Amen."

Sodina tears, putting Lea's hand on her cheeks and squeezing it.

"Thank you, Lea, that was beautiful."

Lea nods, walking back to her bed and lying down. Bridget sits up in the bed, not saying anything but smiles over at Sodina.

The three women lay down as the sun shines through the room as mid-day approaches. Hours pass as Sodina sits up quickly to the sound of the dinner bell.

"Oh, I overslept. I need to get to—" Sodina looks over on the small table beside her bed with a note and a small bottle beside it. Sodina picks up the letter and reads it:

To the kind woman who stormed into my office,

Your potion is here.

May it hold the healing you are looking for.

-Cynthia

Sodina mustered her strength, leaning the bottle towards her nose.

"What does it smell like?" Lea asks.

"Smells earthy and a little like carrots. Kind of strange, but here we go."

Sodina gulps down the potion that tastes like grass, carrots, and potent wine.

"Ugh." Sodina sticks out her tongue.

"How do you feel?" Bridget asks.

"My body feels like there are brief shocks of energy going through my blood cells."

"Maybe it is cleaning it," Lea says. "Give it some time."

Sodina opens her dinner plate, revealing a cooked duck, a bread roll, and a mini cake.

"They did not spare any expense," Bridget comments, chowing down on the duck leg. "Man, this is good. The flavors are out of this world."

"You should use your fork," Lea whispers to Bridget.

Bridget elbowed her gently. "I will eat how I like."

Chrono walks into the room, sweating from training.

"I just spoke to Queen Charlotte, and she will be moving Queen Sarah and our people back down here for safety. They do not want a sneak attack to happen. The demons may scout with some of their winged creatures. Till then, I will not see you guys too much. I will come by to say hi a few times in between training sessions. I went to see some troops they have coming in, and they need a lot of work."

Bridget nods. "As soon as I am able, I will join you."

"That sounds good." Chrono smiles. "You ladies have a good night. I will see you tomorrow."

Sodina, Bridget, and Lea wave as Chrono departs, heading back to his sleeping quarters.

"The evening is still young, but I am tired. I'm falling into a food coma." Sodina looks over to Bridget and Lea. "I am going for a walk because I cannot stay cooped up in this room."

"Do not push yourself, Sodina," Lea says to her.

"Do not worry. I am just going to the front of the castle to look at the stars." As Sodina quietly walks along the facade, she observes the garden shining underneath the glistening light of the moon. *I hope you are okay wherever you are, Slash. I need you now more than ever.*

Chapter 22

Month of Fairy
Day 8

One week has passed since the healing of the Sodina, Bridget, and Lea began.

Tori looks out over the horizon as the town of Lafare comes into view.

"My poor wings feel as if there are about to fall off," she says as she crosses what was once the Bridge of Eden.

If it was up to Tori she would have slept, but Slash was counting on her.

In fact, she felt a heavy responsibility to help humanity. All this stopping and fighting has caused her to make this trip longer than it needed to be.

Tori flies down, landing on the steps of the castle of Lafare. *It was exciting meeting those individuals from the Eastern Kingdom in Mala. They seem to have found a new life here in the Southern Kingdom.*

Smiling, Tori walked into the front doors of the castle before being stopped by a Southern knight.

"Halt!" He speaks to the small fairy. "What is your business here, Lady…?"

"Tori," she tells the knight. "My name is Tori of the Great Forest and I would like an audience with Queen Charlotte."

"Wait here, please." The knight sprints into the castle to the throne room.

After a few minutes he comes back panting and says, "She will see you now."

Tori speeds through the castle and into the throne room, smiling at the queen. "Hello, Your Majesty! Great place you have here."

"A real fairy. Captain Robert wasn't kidding." Queen Charlotte sits up. "What matter of business does a celestial creature such as yourself have with us?"

"I seek a woman named Sodina, Your Majesty. Is she here in your city?"

Charlotte perks up and walks down towards Tori. "She is here with us, healing up from a dangerous journey. I will take you to her."

Charlotte guides Tori towards the healing ward of the castle.

Tori floats happily with the Queen as they enter the room despite her lengthy journey.

"That is Sodina there." The Queen points to a beautiful red-headed woman resting in her bed with her eyes closed.

Tori flies over slowly and Sodina opens her eyes to the sight of a fairy standing beside her.

"Oh! Hello," Sodina yawns. "Who might you be, milady?"

"No wonder he thinks so highly of you! You're so beautiful!" Tori exclaims to Sodina.

Sodina let out a cough. "Who is this 'he', sweet fairy?"

Tori giggled, twirling in a circle. "Your husband!"

"Slash!?" Sodina yells, jumping out of bed. Bridget shoots up out of bed, looking over at Sodina.

"Why are you yelling?" Bridget groans.

"Do not push it," Lea shouts to Sodina as she races into the healing ward. "You're still weak, Lady Sodina!"

"You know where my husband is?" Sodina asks, grabbing Tori's hand tightly.

Charlotte takes a seat near the corner of the room, listening in to the conversation.

Tori nods, looking into Sodina's eyes. "He is alive and well in the city of Artemis."

Sodina's eyes light up and tears start to fall like raindrops during a summer rainstorm.

"He wanted to let you know he is training an army to attack the demonic empire in Glashmere," the fairy continues, now addressing the Queen in the corner of the ward. "Most of the Eastern Kingdom has fallen, Your Majesty. An army is rising in solidarity with the demons."

"An army, you say... Do you know of their number?" Charlotte asks.

"Probably around five thousand strong now," Tori responds. "The demons are building their military and have demons at the end of the Bridge of Eden, keeping guard. It is impossible to build a bridge making the way across, and they know this. In a month, an attack will take place at Dalton. Rinkar and Jerut have fallen as well to the demons, but most of the civilians were evacuated."

"I would advise against evacuation," Charlotte says. "Please tell them to hold on and try to take out the demons at the Bridge of Eden. I have a plan to make it across the gap, and hopefully, it will work."

"Alright, Your Majesty."

Charlotte stands to walk over to Tori by Sodina's bedside.

"Tell them to hold out and give them this message," The Queen began. "The Southern Kingdom will be ready to attack in less than three months. The War Master of Glashmere is here and is training up the troops. We will join them in a joint attack to push the demons back towards the capital. We will have a foot army of fifteen thousand strong to march towards them."

Tori nods in reply. "I will let them know, Your Majesty. They may want to strike still, but Slash and a gentleman named Bartholet are leading the charge. Slash is a good listener and Sir Bartholet is an honest man."

Lea looks over at Tori brightly. "Captain Bartholet! I know him quite well, Your Majesty. He is kind and noble. People follow him without question. He has inspired many in our profession. He is as pure-hearted as they come, and with a large belly to boot."

Tori laughs with Lea. "That's him!"

"Please tell him his best pupil says hello."

"I will," Tori smiles. "I admit I am quite tired, though, Your Majesty. Is it alright if I rest here for a bit before my journey back?"

"Of course," Charlotte replies, showing Tori a bed where she could sleep. "I do appreciate that information, sweet one. Please give young Slash and Captain Bartholet my regards and let them know we will be there to meet them in the coming months."

Charlotte leaves, walking back towards the throne room with Captain Robert by her side.

Sodina walks over to Tori, sitting on her bed.

"I really like your wings," Sodina tells Tori.

A giggle escapes Tori's mouth. "Thank you, Lady Sodina. They came in handy, getting away from some patrols around the demon empire."

Sodina let go a sigh of relief. "It makes me so happy to hear that my husband is well."

"He is quite the knucklehead, though," Tori says in a peppy voice. "He sure is passionate and talks about you a lot."

"I was so worried about him this whole time," Sodina whispers.

"He single-handedly tried to take on one of the demon generals!" Tori raised her hands. "The dreadful Lady Lisha."

"Lisha!" Bridget fumes and clenches her fist as she approaches her friend and the fairy. "That crazy demonic woman. That mad demon almost killed us, and we all attacked her at once."

"Slash took her on all by himself." Sodina shook her head at the memory.

"He is a crazy man after all," Bridget laughs. "I am surprised he was not killed."

"From what I was told, he gave her a good fight but was eventually overpowered," Tori says. "She was toying with him, and they kept him locked up for months."

"This whole time, Slash was in captivity?" Sodina gasps. "Oh, my poor beloved. I know that he did it for me. For Amanda and Lorenz. He feels guilty he could not save them."

Tori nods her head. "He talks about them, too. Sometimes mumbling in his sleep."

Bridget leans back on the bed, looking at Tori. "So, you were there with him during the fight?"

"No, I was there near the very end of the fight," Tori looks at Bridget. "My job is to protect humans from getting close to the demonic realm's grasp. I was watching over the area when he came charging through the forest. I knocked him out because, apparently, he traveled a long way without resting. He would have been done before he even got to Lisha. That did not matter because he lost anyway."

"Sounds like my husband," Sodina sighed. "Always making rash decisions."

"He is now preparing to take back your home, Lady Sodina," Lea says dreamily. "What I would give for a man like that."

"He is truly an amazing man." Tori smiles. "I admire him a lot even if he gets on my nerves."

"Please let him know how much I love him. I cannot wait to be in his arms, and we will take back our home together."

"I will, Lady Sodina!"

"Oh!" Bridget interjects. "Sodina, you almost forgot! Tell Slash that we are close to creating a potion that will heal his great wife of the poison in her veins."

"I am feeling great, but the effects are making me sleepy." Sodina pats Bridget's shoulder. "Thank you for reminding me."

"I will make sure he gets all your messages when I get there." Tori yawns and wraps her wings around her as she falls asleep.

"And I thought Lea was small," Bridget snickers. "Poor tiny magical fairy thing."

"We know that Slash is alive and well." Sodina holds her heart in relief. "I feel better already."

"I cannot wait to meet him, of course, but to up and leave his wife to kill a super powerful demon? I would think twice about that," Lea says pointedly to Sodina.

"I forgave him the moment he did it," Sodina admits. "We could have solved the problem together with Bridget. I longed for him to help me and those emotions of being abandoned linger in my mind."

Lea looks at Sodina, knowing her emotions were pure. Lea puts her head on her pillow. *So sappy.*

"One day, I hope to be as in love with my partner as you two," Lea smiles as she closes her eyes to rest more.

Only an hour later, Tori sits up from her rest. "Well, I should be off!"

"But you just got here," Bridget pouts.

"The demons are not that active at night, so I can make agreeable time flying above the trees. I truly enjoy looking at the moonlight as I fly." Tori smiles, her wings fluttering as she spins into a midnight blue dress for travel.

"We really appreciate you, Tori." Sodina walks up to Tori for a large hug.

"Yes, I know I am amazing." Tori winks at her, wrapping her arms around the human. "I will see all of you on the battlefield in the coming months. I will get word to Slash, and he will be so excited to see you."

Tori waves as her wings flutter faster, propelling her out of the room's window and out beyond the castle.

"What an interesting fairy," Bridget smiles, punching in the air to practice her strikes.

"Stop that, Bridget," Lea scolds the giant woman. "You need to get stronger so that we can fight in this war properly."

"Ugh, you're right." Bridget lies back. "I'm just so jealous that Chrono turned out just fine and gets to lead training the troops. I feel so useless."

"Well, you're not," Lea says. "You're Lady Bridget of the North. Defender of peoples and whatever. You were hurt and you need to heal. You're only human. Or are you a demon too? You may heal faster if you are a demon."

Sodina looks out the window as she drowns out the sound of the two ladies bickering and says a small prayer to Goddess Astra.

Slash, I will be with you soon, my love, she thinks before closing her eyes and drifting away to sleep.

* * *

The days pass quickly as Tori flies past the old Bridge of Eden, Dalton, and towards Artemis.

She had made great time for a fairy her age. Only three whole days had passed instead of the week it took her to get to Lafare.

It was absolutely necessary that she got to Slash and the Captain as soon as possible.

Nighttime had fallen on the third day of Tori's travels as she landed near the gates of Artemis.

What happened here? Tori flies over endless piles of wolfen corpses lying out of the gates. Tori sees everyone going about their lives as usual. The town seemed at ease despite the obvious bloodshed outside the gate. She looks down towards the city square to find Slash and Bartholet enjoying a meal. "What in Astra's name happened here?!" Tori yells down to Slash.

Slash, startled from the sudden outburst, falls out of his chair and lands straight on his butt. "Ouch!"

"You have dead bodies of the enemy one hundred feet from the gate," Tori explains.

Bartholet waves his hand at Tori. "You should not be so hard on him. We have been fighting nonstop since you left. After we killed Xander, more wolfen came. The first day was fifty, then fifty more two days later. Then one more wave. They tried to scale the wall."

"Sadly, some children were playing outside of the gate and were killed when they attacked at mid-day," Slash says as he stands and brushes the dirt off his pants.

"There was no time to save them," Bartholet explains, bowing his head.

Slash looks at Tori, shaking his head. "Yes, so we clearly deserve the break, thank you for asking. Any word from my wife?"

"You have one amazing woman," Tori says, putting up her finger, wagging it in his direction. "You should have never left that woman. She cares deeply about you and does not want any harm to come to you."

Slash sighs in relief. "I'm so glad she's alright. She must be with Bridget."

"She is!" Tori turns to Captain Bartholet next. "Queen Charlotte would like you to hold your attack on Dalton."

"And why should we do that?" Bartholet asks with his mouth full of meat. "We've been training day in and day out for the battle."

"The Queen says that they will march with an army of fifteen thousand strong towards the Glashmere." Tori puts her hand on her hip as she continues. "They need time to train up their ground troops. The War Master Chrono is there with them, training the fresh recruits as we speak."

"What do you think, Slash?" Bartholet looks over at him. "We are co-commanders in this operation after all."

Slash gives him a look and turns back to Tori. "I think it would be best to hold true to that request. There is no need to be rushing into battle without full strength."

"Fine." Bartholet crosses his arms. "Answer me this, though, Lady Tori. How will they cross the Bridge of Eden? It's completely destroyed."

"The queen mentioned that she has a plan that should work, but you will need to clear the troops out of the way at the Bridge. They will launch the attack in the coming months!"

"Hmm..." Bartholet strokes his chin, considering the information. "Queen Charlotte sounds very sure of herself."

Tori nods at the two men, "The queen advises you to get ready. Your wife cannot wait to see you, Slash."

"Until then, all we have to do is survive," Bartholet laughs, looking at Tori. "Easier said than done in these times."

"I am just the messenger." Tori looks at the two men and rolls her eyes. "With me here, we should have no problem fighting off minor demons, but we will have a significant problem if any of the sentinels attack or, worse, a demon general."

"Until that fateful day, let us rest, train, and focus on protecting those in our stead," Slash says with vigor.

Chapter 23

Month of Witches

Day 8

Over the next three months, Chrono trains the Army of the Southern Kingdom. Slash and Bartholet meanwhile train their troops in the city of Artemis. They raise enough forces for a cavalry unit of five hundred horses and four thousand five hundred ground troops. The attacks on Artemis stop after a week of relentless wolfen trying to storm the front gate.

Slash looks out at the night sky with Tori.

"Are we ready?" Slash asks Tori, looking over at her.

"You ask the wrong question, Slash," Tori responds. "Will you be prepared for what you will face?"

"I am. And I am also ready to see my wife." Slash smiles.

"I bet you are." Tori giggles, nudging her elbow into Slash's arm. "Do you need a hug before you do?"

Slash let go a chuckle. "A hug would not be bad, you know."

Tori wraps her arms around Slash as her wings wrap around him.

"Do not die, dear friend. I have gotten to known you over the past months. You are noble and kind. I am happy to have met you. I will fight beside you on the battlefield. You have my wings to push you forward."

"Thank you, Tori, you are amazing. We head out in the morning. It's a few days journey to the Bridge of Eden. We need to get some rest."

Bartholet walks up to Slash, unaware of the mass of people gathering behind him. "Slash, we need to address the troops."

Slash nods before he turns around, looking down towards the people of Artemis.

"Fellow countrymen, I ask you to come together for this battle for our hometown. We were dealt a cruel blow by demons. They killed our king and queen. They killed thousands of our countrymen without a second glance. I ask that you dig deep and fight with all of your hearts for victory against an enemy beyond our comprehension. We will fight against an enemy we know not that much about. We have only seen grunts until now. Faced with our most significant adversity, we must rise above and have hope in each other."

Slash draws his sword and lifts it up above his head. "If you see someone fall down, lift them up. Inspire, empower, and lead by example. We will take back our home. Let us drink and be merry tonight! Rest well, and we will depart in the morning."

The men cheer with resolve, raising their weapons above them.

He really has them riled up, Tori thinks to herself, looking at Slash and Bartholet.

"Good job co-commander." Bartholet pats Slash on the back. "Will you be partaking in wine tonight?"

"I will turn in for tonight." Slash walks down from the steps of the city square and heads to a tent near the city gates. *We will win. I know of it.* Slash closes his eyes to rest, preparing his heart and mind for the journey that lays before him.

* * *

Gareth walks down to meet his three generals bowing before him.

"The humans think they are making their move, but little do they know that they are marching to death's door."

"What will you have us do, my lord?" Neron looks up at Gareth.

"I would like Magnar to lead the charge at the Bridge of Eden. Take our forces in Dalton and intercept them before they reach the bridge. I have heard rumors that they wish to secure the Bridge of Eden and push back towards Glashmere."

"It will be done, my lord." Magnar looks at Gareth smiling.

"It's been a bit too long since I have had a fight, but we will need to keep clean. I guess it cannot be helped with this fight."

Lisha looks over at Magnar, snickering. "You are such a weird individual."

"Keep your chatter down," Neron says.

"You called, Lord Gareth?" A female voice says.

"Claudia, yes, I would like you to accompany General Magnar to Dalton to intercept."

"Yes, my lord, I will destroy humans with elegance."

Claudia twirls as she bows and walks out of the room.

That ditzy demon, how did she even earn a place in the Dark Order, Neron thinks to himself.

"Lisha and Neron, you are to stay here. Nagi is on a mission in the Northern Kingdom. The other members of the Dark Order are on a mission as well, gathering information. You are all dismissed."

Before the others leave, Gareth reaches out and grabs Lisha's shoulders from behind.

"Lisha, come here. Come to my chambers later for your weekly treatment."

"Yes, my lord." Lisha bows. Turning away, Lisha walks out the door, her fist clenched. *You have lost your way, Gareth. I will kill to set you free from the darkness that is destroying your heart. You are not the demon I fell in love with. You care nothing for our daughter. You want her to be your tool.*

* * *

"I will be back soon." Chrono looks at Queen Sarah before kissing her on the lips.

"I will waste no time getting back to your side."

"You better not or I will go crazy," Sarah responds, crying and holding his hands.

"I need to go join my friends at the front of the line now." Chrono waves looking back at Sarah, standing at the steps of the Castle of Lafare.

Queen Charlotte stands ready at the front of an enormous army with Bridget and Lea as Chrono runs up to get on his horse.

Pulling out a sizable magical seashell, Charlotte presses her lip against the corner of the shell.

"Men and women of the Southern Kingdom, we ride today in honor of our fellow countrymen in this continent of Esteria. Their kingdom was ravaged by the demon army. We ride today to rid the Eastern Kingdom of this evil. We will return home victorious, liberating the Eastern Kingdom and giving them their home back. We will cross the Bridge of Eden by using ropes and having catapults launch hooks to the other side. Hopefully, this will lead us across the bridge, building a makeshift crossing. We march to victory."

The army cheers a triumphant war cry.

Bridget looks down at her chainmail dress and broad ax at her hip. A green cloak with a hood adorns her body as she looks over at Sodina. Sodina was wearing a dark purple cape over a green dress and brown pants with tan boots, sitting on her horse.

"I feel so much better," Sodina comments. "And that healing potion helped me greatly. I have not had a relapse since I took it."

"We were so focused on training that I forgot to ask you about that." Bridget smiles at Sodina.

"That was a rousing speech by the queen!" Lea glances over at her friends.

"This new bow made of dragon steel will do me well in battle." Chrono sits on his horse with a gold shield emblazed with the crest of the Eastern Kingdom. "I am ready. Today's the day."

Chrono nods at Queen Charlotte, she smiles in response.

"Let us ride!" Charlotte yells into the shell.

She, along with the others, lead the massive army of 15,000 towards the Bridge of Eden.

Queen Charlotte sits on a black horse in a white dress with a silver chest plate. Her helmet was a radiant pinkish color with small wings on it, and her spear sat on the side of a horse.

Chrono rides up towards her.

"How are your people?" Chrono asks.

"I have left my chief advisor Leanne in charge of getting the people to safety. Also, a small garrison of troops from the Naval Academy will lead the people to safety. Mala is empty except for essential individuals. My people will be okay. My heart beats for them."

Charlotte smiles. "What type of queen would I be if I did not champion for others?"

"We are grateful for you," Chrono nods as he looks out into the night sky.

"Let us ride, War Master, to retake your home," Charlotte bellows.

* * *

The morning comes. Slash wakes to put on his boots and a brown cloak.

"You will not wear any armor?" Bartholet asks Slash.

"It limits reaction time. I'd rather be speedy and dodge attacks than be in a slugfest with a demon because the armor is weighing me down."

Bartholet puts on his wrist guards and puts his bow on his back.

"Let's get going." Bartholet nods at Slash.

Slash approaches the man serving hot tea, grabs a cup and takes a quick sip.

"The town of Artemis, now 30,000 in number, waves to their 5,000 troops leaving to fight the demon empire. These people have no ruler, yet they thrive. Do we need kings? I wonder." Bartholet looks over at Slash.

"They are treating us like ones," Slash smiles.

Tori flies beside the two. "You two have protected all the refugees from Rinkar and Jerut. That is why they adore you. No one has starved, and crime is low."

"I think it was wise to leave 500 troops here," Slash suggests. "Hopefully, no harm will come to them."

"The walls are reinforced," Bartholet says confidently. "We will make haste to the Bridge of Eden and take back that area."

Slash and Bartholet led their 5,000 troops outside the gates of Artemis. Tori flies above Slash, looking down at him.

"I will scout ahead and make sure our path is clear. I will travel back and forth to keep you out of danger as much as possible."

Slash and Bartholet nod as Tori flies off into the distance.

"We are making good time with the weather cooperating with us. There is no sign that clouds will be gathering." Slash puts his finger into the air, feeling which direction the wind is coming from.

"Those wolfen have a particular stench about them. We may run into a few on our way, but it should be no issue." Bartholet pushes his horse harder as he gets in front of Slash.

"Keep up co-commander." He smiles back at Slash.

"No problem at all." Slash pushes his horse to gallop harder. "I bet I will take out more demons than you on the battlefield."

"You think?" Bartholet smiles. "We shall keep count."

The next few hours pass with little issue as Tori reports back from her scouting mission while the army is taking a brief break.

"There are no enemies up ahead for the next few hours." Tori winks at Slash.

Slash nodded, his eyes glaring into the unknown future. "Thank you for checking on that."

Bartholet blows a horn signaling that everyone finishes up their break time and get back on their horses. The march resumes towards the Bridge of Eden. "5,000 horseback archers. My. What a fantastic sight that is," Bartholet comments.

"I agree," Slash smiles.

"You taught them sword skills as well," Bartholet explains. "We ran most of the resources dry in this area, but everyone is armed with a bow and sword. To have 5,000 horses gallop towards the demons will strike fear in their hearts."

Tori looks down at Bartholet and Slash with concern as they know not what dangers await them.

For the next few days, the armies slowly march towards their shared destination.

Charlotte looks back at Chrono, who is looking determined as ever. "We will pass by Mala, then the Bridge of Eden."

Chrono nods, looking back at Bridget, Lea, and Sodina passing on the message. "We will rest there outside the gates and be ready for the battle that lies ahead."

The enormous army passes through the town of Mala and makes camp outside the gates of the city.

Charlotte pulls out her magical shell and speaks into it. "Rest, warriors of the Southern Kingdom, for tomorrow. We face an enemy unknown to us. Please steady your hearts and rest well."

Lea pulls out her copy of the book of Astra. "Chapter 10, verse 1. In times of great trials love those around you deeply and make your heart glad about joy. Verse 2. For in the face of significant opposition, you will find your greatest treasure, your true self." Lea closes her book, looking at her friends around the fire. "We will make sure we rid our home of these demons."

Sodina nods, thinking about Slash. *Just one more day until I see my love.* Sodina folds her hands towards her heart.

Bridget looks around the group of people she now calls family, trying not to show too much emotion.

"You guys, if we do not make it through tomorrow, just know that I love you, okay?" Bridget lowers her head, blushing.

"It's not like you to get emotional, Bridget." Lea speaks softly to Bridget.

"Well, you guys are indeed the first people that cared for me. You did not exploit my talents or hurt me emotionally. You took my emotions and returned to me tenfold, and for that, I will die on the battlefield with you any day of the week. Now I do not plan on dying tomorrow, but you know what I mean."

Chrono, Sodina, and Lea bust out laughing.

"It's not funny." Bridget crosses her arms.

"Just joking with you." Chrono pats her on the back as he walks over to Charlotte.

Charlotte, drinking a cup of tea sitting on the ground by her horse, looks up at Chrono.

"Queen Charlotte, if the worse shall happen to me, please let Queen Sarah know that I fought to my last breath."

"It shall be done, War Master." Charlotte nods as she looks off in the distance towards the path they are to travel tomorrow.

* * *

"We should rest here for the night," Slash speaks to Bartholet.

"We need to have our energy tomorrow because we are only a few hours from the Bridge of Eden."

Bartholet blows his horn, putting his arm up in the air to stop.

"We will make camp here. Pass the word back to the next soldier and so forth."

The men give the word as many of the archers tie their horses to trees while others sleep on them for comfort.

The night sky had a pleasant summer breeze as Slash practiced his sword attacks on a nearby tree.

"My blade will be ready to cut through whatever demons come our way."

"Do not use me too much tonight," Ella giggles, speaking to Slash in his mind.

"I sometimes forget you are with me, Ella."

"How can you forget me?" She says sharply. "I am the one that helped you escape. I rarely get angry, but remember, I am always here to guide you. My spirit may rest because it is difficult to stay awake all this time. Call on me, and I will be there to guide you, okay?"

"You got it." Slash puts his sword away as he walks back to where Bartholet and Marco were sitting.

"I finally found you after all of that traveling." Marco lets go an enormous smile as he passes a cup of soup to him. "I had some fish leftover from yesterday, and I thought it would be good to share it with you."

Slash smiles at Marco, accepting his food, chowing down immediately after. "We are no good if we do not fuel our bodies, you know."

Marco chomps down on his fish sandwich, telling stories to Slash and Bartholet about his childhood. The hours pass as they share stories and drinks.

"I will rest for the night." Slash lies on the back of his horse, closing his eyes.

"I think you should get some rest too, Marco." Bartholet directs him to go.

"I am so full of energy, Bartholet." Marco does a backflip, waving at Bartholet and getting the hint it was time for him to leave.

Tori lay down beside Slash, closing her eyes to rest. *I wonder if they have enough strength to do this. Will a demon general show up? That woman dressed in purple...* She trembles trying to drift off to sleep.

* * *

Then the morning comes. Magnar and Claudia awaken from their sleep in the town of Dalton.

"This should be easy, don't you think? The scouts we sent said all the troops are on horseback. All we have to do is cut the horses out from underneat them and poof, there goes their hope."

Magnar points his spear towards the morning sun. "I will skewer at least a hundred human on this spear today, hopefully their blood will not dirty my armor."

"Oh, you and your blood situation." Claudia smiles, rubbing him on the shoulders. "You need to relax about that and enjoy the bloodshed. Why not get up close and let them have it?"

Claudia's nails grow to a foot long before she retracts them back into her skin.

"You can have fun. I will let the wolfen take care of most of it, and then I will take out the rest."

Claudia's flowing blue dress dances in the wind as she looks at the 3,000 wolfen leaving the city of Dalton, heading southwest towards Eastern Kingdom Resistance.

"We have another 3,000 troops here and another 19,000 in reserves coming up. I heard it was a combination of wolfen, solems, and lesser cyclops," Magnar explains.

"Where did he gather that many cyclops?" Claudia gasps with surprise. "Those things usually have minds of their own."

"Well, they are also dumb." Magnar shrugs. "From what I heard, it is easy to manipulate them with a simple spell."

"I guess so." Claudia shakes her head. "That is an impressive army, no doubt. It will serve us well in crushing this revolt."

"Now we wait." Magnar sits down with a spear in hand, watching the sunrise. "Let's get to the Bridge of Eden in an hour to see if any of them breakthrough. There we will crush their dream."

Claudia licks her lips, nodding in approval. "It will be elegant."

* * *

Slash sits up, eating a piece of bread from his sack as Bartholet blows his horn loudly three times.

"Do the troops know what that means, Slash?" Asks Bartholet. "It means we leave in 3 minutes."

The group of 5,000 men quickly gather their things and get on their horses as the horn is blown one more time, signifying their departure.

"I think many of the men were already awake." Bartholet jumps on his horse, leading the pack.

Slash, Marco, and Tori follow as the rest of the men fall behind them.

"You see that hill up there far in the distance? Once we round that hill we should see the Bridge of Eden. That is about three hours from here."

An hour passes by before Slash seems something in the distance. "What is that, Tori?"

Tori flies into the air to look forward.

"It's a mass of wolfen at the bottom of this hill. Make ready for battle. There are a lot of them," Tori yells down.

Bartholet blows his horn twice, signaling that they are preparing for battle.

"Make ready, men!" Bartholet yells loudly. The words echo back toward the last man as all the men pull out their bows and shoot a volley of arrows.

The wolfen charge, running on all fours as they clash into the horsemen.

"Fight, men, fight!" Bartholet yells.

The 3,000 wolfen and 5,000 warriors from Artemis clash in a wide-open field. Slash jumps off his horse after a wolfen snags it by the neck, throwing him to the ground. Tori flies, lifting Slash as he puts out his hand, creating a barrier keeping the wolfen from attack him.

"Are you ready for this?" Tori looks at Slash.

"Never better." Slash runs forward with Tori as they duck the attacks from wolfen left and right. Slash takes his sword and pushes it through the gut of wolfen, kicking it off the blade and stabbing it in the chest.

Tori flies into the air and shoots a ball of small green mist out of her hand as 10 wolfen fall asleep in a pile.

"Help me!" Marco screams as a wolfen grabs him by the neck, dragging him across the ground, ripping a part of his neck off.

"Marco!" Bartholet guides his horse toward the wolfen, jumping off his horse and stabbing the wolfen in the neck, killing it. "Marco! Marco! Stay with me," Bartholet yells.

Marco breathes heavily, smiling as his eyes slowly closes, his cheeks flush before his eyes completely shut.

Bartholet holds Marco's body, crying as wolfen lunge towards his neck.

"Commander!" A man says, jumping in front of Bartholet, stabbing the wolfen in the chest.

"Sir, you need to rise," the man yells.

"I know," Bartholet yells, leaving Marco's body on the ground. "Kind friend, rest well."

Bartholet whistles as a horse rides toward him and he jumps up on it.

"Keep up the fight, men!" Bartholet yells, pulling out his sword, stabbing another wolfen in the face.

"Die, human!" A wolfen yells, running toward Slash.

Slash steps to the right and cuts the wolfen across the chest with his sword, cutting most of its torso off. "That one is for Marco." Slash holds back tears as he ducks left then right, stabbing two wolfen in the hearts in rapid succession.

Tori hovers above the battle spraying green mist, putting several small groups of wolfen to sleep at a time. "This is exhausting," Tori says, wiping the sweat off her head. *Keep it moving Tori, you push on no matter how much it hurts.* Tori flies down, reaching out her hand as a small tornado of wind lifts 50 wolfen in the air before they fall to the ground, dying from the crash. "So much blood." Tori looks at the carnage that lay before her. Men with arms ripped off. Wolfen gnawing on the necks of men. *This is turning into a slaughter for both sides.*

Two hours passed as the battle raged on. Bartholet, bleeding from his right arm badly, stabs a wolfen in the neck as another jumps on his back.

"Your flesh will taste fantastic in my mouth."

Slash runs up to the wolfen and stabs it in the neck with his blade as the wolfen falls off Bartholet's back.

"Thank you," Bartholet says to Slash. "I have not seen Tori in some time, I hope she is okay."

Tori looks at the battlefield, knowing that the bloodshed needed to end. *After I use this attack, I will not be of any good to Slash for the rest of this battle, but if this goes on, they will lose more people for their cause.* Tori puts out her arms and her wings grow twice in size. "Eternal Rest!" She yells as a large green mist flows over the battlefield.

Slash rips his sword out of the neck of a beast. *We are winning the fight, but not without taking heavy casualties.*

Bartholet runs beside Slash as they push their swords into a larger wolfen standing ten feet tall.

"Mere humans, you will not crush me." The wolfen tries to grab Bartholet but he ducks, shooting an arrow into the neck of the wolfen. Slash runs underneath the legs of the wolfen and cuts a massive gash across its right leg.

"Ugh." The wolfen stumbles as several archers shoot forty arrows into his chest, killing him.

Slash looks down at the second sword he had made for battle but chose not to pull it out. *This is not the right time for it.* Slash runs into another wolfen on the battlefield, chewing on the neck of a dead archer. Slash runs toward the wolfen, cutting its head clean off. Looking down at his blood-stained clothing, he falls to the ground exhausted. As he looks up, he sees a large green mist cover the whole battlefield. *Is that Tori?*

A wolfen runs towards Slash, lunging at him before suddenly falling asleep.

"What is this?" Slash mutters.

"The wolfen are falling asleep!" A man yells. "Kill them where they stand."

Slash reaches into his sack and pulls out a small red potion. *Hopefully this will give me some pep. I had a novice potion master do it, so probably he filled it with nutrients.* Slash gulps down the endurance potion before standing up slowly.

The 500 remaining wolfen, fast asleep, are killed in their slumber by the remaining members of the resistance. Bartholet blows the horn as the men shout in victory. Tori, exhausted, lands on the ground near Slash.

"I used up most of my energy on that attack. You were losing too many men. Once I unleash an attack like that, I become tired and weak. I fear the worse may be yet to come."

"You saved so many lives." Slash looks down at Tori.

Tori breathes heavily as she flies up to Slash, wrapping her arms around him. "You humans are resilient creatures."

"Thank you, friend." Slash kisses Tori on the cheek as he lets go of their embrace. Tori blushes slightly as she sits beside a tree resting.

Two hours pass as most of the men rest while other count bodies.

"Sir, I have the report." A man walks up to Bartholet and Slash. "There are around 3,000 wolfen that died, and we lost 2,500 men and 3,000 horses."

Bartholet lowers his head, looking at the ground. "Thank you for the report."

"Yes, sir." The man walks away from Bartholet.

Bartholet turns to Slash. "Should we bury our men or push forward to the Bridge of Eden? We are banged up bad, but Tori released a healing aura of such that is helping a bit and keeping spirits high."

"We do not have time to bury our men." Slash looks sternly at Bartholet. "I would like to, but we have to keep the move."

"But Marco is dead!" Bartholet screams at Slash, clenching his collar.

Gripping his fist, Slash stares at the ground. "I know that, and I would like to help him rest, but his soul is already in the next life."

"Damn it!" Bartholet yells, screaming to the sky. "This world is harsh to those pure of heart. Let us at least bury our friend."

Slash nods, crying, looking over at the body of Marco near the tree line. Slash walks over to a horse carrying a shovel and digs a grave with Bartholet. Slash takes his cloak and wraps it around Marco's body, picking it up, and placing it in the grave. Bartholet, Slash, and several other men each put a scoop of dirt from the shovel onto the grave until it is covered. Bartholet turns to the small group of men standing before him, tears streaming from his cheeks.

"Do not let the death of Marco or any of our brothers be in vain. Rest up and ready your hearts for more bloodshed. We leave in thirty minutes." Bartholet walks off, his head bowing towards the ground.

"I didn't expect this much rain today, especially with no clouds in the sky," Tori says, looking at Slash tearing up.

"Let it rain Tori," Slash whispers. "Let it rain, my friend."

Tori has tears streaming down her face as she curls up in a ball, crying in front of Marco's grave.

"Slash. Do you hear me?" Ella whispers. "I never told you this, but I can feel the evil when you cut those demons. I can feel it through my spirit. This sword is light, and what you are killing is evil. It affects me. Please be sure to not overdo it using me. Even this sword has its limits."

"I understand, Ella." Slash wipes the blade clean of blood.

* * *

Meanwhile, in the Southern Kingdom.

"We reach the Bridge of Eden in three hours."

The troops behind her yell. "All hail Queen Charlotte!"

"That makes my heart thump with excitement," Bridget says. "I cannot wait to break some skulls."

Bridget puts her fist into the air and yells with intensity.

"Let's go get this win for you, Sodina. I am your shield, my friend." Sodina smiles at Bridget.

Lea looks at her friends, saying a prayer.

"I pray that we are not too late," she whispers underneath her breath.

* * *

Bartholet pulls out his horn, blowing it loudly as the remaining troops line up to depart from the bloody battlefield. Tori flies on the back of the horse with Slash and she wraps her arms around him.

"We ride 2,500 strong toward the Bridge of Eden," Bartholet says, looking over at Slash. "What are our chances of surviving?" Bartholet wraps his hand in bandages as he puts his knife away.

Slash smirked, trying to remain positive. "Well, I feel like we have a splendid chance of putting up a fight. I have yet to draw my second sword. You remember those techniques I was working on?"

"Those techniques where you danced with two swords waving them around like an idiot?" Bartholet laughs.

"Your words wound me." Slash looks over at him jokingly. "Yes, when I did that. Hopefully, I will not have to pull that second sword because it will drain my energy significantly, but I will need it."

Bartholet nods as he picks up speed on his horse.

"Two hours until we reach our destination." Bartholet looks at the afternoon sky with fear in his eyes. *That was something I have never seen before. Those wolfen moving with such rage. The demons hate us. They killed those we love without remorse. Do they have no hearts of their own? Goddess Astra created demons, but I wonder if these creatures were created for killing. Knowing this means nothing. The goal remains the same. Kill them all. Crush and kill them all.* Bartholet, still in pain from having a wolfen bite into his right arm, grips the rope used for guiding the horse. *We will overcome it.*

Two hours pass as Slash and his group turn the corner to find two individuals standing alone in a clearing before the Bridge of Eden.

"Welcome, pathetic humans," Magnar says, laughing. "You have fallen right into our trap. In these trees around you hide more than 3,000 wolfen for you to have fun with. I see your force has taken a significant hit. I wonder if you can take a second wave. We wish to speak to your commander."

"What are you doing?" Claudia whispers to Magnar.

"Having a little fun," Magnar speaks back to her in a humorous voice.

"What are we to do, Bartholet?" asks Slash.

"We go!" Slash, with Tori still on the horse with him, and Bartholet head to the center of the field.

"I think this could go badly," Bartholet whispers over to Slash. "We could be killed on the spot, but I have yet to see our help from across the bridge, so I call this stalling." Bartholet lets loose a slight smile.

Slash nodded firmly. "What a cocky move that is and one that I would not risk my life for, but here we are."

Bartholet and Slash dismount their horses and walk towards Magnar and Claudia.

"We would like you to surrender," Claudia whispers, looking at Tori with interest.

"I thought we killed all the fairies in this region."

"You will pay for that transgression with your life," Tori yells at Claudia.

"We will not surrender," Slash replies, keeping his hand at the ready on his swords.

"You think you have a chance?" Magnar laughs. He slams his spear into the ground towards Slash and Bartholet. "This spear is 7 seven feet long. All I have to do is move a few feet forward and you two would be like vegetables on a skewer."

Slash nor Bartholet flinch at the sight of Magnar flaunting his power. They both turn away, not saying a word to either of the demons.

"Damn human, watch your manners," Claudia yells. "You are standing in the presence of the most beautiful demon in the Dark Order. My elegance should be worshipped."

Slash and Bartholet get on their horses and ride back towards their army. Magnar picks up his spear and throws it towards Slash.

"Slash! Lookout," Tori yells.

Tori puts up her hands, creating a small magical shield deflecting the spear, but not before her right eye is gouged. "Ugh." Tori grabs her eye as it bleeds profusely.

"Tori!" Slash yells, looking back. Slash and Bartholet ride quickly away as Magnar runs up and grabs his spear.

"Attack!" Magnar yells in a loud, bellowing voice.

"Men, fight till you have no energy left!" Bartholet yells, blowing into his horn. "Give them hell!" Bartholet pulls out his sword as his horse gains speed, riding toward the wolfen emerging from the trees. The remaining men on horseback pull out their bows and shoot volleys of arrows into the wolfen closing in on them.

Magnar runs into the battle with his spear, stabbing through a horse. He slams it into the ground with the rider still on it. Claudia extends her nails, grabbing a man, and putting her claws through his neck before she throws his body in the air. Magnar swings his spear in a circle, taking out five horsemen and stabbing another three on his spear and throwing them to the ground.

"Humans are so much fun to kill, but so much blood."

Slash looks over at the power that Magnar is wielding. "Bartholet, those two will be trouble. Try to stay away from them."

Bartholet nods with a look of approval, but his eyes say something else.

Slash steers his horse away to the edge of the battlefield. "Tori, hide in the woods or up on that ledge where none of the wolfen can get to you."

Tori nods, flying up, putting pressure on her eye while doing so. "Be safe, Slash. Do not be reckless."

Slash waves, guiding his horse back toward the battle.

For thirty minutes, the wolfen melee with the resistance, inflicting heavy casualties. Bartholet lifts his head as a wolfen slashes him across the chest, cutting him deeply. Slash looks over at Bartholet, kneeling on the ground.

"This one is mine!" Claudia walks up to Bartholet kneeling on the ground. She holds his neck and drives her razor sharp nails into Bartholet's chest. She pulls it out.

"Bartholet!" Slash screams before running towards him. "You witch!" Slash swings his sword and cuts off the wolfen's head.

Bartholet's body falls to the ground, blood spewing from the open wounds in his chest.

"You will die next," Claudia says, swinging towards Slash.

Slash kneels on the ground and whispers, "Perfect vision."

Tears streaming from his eyes, he sees Claudia in a vision swinging down from an angle towards his skull. Slash rolls to his left and pulls out his second sword.

"Die, demon!" Slash takes his two swords and slices her legs, buckling her to the ground.

Claudia let out a shriek. "Impossible!"

Slash stood up his hair soaked in blood. "Atone for your sins, demon, for this sword shall absolve you."

Claudia yells as she is decapitated before her body explodes into purple mist.

Magnar, halfway across the battlefield, sees the dust of his comrade and swells with anger. He puts his spear through two men and swings them toward the tree line.

"You dare touch one of Gareth's elites. You will feel my wrath, human," he yells across the field.

Slash rushes towards Bartholet and grabs something in his sack.

"Drink this, it will numb the pain," Slash says.

Bartholet slowly puts his hand up. "I want to feel the pain my men felt," Bartholet whispers.

"Fight, Slash. Fight and live. You can lead these men to victory."

Bartholet grips Slash's hand, covered in blood. Slash closes his eyes, holding his friend close. He felt no emotion except anger. Only the anger of losing a loyal friend and brother in arms.

Slash stands up, looking toward Magnar. He points his sword.

"Be careful," Ella speaks to Slash. "You already used your perfect vision for today. The enemy you face is one of Gareth's right-hand men."

"I know." Slash steadies his breath. "I am ready for him."

Slash runs towards Magnar, dodging the wolfen as he sets his sight on only Magnar.

"All of that fighting and it amounts to nothing," Magnar yells at Slash.

"You will die here on your own soil without gaining your land back. How does it feel knowing you will lose everything despite your big boy mannerisms?" Magnar puffs his chest out, pulling out an arrow from his shoulder.

Slash notices the march of several thousand soldiers in the distance. Across the Bridge of Eden were the armies of his allies and friends. *Help had come, but at what cost? He had lost almost all of his men in a matter of an hour. How long will it take them to make a makeshift bridge?* Slash looks out among the few hundred troops he had left.

"Fight, men! Our help has come! Fight until your legs cannot carry you anymore."

Slash and his soldiers charge. Their feet strike the ground like thunder. They scream, holding their weapons up high. It was the hour of reckoning at last.

"Sodina. May this be our last day apart," Slash whispers. "I'm coming for you."

Chapter 24

Month of Witches
Day 9

Sodina squints and sees people fighting in the distance.

"Goddess Astra, what are we to do?" Sodina clenches her fist. "This method of getting across will not work."

Charlotte groans to see the hooks reach their mark, but they were proving not strong enough to build their wooden bridge up. "It was worth a shot. It would take forever for each person to cross on foot. The hooks are digging into the rock over on the other side, but this is a lost cause."

Charlotte looks out at the slaughter happening to the men on the other side and starts to shake nervously.

Slash looks over to the bridge with the hooks in the ground. *They are not trying to cross on ropes, are they? That won't work!* He jumps to the right and slams his blade into the hip of a wolfen, and with his other sword he pierces its back, striking it down.

In that moment, Sodina remembers the words she heard several months prior while she was crashing towards the sea. *This pendant will make way for you. Oh, that's it!* She thinks.

Sodina gasps as she runs up towards the edge of the broken bridge. She rips the pendant off her neck and puts it down at the edge. It glows and as a myriad of colors spew out of it, it makes a rainbow pathway over the water to the other side.

Charlotte looks at the spectacle and stares at Sodina in awe. "How did you do that, Lady Sodina?"

"It was not me, Your Majesty," Sodina responds. "I believe this gift is from another realm. I have faith that we can cross this bridge now!"

The rainbow-colored pathway glitters with light as Sodina takes a step onto it.

Lea holds her breath as Sodina does not fall through the pathway.

Charlotte walks beside Sodina, keeping her footing as well, smiling from ear to ear.

"Let us charge," the Queen yells. Charlotte runs ahead with Sodina beside her.

Bridget and Lea follow, screaming at the top of the lungs as they make their way across the supernatural bridge.

Magnar glares over at the massive force coming over the bridge. "Ha! Humans, you think you have won? Prepare to meet your end!"

"ATTACK!" Magnar shouts and runs toward an approaching human and pushes his spear through him, slinging him through the air.

Slash runs towards the bridge as he sees Sodina and her friends.

"Sodina!" Slash yells, the wolfen blood all over his clothes dripping away as he ran to his wife.

Sodina sprints as fast as she can into his arms, kissing him on the lips. "My love!" Sodina kisses him over and over.

"I'm so sorry, Sodina!" Slash puts his hands through her hair. Suddenly, time stopped for him. He was holding his wife again, but it could only last for a moment.

"You dense fool!" Bridget runs up and wraps her arms around the lovebirds reunited again. "Why did you leave us?! Never ever do that again."

Bridget blushes and pulls away from her friends when Lea runs up beside them, tears streaming down her face.

"How emotional!" The young archer exclaims.

"We have little time for tears, girl," Slash says. "We need to go now."

"I am surprised we were not trampled," Sodina laughs and wipes her tears away.

The War Master approaches the group on horseback and Slash immediately bows at the sight.

"The soldiers parted around you," Chrono speaks. "I see you are well, Slash."

Slash gave him a confident glance. "Extremely well, War Master!"

"We have heard a lot about you," Chrono waves. "But we really must go now."

"Let's go take back our home!" Slash yells.

The group of five turn around, running towards the battlefield.

Slash grabs Sodina's hand and throws her into the air.

"Inferno!" She yells, shooting a stream of fire out of her hand towards a group of wolfen.

Tumbling on the ground, Lea gets up and runs, shooting three arrows and killing three wolfen right in their skulls.

Bridget, swinging her axe, attacks three wolfen, slicing their heads off one by one in rapid succession.

Magnar, looking at the backup army coming, runs towards Slash.

Slash runs in front of Sodina, blocking Magnar's spear from hitting her.

"Get back, love!" He yells. Sodina jumps back, standing back-to-back with Slash. "I need you to enchant my swords now!"

Sodina turns around quickly and chants a spell that lights up both blades in his hand.

"Get away from this demon, love, he is mine," Slash growls.

She nods, going into the battlefield, leaving Slash to battle with Magnar.

Slash runs towards Magnar, slamming both blades towards his head. Magnar puts up his spear, blocking the attack and pushing him off.

Landing on the ground, Slash looks up as the tip of the spear is coming down towards his head.

Chrono jumps in and puts his shield up towards the attack, blocking the spear.

"Ugh!" Chrono pushes the spear back, looking back at Slash.

"Thank you!" Slash smiles as he stands up beside Chrono.

"Such hope!" Magnar laughs maniacally as he picks up a dead human body and throws it at Chrono.

Chrono jumps to the left side as Magnar, already in the air, slams his spear into the War Master's shield again.

Chrono is thrown back twenty feet and he hits the ground hard.

Slash runs behind Magnar and stabs one of the enchanted fire swords into the demon's right leg.

Magnar screams as he pulls out the sword and throws it across the battlefield, forty feet away.

"That one hurt, I will admit it, human!" He says. "But I will hurt you worse than that!"

Lisha looks down at the battlefield from the sky, seeing Bridget fighting wolfen. *I need to find some way to get to hear without drawing too much attention.* She continues to survey the battle, looking for an opening.

Charlotte, riding her horse through the battlefield, pulls out her spear and stabs two wolfen in their skulls. "Do your worst!" The Queen yells. She turns her horse around and puts her spear into another wolfen. Captain Robert was close behind her, slaying as many wolfen cubs as he could while protecting the queen at the same time. Looking up at the hill, she saw the approaching army of more demons. Pulling out her shell she put it towards her mouth. "A second wave is coming." The warriors cry out in unison, fighting harder than ever.

A wolfen grabs a soldier by the neck and tosses the body towards Charlotte, knocking her off her horse.

Charlotte rolls out of the way as a wolfen slams its claws into the ground next to her, missing the Queen completely. She jumps up, swinging her spear towards the wolfen, cutting one of its arms off.

"You will pay for that dearly, human!" The wolfen growls and runs towards Charlotte as an ax is slammed into his neck.

Charlotte looks up to see Bridget drenched in wolfen blood.

"Can't let the Queen perish in this battle," Bridget smiles, lifting the axe out of the neck of the wolfen.

"Thank you," Charlotte shakes her head, looking at the army getting closer. "Let's buckle down and keep at it."

Bridget runs towards another wolfen, rescuing a soldier on the ground about to be killed. She lifts him up off the ground and continues to fight, killing the fat wolfen with her giant ax.

"Archers, follow me!" Lea yells to the Archery Corps. "This one is for Captain Bartholet! Fire, men!"

A massive volley of arrows slam into the oncoming army of cyclops, wolfen, and other demons.

The arrows hit their mark as many wolfen on the front-line fall and the archers prepare for another volley.

"Fire again!" Lea screams, preparing her own bow.

The arrows hit their mark as more wolfen fall and cyclops continue to walk with arrows in their eyes.

The wolfen from the second wave ran on all fours, closing the gap between the archers.

Lea turns to the soldiers, nodding before screaming in unison.

"Charge!" They yell as the archers put down their bows and run towards the hordes of monsters coming towards them.

"They are trying to buy us time." Charlotte looks at the small group of men pushing their horses to the limit while battling certain death.

"We are almost done cleaning up the last of the creatures here," Sodina says after casting a death spell on another Cyclops. Chrono zooms in to pick her up and they ride off toward more enemies.

"I had no idea they would be so tall." Charlotte looks at another cyclops in the distance, picking up trees and hurling them into the battlefield.

Pulling out her shell again, Charlotte lets her troops know to turn their attention towards the army heading towards them.

Charlotte whistles for her trusty horse to come back to her and she jumps on it effortlessly, riding towards the oncoming demonic army.

An enormous twenty-foot tree flies over her head, crashing into several troops behind her and killing them instantly.

Tori sits at the top of a tall tree away from the battle as she stops and stares at Lisha across the battlefield. *I wonder why she has not joined the fight,* she thinks to herself. *It looks like she is observing. I will monitor her and make sure to warn Slash if she makes a move.*

Chrono sits up, wiping the blood off his mouth as he looks down at his shield, now cracked in half.

"Wonderful." He grumbles as he discards it and looks to his right at Magnar standing opposite him in the distance.

An evil purple aura surrounds the vast body of the demon and it blasts towards him.

"Chrono!" Sodina runs over to him and puts her arms out to heal him. "Revival of Goodness!"

She chants as a sizable green mist covers his body to close his wounds. Sodina glares at Magnar and spits a freezing incantation to ward him off as Chrono heals.

"Thank you, milady!" Chrono says. "I feel right as rain. Are you okay?"

"That healing spell really gets to me," Sodina says, breathing heavily. "I have used a lot of magic today, running around healing people. So many cries and screams of pain." Sodina clenches her fist.

"Keep going." Chrono looks at his friend, smiling. "Do not stop."

Sodina nods and runs back into the battlefield, looking for another injured individual to heal.

Chrono picks up his sword, running towards Magnar who was beginning to unfreeze. Slash approaches the War Master with his blades still bursting with flames.

Magnar roars and runs over, ramming his shoulder into Slash, knocking him back 25 feet. Slash coughs up blood as he sits up, looking at Magnar running towards him.

Chrono yells out, "War Dance!" The War Master doubles his speed and cuts off Magnar's right hand, landing on the ground in front of Slash.

Magnar steps back, screaming in pain. "Damned humans! You will pay for that!" He sprints towards Chrono, pulling out a longsword at his hip and slams it vertically towards Chrono, cutting his right arm clean off.

Chrono cries in pain, falling to his knees and holding his shoulder as blood pours from the wound.

"Chrono!" Slash yells.

Slash grabs his sword before Magnar kicks him in the chest, knocking him back fifteen feet. Slash looks up at the sky before blacking out.

Tori looks down at Chrono bleeding and Slash unconscious. *Oh, no, but I cannot help them. Please keep fighting!* Tori thinks to herself.

Chrono, hissing in pain, grabs his sword out with his left hand. Ge looks at Magnar with killer intent. "You will not beat me," he says, panting. "War Dance!" Chrono runs towards a tree behind him, holding his shoulder down to stop the bleeding and backflips into the air above Magnar. "Downward Spiral!" Twisting his body, Chrono points his blade towards Magnar.

Seeing the attack coming, Magnar grabs Chrono in midair by the neck with his massive hand gripped tightly around Chrono's neck.

Squirming, Chrono tries to swing his sword, but his blade cannot meet its mark.

Suddenly, Chrono falls out of the demon's grip as he sees Magnar thrown ten feet away by his pal Bridget, shining victoriously in the sun.

"You okay, War Master?" Bridget smiles, standing up after delivering a suplex to Magnar.

Chrono yells as he holds his shoulder, still bleeding. "Do I look okay?!"

Sodina leaps in and hurries to patch up the War Master's bloody shoulder. She then turns her attention to her unconscious husband and makes him drink a small waking potion. Slash coughs up some blood but sits up and hugs his wife.

Chrono cracks his neck and frowns at the sight of his left side, now without a whole arm. "What's the situation now, Lady Bridget?"

"Well, for starters, my ax has grown dull after putting it through so many demons," she answers. "The battle is not faring well out there. The cyclops are hard to bring down. Charlotte and her army are taking heavy casualties but are fighting to the bitter end."

Chrono nods, sitting on the ground, looking down at his arm again. "Hopefully we can make it through this." Chrono pulls out a numbing potion from his pocket and gulps it down.

They turn to see Magnar speeding towards them again with one hand and Chrono laughs.

"Keep him busy, will you? I have a lack of arm to attend to!" Chrono yells to Bridget.

"My pleasure, War Master!" Bridget runs over to Magnar and throws a punch to his jaw.

"How dare you touch me?" Magnar yells, spitting from the punch.

Bridget throws her fists at him again and takes his right arm, swinging him in a circle and slamming him into the ground.

Magnar coughs up blood as he materializes his spear while lying on the ground.

"No fair, demon man!" Bridget smiles, jumping to avoid him swinging his spear towards her legs.

Standing back up, Magnar shakes his head as he points his spear towards Bridget.

"That bleeding must be getting to you!" Bridget shouts before running forward.

Bridget avoids the vertical attack Magnar launches and punches him twice in the face and once in the stomach.

Stepping back, he grabs his chest and spits up more blood. "How are you so strong, human?!"

"Ready to give up?" Bridget responds, delivering an uppercut to his neck, flipping him once in the air landing him on his back.

Magnar could barely catch his bear the blows hitting his vital organs. *Impossible! How?*

Sitting up, Magnar pulls out a second spear from thin air and puts them together with two blades at the end. "Prepare to meet your end!" Magnar yells as the purple aura around his body glows larger, covering a ten-foot area.

Bridget steps back, grabbing at a sword on the ground beside her to hold in her other hand. *He's getting serious now.*

Twirling the twin-bladed spear around his head, Magnar throws it at Bridget.

Her eyes widen. She has no time to react to the incoming blow and closes her eyes, ready for death to consume her. *Goddess Astra, if you're there, please let it be swift.*

In the blink of an eye, Lisha appears before Bridget with her own spear drawn, deflecting the attack.

"What is the meaning of this?!" Magnar yells at Lisha.

"You will not kill my daughter, fool!" Lisha snaps at Magnar.

Bridget stands there behind Lisha, her mouth wide open in awe.

"I love you, my daughter." Lisha turns to her and puts her hands on her shoulders. "You may not remember me, but I will not let any harm come upon you now."

Lisha snaps her fingers, revealing her tightly fit purple battle lingerie and her high heeled boots under her robe.

"Now, Magnar, if you insist on going on any further, I will be forced to kill you."

Magnar, with his weapon in hand, looks at Lisha with contempt. "Once Gareth hears about this, you will be killed on the spot. Betrayal against our Lord himself is a crime punishable by death."

"I know that," Lisha smiles wickedly. "He has changed for the worse. Have you not noticed? Are you too stupid to comprehend?

Magnar spits, "You weak-minded fool, he is our leader, and you have no right to say anything against him."

Lisha responds by pulling the scythe at her back as Magnar prepares to strike.

Lea rides her horse up to the rest of her party. She was bleeding from a rip in her neck, but she jumps off her horse to run towards Slash.

Slash holds his chest gasping for air.

Lea helps Sodina lift and lie him on his wife's lap.

"I am all out of pain potions," Lea whispers. "I think Slash may have several broken ribs."

Slash tries to move his arms, but they feel heavy.

"Honey, I am here," Sodina coos as she strokes her husband's hair gently.

"I tried, but he is too strong." He looks up into Sodina's eyes and his attention is grabbed by the sight of the demon woman with Bridget fighting Magnar.

"That woman Lisha is protecting Bridget," Sodina says to her husband.

"I do not understand," Slash whispers.

"According to her, Bridget is a demon spawn and her daughter," Lea explains.

Slash's eyes widen as he laughs and then coughs some more in pain, "You have got to be kidding me."

"We are not joking, my love," Sodina answers. "I promise. We ran into her trying to get the precious treasure of the Tree of Woe. She almost killed us."

"That witch will die where she stands!" Slash yells and sits up before screaming in pain.

"You are in no condition to fight, my love." Sodina kisses him on the head gently.

Suddenly, Lea sees Sodina's arms shake as they turn purple and she screams in pain. Sodina pulls away from her husband and falls to the ground.

"Sodina!" Slash shouts. "What is going on?"

"It's wearing off! The potion!" Lea says frantically, looking at her friend's body starting to turn purple all over.

Looking around her sack, Lea tries to find something that will help her friend.

Sodina curls up in a ball in front of Slash, looking into his eyes.

"Fight it, Sodina," Slash says to her. "Please. I know you can."

Sodina smiles, trying to hold back her pain and cries out again.

A loud explosion booms around them and the ground shakes.

A solider rides on horseback toward them, covered in demon blood, screaming. "Someone just showed up and wiped most of the remaining forces. The Queen was severely injured, and they are carrying her back towards the bridge!"

"Oh, Astra, no!" Lea yells.

Slash holds his wife protectively and mutters a small prayer with her.

Magnar and Lisha look over to the left to see Gareth flying over the army, shooting lightning blue rays, killing hundreds of humans at one time.

"Damn it!" Lisha yells, standing back. "You need to get out of here now, daughter!"

Lisha looks back at Bridget and she nods in response.

"I... I will be back to kill you, Mother," Bridget whispers, looking Lisha in the eye as she runs back towards her friends. Lisha frowns and sees Magnar grinning.

Magnar chuckled in pain. "Look at the destruction you caused, Lisha! Your little stunt pulled out Lord Gareth himself! Neron was keeping an eye on you this whole time. Ha ha!"

Gareth looks down at the dwindling enemy forces, but knows he still had hordes of creatures at his disposal. *The humans would suffer greatly.*

"Retreat!" A little man yells, sounding a horn.

Wolfen start running towards the southern army in pursuit, but the last of the Southern army push back towards the rainbow-colored bridge.

Gareth lands in front of Magnar and Lisha.

"Now, what am I to do with a traitor?" Gareth says, looking up and down at Lisha. Gareth flies quickly towards Lisha, grabbing her by the neck and tossing her ten feet into the air. He slams his knee into her chest in midair and punches her into the ground in rapid succession.

Lisha hits the ground, spitting up blood.

Bridget turns around to see Lisha on the ground fighting the demon lord for her. "Mother..." she whispers.

Gareth flies over to Bridget, smiling.

"Oh, it's you," he says in a chillingly quiet voice. "You look just like me."

"I don't think so." Bridget glares at him.

"Once I finish teaching your mother a lesson, I will take care of you."

Lisha sits up as Gareth floats back to kick Lisha in the face, crushing her nose. Lisha screams in pain and throws a punch at Gareth's face as he dodges and elbows her in the cheek.

Slash looks up to see Gareth standing forty feet away from him.

"That bastard!" Slash roars. "I must kill him before he hurts anyone else!"

Ella, are you there? Slash thinks to his minor goddess friend.

Yes, I am, she responds in his ears.

Tears were forming in his eyes. *I need you to transfer what minor power you have into my body, please.*

Ella was silent for a moment. *But, Slash, that may kill you.*

Just do it! Slash screams to Ella in his mind.

Slash glows green as he stands onto his feet to Sodina and Lea's surprise.

"Gareth!" Slash yells as he runs towards Gareth. The Sword of Discernment appears in his hand, glowing brighter green every second.

"What a pathetic attempt to kill me!" Gareth puts out his hand as it glows purple.

"Slash, no! You will die, my love!" Sodina yells as her body is about to explode due to the poison in her veins. She struggles to stand up and run behind Slash.

She falls to the ground completely as the poison reaches her brain. A radiant light sprouts from her and two giant 10-foot wings stretched from her back.

Lea gasped, falling to her knees in awe.

Sodina keeps her eyes on Gareth with renewed power as she speeds towards Magnar with a blade made of light cutting him in half, killing him instantly.

Gareth looks at Magnar's body disappearing.

He charges a ball of purple energy at Slash and Sodina deflects it before it hits.

Fading in and out of consciousness with her wings losing strength, Sodina mutters a prayer. *Goddess Astra, give me the strength to get my friends to safety.*

Sodina closes her eyes as balls of light surround each of her friends as they lift 100 feet into the air and shoot off west towards the Western Kingdom.

Lisha looks up as a ball of light surrounds and lifts her into the air, flying away from Gareth completely.

"What the…" Gareth looks up at the raining sky. *Does this mean a New Age of Goddess Astra's reign is upon us?* Gareth clenches his fist and looks at the bodies. *Based on history, she was never to show her face again after the First Great War. What a mad woman.*

Gareth walks over to Magnar's body and bows his head. "General Magnar, you served me well. Rest now, dear friend. I will slaughter every human that dares lay a hand on my people."

* * *

Later in the day, Lisha wakes near a small pond in the Southern Kingdom at midnight. Rubbing her head, she looks around, gaining her surroundings.

The last thing she remembered was that Gareth was ready to kill her.

Bridget's friend had turned into an angel or goddess. Lisha wasn't sure.

She needed to lie low for a while and hide out. Her stomach grumbled and the general decides she needed sustenance.

Lisha stands up, legs shaking, and walks towards the edge of the pond.

As she reaches the edge, she sees a familiar fairy come into view, lying unconscious on the grass.

* * *

Sodina wakes up her eyes beholding a far-reaching desert, her friends still unconscious on the ground beside her.

"What happened to us?" Sodina mumbles and tries to remember. In her mind, she sees the wicked Gareth, and Slash about to die at his hand. *What was that brilliant light that covered us?* The questions ran through Sodina's mind as she looked into the starry night sky. Sodina clenches her fist, the moon in full view, its radiant light shining over the vast sands of the Western Kingdom. *One thing I know for sure... Our fight is just beginning.*

Made in United States
Orlando, FL
13 February 2023

29949472R20202